HERO

P E R R Y **M O O R E**

HYPERION
LOS ANGELES   NEW YORK

Printed in the United States of America

First Hyperion hardcover edition, September 2007

First Hyperion paperback edition, May 2009

10 9 8 7 6 5

V475-2873-0-14297

ISBN 978-1-4231-0196-3

Library of Congress

Control number for Hardcover: 2009279167.

Visit www.hyperionteens.com

For everyone

CHAPTER ONE

I NEVER THOUGHT I'd have a story worth telling, at least not one about me. I always knew I was different, but until I discovered I had my own story, I never thought I was anything special. My destiny began to unfurl during my very last game at school. What started with an accident on the court ended with the single most devastating look I ever got from my father. And it made me want to die.

At the game, I'd scored twenty-two points, which already topped my personal best by a basket, and I showed no signs of slowing down. Every time I sank the ball, I could hear a lone deep voice begin to cheer a full second before the rest of the bleachers chimed in. Dad's voice was hoarse from screaming, but I could still tell it was him, because no one else there would bother to remind me to follow my shot or get my hands up for defense.

I ran down to the other end of the court and posted up under the basket, and I caught him out of the corner of my eye. He was sitting in the remote upper lip of the bleachers, in his usual spot, away from everyone else. The crowd was sparse up there, which he said gave more room for a man of his considerable size to spread out, stand every few minutes, and stretch his back. The truth was that the extra room also made it harder to tell that people were uncomfortable sitting close to him.

I was surprised to see a young couple sitting near him that night. The husband would occasionally turn around to agree with my dad on a call or congratulate him when I made a shot. They were probably parents of one of the freshmen on the team. Didn't recognize my father yet.

But I got the feeling they found something about him familiar. Like someone they'd seen on TV, in a movie, a local politician, or someone vaguely famous. They would have recognized him right away if he'd been wearing his mask. My guess is he'd probably saved their lives at some point. Dad always ran into people whose lives he'd saved. I could tell because his left jaw would clench, just a smidge, a bicuspid ground into a molar—a telltale sign that he was either going to be ignored, maligned, or dismissed by someone who was only still breathing by the good graces of my father's actions. He never wanted me to see it, but kids aren't stupid. Even if Dad had ever possessed superpowers, invulnerability wouldn't have protected him from the shame of having people look down on him in front of his own son.

I looked over and saw that Dad had his bad hand in his pocket as usual. I couldn't tell from that far away if he was grinding his teeth. The minute the new couple would go to shake his hand, they'd figure it out. The hand always got 'em.

Usually the only person who sat alone at the games was Mr. Carrier, whose wife had shown up at a PTA meeting more than once with a black eye. He always tried to strike up a conversation with Dad.

"Hi, Hal, Bill Carrier. We met when we picked the kids up from basketball camp, remember me?"

"Vividly."

Dad wouldn't shake Carrier's hand, no matter how many times he tried to strike up a conversation. And it wasn't because he was uncomfortable with his deformed appendage, either; it was because Mr. Carrier didn't deserve the courtesy after what he'd been doing to his wife. Dad was like that with his convictions, utterly firm, no gray areas.

Dad had a perfect attendance record at all of my sporting events, except for one game four years ago, and that wasn't because he didn't try to make it. He punched out of work at five on the nose, never a second later, when I had a game. That winter he'd been nursing a severe cough, and on that particular day, he finally collapsed in the parking lot after a nasty coughing fit brought on by helping my geometry teacher push her Tercel out of a snowdrift. In the examination room at the hospital, the doctor told us she'd never seen such an acute case of pneumonia where the patient had been ambulatory, much less alive. My dad came the closest he ever had to smiling when he heard that. He tied his hospital gown tightly around his waist, still the trimmest midsection he knew of for a man his age, and readjusted his shoulders as if he were suiting up to enter battle. He wasn't one to toot his own horn, but you could tell he liked to win, even if it was just against an infection.

He was so dedicated to my games that he even showed up the night he discovered Mom had disappeared for good. He just sat up there in the back corner of the bleachers, same as any other game. He cheered when we were up, he shouted at the ref to get a new pair of glasses when we were down. He waited until after the game to tell me the news.

"Why didn't you say something?" I lowered my voice, careful not to show too much emotion in front of my team.

"No use losing a game over it," he said.

Since I was on such a hot streak this particular night, Dad didn't have a whole lot to say to the ref. Yet despite playing the most spectacular ball of my life, we were about to lose to the Tuckahoe Trojans. Before you laugh at the name, understand that this was the toughest school around. In fact, after some unfortunate postgame assault issues, they'd been banned from the schedule for the past five years. Rumor had it that if they lost a game, they'd break the fingers of the opposing team members, at least whoever they caught. One finger for every point by which they lost. An eye for an eye, a finger for a point.

Needless to say, things were a little rough in the paint that night. I'd been popped in the eye by an elbow during a mad grab for an airball, but I could tell that it wasn't a black eye because it hadn't swollen shut—yet. The jab took me by surprise, first because it hurt like hell, but also because after the guy who threw it popped me, he followed the ball down to the other end of the court, stopped, stared at me with contempt, and then did the strangest thing.

He winked. Like he was flicking me off with his eyelid.

A little on-court hostility wasn't uncommon. Sometimes it could be a great motivator, help get your juices going. But this was different. Somehow this was personal, and the more I thought about it, I knew I'd seen this guy somewhere before.

He was a good two inches taller than I was—a rare thing, particularly because he was my own age. The summer between fifth and sixth grade I'd had an agonizing growth spurt when I grew over a foot in the span of three months. Dad sat up with me during those long excruciating nights on the stretching block (i.e. my old twin bed). He brought me orange Popsicles and laid cool washcloths on my forehead and played cards with me until the pain passed.

About this time I started having the seizures, too. Although the doctor said there was no connection, you didn't have to be a rocket scientist to figure out the link between shooting up out of your body and losing control of it. Soon I would discover that seizures weren't the only strange things my body could do.

So it was pretty unusual for me to play against someone who was even taller than I was. The guy's shoulders were broader and more worked-out than mine, too, like he took the business of physical training much more seriously than most people our age. The line of his jaw jutted out straight and severe. There were deep pools of dark in his eyes, so you couldn't tell where the pupils ended and the irises began. When you looked in his eyes, you saw a darkness that went on forever to some faraway place, where neither you nor I nor anyone else was welcome to go. And I got this sense from the way he leaped up for the ball, just a hair above everyone else, that he was deliberately holding back. Like he could have touched the ceiling if he'd wanted to. When he sprinted, his breath was even and controlled, like he was saving it up for something else, something more important.

For all his size, he was faster than everyone else, too. I hadn't seen anyone come even close to him on a fast break. But even though he was the biggest guy on the court, his shoes barely squeaked and he never stomped the wooden planks of the gym floor after a dunk. You'd never hear him if he snuck up behind you.

Anyway, the most remarkable thing about this kid popping me in the face wasn't that he was bigger and stronger than I was. It was remarkable because it was clear he'd hit me on purpose. He wanted me recognize him, to know who'd thrown the elbow. And when he turned back to wink at me, I finally figured out how I knew him.

It was a memory I would have rather forgotten.

Let me backtrack for a second.

Even though I go to what our neighborhood association hails as a good school, I don't live far from the Tuckahoe Trojans. Years before I was born, when Dad had finally scrimped together enough money for a down payment on a house, he took out a map of the county and pinned it to the wall. With color-coded pushpins, he targeted the areas with the best school districts, and researched the cheapest houses in those areas. He came up with a house he could afford: a modest two-bedroom on the outskirts of what was then the toniest new neighborhood in the suburbs. Our home was also known to our snottier neighbors as "the shittiest house in the whole subdivision." But Dad isn't one to shy away from a challenge, and from the minute he moved in, he went on a tear of home improvements. A slick paint job on the front of the house, a well-manicured lawn, a new mailbox. I'm not sure what Mom did during this. I expect all she had to do was get pregnant and keep things orderly. Dad's sacrifices and fixing-up didn't really add up to much if you didn't have any children to pass on the Better Life to.

Despite Dad's many attempts to fix up the house, our neighborhood seemed to have its own plan to join the other side of the tracks. Last summer, I chipped the blade of our lawn mower on something hard. I turned off the motor, flipped over the machine, and saw a big chunk of the blade was missing. I emptied the contents of the grass bag and discovered the culprit stuck in a wet clump of crabgrass—a crack pipe.

I showed the crack pipe to Dad.

"There goes the neighborhood," he said. You could never tell when Dad was joking.

I wasn't driven to action until after the night those idiots broke in. They had to be on large quantities of drugs because they were evidently the only people in the tristate area who didn't know my dad lived there. God knows, if you counted the hate mail we received or how many times the yard was vandalized, you'd think we had my dad's name lit up in neon letters above the front door.

I'd just had knee surgery to repair some torn cartilage, so I was set up on the couch for a few nights because I couldn't make it up the stairs. Dad's car was in the shop again, so there were no cars in the driveway, no evidence of anyone home.

I'd just finished watching an infomercial about a new skin-care product, which, because of the painkillers, I'd found immensely entertaining and curiously emotional. I turned off the TV and let the darkness from the house seep into my head. High on the meds, I practiced my favorite method of drifting off to sleep. I filled my head with thoughts of the future, of infinite possibility. *There's someone out there who will one day find me and fall in love with me and prove that all this waiting actually meant something. . . .*

There was a smile on my face when the back door exploded open. At first I thought the house had been struck by lightning. I bolted upright on the sofa and tried to get my bearings. I looked out the window, but I couldn't see any rain, and the trees weren't moving in the wind, either. Then I heard quick footsteps in chunky boots and hushed, hurried voices. I turned toward the direction of the voices, and in the doorway to the kitchen I saw the silhouette of two men. Very large men.

I thought about reaching for something to defend myself. The best I could come up with was the poker by the fireplace, but that was clear across the room. I froze. It was the most terrified I'd ever been in my life. When they stepped in the room, I saw there weren't two of them, after all. There were four. One of them had already begun to rifle through our hall closet for valuables. Valuable whats, I had no idea. A couple of old umbrellas, some mismatched mittens from when I was little, Dad's favorite old Tarheels hat? At least they hadn't seen me yet in the darkness. I tried to hold my breath and prayed they wouldn't hear me, but my heart was pounding so hard in my chest I thought they'd know I was there by the vibrations.

One of them walked toward me. I was sure he was going to grab me, but he passed right by and began to unplug our TV.

"Cheap bastards don't even have a DVD player," he said to himself.

I let a little air out through my nose and tried to keep myself from shaking. But there was a guy in the doorway who stopped and looked over in my direction.

"Hey, give me the flashlight," he said to the guy in the kitchen.

The guy in the doorway took a few steps in my direction and stopped for a moment. I saw his posture soften in a sign of recognition, and it sent a chill up my spine. His head tilted ever so slightly to the right, and I knew he was beginning to make out the shape of my head poking up from the couch. He took a step closer.

"Shit," another guy said from across the room. He'd found Dad's trophy case, his medals, all his commendations.

The moonlight reflected off an old medal the president had once given Dad for single-handedly fending off an invasion of telepathic starfish-shaped aliens and illuminated a very distinct impression on the thug's face. Panic.

"What is it?" said the guy who was digging for gold in our mud-crusted closet.

"We gotta leave. Now. You know who lives here?" There was an alarmed tone to his voice, but it didn't stop the man in front of me from closing in.

"Shhh, shut the fuck up!" He crept closer toward me. "Listen!" he whispered. "I think someone's *in here*."

They froze and my heart sank. There was just enough moonlight trickling in through the window behind me to cast a glint off the gun in his hand as he raised it toward me.

I bit my lip. I knew he was going to shoot me, and I fought the urge to wet myself. I heard him cock the gun, and then he lunged for the light switch to flip it on. In a millisecond I knew he would see me, and I prayed it wouldn't hurt, that it would be over quickly. In a flash, light flooded the room.

And there was Dad.

He stood upright in the middle of the room, his massive frame positioned directly between the gun and me. As the guy pulled the trigger, my father's foot kicked the gun up into the air. The sound of the gunshot and the flash of light immediately captured everyone's attention. Dad expertly used the element of surprise—one of his trademark tactical maneuvers—coupled with his intimidating physical presence, and leaped into action.

I'd seen old footage of Dad fighting, and no matter who he was up against, there was a majesty to the way he carried himself, even if the odds seemed to be dramatically against him. Didn't matter how many superpowers the villains had. Didn't matter that Dad had none himself. He was like an ancient warrior dressed in chain mail who knew he could take on an entire modern army with nothing but his trusty broadsword.

In the brightness of the room, you could see Dad's posture was tense and ready, but his face was relaxed, almost at peace. His normally wrinkled, eternally worried brow was completely smooth. I'd only seen it that relaxed after the rare third, maybe fourth beer.

In the time it took for the gun to land in our fireplace, Dad delivered the answer to the question about who lived here. With one decisive gut punch, he took out the guy who'd tried to shoot me. Before the guy in the kitchen had a chance to react, Dad had blinded him with a torn bag of flour from the counter, and proceeded to knock out five of his eight front teeth.

The last guy made a desperate scramble over to the fireplace to grab the gun. He managed to reach it before Dad could stop him. He trained the gun on me and shouted for Dad to stop.

Dad looked up like a lion stalking his prey. He saw the guy threaten me with the pistol. The calm look on his face tightened and his eyes narrowed. He stood up and, with a quick and even pace, marched over to the man with the gun, who by this point actually did wet himself. With his good hand, broad and thick, with callused fingers, Dad took the back of the man's head, like a pro would palm a basketball, and smashed his face through the glass of the trophy case.

After the police had left, Dad replaced the dead bolt on the back door, quietly swept up the broken glass from his trophy case, and poured baking soda on the urine stain in the carpet. It was then that he finally spoke to me.

"I thought for a second, when I first heard something, maybe it was your mother coming home."

I'd had it with my neighborhood; the break-in was the last straw. My dad always said it's one thing to bitch about things that bother you, but it's another thing entirely to get off your butt and do something about it. If I didn't like what was going on in our neighborhood, I should try to make a difference. I went to the community center, over by Tuckahoe High School, and signed up for a tutor–mentor program. There was some mandatory bullshit training seminar led by a sharp-featured woman named Cindy, who visited the center maybe twice a year from the state education board, and she talked to the volunteers like we were first graders. After I gave them proof from my doctor that I had passed my tuberculosis test, I started going to the Student Life Center every week to tutor.

The first few months were rewarding. I mostly helped kids with their math homework and taught them how to read. A lot of times I read books to the younger students. There was one little girl who never missed an afternoon. Sunita had lived in a series of homes; her mother had left her at the hospital after giving birth prematurely. Sunita's birth weight had been so low that the doctors were certain she wasn't going to live, but she rallied, and other than being a little small for her age, I'm not sure anyone would have known the difference. The director of the Student Life Center, Phyllis, said she didn't think Sunita's brain had developed properly, because she hardly ever spoke.

"Listen, Thom," Phyllis said, "I've raised six kids through that age, and the last thing you could imagine is a single minute of any day without all of them talking, usually at the same time. I'm telling you, something ain't right with that girl."

But when she came to my reading group, she always listened attentively, laughed at all the right parts, and grunted for me to turn the page if I was a little slow on the draw. Personally,

I didn't think she was a slow learner. I think she just didn't have that much to say yet.

When I came in one afternoon for my weekly reading session to the kids, Phyllis informed me that this was an important day for the Student Life Center: Cindy from the State and various other community leaders had come to tour the facility for "a very special visit."

"What for?" I said. "A book burning?" I was only allowed to read from a strict list of state-approved "culturally sensitive" books.

"No, even better," Phyllis said. "Budget cuts."

Phyllis warned me that they might stop by while I read to the kids. Everyone was to be on best behavior, since these visits had a direct impact on their annual operating budget. In my mind, this meant I should take advantage of the opportunity single-handedly to win them their funding for those streetlights in the parking lot they desperately needed to stay open late. So instead of the usual lighthearted reading (*Hop on Pop* and *Green Eggs and Ham* were favorites), I decided to impart a little environmental wisdom, and I grabbed a worn paperback copy of *The Lorax* from the bookshelf above Phyllis's desk. That should impress the visitors.

The tour group had already made themselves at home when I walked in. They stood in the back with attentive, stiff smiles on their faces, and seemed to study my every move as I sat down to read. Cindy from the State popped a lozenge in her mouth. I could hear her sucking on it as I opened the book.

"'I am the Lorax and I speak for the trees!'"

I think I was trying a little too hard. The kids didn't make a noise, and I realized this wasn't exactly one of the Doctor's more cheerful books.

Here I had introduced these kids to the rich, colorful world of Dr. Seuss, and in the span of one afternoon, I tore it all down and drove away all the cute, furry creatures. There wasn't a single laugh or giggle in the whole room. You could hear the squeaking sound of sneakers as they pivoted on the basketball court in the gym down the hall. I heard Cindy crunch on her lozenge through her closed mouth. When I finished the last page, which warned the children to take care of their world, I closed the book and asked the group of blank faces, "Well, what did you think?"

Silence filled the room. The group of adults standing in the back craned their necks to examine the kids' reactions.

I imagined the number of kids who returned next week would drop off dramatically, funding would be cut, they'd never get their streetlights. The whole center would eventually be shut down.

I caught Sunita out of the corner of my eye as she rubbed her eyes. Great, I even made one of them cry.

"Sunita, are you okay?" I asked.

She looked up at me with an intense stare, and then the little girl who never spoke opened her mouth.

"THOSE FUCKERS BETTER PUT THOSE TREES BACK WHERE THEY BELONG OR I AM GOING TO FUCKING *KILL* THEM!"

"Why don't we go see what's happening in the pottery class." Phyllis hurried the visitors out of the room. As the tour left, I saw Cindy's mouth was still open.

The next week they asked me if perhaps I'd be happier working with some of the older students. As Phyllis rushed off to round up some troubled students for me to tutor, I checked her shelf for some books to have them read out loud. Nothing jumped out at me. Picture books were too juvenile, and Hemingway, Steinbeck, and Fitzgerald weren't exactly going to score any points for relevance with this crowd. I knelt down and opened the lowest drawer of her desk and dug deep for some workbooks.

"What are you doing in there?"

I jumped and hit my head on the desk. I turned around and saw one of my new students, about my age, standing behind me.

"You scared me." I shut the file cabinet.

"What are you doing in there?"

He had a thick accent, so his family must have only moved here recently. One of the many English-as-a-second-language students who came to the center to learn English. He sounded just like Ismeta, the cleaning lady at school who'd once talked to our class about her experiences as a Bosnian refugee. I always felt bad for the ESL students. I couldn't imagine what I'd do if I had to take chemistry in Bratislava, or learn high-school French in Pakistan. Maybe I could start with the Dr. Seuss after all, I considered. I picked up *Hop on Pop*, and he eyed me suspiciously.

"Oh, I was just looking for something for us to read tonight," I said, slowly enunciating each word. "Do you like books?"

He stared at me. He didn't blink.

"See, that's the great thing about learning English. You get to read some cool books and stuff, so it's not all about boring homework."

He still didn't blink. "Books and stuff?" He repeated the words like he was spitting out poison.

"Yeah," I said. "It's pretty fun when you get into it. Reading and all."

Phyllis hurried back in the room. She hadn't yet noticed the toilet paper on the back of her shoe.

"I see you've met Goran," she said.

"Yes." I smiled. "I have the feeling he's going to pick up English in no time."

Phyllis looked at Goran to see if I was serious and then looked back at me.

"Thom, Goran founded the literacy program for the older kids here two years ago. I asked him to show you the ropes tonight," she said. She leaned in to me and continued, "You should take a look at Goran's poetry if you get a chance. *Harper's* published one of his poems last month."

Goran, arms folded, stared at me with contempt.

Sometimes I am the world's biggest loser.

"Goran, this is Thom, one of our new volunteers." Then she added with a lower, hushed tone, "Keep him away from the Dr. Seuss."

I couldn't bring myself to make eye contact with him when I stood up to shake his hand. He was a full two inches taller than I was.

He shook my hand hard and slow. Hard enough to send a message about his strength, and slow enough to tell me that the handshake—like any other future interaction of ours—would begin and end on his terms. I managed to make brief eye contact and then he let go.

Goran's utter lack of expression made me think he was going to hit me.

He opened his mouth to say something, but stopped short of any words. Instead, he turned and walked down the hall, long determined strides, and I struggled to keep up with him.

After he introduced me to my new students that night, I never saw him again. Phyllis said he'd switched nights because he'd recently taken a full-time job, in addition to his regular schooling and extracurricular activities.

"He supports his family, you know," Phyllis whispered, like it was a secret.

I could barely imagine supporting myself, much less an entire family. I'd bitched ad nauseam when I had to pick up work as a stock boy last Christmas. Lifeguarding each summer at the pool hadn't exactly been a real career motivator or moneymaker, either.

"What does he do?" I asked.

"Security," she said. "He's a night watchman."

I always wanted to run into him again and tell him I was sorry. That I was an idiot and I wasn't thinking when I met him, and I'm not usually like that. Maybe we'd even have a laugh about it—stranger things have happened. But I never saw him again.

Until he popped me in the eye during the basketball game and stole the ball from me.

"Foul!" my dad shouted from the stands. "Are you blind?! Foul!"

I sped down the court, my eye stinging from the sweat that trickled in the welt left by Goran. He pulled up at the top of the key and sunk a three-pointer, which put his team ahead. By the time I got back under the basket, the elbows were flying on both sides. It wasn't out of loyalty to me, either. I'd grown used to the fact that my father's disgrace had isolated me from most of my childhood friends. By high school I'd learned it was easier not to make friends in the first place than to lose them after they found out about my dad. But even if my team didn't care much about me personally, they didn't like someone else getting away with a cheap shot against them. And they certainly didn't like the idea of losing.

I'm guessing that's why Clayton Camp, our Harvard-bound power forward—who graced us with his presence on the basketball court only because it kept him in shape for another All-American lacrosse season—lashed out. I'd just missed a layup, a real confidence builder during such a tight game, and the rebound had bounced in Clayton's direction. Clayton had already slightly bent his knees and lined up his three-point shot, but the ball never reached his fingertips. Goran intercepted the ball with impossible speed. Frustrated and humiliated, Clayton turned around and kicked the back of Goran's heel as hard as he could.

No one at the game that night would ever see a more flagrant foul in his lifetime. Not even the ones who would go on to play ball in prison. As Goran tripped, the momentum from his sprint propelled his massive frame through the air parallel to the floor. He landed on his leg and knee with an eerie crunch and tumbled into the bleachers.

The Tuckahoe Trojans cleared the bench.

Clayton got the worst of it. The Trojans' point guard, a little guy who looked like Gary Coleman on steroids, led the charge. I saw Clayton disappear under a pile of Trojans as they pummeled him. It took almost every adult in the gym to pull the kids off each other and restore order.

Meanwhile, I looked over at Goran, who was doing his best to hide an expression—excruciating agony. He was crouched in a fetal position clutching his knee. He heaved deep, labored breaths through clenched teeth, but he was determined not to cry. If an accident this painful didn't make him cry like a baby, I figured the guy didn't have tear ducts or nerves or something, because when I looked down at the injury, I saw bone.

A portion of his tibia had poked its head out of the skin under his knee. The crowd had cleared away to give him plenty of breathing room. A few kids were yelling and pointing. Most of the parents couldn't even look. One of the mothers—his?—was screaming to call an ambulance. The trainer was one of the only people who hadn't turned away, but he was next to useless. Other than giving Goran a few towels to wipe up the gore, he was practically as helpless as the rest of them. He could tape a sprain, sure, but a mangled leg was a little out of his depth.

I can't explain why I did what I did next. I guess I was thinking about Goran and his full-time job and how he would support his family if he lost his leg. I guess I was thinking how his eyes, still deeply guarded, still opaque, didn't betray the weakness of the rest of his body. I was propelled by a force deep within me that I didn't understand. I knelt down beside him.

"Let me see," I said.

He couldn't speak, he was so racked with pain. I reached out my hand. He looked at me, startled and curious. I hesitated for a moment. Then I grabbed his leg firmly by the ankle.

"Don't touch it!" The trainer winced.

Goran eyes locked on mine. I held on to his ankle and my hands began to move up his leg. I reached the wound and covered it with my palms, bone and bloody bits and all.

His eyes never lowered their gaze.

My hands suddenly felt scalding hot, and all I wanted to do was pull them away and stick them in a pile of snow, but I held on for as long as I could. I felt dizzy, and my eyelids grew heavy. Something was guiding my hands, something I couldn't see or understand, like a Ouija board that actually works.

Finally the whistle blew, and the ref asked us all to return to our respective benches. An ambulance had arrived, and I saw two technicians wheeling out a stretcher for Goran. His breathing had finally relaxed, his face suddenly expressionless again.

He never broke eye contact with me, even when I turned around to head back to the bench with the rest of my team. Bewildered at my own actions, I stopped to catch my breath and spotted my father carefully observing me from the bleachers. He had a peculiar look on his face and held up his hands and pointed them at me. I looked at my hands and saw that I had blood on my palms. Not as much as you'd expect, but blood nevertheless. I saw the new parents notice my Dad standing with both hands out of his pockets. I wiped the blood off on my jersey and crouched down to huddle with the rest of my team.

Clayton earned his first ejection from a game, and after the Trojans sank two free throws from the technical foul, we resumed play. We were losing only by a narrow five-point margin, but I didn't really give a shit about winning anymore.

That is, until that little punk-ass Gary Coleman look-alike clipped me as he drove for the basket. I didn't bother to foul him—if he wanted to score that bad, he could knock himself out, as far as I was concerned. But it was what he said after he clipped me that made all the difference.

After the ball went through the hoop, he looked at me with a prune face and said, "Faggot."

That made me want to win more than I've ever wanted to win any game in my life. I glared at the scoreboard and wiped the crusted saliva from the corners of my mouth. Only two minutes left. I sped past him to the basket. I got the ball at the top of the paint and fake-pumped a pass in his face before driving to the basket for another two.

We stayed down under the basket for a full-court press, man-to-man. Sticking on a single opposing player, shadowing his every move, is the most exhausting form of defense there is. You can't keep it up for more than a few minutes without dropping, but adrenaline fueled me. I wasn't going to let their center get the ball under any circumstance. My arms stretched into the air, blocking any clear path from the ball to his hands. My feet bounced and danced around him. Wherever he went, I was there. The Gary Coleman point guard had trouble getting past midcourt with our press, so with no other option, he lobbed it to their center. I leaped up in the air and snatched it.

I could have passed it off to anyone else on my team; they were all closer to the basket than I was. But I broke into a sprint and took it myself at full speed the entire length of the court, right past Gary Coleman to the basket for an easy layup. I smacked my palm against the glass backboard for emphasis, and the sound echoed throughout the gym. I looked in the stands and saw my father jumping and shouting for me, and the cacophony of the crowd drowned out his voice. I saw that my hand had left a plum-colored smear on the backboard, a combination of my sweat and Goran's blood.

Then my finger began to twitch. This may seem like a pretty harmless detail, nothing more than a little side effect of all that adrenaline and testosterone, or maybe I'd smacked the glass too hard, but for me it's one of the worst things that can happen. The twitching only *starts* with the finger. It rarely stops there.

Suddenly I started to feel like I was hearing things under water, like I was walking through Jell-O. My tongue secreted a metallic, acrid taste, as if I were sucking on a rusty nail, or drinking water from a tin bucket. I swallowed and tried to ignore it, but the warning signs were always the same.

The spotlights hanging from the rafters cast a halo around everything. Then the world around me grew dim. It reminded me of looking through an old View-Master, and the dark outlines around the edge of the picture slowly grew and grew until the entire picture became dark, too.

I put my hands on my knees and heaved and huffed as I tried to catch my breath.

"*Cosmic Boy . . . Lightning Lad . . . Chemical King . . .*"

On rare occasions, I'd been able to stave off the seizure if I caught it early. I practiced some good old-fashioned rhythmic breathing I'd learned in swim class, and I recited to myself the roster of *The Legion of Superheroes*, my favorite comic book when

I was a kid. Back before Dad banned all superhero comics from our house, back before the books detailing my father's adventures had been canceled, all old issues removed from the shelves and discarded. This was how I struggled to regain my composure, to ward off the full throes of the seizure.

"... *Invisible Kid* ... *Colossal Boy* ... *Phantom Girl* ... *Element Lad* ..."

The world began to tilt, and I felt like I was about to spin off into orbit. Like you felt as a kid when you were rolling down a hill, only this hill had no end. I struggled to hold all my atoms together as the world around me grew dark. My feet became numb, and the twitching had traveled up my arm to the side of my face.

Even as far away as he was, my father saw the right side of my mouth quiver. He pushed past the young couple new to town, his ruined hand planted on the wife's shoulder for balance, and jumped over the side of the bleacher to rush to me.

I closed my eyes and took three more quick, sharp breaths.

"*Saturn Girl* ... *Shadow Lass* ... *Ultra Boy* ..."

I looked up, and my vision returned in time to see the basketball sailing for my head. I reached out and grabbed it with my twitching hand. I struggled to hold on to the ball. My fingers sputtered and spasmed like they'd been plugged into a light socket.

The world stopped. I could hear bits of conversations echo off the cinder block walls. The paramedics argued over where to put the dressing on Goran's leg. They could no longer find the spot where the bone had punctured the skin.

My dad raced toward me. I saw there were three seconds

left on the clock. I heard my team, the coach, the stands yell, "Shoot it!"

"*. . . Chameleon Boy, Dream Girl, WILDFIRE!*"

I bit my lip to stop it from shaking, and with all the energy I could muster I jumped into the air and pushed the ball forward. The basketball quelled the twitching as it rolled off my fingertips. The ball sailed through the air at an impossibly low angle. It hit the backboard—loud and hard—and bricked straight back through the hoop with a graceful swish.

The crowd erupted with cheers. The buzzer sounded the end of the game, and I stood there looking at the scoreboard in disbelief. I saw my dad standing in front of me on the court.

"You okay?" he mouthed over the din of the crowd, a skeptical look on his face.

I nodded, and then my teammates pounced on me. My dad took a step back behind the bleachers, and my team picked me up in the air. As I rode on top of sweaty, eager hands, I watched the paramedics wheel Goran out the door, around the side of the gym. It was hard to tell, jostled around up in the air like that, but I could have sworn I saw that same expressionless stare fixed on me as he disappeared around the corner.

Later, fresh and showered, we met our parents in front of the gym. I pushed open the door and savored the moist promise of spring in the evening air. The sun was setting later and later each day, summer would be here soon, and everything would be okay. I rubbed my hand through my wet hair and spotted Dad waiting under the streetlight in the far corner of their parking lot.

The New Parents sidestepped my father to get to their

parking space. I saw the mother lean over and whisper a private word with her husband as she pointed at my dad, a sharp look on her face. Dad put his bad hand in his pocket and jingled his keys. This was the gesture he made whenever he pretended not to notice.

"Good game, kiddo. You really took it to those knuckleheads," my dad congratulated me.

My teammates surrounded me, with some of their parents. The coach even shook my father's good hand.

"Quite a kid you got there, Hal," he said. "Listen, I'm taking the boys out for pizza, before they go off and do what boys do after they win a game like this. Why don't you come along?"

I must have really been a hero that night, because it was the first time anyone at school had invited my dad anywhere.

Before he could answer, a sonic boom roared through the air and threatened to burst our eardrums. We all looked up into the sky at the source of the thundering noise. A group of objects flew across the stratosphere in a perfect pattern.

To no one's surprise, it was a flying formation of people, not jets. It was the League. I spotted Uberman's cape. I always looked for his bright yellow cape first; it stood out best compared to the other heroes in the sky.

"Wonder who they're off to save tonight?" my coach said.

The entire parking lot of spectators craned our necks and watched the colorful saviors streak across the sky. I watched the wonder light across everyone's face, and then I caught my dad looking down at a crack in the pavement. He jingled the keys in his pocket.

After the heroes had disappeared into the horizon, Dad looked up and saw the New Parents standing in front of him.

"I thought it was you," she said, eyeing the mangled hand in his pocket.

He knew what usually came next, but he didn't betray a hint of shame. It was bad enough that it would happen in front of his son. Dad stood his ground.

The mother raised her hand and smacked him on the side of his face with all her might. You could hear the slap echo off the brick gymnasium wall. It made my whole team turn around.

"My *father* worked in the Wilson Tower," she hissed, her face streaked with tears. Her husband quickly pulled her away and moved her to their car.

"We'll catch up with you at the restaurant," I told my coach and team. I always tried to cover up the awkward silence that ensued after these encounters. I walked over to Dad. I knew everyone was watching. The sound of the slap still rang in my ears.

"Throw me the keys, Dad," I said, like nothing had just happened. "My turn to drive."

I could never have predicted what would happen next. I was too busy trying to save my father's dignity.

The Trojans sauntered past us toward their bus. The Gary Coleman point guard pointed at me and announced to his buddy, in the three seconds it took for him to pass us, something that changed everything.

"Oh, that's the gay guy."

He didn't say it with venom. He didn't need to. He said it loud enough so we could hear it, like it was just so obvious. You don't make an *accusation* that the sky is blue; it's simply a matter of fact. The coach's smile dropped, my teammates looked uncomfortably in other directions and tried to pretend they didn't hear what they all had obviously heard.

My father stared forward, a fixed expression on his face. I think he was afraid to look at me. Afraid of what his look would do to me. I heard the keys jingle against the change in his pocket again.

"See you guys later." My voice wavered on the word "later." The slight rattle in my voice betrayed me. It was a sign of shaken confidence, proof that what that little punk said was true.

I saw Dad's eyes widen just a fraction when he heard my voice catch. He glanced at me but quickly turned away. He didn't want me to see his reaction, but I did, and I'll never forget it. In that brief glimpse, I could see what he was thinking behind that fixed stare. There would be no grandkids, there would be no more Creed family bloodline, nothing else to look forward to. From that point on I'd become the last, most devastating disappointment in what he thought his life had added up to—one overwhelming failure.

I looked over to him, a little boy just wanting his dad to look back on him with approval. I wanted him to make some joke about what a loser that other kid was, about how I'd really kicked ass tonight, about how he'd never seen a high score like that. I wanted him to muss my hair and take me home and pop some popcorn so we could stay up late and watch *Saturday Night Live*. I wanted him to tell me everything would be okay.

"We should get going," Dad said, and shook hands with

the coach. He couldn't bring himself to look at me. I felt a tiny spasm in my pinky finger as a tremor slowly rippled up my hand.

I howled and spun, and the last thing I remember was wetting myself before my head hit the pavement.

CHAPTER TWO

WHEN I WOKE UP in the emergency room, the doctor, a heavyset man with more hair growing out of his ears than on his head, was giving Dad a routine list of things for me to avoid. Dad kept reminding him we'd been through this before, but the doctor was determined to finish reading the checklist.

"And last but not least, strobe lights are a big no-no."

Great, there go the disco lessons. I didn't need another list of special foods to avoid, or another series of MRIs, or an adjusted dosage on my medication. What I really needed was to avoid losing control of my bowels in front of my schoolmates.

"Oh, and I almost forgot," the doctor said. "I'll need your son's driver's license."

There are two things I really hate in this world. One is when adults refer to me in third person while I'm in the room. Second is having my license taken away for six months according to the state law regarding seizures. Rarely do I get them both at the same time.

Dad knew this was a severe blow to my independence, but I think he was secretly relieved, too. Playing dutiful parent overshadowed what that bratty little shit had said about me after the game. Dad put some compassion into the performance as he reached out his hand, sympathetically, for me to fork over my license. Any vestige of what had been said after the game was now buried in that special treasure chest where he locked away all his secret shames: His career. His hand. Mom. And now me.

I remember when I was a little boy, Martina Navratilova moved into our town for a brief time, in an expensive compound by the bay, where she could quietly train for the U.S. Open. The local paper did a cover story on her in the features section. With her racket slung over her shoulder, she posed by a crape myrtle bush and gazed wistfully into the sky. My father sat at the kitchen table with the paper that morning with extra care. His bad back had kept him up every night that week, and I knew to tread carefully when his back pain was flaring up. The only thing that pissed him off more than the pain itself was the way the government refused to pay for the medical bills. With his prior dangerous career, they explained, it would be very difficult for him to prove that the damage to his spine was a direct result of combat during his military service.

Mom gave Dad his eggs, sunny-side up, with tiny purple pills on the side of the plate. It took him a few minutes to position the fork carefully between the mangled nubs that remained on his bad hand. He was going through one of those phases where he'd convince himself that, with enough training, he could learn to use that hand. He carefully speared bites of egg and slowly propelled them to his mouth. He dropped the fork onto the plate a couple of times before he finally switched to his good hand. He read the paper and chewed for a while, and pretended like nothing was wrong. Then he looked up from his eggs and held the newspaper article out over my Crunch Berries.

"This is one of the world's big problems, son." He shook his head.

"Hal, leave it alone," Mom said from the kitchen and stifled a yawn.

He looked over at her for an instant. I thought he was annoyed at the yawn, a crime against his scintillating conversational skills. I had no idea at the time why he was really mad at her, what that yawn really meant. That would all come out later.

Mom served Dad more eggs and set a glass of orange juice in front of me. When I reached for the glass, she locked her pinky finger with mine, just for a moment, not long enough for my father to see, but long enough for me to know she was there for me.

"She's what you call gay," Dad continued, despite my mother's wishes. "That means instead of liking men, she likes to be with girls."

"I like girls," I said. It was true: Bretta Zimmer was my best friend in school that year.

"Damn straight," he said.

Mom disappeared down the hall to the laundry room.

"Do you know what you call a man who likes to be with other men?" Dad asked.

I peered down into my bowl. My Crunch Berries were

getting mushy in the milk. I hated mushy Crunch Berries.

"Hal!" my mother snapped from a remote, hard-to-pinpoint corner of the house.

"You call them *queer*." He cringed. "These people will never have a normal life. They are the ultimate downfall of our society, too, because if it were up to them to proliferate, there wouldn't be any reproduction and we would fail to continue as a species." Dad speared another chunk of eggs with his fork. "It's Darwinian."

I watched a Crunch Berry sink to the bottom of the bowl.

"What's Darwinian?" I asked. I tried to keep my eyes on my bowl; I didn't want to make eye contact with Dad. When I did look up briefly, glare from the morning sun caught my eye, and I thought I saw our dirty mop bucket floating down the hallway toward us, but I couldn't see Mom behind it. My eyes must have been playing tricks on me. I quickly looked back down in my cereal.

"Never mind," he said. "All you need to know is that it's wrong. In fact, the only thing you could be that's worse is one of these new, so-called self-professed 'heroes' with superpowers. Sons of bitches wouldn't know their asses from a—"

Sploosh!

The mop bucket floated above my father's head, turned upside down, and showered my father with a filthy, scummy lather. Through the glare of the sunlight, I still couldn't see my mother.

"They're ready for you at checkout," a perky, young nurse whose polished name tag said *Randi!* announced to us. Her ponytail, situated too far on top of her head, sprung out in all directions like a poorly bleached tropical fern. I wondered what she was thinking when they asked her to spell her name for the name tag and she added that explanation point.

"Careful you don't hit on too many of the nurses," Dad said as he wheeled me past checkout. "I don't want to come home from work one night and find the house full of candy stripers."

I mustered a weak smile. Now he was overcompensating. Maybe Dad hadn't buried that postgame comment yet after all.

Since the doctors took away my license, I'd had to beg for rides wherever I wanted to go. School would break for summer soon, and that meant I had my jobs to get to.

If I didn't make the van on time, I'd miss the morning shift on the highway custodial crew. The late guys always got stuck with mowing the median, a much harder chore than picking up trash off the side of the road.

My shift would end just in time for me to catch a local commuter train to the crosstown bus, which left me barely enough time to make it to the mall for the lunch and dinner shift at Schmaltzy's Cafeteria.

I could always tell exactly how late I was by the size of the stack of dishes in the sink beside the Hobart. Good thing I was a fast washer.

The late guy inherited the macaroni and cheese pan. All the scouring in the world couldn't scrape the crust off those things, but I did my best. I picked tiny bits of steel wool out of my hands every night before I crashed.

In a few weeks I'd have to add the summer basketball

league to this crazy schedule. I'd smell like grease and detergent, but if I hustled, I could make it on time. Throw in my nights tutoring at the Student Life Center, and it made for one exhausted me.

The mad scramble for transportation got really old really fast. I was constantly late for everything. I felt bad when I stood up my students one night because the crosstown bus broke down.

And Coach had suddenly stopped speaking to me, which had never happened before. I hoped it didn't have anything to do with the comment that Gary Coleman twerp made. No, it was probably just because I was always late—he hated tardiness. His usual punishment included an agonizing series of wind sprints at the end of practice. But instead Coach did nothing. He gave me the total silent treatment, which was actually worse. One night after practice I just started doing the wind sprints myself, hoping to get back into his good graces.

Dad couldn't help me, either. Not because he didn't want to drive me, but because all my running around usually occurred during the long hours of his never-ending workday, and we depended on his overtime to pay off the third mortgage he'd taken out on the house by then.

Eventually, I just threw in the towel, went to the garage, and pumped air into the tires of my old dirt bike. Hell, it beat walking.

Except for when it rained. Or when you weren't in the mood for public humiliation. One day I was riding my bike to practice after work because Coach had asked to see me early. I was running late so I pedaled as fast as I could. I was more than a little annoyed when I stopped for a red light at a crowded intersection and found myself surrounded by a gang of kids on skateboards. The oldest one must have been at least a couple years younger than me. He was just getting the first whisper of a mustache on his lip.

"You kidding me?" He spoke through a menthol cigarette that dangled from his lips. "That bike's like twenty years old. Mag wheels?"

I rolled my eyes and waited for the light to change. When it changed to green I stood up on the bike to press down on the pedal as hard as I could to distance myself from this bad after school special, but the bike didn't lurch forward like it should have. Something was dragging behind it, holding it back. I turned around and saw the kid with the quasi mustache, his hands gripping the back of the bike for a free ride on his skateboard.

I thought about clocking him, but the only thing more humiliating than riding your dirt bike to school is getting in a fight with a bunch of kids.

"What are you doing, dumbass? Busy intersection, lots of cars."

The kid looked back at his friends and grinned. He was in full showmanship mode now, and it was only going to get worse.

"It's called skitching, asshole," he said to me. "It means I get a free ri—"

WHUMP!

The blur of a car whizzed by and knocked him off the back of my bike. He bounced off the car's windshield and flew high into the air. I didn't see him land, because it was clear on the other side of the street across from all the traffic. His skateboard veered across the intersection, somehow missed every car, and disappeared into a sewer.

The car screeched to a halt; the kid's friends raced over to his side. One of them had the good sense to use his cell phone to take a picture. The driver of the car called an ambulance, and by the time I got there, the injured kid, drained of all color, was coughing up blood.

I moved in quickly, before any of the stunned bystanders could protest, and I grabbed his head between my two hands.

"Hey, kid!" I tried to get his attention. His eyes were glassy, rolling back in his head like a porcelain doll's.

"Hey, dumbass! I'm talking to you!" I yelled at him to keep him conscious, to keep his attention on my voice while my hands did their work. My hands burned as I yelled. "Don't ever do that again, you hear me?!" I shook him by the shoulders, and I felt like my hands were going to melt. "You hear me?!"

Traffic had stopped by now, and people were gathered around me. A gruff man with a tire iron had organized a group of adults to move me away from the injured kid. They began to approach.

Finally, the boy's limp eyelids popped to life and he looked at the panic around him.

"Okay, okay, I'm sorry." He wiped the blood away from his mouth. The coughing had stopped, and there was no more blood trickling out. He even stood up. "Really, I'm sorry. Is everyone okay?"

The ambulance arrived moments later, but I was long gone by then. I heard the paramedics had to treat the driver of the car that hit the kid more than they had to do anything for the kid himself. The driver was apparently in shock, hyperventilating from the whole ordeal, and the kid with the quasi mustache gave her the paper bag that carried his cigarettes so she'd have something to breathe into. The driver accidentally inhaled the receipt, and the paramedics had to fish it out of her windpipe.

I stopped in the parking lot in front of the gymnasium and puked into the bushes. I wiped my mouth. I didn't like throwing up, but I was getting better at this: my fingers didn't even twitch this time.

"You're late," Coach said when I finally arrived, disheveled and worn out. He clutched a tub of potato chips and offered me one.

"Uh, no thanks," I said.

"Listen, Thom. I'm going to cut to the chase here." He shuffled a few papers on his desk. They were yellow with age. "How long have you played center for me?"

"Five years."

"Really? Is that all?" His eyeballs rolled up as he tried to remember, like he was trying to get a look back at his brain. "I thought it was more than that."

I stared at a coffee mug on his desk. It said NUMBER ONE DAD! in big, bright letters, and it was half full with coffee from the morning. The creamer had congealed into a thick film on the surface.

He chomped down on a potato chip, shook his head, and shrugged.

"Well, the point is, I've been looking after you for a long time now, and I only have your best interest at heart."

Uh-oh. Here it comes.

"This little medical problem of yours, it's got us worried. See, we have extremely high insurance premiums to pay here at school. It's getting to the point where I don't know how any athletic program can survive. Do you understand what I'm saying?" He fiddled with a burned chip in his puffy fingertips. He focused on the chip so that he didn't have to look me in the eye. Finally, he popped it in his mouth.

Why wouldn't he look at me? It couldn't be the seizures. People haven't thought you could catch those since the Dark Ages, since they thought all you needed to feel better was a good leeching. Plus, the coach had a daughter with cerebral palsy.

My mind drifted and I looked at a potted plant on his desk. It was made of three branches—the first branch was dark green and normal, the second was pretty normal except for the cobwebs on it, and the third was desiccated and dying. Coach spotted me staring at the dying branch, then watered the plant with the dregs of his coffee mug.

"Thom, I don't think you can be on the team anymore."

What the hell was he talking about, he didn't think I could be on the team anymore?! Did I just have my hands amputated and nobody told me? Of course I could still play on the team.

"Maybe you'd be more comfortable on the junior squad."

I tried to get this straight in my head. He wanted me to go play with a bunch of kids in junior high because I have a seizure disorder?

"It's really a matter of priorities, the safety of the school, your health," he rattled on. "Insurance premiums, liability issues . . ."

And suddenly it all made sense. Why he'd been giving me the silent treatment at practice, why he wouldn't look at me anymore. I'd known all along, but I just didn't want to admit it. He'd heard what that little Gary Coleman twerp had said about me outside the gym after the game, and now he didn't want me around. I made him uncomfortable.

"Because I'm different?" I wanted to hear him say it.

He finally looked at me, and I could see something right behind his eyes. It wasn't a look of disappointment. It was a look of disgust.

"Because you're different." He bit down on a potato chip.

I touched the dead branch of the potted plant on his desk. I fiddled with its brown leaves while I thought about what I should say. I was fuming, burning inside out with anger. I wanted to tell him that I didn't deserve this. I considered begging him to let me stay on the team so I could still play. Then I considered telling him he could take his JV squad and shove it up his—

But then I saw something that told me exactly what I was going to say. As Coach reached for another chip, I noticed that from the depths of his chest a dark, black glow emanated, a murky wave. I can't explain how I knew what it meant, but it was as natural an understanding as you have when you pull your hand away from scalding hot water.

A strange thought occurred to me. A voice in my head said I could reach out and touch the thick, murky darkness and shape it in my hands and roll it like a lump of Play-Doh until it dissolved into my palms. My hands felt hot, seething. But I didn't reach out and touch the darkness. That same voice in my head told me it was too much for me to handle, that it would hurt me. So I didn't go near him. Instead I put my hands in my pockets and stood up.

"If you don't go get a cardiogram soon," I said, "you're going to die." I stopped at the door on my way out and added, "You probably won't even make it to next season."

I glanced at the potted plant—now with three healthy branches—and I slammed the door behind me as I left.

I came home early and stood in the hallway and watched the sun go down outside. Walking upstairs, taking off my jacket, or grabbing a snack required too much effort. I didn't have to work and I wasn't supposed to be at the learning center, so there was nothing to unglue my feet from the floor. My head throbbed, and I wanted to sleep for a million years until there was nothing left to worry about.

Finally I went to Dad's desk bureau, crowded with bills and insurance paperwork, and unplugged the laptop. I took his real estate homework off the top of the computer, and brought it up to my room to check my e-mail. Maybe I'd get a head start on that history paper, too.

Instead I went straight for the porn.

I had strict rules about looking at porn. First off, I wasn't allowed to think about suicide after I looked at it. Years ago, when I'd first figured out I was a sucker for a nice hairy chest, I thought for sure I'd have to kill myself before I was eighteen. The closer I got to eighteen the more I had to rethink that solution.

Second, there couldn't be anyone in the house when I did

it. The last thing I needed was to get caught jerking off to an oiled muscle stud. A few years ago, when our class took a field trip to Washington, Rich Roberson was caught beating off to a men's exercise magazine. He had some lame excuse about how the magazine was left under the bed, and he was just doubled over with stomach cramps or something, but then he came to school after a weeklong absence with bruises all over his face, his arm in a cast, and an awkward limp. He told everyone he had been in a car accident, but people had spotted his family's cars and there was no sign of any damage. A few weeks later, his family sent him away to boarding school and moved out of town.

Third rule: it had to be clean. No horses, no pets, no scat, and absolutely no kids. I never understood the fascination with young hairless boys anyway. I wanted someone big and broad and hairy, a real man like you used to see in magazines and on TV from the late '70s. Mechanics, plumbers, lifeguards, and cowboys with dirty hands.

And lastly, the site had to be worthwhile, otherwise my imagination was always better. One of the sites I most frequently visited was the Hero Fantasy Worship Web site. I don't know anyone who turns my crank more than Uberman, and it's not just the body. Honest. The guy is the paragon of everything a man should aspire to be—the perfect hero. Superstrength, the power of flight, invincibility—all the A-level superpowers. But his strength of character was just so damn perfect, too. Always saying the right thing on the news after a big fight, never too busy to thank his fans. Hell, the man even found time after saving the world to help small pets in various forms of distress. Perfect skin, a great smile with impossibly bright, but not horsey, teeth, and strong, chiseled features. Okay, so his body was also amazing, but I noticed the details others might overlook. For instance, his legs were as big as his upper body, in perfect proportion. I always laugh when I see some muscle guy at the gym who bench-presses some ungodly sum of weight, and then when he hops up from the bench, you see that he's teetering on top of skinny legs, like a Smithfield ham walking on toothpicks. I'd never seen him up close, only briefly, flying through the sky with the rest of the League, but from what I'd seen on TV, his muscular proportions were the same as the drawn, impossibly buff version of him in his comic book.

Once I'd even bought a poster of Uberman to put on my wall. It was a rebellious phase, during my first year of high school. I was at a comic book convention at the Radisson and saw this poster of Uberman, shirtless but still wearing his cape. He had impressive nipples spread across his perfectly built, massive chest. I deliberately left my bag of comic books by a magazine stand so that once all my friends had left to wait at the bus stop, I could run back inside and buy the poster without anyone seeing me.

I don't know what the hell I was thinking. Like I could come home and nail Uberman on the ceiling above my bed. The poster wasn't taboo just because of the sexual implications, either. Anything about people with superpowers was forbidden in my house. We couldn't even talk about them. There was this one time when I was just a kid and I'd first joined the basketball team and Clayton Camp came over to play.

We'd shot baskets in the driveway with the hoop my dad had just hung above the garage. When we got bored, Clayton ran inside and pulled some action figures out of his overnight bag. All superheroes. All superpowered.

"I'll be Uberman, you can be Right Wing." He handed me my action figure. Superpowered heroes were bad enough, but Right Wing was outright treason.

"I don't know if that's such a good idea," I replied. I glanced over at my father hosing down lime in the yard. He stopped by the bushes to chop a garter snake in half with a shovel. He disappeared into the backyard to dispose of the remains.

"C'mon, it'll be fun. We can blow up some people or something. I've got firecrackers." He pulled some low-grade fireworks out of his bag.

We played at the foot of the driveway, near the gutter and behind the bushes, so no one could see us. We used the figurines to simulate our own battle sequence, and with Clayton at the helm, there was a lot of death and destruction.

He went for a firecracker to blow up some of his sister's old Barbies.

"Why don't you use the flare instead?" I cut my eyes toward the yard; I couldn't see Dad. "Something not so . . . loud."

"Good idea," he said. "We'll torch her hair."

Somehow Uberman and Right Wing, despite their combined superspeed, let Barbie's head melt to an expressionless clump of hair and plastic under the heat of the flare.

Clayton reached for the pack of firecrackers and then lit a match.

"Look out, it's Frankie Flamethrower! He's going to finish her off!" Clayton shouted.

"Clayton, don't light the—" I reached for the firecrackers, but he'd already lit a fuse before I got the words out.

He held the firecrackers high in the air away from me and pushed me to the ground.

The wick had almost burned down to the cracker, and I could see in a split second it would explode the entire pack in Clayton's hand. A flicker of panic sparked in his eyes when he looked to his hand and saw how quickly the wicks were burning down.

"Throw it!" I yelled. "Throw it!"

But he was too scared to do anything, like the firecrackers were stuck to his hand with glue. He was frozen.

And a forceful stream of water blasted the fireworks out of his hand and almost knocked him off his feet.

I looked up and saw Dad standing across the yard with the garden hose–gun. He marched over toward us spraying water nonstop from the hose. He never let the stream off of the fireworks until he was certain that there wasn't a spark left. Then he turned the stream of water on the action figures and blasted them into the gutter.

"My heroes!" Clayton watched the force of the water wash them down the gutter.

Clayton slipped in the mud as he struggled to get up. He was crying, still scared, and humiliated. My dad reached out his hand to help him up.

Clayton pushed my father away and ran inside crying. I stared at the muddy handprint on my father's work shirt, and then I picked up the soggy firecrackers to throw in the garbage. That was the last time Clayton came over.

So it didn't seem like such a good idea to put up a poster of a superhero—shirtless or not. I ended up throwing the poster away in a Dumpster behind the Food Lion, but that didn't mean I couldn't go online every now and again to sneak a look.

The Web site promised a host of treats for subscribers, but I wasn't stupid enough to give them a credit card number. My dad had been through enough scandal to last a lifetime, and he didn't need to add gay Internet porn to the list next time he went in to get his hard drive upgraded. Which is why I was super careful to wipe the history of all prior sites before I gave the computer back. I cruised around the "free tour" section, which I'd only been through about one hundred times. The last page had this shot of Uberman, totally naked except for the "JOIN NOW!" strategically placed over his manhood. Most people would feel shortchanged, which I'm sure was the intended effect, and sign up immediately to see what he had underneath that icon. Still, I knew better than to pay for it. Plus, the picture would be totally bogus; it would be Uberman's head superimposed on some other guy's body anyway. I could tell because the nipples were nowhere near as big as they'd been on the poster. Like I said, my imagination was always better, and that picture, with all it suggested, was more than enough for me.

To help fall asleep at night I used to make up scenarios about Uberman. This was a favorite: He'd pick me up from a game after school and drive me home, and we'd be totally in love, and I'd lay my head in his lap as he drove. I'd look up at him, and he'd look back down at me and smile, the corners of his full lips turning up ever so slightly, until he couldn't help but pull over to the side of the road and kiss me.

Another favorite: Uberman rescues me from some terrifying situation where I'd valiantly defended a group of innocent bystanders—kindergartners, physically challenged kindergartners—against one of his arch nemesis hell-bent on the destruction of innocents. Uberman would swoop in right as I dove in front of the death beam to save the children, and in an instant he'd block the beam and kick the supervillain's ass. And I'd knock out the henchman, who had miraculously crawled over to the death ray and was about to push the self-destruct button. Such an act of valor would elicit a personal invitation back to Uberman's pad, where we'd exchange coy pleasantries about our favorite movies, bond over our favorite music, and then he'd whisper words meant only for me right before he'd take me in his perfectly tanned hands and—

"Thom! Where's my computer?" Dad called out. His voice was close, he couldn't be far down the hall. God, he was stealthy when he wanted to be. I hadn't even heard him come home.

I fumbled to pull my pants up.

"Thom, I have my real estate class tonight! I need the computer!"

I struggled to pull up my pant leg and tried to smack the power button at the same time. The result wasn't pretty. I tripped over the DSL line and tumbled over onto my face. I heard a nauseating crunch when the laptop bounced off my bed and landed on the hardwood floor, a few inches away from the soft, cushioned throw rug.

Dad knocked and opened the door in one quick gesture.

"Jeez, Thom, what are you doing in here?"

The good news was that I'd fallen on my front, so you

couldn't tell my pants were undone. But the bad news was I saw Dad look over at the open laptop. That was it, my life was over.

I looked over my shoulder and saw a blank screen.

"Thom, I've told you a million times not to use the computer on the floor. Someone might step on it."

"Sorry."

He paused and looked around the room suspiciously.

"You okay?"

I thought about that kid who'd been hit by the car earlier, how his rib had made the same crunching noise as the computer.

"I'm fine. Really."

"I put that lasagna in the oven for you. I know it's leftovers, but it's always better a few days later anyway." He fiddled with some change in his pocket. "I should be back from class before you go to bed."

"Okay," I said. *You can go now.*

He stood for a minute and looked around the room. I knew he was apologizing for a shitty dinner; I knew he wished he could afford a steak dinner for us every night; I knew he was ashamed his only hope to get out of that shitty factory job was the real estate class at the Learning Annex every third Tuesday of the month. I wanted to tell him I didn't care about any of that, it didn't matter to me what the hell he did for a living, and I wasn't even that hungry anyway. I wanted to tell him I was going through all these changes and some of them scared me, and I really just needed to hear him tell me that everything was going to be okay. But I didn't say a word, because more than anything, I wanted him to leave so I could zip my pants up and fix the computer.

Dad picked at the grime underneath his fingernails for a second and then headed down the hallway to his room.

As soon as he left, I rushed over to the laptop and tried to turn it back on. Nothing. This was bad. Really bad. That picture would still be on it if a repairman turned it back on, and my life would be over. I picked up the laptop and shook it to see if I could hear anything. I heard some loose plastic bits rattling around inside the hard drive, like I was shaking a near-empty bottle of aspirin.

I set it on the bed and tried to remain calm. Maybe I could fix this. I took a deep breath and rubbed my hands over the smooth surface of the laptop and waited.

My hands didn't get hot, and I smacked them together a few times to see if I could ignite a twitch in one of my fingers. Maybe my powers extended to inanimate objects. I looked over at the electrical socket in the wall and thought about sticking my finger in it.

I tried whispering a prayer while I rubbed my hands over the screen.

"I booked us a court tomorrow, if you want to play—" Dad poked his head back in my room. "What are you doing?"

"Um . . ." I took my hands off the computer and rubbed them together. "Just praying my English paper gets an A."

Dad looked at me curiously, like he wanted to smile with me, but that something didn't add up. He walked over to my bed, reached down and grabbed the computer.

"Wait!"

Dad was surprised by the outburst. He folded the laptop shut and tucked it under his arm. He rubbed his eyes and thought about the right thing to say.

"Look, I know most of your friends have their own computer. As soon as I get my realtor's license, I'll be making enough to get you one." He took his thumb and pulled down the skin beneath my lower eyelid, a not-so-subtle gesture to see if I was on something. Then he mussed my hair and said, "For now we have to share."

I listened to his footsteps growing softer and softer as he walked down the hallway, down the stairs, until the screen door slammed shut behind him. I heard him rev up his old Camaro and pull out of the driveway, careful to avoid the cracked pavement at the foot of the driveway. He'd open the computer and see that picture, the gay superhero porn site, and understand everything all in one nauseating moment of clarity. I stared out the window at the full moon and watched it cast shadows that danced on the mulch in our backyard, like skeletons on a freshly dug grave. I knew I had to leave.

CHAPTER THREE

I CHECKED THE CLOCK above the stove, and give or take ten minutes, I figured I had two and a half hours to pack and get a head start before Dad got back. For some odd reason, the first thing I put in my bag was a six-pack of canned juice and some protein bars. It wasn't like I was going camping, but I thought it would be a good idea to take some food anyway. Next, I found myself throwing a can opener in the bag. It seemed like something everyone should have.

I tried not to look at photo albums as I hurried past Dad's trophy case. There were more important things to bring, and I didn't have a ton of room for pictures. I grabbed a medium-weight jacket from the closet and climbed the stairs, three at a time.

In my room I grabbed the Swiss Army knife my dad gave me for Christmas. I stood there picking at a hangnail as I tried to think about what my life would be like once I left, where I'd live, where I'd work, how I'd finish school. I caught myself thinking about falling in love with someone who I hoped was out there right now thinking about the possibility of me, but I quickly banished the notion. It was that kind of thinking that landed me in this situation to begin with. Hope can ruin you.

I packed exactly seven clean pairs of socks and underwear. I wanted to take more so I wouldn't have to do as much laundry, but the bag was only so big and I needed to be able to sling it over my shoulder without it slowing me down. The hardest part was actually figuring out which clothes to take. I'd need something nice for a good job interview, and my sport coat and tie didn't fold up nicely in the bag. I folded the jacket seven different ways from Sunday before I just wadded it up beside my sweatpants in a corner of the bag. In the bathroom I threw my toothbrush in my dop kit and stopped at my reflection in the mirror. I grabbed some tweezers and plucked at a stray hair growing in the middle of my eyebrows. I'd never seen a hair there before, which could only mean there'd be more, so I tossed the tweezers in, too.

By the time the moon had drifted above the window's line of sight, I decided my food choices hadn't been wise. I could drink water for free anywhere and therefore should ditch the drinks and pack more food, maybe some canned goods, maybe some peanut butter.

I headed downstairs back to the kitchen, but stopped by the shelves with the photo albums. I reached up high and dragged one of the albums off the dusty top shelf.

I opened to a page of me at eleven months drinking a

can of Pabst Blue Ribbon. The tradition continued through my childhood. My dad used to cook out on the grill, when it began to get nice outside in late May, when the gardenia bush began to bloom. He'd come home from work, sometimes whistling a Johnny Cash song, and you'd never know he had any troubles while he dragged out the industrial-size sack of charcoal and filled up the grill, lighting it just so, because only amateurs used lighter fluid. Then we'd wait at least an hour to get the coals perfect, a radiating core of molten light in the middle, before we could actually put the burgers on. It drove Mom crazy.

Mom would pass the long wait by shooing away flies from the cheap meat patties and slicing onions and looking out on the horizon for something that never seemed to come. While he waited for the embers to light in that perfect configuration, Dad would enjoy a beer (or two) on the deck he'd built with his own two hands. And he'd ask yours truly, each time, to go inside and grab the beer he'd put in the freezer. And each time I'd shake it up as much as possible before I brought it out to him.

Sometimes I'd toss the can up in the air and spin it like a baton, sometimes I'd jump up and down with it, sometimes I'd roll it down the kitchen floor like I was bowling. I'd walk out onto the deck slowly, as if there was nothing to hide, and I could always tell he knew what I was up to. That was part of the ritual, part of the game. I'm sure he could read my smirk when he took the beer out of my tiny hands, but he played along anyway. Sometimes he'd hold it over the grill and pretend like he was going to explode it over my burger, sometimes he'd ask me to open it. Sometimes he'd chase me around the deck threatening to spray it in my direction, and sometimes he'd open it up and act surprised when the spray caught him in the eye. He was consistent about one thing, however: he always let me take a sip, safely out of Mom's line of vision, before he set the hot dogs on the grill.

I came across a picture my mom's sister had taken of us at a cookout where I'd accidentally given Mom the can of Dad's shaken beer. Aunt Mary Sue snapped the shot the instant Mom opened the beer, and the entire picture exploded with a foamy spray on top of elated, surprised faces. That had always been my mother's favorite picture, and I stared at a chocolate smudged thumbprint in the corner that proved it.

I leafed through the rest of the album and pulled down another one. This one had a series of shots Dad took on one of our frequent train-watching trips. Dad loved to follow trains, take pictures of the engines, wait at crossroads in deserted towns for some old, rarely seen engine to whirr past us. Mom would pack a picnic lunch, and we'd pile into the car and bounce along a deserted main street in some choked-out old town, with me crawling around the weeds near the tracks looking for june bugs and railroad spikes while Mom and Dad drank beer and munched deviled eggs until the train passed. By the time I was a teenager, those trips felt like punishment, but in the pictures we were nothing but broad smiles in desiccated towns. We laughed with unbridled joy whenever the trains finally whizzed past and sent the wind whipping through our hair.

I rubbed my finger over the picture of my mother at my kindergarten graduation. Time seemed to have faded it. My mother stood behind my father in the back row of the audience, and her image had become blurry. I remember how uncomfortable my mother was with having her picture taken. She must have fidgeted each time someone snapped the shot; that would explain the blur. I flipped through the rest of the pages and noticed that while the shots seemed clear, Mom's image in them had become increasingly faded. She'd been growing fainter and fainter by the year, and I was surprised I'd never noticed it before. By the time I saw the picture from my first-ever basketball game, you could barely see her at all sitting behind my father on the bleachers.

I checked my watch. I'd been stupid to look at old pictures. I should have been on the road long ago. It was a quarter of eleven, and I hadn't even figured out what I was going to do for money.

I flipped the album's pages to my mom's favorite shot—of the beer can exploding on us. I peeled back the cellophane so I could remove the picture and noticed a little strip of paper poking out from behind it. I stripped the photo off the sticky page, and there it was.

I couldn't believe what I saw.

I glanced around the room. Maybe there was a camera, maybe this was a practical joke. It had to be. But when I looked back down at the page, it was plain as day.

A note.

The edges of the paper were almost as dry and brittle as the picture. I tore off all the other photos, one by one, and discovered underneath each a hidden treasure of pictures, another set of photos I was never meant to see, until now.

I stared down at the note in my hands, my fingertips numb, and the words, written in my mother's perfect, deliberate cursive, burned in my mind:

To my son. Know yourself.

I tucked the stack of photos into my bag and ran out the door.

CHAPTER FOUR

AS THE BUS PULLED OUT of the terminal, I remembered I'd forgotten to drag the trash can to the curb for pickup tomorrow. That would be Dad's first clue I was gone. I'd managed to say good-bye to the house, and I remembered thinking that I was forgetting something as I watched the bats dance in and out of the glow of streetlights. It was too late to worry about anything else but leaving now.

I settled into an empty seat in the back of the bus by the bathroom. The faded cushions smelled like an ashtray, and I leaned my head against the window and stared back at the terminal as we pulled on the highway. I reached down for my bag and pulled out the stack of pictures I'd swiped from the album, a secret history. I craned my head above the seat to make sure no one in the bus was looking back in my direction, and then I started leafing through the piles.

The first picture of my mother wasn't really a picture of her at all, but of her boot. It was an original black-and-white photo from a newspaper clipping, and there was a chubby, middle-aged woman with a bad perm dressed like a female wrestler in a Halloween mask, and what looked like cardboard, polka-dot wings hastily pinned to the back of her unitard. The chubby woman lay flat on the ground, knocked out, a single stylish boot pinning down her chest. She was wrapped in a lariat pulled taut into the air above her by an unseen force, like her assailant had been magically airbrushed out of the picture, except for the boot.

Inscribed on the picture was the following message:

Congratulations on nabbing your first villain. Keep up the good work! Yours in courage, Captain Victory

I kept staring at the pictures in disbelief. I didn't blink once for at least an hour. My mother had been a hero. All these years, and I had no idea. The questions were just beginning to take shape in my head. Why had she hidden it from me? Did Dad know? Is this where my powers came from?

I flipped over the picture and found a newspaper article folded and taped to the back. The headline read, "Metro City Mystery Figure Foils Ladybug's Larceny!"

The next shot was taken when Mom was around my age. I'd never seen any pictures of her when she was a young woman, before she met my father. You know how women can be with their pictures. Most of them don't like to be reminded of how they looked thirty pounds ago.

But there was a specific reason I'd never seen these. Dad simply would never have allowed it. Not after what happened to him. Not after he'd laid down the law in his own house about superpowers.

There were more pictures of my mother, her body lithe and fit in a tight costume, in various victory poses with her own rogues' gallery of victims: The Ladybug, Miss Malevolence, Zorba the Meek, Morning Glory and her henchmen, the Pansies (no comment), and this chick called the Quarrel Queen, who had some sort of sonic scream device that poked out of her stomach. God, what a bunch of losers. In those ridiculous outfits did they ever pose a real threat to anyone?

There were a series of group shots where Mom must have joined a C-list group of costumed heroes called C.R.I.M.E.B.U.S.T.E.R.S! Looked like she was teamed up with a guy who could shoot fire out of one hand and make ice cubes with the other. The entire group was young and tan, their bellies trim, held in effortlessly, and you could tell by their persistent smiles that they were always aware when the cameras were on them. There was a picture of the governor himself awarding them with medals of valor. The "Ones to Watch" article heralded Mom as one of a group of new up-and-coming heroes poised to take over where their golden age predecessors had left off.

There were also pictures of Mom in her civilian identity when she graduated from teachers college. She posed with a group of friends holding their diplomas and throwing their hats in the air. In the group, Mom was the only one looking at the camera, her graduation cap still on her head, a serene smile on her face, her lips slightly pursed, like she knew something they all didn't.

And then I saw how my parents had actually met. The banner above them read "LEAGUE TRYOUTS." I had no idea my mother ever got this close to the big time, but there she was up on the platform receiving her official probationary certificate from my father, Major Might. Mom looked elated at receiving official League-tryout status; but what you could see in her eyes was the way she looked up at my father. Here she was, fresh out of teachers college, holding a small idea of wanting to fight for truth and justice with her bag of invisible tricks, and a mountain-size crush on Dad, one of the most popular heroes of his time.

In the next group of shots, you could tell she'd become chummy with everyone on the League. She'd spent this day wandering around their secret clubhouse snapping candid photos. Elastic Elbert caught with his coiled arm down the toilet as he tried to unclog it; Warrior Woman putting on mascara and slathering on some anti-wrinkle cream—showing that maybe that ageless Greek-goddess beauty didn't come without a little effort; and the Nucleus and his sidekicks, the Electrons, engaged in their weekly poker night, cigars dangling from each of their mouths, brown liquor drinks resting on the table. From the surprised look on all their faces, you could tell my mother had uncanny access, a level of intimacy the mere mortals of the world would never have.

The subjects in the last picture of the series she had more respect for: she'd clearly asked them to pose. In the same fluid cursive handwriting, she'd written on the white border at the bottom of the graying photo, *Three generations of my favorite heroes.* Captain Victory, the elder statesman of the group, and according to history the world's very first costumed hero, had his arm around his former sidekick, my father, Major Might, who in turn had his arm around his current sidekick, the Right Wing. Each one flashed a handsome smile for my mother, chins held high. Perfect teeth. They each had a raised fist in the air with the three middle fingers up, signifying three generations of the world's most virtuous warriors for truth, justice, and a better way. I studied my Dad's smile in that photo and decided I'd never seen him happier, or more proud.

I remembered the old guy, Captain Victory. He'd been the only one to lend my father money after he couldn't get work and the bank seized our house. Up until a few years ago, when I started to get serious about sports, Dad had dragged me with him to the nursing home to visit his mentor every weekend. All I remember was the rotten smell of that old folk's home, sickly-sweet wafts of disinfectant meant to cover up the putrid smell of decay. The old man couldn't talk by then, so mostly my dad would bring in pictures or read the newspaper to him, stopping after every other story to grimace at the state of the world. Then Dad would give me a dollar and send me down to the cafeteria to get a bowl of Jell-O cubes, and I'd sit there and watch Dad try to spoon a few shaky cubes into the old guy's mouth.

There weren't too many shots of Mom in her costume after that. I guess it was always a challenge to snap a good shot of an invisible superhero in action. Then there was a brief piece in a magazine column that asked, "Whatever Happened to Invisible Lass?" The subtitle speculated that it was "The Ultimate Vanishing Act." Apparently, Mom had been as careful to hide her civilian identity from the public as she'd been in hiding her public identity from me. There was never another mention of the Invisible Lass, and just like that, she was gone.

I flipped to another shot and that's where my parents' wedding pictures began. I lifted the picture of Mom stuffing a piece of grocery-store wedding cake into Dad's mouth. The hidden pictures stopped there, back to the normal order of things. After a series of honeymoon pictures, mostly of Mom sunbathing and Dad on water skis, I saw the first shot of my mother in a maternity dress, her belly swollen with me crouched up inside her. She was taking a turkey out of the oven and holding it up proudly, while my dad was pointing at her tummy, a goofy grin on his face. I had never seen that expression on Dad before.

So this was it. This must be why I could do these superhuman things. I had inherited powers from my mother. I wasn't losing my mind at all. I shut out a nagging voice in the back of my head that said *Thanks a whole lot for up and leaving me on my own right now when I could really use someone like, oh I don't know, my* mother *to talk to about these major events happening in my life.* Instead I held the clippings and pictures in my hand and rested my head on the sticky bus window and looked up at the stars and thought about the future.

I woke up and wiped a thin trickle of drool off my cheek. In front of me I noticed a three-hundred-pound lady in a pineapple-print muumuu, who snorted every time the bus hit a bump in the road. She munched on a Fudgsicle and stared out the window. Beyond her was a young mother with thinning hair threatening to discipline her little girl with an oversize hairbrush. The kid couldn't have been more than five, and she was whining about wanting to go to bed. She had her tiny index finger shoved up her nose, and with her other finger she picked at her long, unwashed hair, in desperate need of some baby shampoo and an industrial-strength detangler. We made brief eye contact, and she immediately stopped complaining, just before her mom smacked her in the thigh with the back of the plastic brush. The little girl howled and yanked the brush out of her mother's hand and moved to smack her back when—

SCREEEECH!

The bus skidded across the highway. The passengers screamed as the rear of the bus fishtailed into oncoming traffic. The force sent the fat lady's face into the window, and her cheek smeared the Fudgsicle across the pane of glass.

The bus had barely come to a halt against the guardrail when the door burst open and a flurry of dark capes whooshed in.

Transvision Vamp, eyes glowing, whirled around, flicking her black cape over her shoulder, and glared at us. I had never encountered supervillains in real life before. I didn't recognize this crew, never seen them on the news. They couldn't be A-listers.

Vamp glanced at the driver momentarily, her eyes blazing red.

"Drive."

The bus driver floored the gas, and my head smacked the greasy headrest as we sped off.

She turned her attention to the passengers.

"Keep quiet and no one dies," she purred. Her eyes bored into us, and we felt glued to our seats.

Behind her stare, the bus driver reached discreetly for his cell phone.

"Don't try it, asshole," Snaggletooth lisped around his lone fang. He was hanging from the ceiling by his claws. He dropped down and speared the cell phone with one claw, grabbed the bus driver by the collar with his other claw, and casually tossed the driver out the door. He slipped into the driver's seat and slammed his paw on the gas pedal.

The lady in the muumuu screamed as we watched the driver fly by us horizontally outside the bus. We sped forward past him, and his mouth and eyes widened into gaping ovals. I stared at the driver, suspended in midair for a brief moment, and to my surprise the moment didn't pass. He just hung there, frozen in time, except for the yellow lines that sped past underneath him.

We looked up and saw he was hanging by someone's hand attached to his belt. An elongated arm and hand slowly pulled him around the bus and inside through the back window. I felt something wriggly and slick under my feet, but my eyes followed the long ropy arm as it began to retract and wander past the bathroom, under the seats, and across the aisle, until it met up with its owner—a short but muscular guy in a scaly green outfit—right under my feet!

"We said no victimss!" Ssnake hissed at Transvision Vamp, like a grade-schooler tattling on his classmate to his teacher.

Transvision Vamp massaged her temples with her fingers, and her stare turned a shade of ultraviolet as she peered beyond the passengers into the night behind the speeding bus.

"Do you see him?" Snaggletooth asked in a high-pitched

voice, panic setting in. His hands shook on the steering wheel and his claws dug into the hard plastic.

"Shut up, asshole, she's looking!" Ssnake craned his neck out of joint and stretched his head out the driver's side window for a better look. "He was right behind us. He can't be that far."

"Oh man, he's gonna kill me, he's gonna kill me, he's gonna kill me!" Snaggletooth slammed both paws on the gas.

"Wait, I think I see something." Transvision Vamp made her way to the back of the bus.

"What is it, what do you see?" Snaggletooth couldn't seem to get a grip.

"Will you calm down and keep your eyes on the road!" Ssnake brought his head back in the window.

"Screw you, I'm driving as fast as this piece of shit will go. I'm not getting caught by that guy, you don't know what he did to Frank. He caught him robbing that nursing home . . . before the police got there. . . ." Snaggletooth wiped beads of sweat from his forehead.

"That's urban legend." Ssnake tried to talk him down.

"Maybe." Snaggletooth inhaled deeply through his nose, shook his head, and pressed his knees together. "All I know is I plan on keeping both balls and using 'em until I'm an old man."

"Will you both shut up!" Transvision Vamp wiped a smear of lipstick off her front teeth and put her hands on the frame of the back window. "I think I can see the trail he left. Ssnake, hang me out the window so I can get a better look."

I struggled to move in my seat but couldn't. With these guys in the back of the bus not paying attention to us, if I could get up, I knew I could take the driver, I just knew it. An old man in the seat behind me began to hyperventilate. I managed to lift my arm up, reach back, and place my hand on his shoulder. I felt my hand burn as his wheezes subsided.

But my toes started to twitch.

Phantom Girl, Karate Kid, Dream Girl . . . I had to calm down. I could do this.

My leg muscles tensed, but I couldn't fire off the right signals in my brain to make them work.

Ultra Boy, Element Lad, Colossal Boy . . . I yanked my butt off the seat like I was pulling myself off flypaper and stood in the middle of the aisle.

Transvision Vamp and Ssnake were leaning out the window in the back, and Snaggletooth's attention was fixed on the road ahead of him. I struggled to put one foot in front of the other as I made my way up the aisle toward the driver's seat.

The lady in the muumuu covered her mouth with her hand to stifle a scream, and her eyes bulged as she shook her head at me. I kept going.

Matter Eater Lad . . . Light Lass . . .

I was just a few feet behind Snaggletooth now. I looked at his reflection in the rearview mirror, and I could see the panic in his eyes as he blazed the bus forward. With a little luck, he wouldn't look up in the mirror and see me. A few more seconds and I'd be on top of him.

"I found the trail!" Transvision Vamp shouted from outside the speeding bus.

"Oh God, where does it lead to?" Snaggletooth stammered, his eyes still on the road in front of him.

Star Boy . . . Shadow Lass . . . I took another step forward and raised my arms to strike.

Then something caught my attention through the front windshield.

"Hold on, I'm following it now!" Vamp shouted, the urgency increasing in her voice.

"Shit shit shit shit shit shit." Snaggletooth smacked the wheel in a vain effort to make the bus go faster.

I squinted and looked carefully through the windshield. A pair of eyes, a piercing gaze, stared into the bus from the darkness outside, like someone was hanging from the top of the bus. The eyes darted around, surveyed the scene as fast as possible.

Then the piercing eyes locked on to mine and I froze, standing there in the middle of the aisle, my arms raised ready to strike.

"I said, where does the goddamn trail lead—?" Snaggletooth shouted.

Transvision Vamp shouted frantically from the back of the bus. "The roof, he's on the roof!"

Snaggletooth turned his head around to look up at the roof. And he saw me.

I let out a small gasp of air, and I could hear him growl as his muscles tightened, ready to pounce. Snaggletooth sprung at me off his hind legs, claws aimed at my eyes.

Suddenly the front windshield burst into a thousand jagged fragments, and a man dressed in black swung himself into the bus. With lightning speed he leaped forward and tackled Snaggletooth before he could sink his claws into my pupils.

The Man in Black, who had just saved my life, rose before

Snaggletooth could catch his breath and began to land a flurry of staccato kicks in Snaggletooth's gut. Snaggletooth wheezed for air. The bus swerved back and forth, and the passengers screamed as we were thrown from side to side.

Ssnake slithered between my legs, his body gyrating forward in a swift, liquid line to the front of the bus. He popped up and resumed human form in the empty driver's seat and grabbed the steering wheel, which had begun to drift dangerously out of control. The bus smacked into a small Honda and sent it spinning into the guardrail.

The Man in Black delivered a devastating final kick to Snaggletooth's chin, knocking him up into the air. He landed face-first on the floor, and chipped off the end of his fang.

I stood up, wanting to help. A laser beam of light whizzed in front of me and blew a hole through a succession of seats. It stopped me in my tracks, and the passengers dove in all directions. I followed the beam back to Vamp's smoking eyes. She fired repeatedly at the Man in Black, who flipped from seat to seat, dodging the blasts. He bounced up the seats, making his way closer and closer to Vamp. She backed up against the wall, her eyes glowing green with panic. Ssnake was too busy driving to help; Snaggletooth was out cold on the floor; and she was about three seconds away from a hand-to-hand encounter with the most brutal vigilante on the planet. In desperation, she let loose a torrent of eye blasts at the passengers.

The lady in the muumuu shrieked and tried to wedge herself under her seat, and I dove to the other side of the bus. The mother grabbed her little girl and started to stand. The blasts ripped through their seats.

The young mother's face went white, and the little girl screamed. I saw that the mother suddenly had a chunk missing from her side. She clutched the wound, which was gushing thick, dark blood, like motor oil pouring out of a leaky engine. The Man in Black turned around to help, but I was already on it. I had her flat on the floor, my hands pressing firmly on the wound, my palms smoldering as they began to cauterize the gash. Blood spurted on my face. This was worse than anything I'd ever been able to heal, and I could feel the effort sapping my energy. A wave of nausea bubbled up in my stomach, and I fought the urge to barf. The little girl crawled under the seat and whimpered.

The Man in Black grabbed the oversize hairbrush off the floor and disappeared into the shadows under his cape and reemerged right in front of the screaming Vamp. Before she could react, he swiped the sharp bristles across her open eyes, blinding her in an instant. A scaly green leg wriggled past us on the floor and knocked the Man in Black's feet out from under him. Ssnake's elongated hand followed and kept the Man in Black busy, while Vamp wiped madly at her eyes, struggling to regain her sight.

I looked at Ssnake, trying with his appendages to drive the bus and fight the Man in Black at the same time. I saw him mouth "Screw it" to himself, and he took his remaining hand off the wheel and wriggled it back to Snaggletooth and smacked him hard in the face to wake up.

Snaggletooth opened his eyes and jumped up as the Man in Black took Ssnake's hand and foot and tied them in a knot. He threw the knotted limbs around Snaggletooth as the beast leaped for him.

"Snaggletooth, no!" Ssnake screamed, but it was too late. The Man in Black ducked, and Snaggletooth sailed above him out the back window, yanking Ssnake out of the driver's seat by his knotted limbs and carrying him with him. Ssnake's free hand caught the back of the bus, and the two villains flew up into the air, attached to the bus like a kid's balloon that had been tied there after a carnival.

A dark cape flashed past me, and before I could blink, the Man in Black was back in the driver's seat fighting with the gears to regain control of the swerving bus. He looked up into the mirror and his piercing eyes bounced from me to the young mother. I met his eyes and nodded urgently, like I was doing the best I could. My hands burned and I felt like I could drop from exhaustion at any moment, but I couldn't seem to make them any hotter. I was already reaching my limit.

"We have to get her to a hospital!" All that first-aid training really paid off.

The Man in Black pointed forward to the bridge in front of us, and beyond that to the city. We'd be there in just a few minutes if I could keep her alive until then, stretch my powers just a little further. The Man in Black leaned forward, determined, and pushed the bus to go faster.

We could make it—we were almost at the top of the bridge, the city hospital just seconds away once we were on the other side.

Suddenly a blast of energy ripped through the floorboards; crackling and spitting sparks, it began to slice the bus in two from rear to front. Transvision Vamp, undeterred by the blood dripping from her eyelids, was back in business, her eyes aiming a blast down the center of the aisle.

The Man in Black looked up at me in the mirror, his eyes pleading.

I looked down at my hands, blood from the wound seeping up between my fingertips. The young mother's eyes were rolling back into her head, so I pressed harder. The extra effort made me feel like my head was going to explode. The crack in the aisle from the Vamp's eye blast was getting closer and closer to us.

"Help me!" I shouted.

The Man in Black's eyes look down in resignation for a split second before he bounded out of his seat and threw himself back at Vamp. He backhanded her before she could finish ripping the bus in two, but not before Ssnake and Snaggletooth had pulled themselves back on board. Ssnake spit a glob of venom at the Man in Black, who leaped above it. The venom landed in a splat on the floor, and partially on top of the old man's steel-tipped shoe. It burned and dissolved the matter underneath it like acid. The old man screamed; his shoe hissed with smoke.

I reached over to him, one hand still firmly attached to the young mother, and I covered his burning foot with my palm. I clenched my teeth in pain as my hand burned.

Snaggletooth took a swipe at the Man in Black, and the vigilante flipped up into the air, landing far up the aisle. The puddle of Ssnake's spit had burned another hole through the floorboard. Snaggletooth lurched forward, and one of his legs dropped through the hole. He screamed in pain as his femur snapped. I squeezed the old man's foot tighter, determined not to let his foot dissolve.

"Ssnake, get us off this thing!" Vamp rubbed her chin.

"I'm trying!" He caught a deep punch to the kidney from the Man in Black.

The Vamp rubbed her temples and aimed her vision at the apex of the bridge the bus had begun to climb. In an instant, she sent a shock blast that rippled fissures into the pavement. The bridge began to crumble.

We all looked forward in horror as the bus sped toward a gaping hole in the bridge.

The Man in Black swiftly struck Vamp in the windpipe with the side of his hand and jumped back into the driver's seat. He navigated the bus through the holes in the bridge like we were speeding through an obstacle course in a minefield.

I struggled to hold on to both the young mother's bleeding side and the old man's dissolving foot. Below me, the middle of the bus was splitting in two, and it slowly began to stretch me apart like saltwater taffy. In a few seconds I was going to lose one of them, or drop in through the split in the floor, or both. I thought about what my dad would do in this situation, but I couldn't think fast enough. I didn't know how much longer I could hold on. I looked up at the Man in Black's eyes in the rearview mirror. I couldn't see an expression under his cowl, but I knew his eyes were telling me to hold on, the holes in the pavement ahead of us didn't matter, we were almost there, I could do it.

Beneath me the two halves of the bus parted.

"Look!" The little girl pointed out the window. At first they looked like a flock of giant birds.

Suddenly, a rainbow of colors lit up the night outside of the bus. Sparks of light reflected off the little girl's face, and a fireworks display of bright colors exploded around us.

The birds swooped down closer, and I realized they weren't birds at all.

It was the League.

CHAPTER FIVE

UBERMAN DOVE DOWN from the stars ready for battle, his body aimed, his muscles poised and rippling under his costume. His cape and long hair moved in silky waves behind him as he flew.

The Spectrum, who was the League's most easily recognizable hero next to Uberman, emitted a tangible rainbow bridge of color from his fingertips that let the bus glide smoothly over the last deadly holes in the bridge.

Then Uberman landed on the front of the bus with a graceful *plink*, lifted us, and suddenly we were airborne. The passengers on the bus cheered. The Man in Black, now useless in the driver's seat, looked at me through the rearview mirror. I caught myself looking up at Uberman with sheer awe.

The Man in Black sprang from the driver's seat and went after the villains in the back. Ssnake was the only one who looked like he could put up a decent fight at this point; Snaggletooth and Vamp were down for the count. When he reached them, the Man in Black hesitated for a moment before he threw a punch and looked back in my direction, just enough time for Ssnake to wrap his protective arms around his partners and pry open an emergency window exit.

The Man in Black didn't try to stop them, and suddenly he was beside me. I could feel the heat of his breath on my neck. He grabbed my hand, hard, like you would discipline a child.

I'd been so busy staring at Uberman that I'd taken my hand off the young mother's wound. The Man in Black looked deep in my eyes. I was so mortified that I'd let my attention wander, I wanted him to pull off his cowl and say something. Instead he placed my hand back on the mother's side. She was now unconscious. My powers had been more effective than I'd expected, but as soon as I'd taken my hand off, the wound had begun to gush again. Now I kept my hand firmly on it. I couldn't look the Man in Black in the eye after that.

Ssnake enveloped his partners in one single swipe, bundled them to his chest, and spread out his back, king cobra–style, like a parachute. The bottom half of his body morphed into a coil, and he bounced from the bus like a loaded spring. The Man in Black came within a millimeter of snatching Snaggletooth's paw as they floated away and disappeared into the darkness.

Another slight jolt to the bus, and we looked down through the gaping split in the floor and saw the river below us as we flew through the air. The lady in the muumuu held her hand to her chest and crouched down by the wall, like she was afraid she might fall through. Then we saw Warrior Woman piecing the floor back together like a zipper, one chunk at a time, and all the passengers began to applaud.

Uberman opened the door politely.

"You're safe now, folks, back on good ol' terra firma."

There was a flash of silver, and suddenly Silver Bullet stood above me.

"I'll take it from here, young man." He scooped the bleeding young mother into his arms and whisked her off, presumably to the nearest hospital.

In the seat next to us, her little girl pulled on one of the tangles in her hair. Tears began to well in her eyes.

"Where's he taking my mama?"

"Wait," I called out. "You forgot about her—"

Another whirr of light, this time golden, and suddenly Golden Boy, Silver Bullet's longtime sidekick, appeared in front of me.

"We never forget," he said without an expression. In a flash he'd cradled the little girl and was off, kicking up some dirt and grime from the floorboard in my face. As I rubbed a tiny piece of gravel out of the corner of my eye, I wondered if he'd done it on purpose.

I stood and dusted myself off and saw that the lady in the muumuu was already deep in the thrall of Uberman, who was unwedging her from one of the seats.

On the street outside, reporters, cameramen, and adoring fans swarmed the League. The lights lit up Uberman, Warrior Woman, the Spectrum—aka Dr. Roy G. Biv—and then the sea of media parted to make room for the longstanding leader of the League.

Justice raised his hands high, a command to listen, and the crowd obeyed.

"Nothing to see here, folks. Just doing our jobs."

He spoke plainly in the voice of the common man, but with just enough grave authority to give his words weight.

Justice had been the League's leader ever since I was alive, but the guy was in better shape than I'd ever be. He had to be only a few years younger than my dad, and I wondered about the secret to his longevity in a business that seemed to spit out a new, rabidly popular teen superhero group every year or two.

The mob of reporters was shouting questions on top of each other. It was bedlam.

"We'll comment on all that and we'll answer all your questions at the proper time. Right now you'll have to please let us go about our job protecting you, the people."

Justice was a real pro with the press. His voice remained calm and reassuring. Despite the pandemonium, he never got testy, never raised his voice. I thought I heard a few reporters shout out some questions about his feelings on "the death," but I couldn't figure out what that was all about, since as far as I could tell there were no casualties on the bus.

Then I remembered the young mother and my heart sank. I couldn't believe how dumb I'd been to take my hand off her, even for a second. If she died, it would be my fault.

I saw Uberman over by the police barricade lines as he signed autographs for throngs of women who screamed for his attention. He was in the process of asking a woman with fake lips how to spell her name.

"Is that 'Bambi' with one 'i' or two?"

I looked down at my hands and saw them shaking with leftover energy. My heart was still pounding, the adrenaline still pumping through my veins, and I wanted to run a few laps around the block to burn it off. There were no reporters around me, so I actually dropped to the ground to do push-ups.

"Nice job back there, kid."

I looked up, and Uberman was standing above me. My heart leaped into my throat and I hopped to my feet.

"Uberman. It's an honor to meet you." He was going to let me touch his hand. I couldn't believe it.

I wiped the gravel off my palms and shook his hand. I stood there awed and speechless.

"This is the part where you're supposed to tell me your name."

"Oh," I said. "Thom, my name's Thom. I was just, you know, taking the bus because my car broke down and—"

"Some pretty nifty powers you have there, Thom. You'd better be careful or you might put me out of business one day." He gave me a big chuckle and a mock punch to the shoulder. Humor wasn't his strong suit—he should stick with earnest. Still, who cared—God, he was *touching* me. My hand was buzzing from the contact with his skin.

He wiped a long strand of luscious platinum hair out of his face and smoothed it back over his ear. An eternity passed as I stood there studying his face, trying to memorize every detail, every perfect feature. He didn't seem to mind. He let my eyes wander over his face. I was like a kid watching a Disney cartoon for the very first time, absolutely mesmerized by the wonder of it all.

The lights from the camera crews lit up his face. Okay, so maybe his eyes were a little too far apart, and maybe that nose had been shaped so perfectly with a little help from the right nose doctor, using the old "deviated septum" excuse. I was still about to pass out from his beauty. My eyes worked him from his chin to his chest, from one ear to the other, and he soaked up the adulation like you'd bask in front of a sunlamp.

My eyes ended up right above his left ear, where I spotted the Man in Black standing far behind him in the shadows by a piling underneath the freeway overpass. He was far away, small in the distance, but I could tell he was looking right at me, and even with his mouth covered by his dark cowl, I could tell he was frowning at me. His eyes worked like a mirror, and I could suddenly see myself standing there, my mouth open, gawking at Uberman with a dull grin plastered on my face, drool practically spilling off my lower lip.

My eyes darted back and forth, distracted, between Uberman's bright face and the Man in Black's burning stare.

"What is it?" Uberman whipped his head around to see what could possibly interrupt a fan's dream chance to worship him.

But the Man in Black was gone, vanished into the shadows. Uberman turned back to me, and I felt guilty for not asking this sooner.

"Is she okay?"

Silver Bullet suddenly appeared next to us. "Is who okay?"

"The woman you took to the hospital."

Golden Boy suddenly materialized at Silver Bullet's side,

his voice like an echo. "Of course she's okay. We took care of it."

I didn't like the way this Golden Boy said *we*, as in *not you*. Even though he was wearing a mask, I could tell by his voice and attitude that he wasn't all that much older than I was. He stood with a strong, rigid posture, arms folded across his chest.

"C'mon, Francis. We've got to go. Justice called a press conference." Silver Bullet tugged on Uberman's cape.

"Okay, okay, just a sec," Uberman said to his less-popular teammate in a tone that reminded him you don't get to be Uberman by shortchanging the fans on their star-time.

Francis? His name is *Francis?*

Uberman shook my hand again and smiled sincerely.

"I appreciate all your help, Thom. Keep up the good work."

Silver Bullet and Uberman headed back into the crowd. Golden Boy deliberately knocked his shoulder into mine as he breezed past. I stumbled, tripped over my feet, and the next thing I knew I was sprawled out on the pavement.

The pictures in my jacket flew out of my pocket and scattered like a game of 52 Pickup.

"Goddamnit!" I cursed like my dad.

Uberman and Silver Bullet turned around and saw me on the ground, my family photos everywhere. They looked to Golden Boy for an explanation.

"Oh, I'm so sorry." Like he'd just noticed. Jerk. Then, playing the good Samaritan, he began to zoom around snatching up my pictures off the ground. I was sure Uberman and Silver

Bullet must have thought I was a clumsy goof who couldn't keep his balance in the presence of such greatness. Suddenly I was back on the basketball court and I wanted to knock that Golden shithead onto his Golden ass.

I got to my feet, wiped more gravel off my cheek, and felt really stupid. The heroes crouched low to the ground and picked up my pictures. I saw Silver Bullet glance down at one of the shots and freeze for a second. It's still the only time I've ever seen him perfectly still. He looked down at the picture, then up at me, and then down at the picture again.

A second later I saw him pull Justice aside from the crowd. He pointed at the picture and then nodded toward me. Justice looked over at me, and I held my hand up above my eyes to block out the glaring lights of the cameras. All of a sudden I wished I knew some of the Man in Black's tricks, namely how to disappear into the shadows.

Uberman and Golden Boy each handed me a stack of my photos, and the next thing I knew I was shaking hands with Justice himself. Warrior Woman and the Spectrum stood shoulder to shoulder behind him.

"I believe this is yours." Justice handed me back my picture. "And I hear congratulations are in order. Is this your first save?"

Here they were, the League themselves, Justice himself, talking to me after a daring rescue. This was every kid's dream, and I was living it at that very moment. I should have been soaking it up, but there was a queasy feeling in my stomach, and once again I knew I was the world's worst liar. I couldn't take much of the credit.

"I helped out a little, that's all." I plunged my hands into my pockets. "It was mostly that other guy." I nodded to the shadows in the piling by the overpass. "The one in black."

Warrior Woman and the Spectrum shared a look.

"Dark Hero?" Silver Bullet snapped. "You don't want his kind of help."

"He shouldn't even have the right to call himself a hero, not with those tactics." Apparently Golden Boy had to say something nauseatingly kiss-ass every time Silver Bullet spoke.

Justice looked down at me. For the first time, I realized that he hovered a few inches above the ground, which made him slightly taller than everyone else. I had seen him on TV before and knew that he always hovered in the air, but until I saw him in person I didn't understand the effect. You always had to look up to him.

"It's okay, Thom. It's just that he gives people the wrong idea about what we do, always keeping to the shadows like that, administering his own brand of justice like he's above the law."

"Like he has something to hide." Warrior Woman spit-shined her helmet.

"We have to be very careful about the message we send," Justice said. "There are a lot of people who look up to us, you know."

I felt all eyes on me again, and thought about my own secrets, and I wished I'd fallen through the holes in that bridge after all. I shifted my weight uncomfortably to my other foot.

Justice then lowered himself to the ground and handed me a card.

"Thom, I came over to meet you because we think you have potential. With the right work ethic, the right amount of practice, and the right influence, you could be someone people really look up to." He squinted and studied my face for a reaction. "How would you like that?"

I stared at the card in my hands. It was an invitation to League headquarters for a tryout. I thought for a second that he'd handed it to me by mistake.

"You want *me* to try out for the League?"

Justice smiled. "Only if you think you're ready."

I scanned each of the heroes' faces to see if they were serious.

"It would just be a tryout, for probationary status." Justice glanced at Silver Bullet, and I could have sworn I saw the speedster wink at light speed. "If the tryouts go well, you'll be paired with a team to learn how to use your powers, train to be a hero."

"Um, okay, sure. Thanks!" It hadn't struck me yet that Dad would kill me if he knew any of this were taking place. Holy shit.

Justice gave me a warm smile and put out his hand to seal the deal.

"That's fine, Thom, just fine." He shook my hand vigorously but carefully. It made me wonder if he had to be vigilant about his superstrength all the time. He probably could have ripped off my arm if he wasn't careful.

"Uh, these powers of mine, well, they're really new, and I'm not all that good with them yet." I watched Justice levitate a little higher above the ground. I didn't want them to expect too much of me.

"It's all right, son, we'll help you. See you next week."
Justice returned to the press.

Silver Bullet pointed at the invitation. "The time's wrong.
We're going to meet in the afternoon instead," he explained,
"because of the funeral."

"Oh, okay." I nodded like I knew what he was talking
about, even though I didn't. What funeral?

The rest of the League shook my hand and left, until it was
just me and Golden Boy. I saw Silver Bullet nudge his sidekick
forward before he sped off.

We stood face-to-face, and I noticed we were the same
height. His serious expression didn't crack; mine didn't either.
Neither of us said a word, and I wasn't about to break first.

Then I saw something well up in his chest like he was
about to say something, and he shook my hand.

"Good luck."

He sped off, and I tried to decide if he really meant it.

After everyone left, I looked down at the picture Justice handed
me: Mom's favorite picture. Mom, Dad, and me, surprises on
our faces as the contents of a can of beer exploded under
pressure.

On my way home, I thought I saw the hint of a cape disappear behind a corner. Maybe Dark Hero had witnessed that
whole episode with the League, too. Maybe he could explain to
me what had just happened.

CHAPTER SIX

I DECIDED I WASN'T going to run away like my mom. I wasn't sure how I was going to get past this computer revelation with Dad, but I knew I had to. I had a new purpose, something else to hide from Dad: I had League tryouts to attend.

I leafed through the pictures of my mother and the life I never knew she had. Running away was about the dumbest thing I could do. I hated people who ran away from their problems.

As I rounded the corner to my house my stomach growled. I'd be woozy the whole way home after using my powers, and now that the adrenaline buzz had worn off, I just wanted to pass out in my own bed for the next twenty-four hours. But that meant I had to go inside, and that meant I was going to see Dad.

The first excuse I came up with was lame. *Oh, you mean those pictures on the laptop. Well, it's this creative writing research assignment for school; I'm supposed to write from the point of view of a stupid lovesick girl.* No way would he buy that. Then I thought about outright denial. *What porn site? What are you talking about?* Then I'd give him a look like *What's wrong with you for asking a question like that?*

Then I thought I could be a little more inventive, maybe throw him a curveball first. *See, Dad, it's like this, I was driving some friends home from this party because they'd had too much to drink, and I guess that since they were so drunk I didn't realize that by comparison I probably shouldn't be driving either—I never even saw that kid on the skateboard, he just came out of nowhere, and then we didn't know where to bury the body so we put it in the trunk and—JUST KIDDING! I didn't kill anyone, really, I just like dudes instead of girls, that's all. . . .*

A wave of doubt washed over me, and I felt like I was going to yak in the bushes when I saw our little house at the end of the street. I thought about the look Dark Hero gave me while I was talking to Uberman. Like I was a big poser, like I was just some kid who didn't really save anyone on that bus. I didn't really even know how to use my powers yet. Try out for the League? Who the hell was I kidding? And what would they say when they eventually found out there was a reason I never had a girlfriend?

Then I saw Dad's car in the driveway. I heard the motor humming and decided to wing it. As I got closer, I saw Dad in the front seat, only he wasn't moving. He was perfectly still.

I looked in the window and saw his head slumped over on the steering wheel. The hair on my arms stood up. I listened to the motor whirr and watched for movement, but I didn't see any. I reached through the open window and nudged him on the shoulder. A moment passed and he didn't move.

The back of my neck tingled, and I reached out to nudge him again.

Then he bolted upright in his seat and looked out at me. His eyes were wet, his face red and swollen.

Oh, God, this was way worse than I'd expected. He'd been bawling. I'd never seen him like this, not even when Mom disappeared.

He looked up at me with pleading eyes. I opened the car door, lifted his arm around my shoulder, and helped him to the sidewalk, up the steps to the front door. He'd exhausted himself from all the crying. His arms drooped like limp noodles over my shoulder.

"I'm sorry, Dad, I'm so sorry." It was all I could say. So much for improv.

I helped him into his La-Z-Boy and propped the leg rest up for him. He stared forward with a blank expression.

"You want me to get you something to drink?" If he wouldn't take a beer at this point, I certainly would.

"Dad, I'm so sorry. I was just . . . It's just that . . . I—" I kneeled down on the floor. It seemed more appropriate to be on his level. I sighed, and for a second I wanted to cry, too. I couldn't stand destroying what remained of his dreams like this. I had no clue how the hell I was going to fix this. He couldn't even look me in the eye.

Instead he reached for the remote control with his bad hand and mashed the messy lumps of flesh that used to be his fingers onto the buttons. Then I heard the report on the TV.

"Again, for those of you just joining us, Captain Victory dead at ninety-seven."

My head jerked toward the set. They were playing a montage of the young Captain Victory, ancient footage from his glory days, fighting Nazis, leading the charge up the beach on D-Day. Footage of Captain Victory, founding member of the League, as he welcomed in a new era of superpowered heroes, shaking hands with Justice and Uberman. I noticed in all the clips that Dad had been conveniently edited out, although I did catch a glimpse of his boot in one segment of the League locked in battle with the Secret Society of Supervillains.

Dad wasn't crying about what he'd found on the computer at all. I hadn't shattered his last hope for happiness.

He'd lost his one, true hero.

For the first time in my life, I thought Dad looked old. His face was drained of all color, his frame seemed less bulky than frail, and all his energy had left him. He suddenly seemed about thirty years older, and I wondered if this is how it would be one day when I was the one spooning him the Jell-O cubes in the nursing home. His arms shook as he pushed himself up from the chair, and I thought his legs would buckle.

"Where are you going?" I asked.

He kept walking.

"To get my costume."

He polished the buckle to his utility belt first. Then he ripped off part of his rag and gestured for me to help him polish the buttons. About an hour into it he decided it was time to speak.

"You're awfully quiet. Want a beer?" Dad had already had a few.

I really wanted one, but the thought of sharing a beer with Dad seemed really strange. I was torn, though, because he didn't usually offer.

"I'll pass."

I heated up the kettle and brought him a cup of Sleepytime Tea instead. He didn't seem to notice it wasn't a beer, and he set it down next to his medals.

"First person I ever wanted to be was Captain Victory." Dad smeared some polish neatly around the edges of a button and lost himself in a memory. "He had no reason to care about a kid like me."

I reached for the jar of polish.

"How did you meet him?"

Dad chuckled to himself. "I figured out who he was, his secret identity. We used to play heroes at the home when I was little. At first, I never got to play Captain Victory; that was an honor reserved for the oldest boys. But everyone else found homes, and soon I *was* the oldest boy, so I got first pick whenever we played." Dad rubbed a glob of spit on the button to make it shine.

"I guess I just paid attention, looked where no one else did. Hell, I'd followed every single story, bought every decoder ring for years. I remember seeing his picture in the paper as Captain Victory, and holding it up next to his byline—he was a great newspaper photographer, too, you know. Back then I guess it was all so new, they just made it up as they went along. He wore a pair of glasses—that's it—to cover up who he really was." Dad stopped rubbing the button for a moment and shook his head. "Can you believe that? All that stood between him and every Dr.

Ice, Mr. Metal, or Nazi Ned figuring out his real identity was a pair of eyeglasses."

I looked up at my father and thought about how careful my mother had been about hiding her private life. I wanted to ask him about her, but I couldn't even speak. This was the most he'd opened up to me. Ever. I stared down at my button. My fingers were cramping and I didn't feel like polishing anymore.

"So I made an appointment with him at the paper, told him I had an important tip. I was probably only fifteen at the time— God, I had some balls. I put on my Sunday finest, marched right over to his desk in the newsroom, and sat down. He didn't even bother to look up from his phone call. He put his hand over the receiver and told me he was really busy and that he didn't usually take anonymous tips, especially from kids, and this would have to be quick, and what was it I knew that was so important, anyway. I told him I knew who Captain Victory really was. He hung up the phone and looked at me. Then I pointed at him, sat back in my seat, smiled, and said with utter confidence, 'I knew it.'"

I caught myself smiling at the thought of Dad as a teenager, taking the piss out of some too-busy journalist and figuring out one of the world's great mysteries, just because he believed.

"So I told him either he would take me on as his sidekick and teach me everything he ever knew . . ." Dad took another sip of his tea. "Or I'd go to the rival paper with the story."

I choked on my drink. "You *blackmailed* him?"

"Basically, yeah."

Dad caught himself smiling at the memory and then suddenly stopped, probably when he began to think about whatever happened to that brave little fifteen-year-old from the Barry Robinson Home for Wayward Boys who knew exactly how to get what he wanted in life and wasn't afraid to go after it.

"Be right back." He headed upstairs, and I heard him rooting around in his closet.

He jogged down the stairs and sat back down on the floor, his costume still laid out in front of him, and handed me a box of old pictures. Mom wasn't the only one with a secret stash.

"He said he'd take me on as his protégé on one condition: that one day I'd return the favor and take on my own sidekick."

In my head I could see that secret picture Mom had taken of Captain Victory, Dad, and his sidekick, Right Wing, each of them holding up three fingers for the camera, three generations of heroes.

For as long as I could remember, this period of Dad's life had been a blind spot. He'd never said more than two words about his time as the world's worthiest hero, and I learned very young— after only one spanking, in fact—never to ask. But sure as it was almost sunup, here he was sharing with me the details of his origin. I guess death brings out all sorts of things in people.

I leafed through the pile of pictures, Dad and the Ol' Vic fighting the good fight. Their own rogues' gallery of villains, the serious ones, the ones everyone remembers. Sure, they foiled a major bank robbery attempt here, a jail breakout there, but really they were all about saving the world. It was cool to see Dad smiling in so many of the pictures. It made me wonder if I would look back at old pictures of myself and realize I hadn't smiled very often when I was young.

Dad slipped the shirt part of his costume over his T-shirt

and fastened the buttons from bottom to top. He sucked in his gut and looked at himself in the mirror on the wall.

"How do I look?"

The third button down, right above his solar plexus, popped off the shirt, flew across the room, and landed with a splash in his cup of tea.

For a second I didn't know how to react—would this set Dad off? Then, with no warning, we both exploded into a fit of laughter. Dad actually had to kneel down on the floor to catch his breath, he was laughing so hard. It felt good to laugh this way with Dad. Healthy and real.

He reached over for the mug, gulped down its remaining contents, and flashed me a big smile with the button wedged firmly between his teeth. That set me off laughing again, and Dad was chuckling so much—his shoulders bouncing up and down uncontrollably—that he had trouble threading the needle to sew the button back on. I watched him struggle with the needle and thread as he laughed, and my mind flashed to a memory of how Mom used to sew on a button in seconds flat without even taking her eyes off that spot she always seemed to be looking at outside the window.

"Can I ask you a question?"

Dad caught his breath and nodded. "Sure."

"How did you do all those great things? I mean, without superpowers or anything."

I saw a smile creep into the corners of Dad's mouth.

"Well, I worked very, very hard training and preparing. There's no room for error in that line of work, so I was supremely dedicated. And whenever I really needed to step up, I just believed in myself. That was usually all it took. Then I could do whatever I wanted."

I thought for a minute how nice it must be to believe in yourself.

"Hey, Dad." I cleared my throat. "Why do you think I never get sick?"

"That's two questions." The smile that had been forming in the corners of his mouth was gone.

I'd never felt this close to Dad before, and I really wanted to talk about what was on my mind, about all these changes happening inside me.

"I haven't been sick since I was little and had strep that time, not even a cold. It's pretty unusual, isn't it?"

Dad looked down and poked the needle through the hole of the button.

"I don't know, I guess we eat pretty well, and you get a lot of exercise."

"Yeah, but Dad, c'mon, when was the last time you remember me getting a sniffle? You've got to admit it's pretty extraordinary."

He pulled the needle through the thick, stubborn cloth.

"I'm not sure I'd call a kid with a major seizure disorder the picture of perfect health. What are you getting at?" He pinned me with his eyes, his head still.

I wanted to tell him everything. I wanted to tell him about that guy at the basketball game and how he looked at me so strangely, how it made me feel so weird, how my hands burned when I put them on his leg, and then how he suddenly wasn't hurt anymore. How I thought I had the seizures under control, because they're just a by-product of these new powers, and guess what, I just had my first real rescue on this bus, well, sort of my first rescue, and then I met the League, and they invited me to try out. Your own son, can you believe it? I wanted to tell him that I'd found Mom's old pictures.

"Why did Mom leave?"

Even before I finished asking, I knew it was a question my father wouldn't answer.

Dad looked back down at his button. He inhaled deeply, sighed, and rubbed his weary eyes with the nub of his hand. He looked down at the melted flesh where his fingers used to be and pretended to check his watch.

"We should get some sleep."

And just like that the walls were back up. I sat perfectly still and watched Dad collect the beer cans, then I took the mug and put it in the sink. Dad tossed the cans in the recycling bin and told me to leave the dishes, he'd wash them tomorrow.

I crawled into bed, and the sheets felt cool and smooth. I didn't bother closing the shades because I wanted to look at the moon for a while and turn my mind off.

I was drifting off when my door creaked open. Dad poked his head inside.

"I don't want you to worry, Thom. You'll find the right girl to settle down with one day, and you'll make it work. You won't make the same mistakes I did."

Then he gently closed the door, careful not to make a noise, and I didn't hear the floorboards as he crept off to bed. I turned over and faced the window with my eyes wide open in the moonlight.

CHAPTER SEVEN

I WOKE UP EARLY, a whole hour before my alarm. School was out, but I still got up early. I had butterflies in my stomach about going to the League tryouts. I bolted upright in my bed with one overwhelming thought: what was I supposed to wear? I shook my head. What a girl. Even so, first impressions are everything, and I didn't really know what was appropriate for this kind of thing. Do you wear a costume? Something so you're ready to fight and go through some combat training drills if that's what they ask you to do? Or maybe it's more like a job interview, where you wear your nicest clothes to show respect for the others who are higher up on the totem pole.

After a quick shower I laid out two separate outfits on my bed. First my coat, tie, and khakis, my one nice outfit for all respectable occasions—weddings, funerals, or school pictures. Next to it, I spread out my old wet suit, which I hadn't used since last summer, when I decided that although riding a wave was pretty fun, fighting fifty punks named Laird all day for the same dinky set of waves wasn't all it was cracked up to be. The wet suit might be put to better use fighting crime instead.

I zipped up the wet suit and stared at myself in the mirror. It looked enough like a costume to pass. I glanced at my bed-sheets, and instantly decided there was no way I'd wear a cape. Dad had always told me that unless you know how to move with a cape, they just get in the way. More often than not, he said, they were the tip-off of a real amateur, and the last thing I wanted was for everyone at tryouts to think I was an amateur. I looked at myself standing there in my wet suit, my basketball high-tops on my feet. I chucked the high-tops in the back of my closet and put on my black army boots instead. They looked tougher and they didn't stand out as much as the white sneakers.

Then I had a minor panic attack. What if everyone else wore respectable clothes? Would they think who the hell does this clown think he is, the Silver Surfer? I nearly pulled my left arm out of joint trying to get my white oxford shirt over the wet suit. As long as I didn't breathe too much, I was able to button up the shirt and put on my tie. My arms sort of stuck out, propped up by the cushionlike effect of the wet suit underneath. I looked at myself in the mirror.

Not bad.

I heard the door close downstairs and I looked out the window and spied Dad, impeccably dressed in his old uniform, as he walked out onto the front porch. It was so early that the paperboy was pulling up to our driveway on his dirt bike. The kid took one look at my father and did a double take, like he was trying to figure out if today was Halloween or not. With his good hand, Dad took the newspaper out of the dumbstruck kid's pouch, and with a gentle flick of his wrist, casually tossed it over his shoulder so that it landed perfectly square on the front door-mat of our porch. Dad pulled the car keys out of his utility belt, climbed into his old Camaro, fired it up, and slowly pulled out of the driveway. The paper boy didn't move a muscle until Dad's car had disappeared down the street.

I wandered into Dad's closet and pulled an old sport coat from the back rung. It was dark and caked with dust, but it fit nicely over my wet suit, so I wiped it down and put it on. Downstairs I grabbed my backpack, shoved a piece of toast in my mouth, and saw a note Dad had left for me on the front hall table.

Thom, gone to the funeral. Good luck at the game today. Sorry I won't be able to make it.   —Dad

I had told him I had an away game this afternoon a couple hours' drive across state. Under normal circumstances he would have picked out the lie with just one or two questions, like for instance, Hey, what's the name of the school? But in his state all he could do was apologize for not being able to make the trip. The toast felt funny in my stomach; it didn't mix well with the guilt.

The bus is the slowest mode of transportation ever. It dumped me off downtown about half an hour late, so I ran to the park. When I finally got there, the memorial service was already halfway over. The park was overflowing with people, most of them either weeping or trying to get a look at the celebrities in the front row. I'd never seen so many people in one place in my life, and it was weird to see them overcome with emotion for someone who was a complete stranger. I nudged my way past a candlelight vigil and a large family whose mother was passing out sandwiches to all the kids from a giant igloo cooler. Then I nearly tripped over an elderly woman in a wheelchair, who apologized for getting in my way.

"He saved me during the Disastro Attack of '63. Picked me up and scooted me right out of the path of that death ray, he did." She nodded like of course I would remember the incident, like my scrapbook was filled with her clippings, and I smiled back politely before I climbed past her through the crowd.

Silence spread throughout the masses, and I saw all heads turn up and look to the sky. The League descended from the clouds and landed on the stage. Justice hovered up to the microphone to deliver the eulogy, and I heard a female fan's distant scream from the outer reaches of the crowd, over by the Porta Potties.

"We love you, Uberman!"

A cool trickle made its way down my forehead, and my eye stung with the salt of sweat. The wet suit was boiling hot underneath the sport coat. I wiped my brow with the sleeve of Dad's old jacket and tried to listen, but the reverb was so bad on the sound system, only the closest few hundred people could actually hear Justice.

There was an endless train of testimonials from people who all thought they were more famous than the next. A few ex-presidents who'd kept in the public eye mostly as guests on cable news shows, some old movie stars, a couple of young journalists who waxed on about Victory's legacy, with words like "resonate" and "zeitgeist." All I could think about was how I never remembered seeing a single one of these people anywhere near that dank nursing home whenever Dad and I visited the old-timer.

My nostrils filled with a familiar smell, and my eyes scanned the grounds for the gardenias. The smell always reminded me of my mom, since they were her favorite flower. I didn't see gardenias anywhere nearby, but I knew they must be there.

I looked at my watch and suddenly I was worried about getting a head start on the crowd. I didn't want to be late for tryouts. Plus, I needed a Gatorade. I slung my backpack over my shoulder and turned to leave, when I spotted my father crouched behind a lighting crew, where he'd managed to steal a spot near the stage. He knelt on one knee, and his eyes looked heavy as he listened intently to each speaker. He didn't see me.

The slew of celebrity mourners streamed off the stage after the service, and I lost sight of Dad in the crowd. I was nervous that he'd bump into me and ask why I wasn't at my game. I wiped more sweat off my forehead and contemplated making a run for it, but my eyes caught a glimpse of Uberman, still up onstage with the rest of the League as they paid respects to family and friends of the deceased hero. I'd never seen Uberman with such a look of genuine sadness on his face. He tightly hugged a girl who I assumed to be one of Captain Victory's attractive great-grandnieces, and she cried into his chest, right in the spot where I'd always imagined my head would rest at night when he and I drifted off to sleep together in our beach house, with our golden retriever puppy nestled peacefully at our feet.

Suddenly I saw Dad behind Uberman at the foot of the stage. He approached Justice, who was engaged in conversation with the mayor, and tapped him on the shoulder. Suddenly my stomach felt sickly and sweet, and although I couldn't put my finger on it, I thought it was really wrong for these two to talk. It could only lead to disaster or shame or both.

Justice glanced over his shoulder and saw my father in his old uniform. Neither of them said a word at first. They just looked at each other, until finally the mayor filled the awkward silence and excused himself to join another conversation on the other side of the stage.

I couldn't tell what was passing between them. My dad didn't give much away—if he'd gone in for gambling, he would have been a world-class poker player. Justice wasn't giving away much, either. I moved up behind the trunk of an ancient oak tree for a closer look.

Then Dad did something that freaked me out. He balled his good hand into a fist and lifted three fingers into the air.

Justice met the gesture, raised his own fist in the air, and lifted three fingers. Then just as quickly, Justice lowered one. Now there were only two. They both grew solemn and looked down at the ground between them.

It felt like the wind had been knocked out of my lungs, and I actually gasped out loud. Suddenly I understood exactly what was happening. Exactly who they were to each other. I couldn't believe I hadn't recognized him when I met Justice in person.

Dad and Justice were re-creating Mom's picture, three generations of the world's greatest heroes. Except now only two remained—my father and his sidekick. I ducked behind the oak and rested my head against the giant trunk and caught my breath. I'd witnessed something I was never meant to see.

Justice had been the hero formerly known as Right Wing.

He gripped my father's hand in a firm shake, the kind old war buddies give each other when they meet years later. Survivors.

I didn't know what to make of this. I guess it made sense that Dad never mentioned he knew the leader of the League, what with his devout bias against superpowers. Still, you'd think it would have come up at some point.

I stole away from the tree and tried to block all the new questions out of my mind. All that mattered was the League try-out, and I needed to get my head together for it. I weaved in and out of folding chairs stacked in piles like giant headstones, and hurried out of the park. I caught the next bus and headed across town to the secret location.

What was it that felt so wrong about what I'd seen? Why did I have the same feeling you get the first time you hear your parents having sex?

Shit, my watch had stopped again. I didn't know how late I was. As soon as the bus stopped, I sprinted the rest of the way there. Sweat poured down my forehead, and my two outfits clung to my body like a wet, heavy blanket.

When I arrived at the address on the invitation—an abandoned tire warehouse with broken windows and rusted doors—I was sure it had all been a joke, an elaborate setup to humiliate me.

Then I realized I wasn't important enough for anyone to go to all this trouble just to make me feel stupid, and I rang the worn button marked "delivery."

Without a sound the door swung open, and I hurried down a sleek, steely hallway to an open elevator. I stepped inside and noticed there weren't any buttons for the floors. The doors began to close, and I briefly thought how stupid I'd been to go to some strange place and put myself at such risk without letting anyone know where I really was. If something were to happen, who would know to come looking for me? As far as Dad knew, I was at a basketball game out of town. My mind raced with possibilities—what if it was one of Dad's old adversaries out to exact revenge? That seemed like a hollow endeavor to me, especially after all Dad had been through in recent years, but you never knew. I felt my heartbeat quicken when it struck me that Mom, too, probably had droves of her own old adversaries who wanted payback for the years they'd spent in jail. I tried to relax by breathing deeply through my nose.

Finally the elevator door opened, and I walked across the slick marble floor of the waiting room in front of me. I stopped in front of the reception desk. The receptionist, a pert little thing who looked more like a morning television personality than a supertemp, uncapped a black Sharpie Magic Marker.

"Your name, please."

My eyes scanned the waiting room full of wannabe heroes. Some of them read old issues of *Men's Health* and *Cosmo* from the magazine racks. Some of them stretched out, hoisting a leg over any free spot they could find on a sofa or side table. Some practiced whatever it was they were going to do to impress the

League. One guy chatted away, a little too loudly if you ask me, to what sounded like a broker on his cell phone. I couldn't tell if he was looking at me through his Ray-Bans, but I was pretty sure they were purely cosmetic, not meant to contain gamma radiation or anything like that. A couple of costumed crusaders laughed at an off-color joke by the watercooler.

"I need a name, please." There was the hint of a sharp edge to the perkiness.

"Um, it's Thom."

She looked up from her "Hello, my name is" sticker and stared me in the eye.

"Thom Creed?" I ventured. Shit. Only teenagers end statements with question marks like that, and I really didn't want to come off sounding like a dumb teenager who didn't know what he was doing.

She popped the cap back on the Sharpie and smiled tightly.

"I mean your *alias*." Her lips were pursed, and I couldn't tell if she thought I was just a total amateur or if I was messing with her, or both.

"Oh, right, my alias." It had never occurred to me that I might need one. I glanced around the room for some sudden inspiration, but all I could come up with was "The Potted Plant," "The Fruit Platter," or "Free Subscription!"

"Justice invited me," I said. "The rest of the League, too." Like that would excuse me from this whole silly name thing.

She slid her trendy horn-rimmed spectacles down her nose and gave me the once-over twice. Then she leaned back in her chair and opened the Sharpie and began scribbling something on the name tag.

"Suit yourself." She unpeeled the sticker and smacked it on my lapel. "We'll be calling you in groups every fifteen minutes: have a seat. By the way, love the tie. Next!" And she was on to the next person waiting in line, some guy with oversize purple wings.

"Oh, hi, Lester!" She leaned over the desk to kiss him on the cheek. "How're Fran and the kids?"

I managed to find a quiet little spot over by the potted plants. I looked down at my tie and realized I was the only person there without a costume. I thought the act of disrobing in public would be a little embarrassing. Maybe I'd go to the bathroom and change in a stall.

My collar was soaked with sweat. I walked over to the refreshment table and swiped a few napkins to dry off my forehead and the back of my neck. I wished I'd taken the time to get a Gatorade.

I joined the line at the watercooler to pour a cup. When it was my turn, I couldn't seem to get the nozzle to work, and the line behind me was growing impatient. I tried to distract the guy in back of me with small talk. He wore a high-tech visor, a tight blue Lycra suit with the symbol of an icicle on his chest, and a permanent frown.

"Hey, how crazy is this watercooler?"

He stared at me. I cleared my throat.

"Do you know how to work this thing?" I asked.

"Most people *pull* the nozzle." I, of course, was pushing it.

I heard a few would-be heroes snicker behind him. I pulled the nozzle with force, and a torrent of water knocked the cup out of my grasp. The water splashed up on the guy with the visor and immediately froze upon contact with his skin. The line of heroes glared at me. I picked up my cup and skulked back to my space. No one bothered to look at me after that, and right then I really could have used a familiar face. Most of the candidates were at least ten years older than I was.

In fact, the only person in the room who looked close to my age was the pizza delivery girl who'd just walked in. I watched her check in with the receptionist, and then she came over and sat in an armchair next to me. She set her stack of pizzas in her carry bag down on the floor beside me and picked up a magazine with a cover story on NASCAR racers. She crossed her leg and bounced one foot up and down as she read and chomped on a piece of gum. Her face seemed perky and friendly. I glanced down at her tiny body, and I thought she was probably a cheerleader or a high school gymnast when she wasn't busy delivering pizzas to hungry superheroes.

"I'll take mine with extra cheese," I said in her direction.

She stopped reading the magazine and looked straight ahead, like maybe a mosquito was buzzing in her ear but she wasn't sure yet. Then she turned in my direction.

"What did you say?"

"The pizza, I said I'll take mine with extra cheese."

She adjusted her blond ponytail, which poked out of the back hole in her cap, and glanced at my name tag. Then she went back to her magazine.

"I was just saying that I'm glad someone had the good sense to order some real food." I lifted up the corner of a pizza box for a peek. "What you got in there?"

She swatted my hand away with the magazine.

"Hey, hands off!"

She hoisted her delivery bag, and I heard her mutter

"twinkie" under her breath as she moved to a new seat on the opposite side of the room.

I looked up sheepishly and saw practically everyone in the room staring at me. Even the guy with the cool shades got off his cell phone to see what was the matter.

I bent down and pretended to tie my shoelaces just so I'd have something to do. Her insult stung, and I kept thinking about the venom in her voice, the way she'd said "twinkie," emphasis on the "twink." I stole a look at her and saw that she was wearing a name tag with a code name: "Miss Scarlett." Once again I was the village idiot. She wasn't delivering pizzas. She was trying out for the team.

"*Psst.*"

I straightened up. Who was pssst-ing me? I looked over my shoulder to the right and saw some guy having a major sneezing fit. He pulled a couple of tissues out of the utility belt on his costume. He blew his nose loudly, checked the contents, and then pinched his nose to stop the bleeding.

"*Psst!*"

I looked in the other direction over my other shoulder and saw an old lady waving me over in her direction. She had her skirt hiked up above her knees and was massaging her left calf muscle. A network of spider veins spread down her legs and disappeared under her boots.

"Be a doll, kid, and help me pop my knee back in joint."

Her name tag read, "Hello, my name is . . . Old Enough to Know Better."

"Don't you need an alias?" I asked.

She looked at me and chuckled. "Nope. Now go

ahead, reach down, grab my thigh, and give my boot a good yank."

Some of the heroes looked up from their magazines and wondered what the heck this kid was doing reaching up this old woman's skirt.

"Don't be shy. Give it some oomph."

More people were staring by now, and I figured the harder I pushed the sooner I'd get it over.

"Yeah, that's it, that's it. Owwwwwww!"

Her knee made a nauseating pop, which reminded me of the sound my ankle made when I rolled it during state finals last year. She leaned back in her seat and smiled.

"God, thanks for that. Pass a tired old woman her cigarettes, will you?"

I handed her a padded flip-top cigarette case, and her arthritic fingers popped open the fastener, pulled out a Pall Mall, and fired it up with the alacrity of a woman half her age.

"Knees been doing that ever since I got the replacement last year. Kinda burns whenever you do that thing with your hands, huh?"

I nodded and thought about it for a second.

"How'd you know I could do that?"

She inhaled a deep drag from her cigarette.

"I see the future." She exhaled to the side, careful not to blow smoke in my direction.

"I'm Ruth. Nice to meet you, Thom." She shook my hand, and smoke came out of her nose. The guy with the sneezing fit and the nosebleed on the other side of the room began to cough.

"How'd you know—? Oh right, you can see the future." Powers are weird.

"No." She took another long drag and gave it the longest granny ash I'd ever seen. "I can see your name tag."

Embarrassed, I looked down at my name tag. The receptionist had written my name in big bubbly cursive letters.

The receptionist appeared in front of us and leaned down with a patronizing smile.

"Excuse me, there's no smoking in here." She extended a cup of water in our direction for Ruth to put it out.

Ruth held up a finger—not the one she really wanted to hold up.

"Just a sec."

She took one last, deep drag on the cigarette that burned it all the way down to the filter.

"There." She popped the cigarette butt into the glass and it made a little hissing noise when it hit the water. "Perfect timing." She gave the receptionist a quick look and said "Thanks," but really meant "You can leave now."

Then a woman in an expensive but ill-fitting business suit and a tight perm entered and called for our attention. She introduced herself as "Sooz" from human resources and passed out a phone book–thick stack of paperwork for us to sign, and began to explain the contents of the packet. Confidentiality agreements, liability forms, nondiscrimination clauses (which I noticed left out anything about sexual orientation) . . . My eyes had glazed over by the time she got to the personality inventory.

I looked over to the door. Where was Uberman? What was he doing right then? Did he remember me?

Sooz caught me daydreaming and clapped her hands twice. "C'mon people, listen up, this is really important!"

I looked over at Ruth, fast asleep in her armchair next to me. The guy who'd been sneezing nonstop in the corner raised his hand and asked Sooz where the bathroom was and ran from his seat as soon as she pointed him in the right direction.

About an hour later, I looked down at my packet and saw that I'd only completed about half of it. Sooz wandered into the room and looked over everyone's shoulder. She stopped at the pizza delivery girl.

The pizza girl looked up from her paper at Sooz.

"Mind your own fucking business."

My mind drifted over to the door with the League's inner sanctum beyond it. Their secret meeting room, their simulated combat–session gymnasium, their museum of treasures from past adventures, the living quarters of the team. And what would Uberman's room look like? Something modern and architectural, I'm sure. No clutter, but lots of style, a Spartan simplicity so he could wake up and pound out a thousand push-ups and sit-ups before a full day of saving people. Later, he would crash on his platform bed to read a thoughtful and sensitive novel before falling asleep, preferably to some soothing music of my choosing.

And where was Justice? Every time I closed my eyes I'd see him standing with my father, both of them stoic on the platform, neither of them saying a word, just holding up three fingers that became two.

Some other questions began to form in my mind. Like where was Justice when my father, his mentor, was disgraced in the eyes of the world? Where was he when Dad couldn't get work? Where was he the month after Mom disappeared and Dad had to drink himself into a stupor just to pass out for a few hours of sleep at night? What the hell did anyone need a sidekick for if they weren't there for you when the chips were down? Dad had been there for Captain Victory to the very end, even through the depressing nursing home years. It's easy to be there for someone when everything's coming up roses, but how about when someone really needs you?

Suddenly all I could think about was finding this guy and telling him who I really was, and that I needed some answers before I went any further with this whole charade, and if that wasn't something he felt like he could talk about, then he could take his super tryouts and shove them up his—

"Welcome, everyone, welcome!" A warm, booming voice echoed as Uberman glided into the room. I leaned forward on the edge of my seat and smiled. I couldn't wait for him to recognize me.

"We're ready for the first group." He looked down at the clipboard in his hands. "Let's see, Mass Master, Compu-kid, Kung-Fu Karla, and the Human Stain."

Uberman shook their hands and ushered them through the door, which closed automatically behind him. I folded my arms and dropped back into the chair and racked my brain about the things I was going to do to impress them.

CHAPTER EIGHT

"WAKE UP." Someone nudged me. "Kid, wake up, they're calling in a new group."

"Chemical Kid! Miss Scarlett! Polar Paul . . . !" The receptionist called names off the list. I sat up in my chair and looked beside me at Ruth.

"You got a little something there." She pointed to my chin. I wiped the drool off.

"Mighty Mite! Typhoon Timmy! Vicious Violet! and . . ." Other heroes leaned forward in their seat, in hopes their name would be next on the list. She paused before she read the last name.

"And Thom."

I looked over at Ruth, my eyes wide.

"That's you." She pointed at my name tag with her cigarette.

* * *

Inside I found myself in the fanciest gymnasium I'd ever seen. State-of-the-art equipment, clean geometrical lines, like something you'd see in *Architectural Digest*. It didn't even smell bad.

A flash of bright metallic light, and Silver Bullet stood before us, stopwatch in hand. He explained that today we'd be going through a series of tests. The League would evaluate us at each stage, and from every heat, they'd select some of us to continue on to the next round. By the end of the tests, he said, they'd make their final decisions about who made the probationary roster. I looked around at the faces of my competition and wondered if everyone else wanted this as bad as I did. And if they were as scared as I was of not getting it.

Silver Bullet continued on for a while about the importance of maintaining perfect physical shape, especially with all the power dampeners out there. "The technology is available to any low-level metahuman brazen enough to call himself a villain these days. You have to be ready to fight all the time, even without your powers."

He explained the first stage was to be a simple test of our physical fitness and lined each of us up at various stations throughout the room.

I wanted to raise my hand and ask him if there was a locker room where I could take off my suit, but he'd already reset the stopwatch, ready to go. My sleeves were wet from wiping my forehead. I used my skinny black new-wave tie instead, and it shone slick with sweat.

Silver Bullet fired a starter pistol in the air, which seemed like a ridiculous thing to do for a tryout, and we all broke into a sprint. For all the gym's high-tech gadgets and haute design, our first station was just a cleaner, newer version of the same obstacle courses I'd been doing in gym since I was a little kid. Hop quickly through some tires, run a few laps, leap over a few hurdles, climb a rope wall, and there you are.

I was so focused on doing my best that I didn't even notice until I got to the rope that I was a full two lengths ahead of everyone else. Granted, Mighty Mite had to move a lot faster with those puny legs, but I was still kicking ass. I looked over my shoulder and saw Vicious Violet kicking the hurdles into the wall instead of leaping over them. I'd already won the heat by that point anyway. Not bad for a first-timer. I caught my breath and watched Silver Bullet scribble some marks on his clipboard. Looks like all those years of basketball and sports might actually pay off after all.

The next station was even more like gym class. All he wanted us to do was bang out as many push-ups, pull-ups, rope-jumps, and sit-ups as we could during the allotted periods of time. Again, I nailed it, beating everyone in every event until we got to the sit-ups, when Silver Bullet asked us to partner up.

"I'm not doing it with him." Miss Scarlett, the pizza delivery girl, pointed at me. Everyone else had paired off, and it left just me and Miss Scarlett, and she wasn't having it.

"You're also being graded," Silver Bullet said, "on team-work."

Miss Scarlett smiled at him, a cute, flirtatious grin, and he smiled back. Then she grabbed my hand and pulled me aside and whispered, "If you look down my shirt, I'll fry your testicles." Her eyes sizzled when she spoke.

I went first and did more than one hundred sit-ups in a minute, with Miss Scarlett kneeling on the tops of my feet as an anchor. I felt the strain in my abdomen and knew I'd be sore tomorrow. I might be winning these heats, but I'd need to get in better shape if I planned to make the big time. No more mint chocolate-chip after dinner, maybe an additional workout at the rec center each morning before school.

When it came time to switch, Miss Scarlett lay on the ground and tucked her shirttail loosely in her waistband and zipped up her red delivery jacket. As I knelt on her feet, she glanced around the room at her competitors, and I thought for a second that she looked like a nervous little girl who'd always been picked last for kickball. Silver Bullet fired his popgun, and while everyone else cranked out their first twenty or so sit-ups with relative ease and speed, Miss Scarlett took her time, pulling herself up to her knees slowly and gingerly. My knees began to tingle, and she looked at me with flames in her eyes. Suddenly my knees began to burn like they were on fire.

"Ouch!" I pulled away. "You burned me!"

"No, I didn't!"

Silver Bullet sped over to mediate.

"That hurt," I said. "What's your problem!" If she'd been a guy and this had been a basketball court, I would have pushed her back.

"I told you, I didn't do it." She got up in my face. "But I might do it *now*."

"Okay, easy now, you two." Silver Bullet pushed us apart. "That's enough teamwork for today."

* * *

I was still steaming when I walked in the room for my interview. I saw the judges, various members of the League, cracking up with laughter. Miss Scarlett got up from the interviewee seat, smiled and thanked them for their time, and told them if they thought that last one was funny, then just wait until she told the one about the time she'd had to put out the fire at the Sheraton when they double booked the Shriners and the Star Trek convention on the same weekend. The heroes laughed again and bid her a fond farewell, and I could tell she'd charmed the pants off them. She turned to me and brushed a stray strand of hair out of her face with her middle finger.

"I left the seat warm for you."

She breezed out of the room, and I sat down and faced Warrior Woman, the Spectrum, and King of the Sea behind the table. They caught their breath and settled down from all the laughter. Warrior Woman, still chuckling, wiped a tear out of the corner of her eye.

"Boy, she's kinda nutty, huh?" I threw it out there, hoping to break the ice. Their smiles evaporated, and they inspected their new candidate.

"How so?" the Spectrum asked.

Uh-oh.

"What is this saying, nutty?" King of the Sea asked the others through his gills.

"It's just an expression, that's all." The interview hadn't even started and I was already treading on thin ice.

Warrior Woman folded her arms across the aegis on her chest and furrowed her brow.

"Maybe we should just get started."

I cleared my throat and folded my hands together on the table. If I'd been at church, it would have looked like I was going to pray. My neck itched like crazy under the wet suit collar.

They shuffled through a stack of folders and searched for my file, and the Spectrum asked the first question.

"What's your power, son?"

I opened my mouth to answer, but then he pulled out a lime-green folder from the bottom of the stack.

"Bingo, I got it. Says here you can turn into sand. . . ."

"Um, no, I think that's someone else."

"You can't turn yourself into different silicon-based forms? A giant slide, for instance? A sandstorm?"

"No, that's not me." I scratched under my collar.

"Are you sure?" the Spectrum asked. He flipped through the stacks, looking for the right file, and knocked some papers onto the floor.

"Pretty sure."

"So you're saying you cannot turn into any shapes with your power," gurgled King of the Sea, a real quick study. "Interesting."

"No, that's not what I do."

Warrior Woman leaned forward and stared me down.

"Then maybe in the interest of time you could tell us what it is you do, hm?"

I thought she was going to swallow me whole at any moment. I scooched my chair back a little, and it made a high-pitched squeak like I was scratching a chalkboard.

"I heal things."

They shared a look.

"What kind of things?" Warrior Woman fired off.

"People mostly. I did save a plant once."

They shared another look.

"A plant?" the Spectrum asked.

I wanted to wipe the sweat off my forehead. Miss Scarlett really had heated up the seat, and I was boiling. But I didn't want them to think I was nervous, so I didn't call any attention to the sweat on my brow. I wanted them to find me self-assured and confident.

"If someone's hurt, I can touch them and my hands get really hot, and that's when it starts."

The Spectrum scribbled some notes on a pad of paper and asked me a question without looking up. "And what happens when you absorb the injury?"

"What do you mean?"

"Where does all the pain go once you're done with the healing?"

I bit my lower lip. I'd never thought about it.

"Can you then teleport, convert your skin to diamond, fire beams of energy from your eyes, things like that?"

I swallowed and wished they'd left a cup of water for me on the table.

"Well, it used to trigger seizures after I was done, I guess."

"Seizures?" They shot each other a look.

"You guess?" Warrior Woman asked.

"Well, I used to. I haven't been getting them lately."

They gave me long looks, and then with serious faces scribbled notes on their pads.

The more I thought about it, the more I realized I really didn't know where all the hurt went when I healed. In fact, I didn't know all that much about my powers at all. What the hell was I doing here?

"One more question." Warrior Woman broke the silence. This was shaping up to be a very short interview, and that couldn't be a good thing. "Why are you here?"

I wanted to stop everything right there and ask to see Justice and talk to him about my father. I wanted to bump into Uberman in the hallway and have him whisk me away to the moon or Mars or somewhere far away, where he could point out different galaxies he'd been to. I looked each one of them in the eye and searched for the right words.

"I don't know exactly how I'm going to make the world better yet, but I know I'm going to try."

After a tense beat, the Spectrum nodded. The others exchanged a look and scribbled more notes. Maybe it was a little on the earnest side, but it was the truth. I think even Warrior Woman gave me a good mark for that one.

Sooz from human resources came out again and passed out another form. She explained that we had to sign one last release form before we were allowed to enter the Simulated Training Arena, known as the S.T.A.

"Even though all interaction will be computer generated," she explained, "if you sustain any injury, holographic or otherwise, we're not liable."

Most of us signed the form and lined up to wait for the door to open. Vicious Violet shredded the form to bits and said there was no way that she was going to sign her life away. Mighty Mite landed on my shoulder and whispered that Violet was only raising a stink about it because she didn't know how to read or write, couldn't even sign her own name. I had a sudden pang to help, like I did at the center. I could have her working those talons around a pencil and making neat cursive letters in no time. Of course, I wasn't sure how I was going to ask without her trying to eat me.

Polar Pete, a short, pudgy guy who looked like he'd be more at home at chess club than a superhero tryout, was sweating more than I was, and his power was all about cooling off.

"Wh-what do you think they're going to do to us?"

"I don't know," I said. "Probably some simple drills to see how our powers work. I wouldn't worry about it too much." But that kind of anxiety was catchy. I didn't like thinking about it.

"I heard someone in the last group was wheeled out on a stretcher." Polar Pete wheezed and took a hit off the inhaler attached to the belt around his parka.

I was determined to appear brave when that door opened and revealed whatever dangerous scenario they had cooked up for us. I relaxed and breathed deeply through my nose and stared at the door.

"Nice tie." Miss Scarlett shoved past me to the front of the line. "Very heroic."

Our group of wannabes held our breath as Sooz collected the waivers and pressed a button on the wall. The door slowly began to lift, like a fancy stainless steel version of an automatic garage door.

"C'mon, guys, let's do it!" Mighty Mite piped from the floor in a tiny voice that sounded like he'd just taken a few hits off a helium balloon.

At the last minute, I stepped in front of Miss Scarlett. No way was I letting her push me to the back of the bus.

Our muscles tensed as the door opened all the way. The stainless steel floor and walls of the room slowly faded away, and the next thing we knew we were standing right in the heart of the city. Typhoon Timmy dodged a taxi cab as it zoomed past us. Other tryout groups turned and looked in our direction. The League had assembled us all together for the last big test. I saw Ruth, the old woman from the waiting room, massaging her knee by a hot dog stand. She bought a foot-long.

"Okay, guys, listen up." Golden Boy suddenly appeared in front of us. "Here's the scenario: Sergeant Psycho has taken over the city and induced a widespread hallucination of mass hysteria. There's panic in the streets."

"No problem." Vicious Violet grinned and sharpened her fangs with a manhole. "I'll calm them down."

"We'll be watching you from the console room." Golden Boy pointed to a window high above at the far end of the room. "You will be graded on ability and teamwork, and your primary goal is to ensure the safety of the crowds."

We looked up to the control room and saw the League sitting at their judges' table. Miss Scarlett winked at them. Uberman waved back.

"Oh, and one more thing." Golden Boy turned to us before he left. "Sergeant Psycho and his Super Soldiers have hidden a dirty bomb somewhere near the traffic square. You have five minutes before it explodes and takes everyone with it."

"Five minutes!" gasped Mighty Mite.

"And counting." Golden Boy looked at his watch and disappeared in a gold flash.

Good thing they're starting with the small stuff. What do they do for real training exercises if you make the team? Thwart thermonuclear war? Discover a cure for cancer?

Ruth sidled up to me and nudged me in the ribs. "Piece of cake," she said through a bite of hot dog.

"Help me, help me, help me!" A legion of tourists ran screaming past us and knocked over innocent bystanders in their path.

"We'll take care of this." Typhoon Timmy puffed up his chest and nodded at Polar Pete. Pete raised his hand and a giant wall of ice surrounded most of the stampeding tourists. Timmy summoned a whirlwind to scoop out of harm's way a group of young visitors who were waiting in an endless line for half-price tickets to *Rent*.

Another stampede of out-of-towners ran past a building under construction and knocked over the scaffolding, which sent the construction workers tumbling from above. Chemical King and a group of others took to the sky and caught them. Still others engaged various Super Soldiers in combat. Miss Scarlett bent her knees, ready to leap up and join the battle in the sky.

"You know, I've got this really bad hangnail," she said to me and sucked on her pinky finger. "Maybe you could help me with it after I'm done with the real fighting."

And then she was airborne.

I looked up at the console room and saw the Spectrum and Warrior Woman nod at each other and then scribble down something. I wanted to jump in and join the fray and make a difference. I needed to make an impression, fast.

I looked over and saw Ruth pop the last bit of hot dog in her mouth. Three overfed tourist kids ran by squealing like pigs.

"Aren't you going to do anything?" I asked.

Ruth looked up at me and dabbed at a glob of mustard on the corner of her mouth.

"Don't get your knickers in a twist, kid. They're just holograms." She swallowed the bite. "First thing you gotta do is find that Psycho guy and take him out. Then find the bomb, and we all go home early." She finished wiping the mustard off her face with a napkin.

I ran into the crowd and waved my arms wildly and shouted for the flying heroes to come down. I yelled that we needed to find Sergeant Psycho and cut off the hysteria from the source, but no one would listen. So much for teamwork.

"Four minutes!" I shouted. "We only have four minutes left!"

No one bothered to come down from the sky. Each hero was busy doing his or her best to rescue any person from harm, or kick the ass of whatever Super Soldier they could get their hands on, like whoever had the most saves or knockouts at the end of the battle would win the game. A whole lot of good that would do us when the city blew up.

I turned back to Ruth.

"How are we supposed to find this guy?"

Ruth struck a match off the bottom of her shoe and lit a

cigarette. "You heal things, right?"

I nodded my head and waved for her to hurry up with wherever she was going with this.

"Well." She took a long drag. "Then you must be able to see what needs healing. Just look for the highest concentration of people who aren't right in the head."

Why didn't I think of that? I took a deep breath, massaged my temples for effect—just in case the League was watching me—and squinted at all the panicked people in the streets. Sure enough, if I concentrated, I could see an oily blackness swirling around in their heads where their brains were supposed to be. My eyes scanned the crowd and I saw smatterings of people with the black brain goo running away from us and getting corralled in small groups of twos and threes by some of the wannabe heroes.

My eyes made their way to the center of the square, and I saw more and more people with the blackness in their heads. The largest concentration of swirling blackness appeared in a throng of people standing around a fountain. There must have been hundreds of them, and they were rioting, their brains submerged in oily darkness. The source of the blackness, the largest concentration of dark matter, was crystal clear to me.

I pointed to the fountain.

"He's over there!"

There in front of the giant statue in the middle of the fountain of Ares, god of war, stood Sergeant Psycho. He cradled his helmet under his arm in emulation of the statue behind him while he commanded his troops in battle. He had one of those crazy gleams in his eye, the kind where the tops of the pupils don't reach the eyelids. He was safe, blanketed from us by the rioting masses infected by his insanity.

"What next?" I asked.

"Look for what seems out of place." Ruth's attention drifted for a moment to another street vendor. "Do you smell French fries?"

I stared closer. There was something off about the statue. Not off as in how strange it is for a major city of a family values–country to have a fountain with a giant statue of a naked pagan war god at its center, but something else.

The stone was a pale grayish beige, the same light-color khaki you see in the preppy clothes stores, so I thought it was strange that some graffiti artist had gone to all the trouble of painting the helmet black.

"Ruth, the bomb, it's in the helmet on the statue!"

Ruth picked through a tub of fries and plucked the burned ones out.

"What do we do now?" I shouted at Ruth. "We're running out of time."

She calmly held three fingers in the air, then two fingers, then one, then . . .

WHUMP!

It was the guy from the waiting room who'd had all the sneezing fits and nosebleeds. A Super Soldier had casually tossed him aside from the fray.

"Sorry." He sniffled and wiped his nose with his sleeve.

"Quick, what do you do?" I asked.

"Uh." He sniffled again. "I make people sick."

Ruth and I shared a look.

"What's your name?"

"Larry, Typhoid Larry."

"Larry, I'm Thom, and this is Ruth. Nice to meet you." I shook his hand and helped him up. He seemed surprised that I would touch him. Ruth held up her hands and wriggled her fingers like she was saying *Nice to meet you, Larry, but keep your germs to yourself.*

"Larry, I need you to take out everyone around that fountain for me, especially that crazy guy in the middle. Can you do that?"

He grinned. "I can do that."

He walked to the edge of the crowd and his body began to shake and he broke into a sweat. He pressed his lips together and his cheeks began to puff out like a bullfrog. Then he doubled over, grabbed his stomach, retched, and threw up on the shoulder of one of the crazed rioters.

This caused the rioters to begin dropping, one by one, to their knees and throwing up on each other. They dropped in a chain reaction, like a coil of projectile-vomit dominoes toppling each other over, until finally, at the top of the crowd, Sergeant Psycho's knees buckled and he went down in a pool of his own vomit.

I jumped over the convulsing bodies to the center of the fountain and climbed the statue. I glanced at my watch; we only had twenty seconds left. My hands began to heat up, and I felt drawn to touch the bomb inside the helmet.

"Thom!" Ruth sidestepped a puddle of throw-up. "I'm not sure you should touch that thing."

"We only have ten seconds left!"

I looked around at all the heroes engaged in combat or rescues, then glanced over at the control booth. Each member of the League was leaning forward and watching expectantly to see what I'd do next. I saw Uberman bite his lip with concern, and at that moment I wanted to impress him more than anything in the world.

My hands were scalding hot now, begging me to place them on the cool, smooth sides of the helmet. I set my palms down on the bomb and I could immediately feel the energy course through them.

Suddenly the lights of the city flickered like strobe lights. The crowds of people began to digitize, like when you get dirt on your DVD and the scene pauses and the images become pixelated. I smelled burned plastic and saw a trickle of smoke rising from my hands. Then I heard a sickening whir, and the entire hologram of the city, people and all, faded away. *Whhhhhhhhrrrrrzzzzzzt.*

The next thing I knew we were enveloped in darkness.

"Thom?" I heard Ruth ask, but I couldn't tell from which direction.

Suddenly the floorboards ignited and exploded, revealing machinery on fire underneath. The tryout heroes screamed and dodged the flames and shrapnel. An emergency siren howled, and I blacked out.

"You short-circuited the entire S.T.A." The Spectrum wrapped a bandage around my forearm, where a stray piece of shrapnel had grazed me.

"I short-circuited your what?" I asked.

"You burned out the whole Simulated Training Area," Warrior Woman said. "You're lucky no one was hurt."

{ 125 }

"If Silver Bullet and I hadn't been able to extinguish the fire with our superspeed, I hate to think what might have happened," Golden Boy chimed in. He dropped an empty fire-extinguisher next to my foot, and it landed on the floor with a clang.

Silver Bullet pinched the space above his nose between his eyes as if a migraine were coming on. "This is going to take *months* to rebuild."

I sat up and saw the entire group of tryouts surrounding me in what remained of the burned-out room. I tugged at the bandage on my arm.

"You're fine, it's just a scratch," the Spectrum assured me.

I wasn't fine, though. I was more humiliated than I'd ever been in my entire life. I could have been stark naked and I wouldn't have felt any worse. It wasn't only the hundred young wannabe heroes who stared at me like I was the world's biggest loser, but each member of the League was there, too, Uberman included. I tried to make eye contact with him, but he dodged it.

"Okay, people, let's go!" He shouted and clapped his hands once. "Free refreshments in the commissary!"

Miss Scarlett nudged past me.

"Nice going, Supergirl."

None of the other candidates would even look at me as they filed out of the room.

Ruth helped me up.

"Went a little overboard there on the whole save-the-day thing, don't you think." She lit a cigarette and offered me one. I waved it away.

"Still." She sucked in a long drag. "Didn't see anyone else stopping that bomb from going off. Did you?"

I thought about it and she was right. I wanted to say thanks, but my mouth was dry, the corners caked with white, the result of too many nerves.

"Here, I've got some diabetic candy in my purse somewhere." She offered me a hard candy, and I unwrapped it and popped it in my mouth. It tasted like stale butterscotch. "Let's go to the commissary." She put her arm around my shoulders and led me off.

I saw we were going to pass Uberman, who was standing at the door, and I wanted to tell Ruth that we should go another way or wait a minute or two, but I didn't want her to pick up on the fact that I was avoiding him. The woman was pretty damn intuitive, and I knew she'd put two and two together.

"Thom."

Just before we got to the door, I turned around and saw Larry.

"Not now, Larry." I turned back toward Uberman. Soon I was going to pass by him close enough to smell the peppermint on his breath.

"But, Thom—"

I turned around exasperated. "What?"

"I've been trying to tell you I was happy you shook my hand; people usually don't like to touch me."

"Why's that?"

I felt an uncontrollable urge bubble up in my stomach, and the next thing I knew I'd thrown up right in front of Uberman.

* * *

The refreshments they served were worse than the kind we got in school whenever they had to throw together some lame reception for parents night. I took a halfhearted bite of a cookie to get the taste of throw-up out of my mouth and chucked it in a wastebasket when I couldn't figure out if it was peanut butter or gingerbread. Ruth took a sip of her Kool-Aid and handed me a Dixie cup.

"Here, drink this, it'll make you feel better." I took a sip, and they must have put way too much powder in the drink, because it burned my throat as it went down.

Sooz from human resources stood at the podium in the front of the room and tapped the microphone. High-pitched screeches whistled through the room.

"Is this thing on?" Feedback howled, and everyone covered their ears.

"If I can have everyone's attention, please." She put her finger over her lips and shushed the crowd. The chatter died down, and a hundred eager heroes listened attentively in hopes that they'd hear their names called for the next round.

"You can all continue enjoying the refreshments. In a few moments, we'll be posting the results. Thank you." Good thing the woman didn't do crisis intervention and management. The poor thing had zero people skills, and I'm not even going to mention her hair.

"I just wanted to say thanks for coming in." Golden Boy was upon me in an instant and he shook my hand intently, the hint of a smile creeping around the corners of his mouth. "Sorry things didn't work out."

The news hit me like he'd flung a pillowcase of bricks into

my stomach. After I ruined all that expensive equipment, I suppose I didn't really harbor much hope for making the cut, but still, to hear that they didn't want me after all was incredibly painful, especially coming from this jackass. I did my best to make sure none of my emotions showed on my face, and I shook his hand back.

"Maybe next year," he said, and then sped off. I wish I'd yacked on his boots.

Sooz and the receptionist caused quite a stir in the crowd when they brought out the lists. The heroes gathered around them and tried to get an early glimpse as they taped the lists on the wall. The two women disappeared in a sea of costumes as the entire room converged on the spot.

Miss Scarlett flew up into the air, flipped over, and pumped her fist and hollered "Whoo-hoo!" Guess she made it.

Some wannabe heroes reacted with elation; others hunched their shoulders, despondent. I didn't see any reason to stay and punish myself any more than necessary, so I put Dad's coat back on and made my way to the door. On the way out, I saw Ruth standing in the corner, her back turned to the crowd. She pulled a flask out of her poncho and poured the remainder of its contents into the Kool-Aid.

I stormed down the hallway and looked for the nearest exit. I mean, who were they to cut me? Sure, I didn't know what the hell I was doing, but I had to have more sense than the pizza delivery girl. Besides, they were the ones who'd invited me to join in the first place. I didn't ask for this, and it wasn't fair for them to get my hopes up like that. They were seasoned enough to know whether I had the right stuff to make it before I came to embarrass myself. Maybe this was someone's idea of a sick joke; maybe the reason I'd never heard of Justice was because he and my dad hated each other, and maybe the reason Justice invited me in the first place was to be cruel to the son of his ex-mentor. What kind of a prick does something like that? I mean, shouldn't he be figuring out new ways to save the world instead of spending his spare time humiliating kids?

And where the hell was I, anyway? I looked down the corridor, a long stretch of industrial pilings and detritus that cast long shadows on the concrete. I thought I saw something moving in the shadows. I spotted an exit sign at the end of the complex, and I could have sworn I saw a black cape swirl behind one of the pilings, but I was too mad to care.

I was the one who'd stopped the threat and saved the day back in the Simulated Training Area. I deserved to make that team more than anyone else. I wasn't going to let them get away with this. They weren't going to walk all over me. I turned around. I was going back to give those assholes a piece of my mind.

I walked back into the reception room. and pushed through the crowd toward the dais and the podium. I bumped into Polar Pete, who sizzled when he smacked into Miss Scarlett, who was busy telling more stories about herself to a captivated Warrior Woman.

Justice hovered on the dais, his back to the crowd, in intense discussion with Silver Bullet and Golden Boy, who were probably plotting new ways to torture me, new ways to kick dirt in my dad's face. Golden Boy didn't like the plan, because he was shaking his head.

Well, they were going to have to do a whole lot better than this if they wanted us Creeds to feel bad. If they thought they could hurt me or Dad just by messing with my head at a tryout and cutting me from the team, they had another thing coming. If there's one thing we Creeds knew how to succeed at, it was failure.

I approached Justice, ready to chew him out. I was going to tell him off for abandoning my father when he needed him the most, remind him that he was supposed to live up to his name, and not just when the cameras were rolling. I poked Justice on the shoulder with my index finger like I was mashing a beetle into his back. He turned his head, and I spun him around by his shoulder. Shock registered on Silver Bullet's and Golden Boy's faces. My lower lip trembled and a new thought suddenly entered my head. Screw the speech; I wanted to clock him. I clenched my fist, and Justice looked at me, surprised.

"Congratulations, Thom. You made the team."

CHAPTER NINE

SOMEONE FOLLOWED ME on the way home from the tryout. I wasn't sure at first, though. It wasn't until I got to the parking lot of the gay bar that I was certain.

I'd passed by this strip mall about a hundred times since I'd found a message scrawled on the side of a stall at the Exxon down the street, that this was where men came to meet men and do whatever happens next. I still hadn't worked up the courage to set foot inside. So far the most I could do was come to the parking lot and watch to see who went in and who came out. There was this one spot on a generator out by the Dumpster where I'd pull myself up to sit and watch. Since the light above the generator was burned out, people rarely noticed me up there.

I knew I probably wouldn't meet my soul mate in the parking lot, or even inside the bar, for that matter. But I felt a glimmer of hope—maybe tonight would be different. Things had been going well, and I wanted to celebrate. If the League wanted me, maybe someone else would, too. Why not reward myself with a little people watching, at least? What harm could it do? Besides, it wasn't like I was going to go inside or anything. Just the thought of going in was enough to make my insides drop into my bowels. I hoisted myself up on my usual spot on the generator, wiped the grime off my palms, and wished I'd brought some gum or water, because I already had cotton mouth.

I watched a bat flutter in and out of the glow of a streetlight until I finally grew a pair of balls and decided to go in. My boots landed in the gravel with a loud crunch. I put one foot in front of the other and fixed my eyes on the front door of the bar. Abruptly, without a sign of who threw it, a rock landed near my feet.

Someone was following me. I froze in the light of the streetlamp and listened. I could hear the wings of the bat flapping above me, but nothing else. I crouched down and ducked between two SUVs and waited. A shadow moved by the generator.

I could either make a break for the front door of the bar or I could crawl around the labyrinth of parked cars until I reached the entrance to the parking lot and run like hell for home. I looked at my watch. My dad would be expecting me back from my game soon. My tongue felt numb and my teeth began to chatter. There was no way I could go inside; I'd be trapped.

Then I heard footsteps in the gravel, and the crunching sound grew louder as they approached. I rolled under one of the

SUVs, popped up on the other side, and made a fast break for another row of cars closer to the parking lot entrance. The footsteps stopped.

I looked over at the entrance. I could make it with one more sprint through the last row of cars. I started running full speed. My hand latched on to the side of a Subaru. I spun around the last car, slipped on the gravel, and skidded before landing in a cloud of dust. I coughed and peered through the dust behind me into the darkness. I couldn't see anything for a second, but when the dust cleared I thought I saw the fluid contours of fabric, a cape maybe, flowing in the distance. Maybe my head was playing tricks on me for doing something I knew I shouldn't be doing. This was clearly not my scene; I was here out of desperation. Didn't I have standards? Didn't I want more than this? Suddenly the thought of someone finding me here turned my stomach. What would Uberman think? I sprinted as fast as I could out of the parking lot, past the neon Purple Cactus sign, and when I was too exhausted to run anymore, I stuck close to the bushes and jogged with my head turned over my shoulder, suspicious of any shadows the rest of the way home.

I yanked off my tie and toweled off my face with it as I walked up the driveway. Who was following me?

I bet it was that rat fink Golden Boy. Probably volunteered to do the League's routine security check. I can hear him now: *I don't think we should just run his Social Security number, not this one. Trust me, I have a feeling.*

I thought about my fist connecting with his jaw, and the anger felt good. For a second. Then I felt ashamed about enjoying the thought of a fight. Anger was just a momentary cover-up, an emotion that masked your true fears. What really scared me is that maybe it was Dad who was following me. I was hiding more and more things from him every day.

"How'd you do, kiddo?"

"Good," I said. I followed his voice out back to the deck. "We won."

Dad flipped a burger on the grill and pressed down on it with the spatula. The grease dripped on the charcoal below and sizzled.

"How'd *you* do, kiddo?"

I hoisted myself up on the wood railing of the deck and sat. "Fine." I watched my legs dangle beneath me. "Scored fifteen points."

"Hm." Dad moved a burger over to the middle of the coals. "How'd you do on D?"

"Twelve rebounds." This was becoming an interrogation.

Dad looked up from the burgers and studied my face.

"Nice jacket," he said.

Shit. I'd forgotten to change clothes. "Sorry, Dad. Can I borrow it?"

"Sure, all you have to do is ask."

He flipped another burger on the grill.

"You look awfully hot. You didn't shower?"

Was he testing me? The man could always tell when I wasn't telling the truth. But if he was the one who'd followed me to the parking lot, how could he have gotten back here in time to have the charcoal going like that? Dad's fast, sure, but that fast? He didn't have superpowers, like me. There was supposed to be a limit to what he could accomplish. But he was so stealthy. . . .

"Why don't you go get us a cold beer."

Oh, God, he said *us*. He definitely wanted to talk. This was it, he knew everything.

How could I have been so stupid? I was so distracted about the League tryouts that I'd totally forgotten about the broken laptop. He probably took it to a shop and had some computer guy behind the counter fire it back up, only to see a naked shot of Uberman and his giant man-breasts fill the screen.

"No thanks." I swallowed and felt my Adam's apple run up against the collar of my wet suit. "I'm not thirsty."

"Okay, then." He flipped a burger into the air. "You can get me a new one." Dad crumpled his empty beer can in his good hand.

I walked into the kitchen and thought about walking straight out the door and making a break for it. Instead I found myself walking to the fridge and opening the door, like I was a robot Dad had built in his garage workshop and programmed to get him beer. The cool air of the refrigerator felt good against my hot face. I grabbed a beer sitting out alone on the shelf as if he'd left that one intentionally for me.

I closed the door and paused. Something was odd. I opened the door again and looked inside and saw that the beer had been sitting on top of a laptop computer. A brand-new laptop computer.

"Dad, someone left a laptop in the fridge."

I tossed him his beer across the deck. He stuck out

his good hand and caught it without looking up from the grill.

"How about that." Dad grinned and turned to me. "I got a big promotion, Thom. They made me a foreman." He tapped the beer against his leg, excited about his news. "And they gave me a sizable raise."

My mouth grew into a wide smile. I hadn't seen Dad this happy, this appreciated, for as long as I'd been alive.

"That's great! Congratulations! You didn't have to get us a new computer, you know, we could have managed with only one."

"I didn't get *us* a new computer. I got *you* a new computer." Dad tossed the beer back at me, and I snatched it out of the air. "You'll be going off to school soon. Certain things a young man needs these days to get ahead." Dad took the burgers off the grill and set them on the platter. "And I intend to give you all of them. Things are finally looking up." He inhaled deeply and savored the crisp edges of the burgers.

"What about the old laptop?" I asked.

"I'll pick it up from the shop tomorrow."

"I'll get it," I was quick to offer, maybe too quick.

"With what?" Dad made a skeptical grimace. He was the breadwinner.

"I got a new job."

"Another one?"

"I mean, I just picked up a few extra shifts at the cafeteria. Let me pay for it. Please?"

Would he pick up on this? It was only a half-lie. With my League probationary stipend, I did have enough money to get the laptop out of the shop. And I really did want to take care of it—even if there wasn't anything to cover up—to thank Dad for getting me a new computer I didn't deserve.

"Okay," he said. "You can get it." He smiled, pleased at the responsible, grateful son he thought he was raising.

I couldn't believe it. All his dreams about me and my bright future were still on. He didn't know a thing. Now I felt worse than ever about lying to him. If I made the League, I wouldn't exactly be packing up my laptop and extra socks and underwear to move to the state university next fall. The League's state-of-the-art technology would make a laptop about as relevant as Pac-Man. Still, I was thrilled for him about the promotion. I believed everything could work out somehow.

"You okay, Thom?"

He looked at me, his eyebrows raised, a little sad, a little concerned. His sincerity made my stomach rumble with guilt. You can always tell when someone asks how you're doing if they really give a shit, if they really want to know. "You seem like you've got a lot on your mind lately. Now I'll have to work some crazy hours while I'm getting used to the new responsibilities, but if you ever want to talk, just say the word and I'm here, okay?"

I pressed the beer to my forehead and felt the cool condensation on the can drip down my eyebrows.

"Okay."

He grabbed the platter and grilling utensils and headed for the back door. With his hands full he said, "Hey, pop open that beer for me, would you?"

I wanted to take the platter out of his hands and ask him to sit down because there was so much I needed to talk to him about. I considered telling him everything, but I couldn't make any sound come out of my mouth. Suddenly I didn't even know how to begin a sentence.

I grabbed the aluminum tab and flipped it open. The beer exploded and sprayed fizz and foam all over my face.

Dad smiled and opened the back door with his foot.

"Gotcha."

CHAPTER TEN

MY ALARM WOKE ME up at 5:25 a.m., and instead of hitting SNOOZE, I hopped out of bed, threw on my sweats and sneakers, brushed my teeth, and went for a run. I chucked a full half-quart of Breyers mint chocolate-chip ice cream in the garbage on the way out the door. Had to be in perfect shape if I was going to make the League. They were a pantheon of the world's greatest heroes; there would be no second-stringers and no love handles.

Running always gave me time to think. It wasn't like practicing with a team, when I always worried if I was fitting in with everyone else. When I ran, I never thought about screwing someone else up or ruining the team's chance to win. It was a solitary activity, and sometimes that felt nice.

It also felt nice to think about my first practice with my very own tryout squad for the League. I wasn't worried yet about competing with the other squads for the few slots on the big team. I was just proud to be a part of a team, and I was ready to dedicate myself to something I believed in, to work hard enough to see what my best could be. The sun was coming up, but the streetlights were still on, so I jogged at a strong pace, bathed under an even glow. I wondered who else would be on my squad. Pure excitement drove me to run all the way across town, and I found myself in the parking lot of the rec center where I tutored. I finished off my marathon with a few wind sprints. It was so early in the morning that hardly any cars were there, which left me plenty of room to run.

Light poured out of the windows to the gym, and I figured I had time to fit in some weights before my shift and tryouts. I jogged inside, and my sneakers squeaked against the shiny floor of the hall and the noise bounced off the concrete walls. I turned the corner and stopped short of the court when I saw something coming at me from the opposite end of the hall. It was a basketball, and it rolled at me until it came to a full stop right beneath my feet.

I picked it up and rubbed my heated palms over its rough, cool exterior. Then I heard the thudding sound of a basketball bouncing against the wood floor of the gymnasium. I followed the sound as if it were an old friend beckoning me to come play. In the gym I saw one guy far down at the other end of the court. He dribbled effortlessly to the basket and sailed high into the air and dunked the ball. Sweat sprayed from his hair and T-shirt when he landed on the floor. He turned and saw me standing in the doorway with the ball.

Even from that far away I could tell from his piercing stare that it was Goran. Silently, he walked over to me, palming the ball in an exaggerated dribble as he caught his breath. Soon, he was just a few yards away and he stopped. Neither of us said a word, and all I could hear was the sound of both of us trying to catch our breath after pushing ourselves so hard. His eyes never let go of mine, his expression gave nothing away. If someone had seen us, they could have mistaken us for two kids auditioning for a western, our hands on our basketballs pressed firmly on one hip, ready to see who would draw first.

His face reminded me of that time he shook my hand and I thought he was going to hit me. I wondered if my face reminded him of the same thing. My eyes drifted down to his legs, and I studied them for a moment. There was no scar.

In the blink of an eye, he took the basketball to his chest and flung it at me full strength. I saw the ball hurtling toward my face, and I instinctively dropped the ball I was carrying and held up my hands. The ball hit my hands with a large smack, and I felt my palms sting. My heart thumped as the ball struck my chest.

"Go on," Goran said. "Shoot it."

He held his chin high and walked forward a few steps so that he was standing right in front of me. He stood so close I could see the sweat bead up on his forehead into a swollen droplet that trickled down to his eye. But he didn't blink. He was waiting to see if I'd accept the challenge.

I looked down at the ball in my hands and sighed with a deep resignation. I relaxed my posture so that he could be sure I didn't want to play these stupid games with him.

Then I faked the best jump shot I'd ever faked, and when Goran predictably leaped up to block it, I drove past him to the basket for an easy two. With one hand, I picked up the ball and winged it back at him hard.

"Your turn," I said through clenched teeth.

Thus began our one-on-one, a clash of the titans, an epic battle for dominion over the Tuckahoe Rec Center basketball court. If I made an easy jump shot, Goran would answer it with a three-pointer, while the sound of my swish still echoed in the rafters. I'd smack away one of his shots before he launched it, and he'd block my way to the paint as I moved toward the basket on the next go.

Things got even more heated from there. It was the best basketball I'd ever played in my life. If a recruiting agent had been there, we'd both have had contracts in front of us before we left the gym. My diaphragm heaved, struggling for oxygen, and the harder we played, the harder each of us wanted to win. We played in silence, no histrionics, no trash-talking. Either we were bitter enemies locked in a battle to the death, or we were best friends who felt totally comfortable spending time together without saying a word.

Finally, with the score tied at sixty-eight—an incredibly high score considering we'd only been playing for an hour—I guessed the right direction on Goran's next drive, knocked the ball out of his hands, and managed to grab the ball first when we both dove for it. As I dribbled the ball and thought about my next move, I briefly looked down at my watch. Even if I left now, I'd still be running late for my first job, and if I was late for my jobs, I'd be late for my first official League probationary practice, so it was time to end it right here.

I pumped another fake shot, which Goran fell for again—

I'd learned a few tricks from Dad in the stealth department—and drove around him the other way. Still, Goran had already learned to read some of my other moves well, so he was on top of me in an instant. I was so shocked by his reaction time that I made the cardinal error of picking up my dribble.

Now I was stuck. I had no choice but to pull back and launch a Hail Mary three-pointer, and I knew he'd be able to see it coming and block the shot, maybe even without his feet having to leave the floor. Instead I watched the ball leave my hands unobstructed, and it sailed up toward the basket. I looked around for Goran and found him casually walking off the court toward the door. I turned to him and opened my mouth, about to ask him why the hell he stopped.

Neither of us looked to see if the ball went in the basket.

All his intensity had melted away in a single moment. A little boy in a karate uniform approached him and stopped just short of Goran's feet. Wrapped in his white robe, the kid looked more like a bedsheet was trying to eat him than a future martial arts champion. The little boy paused before Goran, uttered something in some sort of Asian language, and then bowed with his hands together. Goran responded, put his hands together, and bowed back at the boy.

Then the kid whirled around and threw an impossibly high kick that would have connected with Goran's jaw had he not thrown his hand in the hair to block it. The kid answered with a punch to the gut, which Goran again deflected. Finally, the kid jumped in the air with a scream and threw another fist at Goran. Goran blocked the punch with ease, but that had been the kid's plan. With his other hand he flicked Goran's nose. The boy landed and giggled. Goran held his nose, with his mouth open in surprise.

"Nice one."

He held up his hand for a high five, and the little boy gave it a proud smack. Then they returned to their initial positions and bowed respectfully to each other.

Goran's brow furrowed. "Where's your bag?"

The kid looked around and bit his lip.

"Go get it," Goran said. "You can't be late for camp." He mussed the kid's hair, and the little boy bounced out of the gym in a swirl of flowing white.

Goran turned back around to me and didn't say a word about the game. Instead he looked me up and down.

And then he smiled. At first it was just one side of his mouth, but then the other side raised up to join it, and he gave me a toothy grin. Not perfect teeth; you don't get those when you grow up in Croatia. But I'd never seen him look like that: equal parts boy and man. Happy.

"Same time tomorrow?"

I studied his smile. I was still trying to recover from our game, and I was panting so hard I couldn't speak. I nodded my head.

The kid appeared in the doorway with his backpack. Goran knelt down, the boy hopped on his back, and Goran sped out of the gym, piggybacking the kid off to camp.

I put my hands on my knees and struggled to catch my breath. It was a long time before I could breathe evenly again. All I could think of as I sprinted home, soaring across curbs and crosswalks, was one thing.

He smiled at me.

CHAPTER ELEVEN

AT FIRST I THOUGHT there'd been a mistake. I crowded into the elevator with a group of heroes on their way to their respective meeting rooms. I tried not to look too excited, but I couldn't help it. I was about to meet my very own team for the first time. My eyes scanned the different faces crammed in the elevator, and I wondered which ones were on my squad. Most of the heroes emptied out on Level A. Level B saw almost everyone else depart. I was left in the elevator with Melancholy Polly.

The door opened on Level C, and she asked lethargically, "Aren't you coming?"

"Oh, no thanks," I answered. "My group's on level D."

"Level D?" She scrunched her nose like she smelled something bad. "I didn't know there even *was* a level D."

* * *

"Hi, is this the tryout group?" I had an eager smile on my face and a smudged list in my hand.

"No, that's down the hall," a familiar, raspy voice said. "This is the League's Narcotics Anonymous Group."

I looked up from the list to see Ruth, the seer, who cackled herself into a smoker's hack at her own joke.

"She's just kidding. You're in the right place, grab a chair." Typhoid Larry sat shivering on his cold metal folding chair. I reached out to shake his hand, but he only regarded it with a sigh. I remembered what happened last time I touched him and pulled my hand back.

There was one empty seat, so I sat in it. Unfortunately, it was positioned right next to Miss Scarlett, who smelled like pepperoni and sausage.

"Great," she said, and rolled her eyes. "Maybe we can get free tickets to the ballet now." She turned her back to me.

I looked around the room and thought certainly this was just a holding area for a much larger tryout group. They'd be joining us any second. Surely this wasn't our entire team: an old lady who, between smokes, said she could see the future; a girl who smelled like pizza and hated me; and a guy who made people sick. This couldn't be everyone. We at least had to have a team leader or something.

"You're in my seat."

I turned around and saw Golden Boy standing above me.

"You can either get another folding chair from the broom closet down the hall," he said, "or you can sit on the floor. We're about to get started."

Golden Boy introduced himself as Kevin and explained

that despite years of service as Silver Bullet's trusty sidekick, he'd been saddled with the responsibility of turning us into "real" heroes. He explained that over the course of the next few months, we'd be competing with the other tryout teams to see who'd advance to the next stage. Now that he'd told us a little about himself, which in fact was very little, he asked each of us to say a few words about ourselves.

Scarlett launched into a retelling of her unremarkable origins before Golden Boy had a chance to complete his sentence.

"I grew up next to the Surry Nuclear Power Plant." She took a squeeze tube of cheap moisturizer out of the utility pouch on her belt and began rubbing it in her hands. The smell, a sickly-sweet combination of too many flowers, almost covered up the aroma of pepperoni. "So the morning after my twelfth birthday, I woke up and found I had a rack on me that'd make Dolly Parton blush, and that I could fry things in the skillet without turning on the burner." She rubbed the excess lotion from her hands into her cleavage. "I work at Rasheev's Pizza Delivery over in Kempsville, but I'm hoping I'll get to quit soon. Seemed like a good gig because I can keep the pies warm. Better tips. How much we get paid if we make the team?" She looked to Golden Boy for an answer.

"Um." Golden Boy leafed through a binder in his lap. "I don't know if that information's in here."

"What about benefits? Medical, dental, 401(k)?" Scarlett was quick to ask.

Golden Boy perused the official League tryout manual at superspeed.

"It doesn't say. I'll have to have Sooz get back to you."

"You do that." Scarlett unfolded an aluminum wrapper, popped a stick of fluorescent gum in her mouth, and began chewing. "Okay, I'm done."

"Let's see . . ." Golden Boy leafed through another pile of folders, apparently dockets on each of us, the background information we'd filled out, data, and results from our tryouts. "Larry, how 'bout you go next."

Larry popped two aspirin and chased it with a swig from a tiny bottle of Pepto-Bismol.

"Where's the bathroom on this floor?" He sneezed, and Miss Scarlett fanned away the air with her wet hands.

"I'm Ruth, I see things, and that's all you need to know. Who's next?"

Now I was the only one left. I thought about what I was going to say: Oh, hi there, I'm Thom. I just want to say what an honor it is to be a part of this prestigious team. A leader that wants to kick my ass, some bitchy girl with a major attitude problem, a geriatric precog, a guy who should probably be quarantined at the Center for Disease Control, and me, just your average, ordinary, gay teen superhero. Surely we're what the founding members had in mind when they banded together to form the world's premier superhero group. What's not to be excited about?

"I'm Thom." I scratched a dry patch above my elbow. "I can heal things. Sometimes."

The rest of the day was spent getting certified in CPR and first aid. It was redundant for me because I'd been getting my certification renewed every year for the past few summers as a lifeguard. Larry got in a fight with the Red Cross volunteer because he wouldn't put his lips on the dummy to practice mouth-to-mouth. I, for one, thought he was being awfully considerate of his other teammates.

When it came her turn to practice on the dummy, Ruth took a deep drag and blew smoke into the doll. She fell into another coughing fit, laughing as smoke came out of the dummy's ears. The Red Cross volunteer was unamused. I hoped the next practice would offer a little more challenge, maybe we'd even see a little action soon.

Golden Boy suggested that next time we try a few icebreakers to get to know each other. Ruth balked at the idea of the trust fall, so Scarlett suggested suck-me/blow-me.

"What's that?"

"Yeah, right," she said. "Like *you* don't know."

I still didn't know what she was talking about, but I definitely knew I didn't like the way she implied that sucking and blowing were things I'd know more about than anyone else.

After the workout session, I went to the guys' locker room on our floor to shower, and I heard voices while I was toweling off. I crouched behind the last row of lockers and saw Golden Boy follow Silver Bullet into the room. Silver Bullet was carrying a crate full of personal items.

"Why can't I keep my locker upstairs with you guys?" Golden Boy had a slight whine to his voice. Maybe he was younger than I thought.

"Look, Kevin, Justice was very clear. This is the way it needs to be for now. I know it's hard, but I expect you to handle this with the dignity and valor of the hero I've taught you to be, understand?"

Golden Boy puckered his mouth like he wanted to say something but was too frustrated. Finally, he relaxed and nodded.

"Look at it as an opportunity," Silver Bullet said. "This team is like a lump of clay for you to shape. If you do well with them, you'll be back on the team in no time."

Silver Bullet handed Golden Boy the personal items from his locker. I could make out a few trophies, a couple of pictures of sports heroes, some socks. I barely blinked and Silver Bullet was gone. Golden Boy stood there alone with his stuff and faced his new locker, a blank stare on his face. Then he dropped the crate and it landed on the concrete floor with a loud smack that made me jump.

Golden Boy looked up and saw me, my towel wrapped around my waist.

"What the hell are you looking at?" He leveled me a look of death. I turned around and finished changing and got out of there as quickly as someone without superspeed could.

Miss Scarlett blew past me on her way out of the womens' locker room.

"Make way, loser, I'm late for work." She swung her pizza carrier and swiped me in the back of the knee, and I crumpled down to the floor. I closed my eyes, savoring the comfort of the cold, hard tile.

"You know, they have cots in the back if you really want to lie down." I looked up and saw Ruth standing over me. She lit a cigarette and pressed the elevator button. She went fishing for her keys in an old Jazzercise gym bag slung over her shoulder, and I figured it was a good time to make conversation. Out of everyone on this team, she seemed to hate me the least.

"Those things will kill you, you know," I said, and pushed myself off the floor.

Her expression was hard to read.

"Not me, they won't." She took a long drag.

"I had an uncle who died of lung cancer. He didn't think they'd kill him, either." I realized I was doing a pretty lousy job of making a new friend, but I kept going on with it anyway because at least she hadn't knocked me back down on the floor yet.

She gave me a look like she thought I might be pulling her leg.

"I can see the future, remember? Superpower . . ."

God, I really am an idiot. She took another drag and muttered something to herself under her breath as she fiddled around in her purse for a mint. She scraped some lint off the candy and popped it in her mouth.

"So what's going to happen to me, you know, in the future? Do I make the team?" I knew it was a stupid thing to say before I even finished saying it, but I just wanted to keep the conversation going. She shot me a weary look that said, *You can't possibly think you're the first person to ask me that.* I looked in her eyes and couldn't figure out if I saw disappointment or aggravation. I like to think that she expected more of me.

"It doesn't work that way," she said, the same way she'd talk to a puppy who'd just peed on her rug.

"You mean you can't always see the future?" I asked.

She turned the candy over in her mouth and let a deliberate silence fill the air.

"Oh, you mean you just *won't* tell me," I said. What was I doing now? Challenging her? She eyed me for a second.

"You can't slip a coin in me and expect me to tell you everything you want to know," she said. "Cigarettes and booze, maybe, a couple of Vicodins or Percodans, definitely. But coins, no."

I laughed out loud and thought I saw her crack a smile, just barely, in the left corner of her mouth, hidden by the long ash of her cigarette. "Here, step into the light, let me look at you."

She spun me around and gave me a serious once-over. I waited a long beat for her to say something. It felt like a year's worth of years passed in that moment, and I wondered what exactly it was that she was seeing. Or was it that she was seeing something so horrible that she was trying to figure out the best way to break the bad news to me.

My mind raced with possibilities. She could have been seeing good things, too. Maybe I ended up living in a beach shack on a tropical island with Viggo Mortensen and we'd go horseback riding on the shore every day. No, more likely it was bad. Maybe I got sick: Parkinson's, maybe; heart disease. Did I ever get a chance to have kids? Did they die before me? Was I going to be bald before thirty? Would I ever get to see my mom again? Or maybe she saw who was following me—the outcome revealed in the future in such a terrible way that it rendered her speechless.

"You got secrets."

She stated it matter-of-factly. My eyes grew wide. I couldn't help it. My stomach dropped, and I suddenly wished I'd listened to the directions when Golden Boy showed Typhoid Larry to the nearest bathroom. She knew. She had to.

"I hate secrets," she said.

The elevator door opened and she stepped inside and hit a button.

"I'll tell you this much," she said. "You got your work cut out for you."

She patted my head, making me feel like the incontinent puppy I was. Then the elevator doors closed and she disappeared.

CHAPTER TWELVE

I HAVE A BAD HABIT of trying to carry too many things at once. It almost got me fired my first day on the job at the Picadilly Cafeteria when I stacked too many dessert plates in the plastic bin so that a giant blob of blueberry pie and chocolate pudding leftovers teetered on top of the last saucer. The saucer flipped over and spilled the mess into some old lady's lap. And it turned out to be my manager's mother.

So today I was trying to be fast and efficient, but careful not to spill. I kept my eye on the clock. If I could clear the tables from the lunch rush fast enough, I could get a head start on the dish washing, which would put me out of there with a full twenty minutes to spare to make it to the League headquarters. Maybe I'd even be early.

I'd vowed never to be late again, that's for sure. The one and only time I showed up late for my League probationary training, I was called in for a one-on-one sit-down with the heavy hitters.

"They're waiting for you," Golden Boy said, looking down at his watch.

"Sorry I'm late, I—"

"Just go, you've already kept them waiting long enough." Golden Boy swept me through the door. I wanted to smack that smirk right off Scarlett's face as I passed by her.

Inside I discovered it was worse than I'd expected. It was the whole League. All of them, seated on the dais, a tribunal staring at me. I swallowed. This was it, I was going to be let go. I should have known better than to keep two jobs on top of my training, but we needed the money. I didn't want to make excuses. I thought about my father, and I decided to stand my ground.

"Have a seat," Justice said from his lofty position. I could feel their eyes bearing down upon me. I thought I even heard Warrior Woman growl.

I closed my eyes and cleared my throat, ready for the worst. When I looked up, Silver Bullet was standing right in front of me.

"Hold out your hand," he said. His face betrayed no emotion.

What was this? Were they going to whack my knuckles with a ruler?

I tentatively held out my hand, scanned the eyes of the League on the dais in front of me.

Silver Bullet slipped a ring on my finger.

"Congratulations," Justice said. A few smiles crept over their faces. "Your League probationary ring."

I stared down at the ring, couldn't believe it was on my finger.

"This is an outward symbol of an inner belief, a reminder that wherever you go, you're part of a team." Justice hovered closer to me. "It also serves as a tracking device, if you're ever in trouble and you need help." He floated directly in front of me, slightly above my eye line and then descended to my level. "And most important"—he shook my hand—"it has the League emergency signal."

The next day I dropped the ring in the sink at work and thought for sure I'd lost it. I searched everywhere, even unscrewed the pipes, but nothing. Before I went into a full panic, I heard a funny noise from the Hobart dishwasher. I'd just put a load in, but something sounded loose in the machine, like a piece of dish had chipped off. I heaved open the door to the industrial-size machine and pulled out the trays of plates and mugs, and there in a coffee cup was my ring.

I glanced over my shoulder to make sure no one could see me and slipped the ring back on my finger. Still hot from the wash cycle, it burned my skin. But I didn't care. It actually felt good. I hoped it had burned a place onto my finger so it would never fall off again.

Since today I was in a hurry, I contemplated stacking one more dinner plate on top of the dishes in my bin, but decided against it. One more sweep in the dining room, I could get started loading my dishes and be out of there by—

"Hello."

My heart did a somersault.

Goran sat in a booth, his little brother across from him picking at a piece of corn bread with his fork. He wore his security guard uniform, which made his shoulders look even broader. I looked for bags under his eyes from working the late shift, but I couldn't find any. Even in the dismal lighting of the Picadilly Cafeteria, his dark eyes lit up the room.

Then he smiled at me again.

I opened my mouth and somehow managed to say "Hi."

"Thom." My shift manager pulled me aside by the arm, and I almost dropped all my dishes. "I need you to stay late, Manny went home sick."

Trying to hide my disappointment, I wiped the sweat off my forehead. I looked over at Goran, who pretended not to look at me as my boss ordered me around. Out of the corner of my eye, I thought I saw his little brother snickering at me.

"Look, just finish Manny's dishes and you can go, okay?"

"Okay," I said, and hurried into the kitchen with my tray.

I loaded that Hobart faster than any human ever had before, Manny's dishes, too. I noticed my reflection in the sink full of rinse water and saw that when I'd wiped the sweat off my brow, I'd accidentally smeared whipped cream from a chocolate pudding dish all over it. That must have been what Goran's little brother was laughing at. I didn't have time to feel the embarrassment; I scrubbed off the mess with the corner of my apron and studied the tall stack of pots and pans that still needed to be washed. How was I ever going to get out of there on time?

"Someone's looking for you out front," my manager called out to me. "Says he has a tip for the busboy." I dropped my shoulders. I didn't have time for this. Plus, I was a total mess and I really didn't like the thought of Goran giving me some token tip because I looked so pathetic at work. It was patronizing, and it made me mad. Who did he think he was, anyway?

I stopped short of the register, surprised because my father had never come to see me at work before.

"Hey, kiddo."

"I'm kinda busy, Dad." I glanced down at my watch. "I'm trying to get out of here."

Irma behind the register rang up Dad's to-go meal. This was totally unlike him. He never spent money on lunch. He prepared a brown bag every day, which he ate alone in the factory cafeteria. What was he doing here? Was he checking up on me?

"Just wanted to give my favorite busboy a tip." Dad pulled a twenty out of his pocket to pay Irma. He handed her the money first, and then took the bag with his good hand.

I cleared empty serving trays from under the sneeze guards and stacked them in my arms. I spotted Goran and his little brother looking over the dessert section. Goran paid careful attention to his brother's selection, but I could tell he was eyeing me with his peripheral vision.

Suddenly I didn't like the thought of him and my father being in the same room. Especially with me in it.

I took more pans and added them to the pile, which was growing too big for me to carry. I hoped that if the stack grew above my head, no one would be able to see me.

"I was thinking about taking a night off to come see one of your games," Dad said with a fixed stare.

"No, that's okay." I almost dropped the pans. "It's just

summer league." I felt my ring catch in the handle of the Salisbury steak pan, and it almost yanked my finger out of joint.

Dad looked at the floor. Irma offered him his change, and the line behind him waited impatiently for him to take it. His mind was on something else, because he reached out for the change with his bad hand.

From behind the stack of trays I saw the shocked faces in line when they spotted the melted clump of flesh that used to be Dad's hand. I saw Goran pretend not to notice. His little brother's jaw was open. Goran quickly grabbed the kid's hand and pulled him in for a private conference. He wouldn't make eye contact with me.

All of a sudden a charge took hold of my body. A shock that only I could feel. It took me by surprise, and I almost dropped every tray in my arms.

It was the alarm on my League probationary ring vibrating. The emergency signal. My heart sank. I had to answer it, but I couldn't let my dad catch on.

"Dad, I've really got to go." I hoped he wouldn't notice the strain on my face, the vibrations emanating from my ring.

Dad studied me for a second, saw the dishes teetering in my arms. He gave me the once-over, and I did my best to slip my hands underneath the stack so he wouldn't notice the ring.

Then he steeled himself against the usual reactions—whispers, harsh looks—from the people behind him, set his lunch down, and took the change from Irma with his good hand. He leaned over the counter and shoved a ten dollar bill in my shirt pocket.

"See you at home."

As he walked out, Dad passed by Goran, who had finished talking with his little brother. Both of them were trying their best not to look at him as he passed. Dad noticed Goran, stopped for a second, and then suddenly whipped his head around to look back at me.

I looked down, hoping he hadn't caught me watching; hoping he didn't realize that I couldn't bear the thought of Goran and my father sharing the same space, breathing the same air, existing that close to one another. Dad turned and left, and I struggled to keep the stack of trays from falling as I carried them back into the kitchen.

I dropped the trays into the sudsy water and leaned against the sink for just a second to catch my breath, utterly spent, exhausted. Then I ran out of there as fast as I could to answer the alarm.

The crisis turned out to be a big disaster.

I met up with Ruth at the docks, where Golden Boy and Typhoid Larry had already confined the situation to a manageable space.

"You're late," Golden Boy chastised me.

"I'm sorry, I—"

"You'll have to do better than that next time. If you get a next time."

"Isn't that—?" I thought I recognized the men on the docks.

"The Wrecking Balls." Ruth finished my sentence and studied them with concern. She stamped out her cigarette with extra oomph.

I'd seen them in the news before, local, not prime time. They were really nothing more than retired professional wrestlers who couldn't come up with a reasonable occupation that paid as well. Their biggest problem seemed to be their lack of finesse. They'd hold up a bank or a drugstore by bulldozing their way through. If they'd used their noggins even just a little, they could have been untouchable: a few of them actually did have superstrength and limited invincibility. But it was almost as if they'd rather get caught than execute a clean getaway, if it meant they got back on camera. The problem was they had a tendency to cause a lot of damage in their wake, and bystanders had a way of getting caught in the crossfire. In this case, the Wrecking Balls had decided to hold up a bank where Typhoid Larry happened to be cashing his paycheck.

Larry raced over, breathless, and told us what had happened. He'd had the good sense to give the Balls a wicked dose of hives in the lobby of the bank, and this had stopped the robbery in midprogress, but he'd left all his cash back at the counter.

"Don't worry," Ruth said, touching her fingers to her temples to make it seem more dramatic. "The money's still there. How many of these guys do we have to worry about?"

"I—I don't know, six, maybe seven. I took one out over there by the crane, gave him acute emphysema." Larry put his hands on his knees to catch his breath. "I think I went a little overboard. Can I borrow your inhaler? I don't want him to die or anything."

Ruth fished around in her pocketbook and forked over her asthma inhaler. "Don't use it all up; Medicaid only gives me one a month." She snapped her purse shut.

Larry took off back to the fight, and I watched Golden Boy weave in and out of the melee. He'd been smart to move the fight over to the docks, where the chances of hurting anyone were kept to a minimum. There seemed to be seven of the Balls, but it was hard to tell since they all looked similar. Long shaggy hair, big steroidy bodies, and skintight, spangled wrestling skivvies. I didn't know how they managed to walk out in public in those outfits, much less try to rob a bank.

Golden Boy held up his hand like a point guard calling a play and flashed the signal for the Fastball Special. We'd practiced it over and over in the League's S.T.A., but it was the first time we'd tried it in the field. The idea was that while Miss Scarlett distracted our enemies with a blinding flash of light, Larry would work up a really good illness, whereupon Golden Boy would pick him up and carry him with superspeed to infect each of our dazed enemies. Ruth would be on hand to predict which ones to infect first, and that would offer our best chance of success before Scarlett's dazzling effects wore off. According to the rest of the plan, Ruth would then predict where Golden Boy would end up, and tell me where to stand to grab hold of him immediately to heal away the sickly side effects of carrying Typhoid Larry at his most infectious.

I'd never liked this plan.

Primarily because there wasn't much for me to do. My power wasn't really an offensive weapon, so I understood my part, but I wanted a taste of the action, and I resented Golden Boy for not dialing me in. How was I supposed to prove myself if I didn't get to do anything? Still, if nothing else I was a team player, so when Ruth directed me to post up on the other end of the dock, near the back entrance of the local hospital, I obeyed.

I sighed and waited for Miss Scarlett to kick it into high gear. She loved giving a good show, and this was no exception. On Golden Boy's countdown, she took off into the air like a rocket and exploded into a one-woman Fourth of July fireworks display. Then she whizzed through the air past each of the Wrecking Balls, cutting it awfully close to their faces. If they hadn't been so tough-skinned, I'm sure she would have burned their noses to a crisp.

"Suckers," she shouted as she flew past them, setting off potent bursts of light.

At the end of the line, she pulled up into the air and stung the last and fattest one in the ass with a tiny radiation blast for good measure. I saw her lips mouth two words as she did it. "Lard ass."

Ruth conferred with Golden Boy, and then she pointed out the best path for him to run, starting with the fattest guy and ending with the hulking, ripped, blond guy who was rubbing his eyes not so far away from me. Larry cleared his throat vigorously, working up an especially viscous phlegm globber. Before he could cough anything up, Golden Boy grabbed him in his arms and they were off. I was restless to get in on the action, but I understood my job was to wait, so that's what I did.

Soon the first three Wrecking Balls were on their knees, doubled over in pain, gripping their stomachs from Larry's power. The youngest one was actually kinda cute. Kinda like a beefier, tackier version of Uberman. How'd he end up with these losers? What in his life made him take this turn to wear gaudy tights, take steroids, and rob banks? Maybe he just needed better opportunities, maybe he just needed someone who believed in him—

Suddenly I spotted Ruth hurrying toward me, waving her hands frantically. She stopped short.

"Uh-oh," she said.

"Uh-oh what?" I asked.

WHUMP! The seventh wrestler, the blond one, knocked me over on my back. The next thing I knew he had me pinned to the pavement. His ham-hock knees pressed painfully into my arms as he sat with his full weight on my chest. I struggled to catch my breath, and I could see out of the corner of my eye that Golden Boy and Larry had finished their run. Larry collapsed, drained from exerting so much energy.

Golden Boy looked around anxiously for me, his neck craning in all directions at superspeed. His face started to twitch, and panic was setting in. I was nowhere to be found. He dropped to the ground on all fours like a dog, grabbed his stomach, and began heaving out his guts.

This wasn't good. I'd failed to do my part, and now there were three of us down. That left only Ruth and Scarlett to take on the rest of the Wrecking Balls, and it was basically all my fault.

"Get up! Get up! Golden Boy's down!" I heard Miss Scarlett screaming at me. I looked up, searching for something to grab hold of, but all I could see was the big blond wrestler's crotch bearing down on me in a sweaty, spangled jockstrap. The meathead's hands wrapped around my neck, and he began to choke me. I kicked my feet and tried to call out for help, but I couldn't even catch my breath.

"Aim for his nads!" Ruth screamed. Aim for his nads with what? My strong sense of integrity?

Then suddenly we were airborne. Scarlett hit us full speed and lifted us off the ground.

"Drop him," she screamed at the meathead, "or I'll fry your balls off!" She shot a flame to underscore her point.

So he dropped me.

It was a long way down. I crashed through the sunroof of the children's burn unit in the hospital. Fortune smiled upon me: a giant Pink Panther stuffed animal broke my fall when I landed on it. A little girl with half her face melted off looked up from her coloring book and yelped.

"Who are you?"

I could see excitement in the expressive half of her face.

"I'm Thom," I said. "Sorry to make such a mess. Watch out for the broken glass."

"Are you a hero?" she asked.

I looked around at the roomful of children, most of them covered head to toe in scars, melted kids in shorty pajamas playing with building blocks and crayons and construction paper. They stared at me with awe, like I'd dropped in on their rehab unit from a cloud.

"I hope so."

I rushed over to the window to look at the fight on the docks below. The orderlies and nurses had rushed in by now, and they were gathered with all the patients, watching the battle. Golden Boy and Larry, still helpless because I hadn't been there to heal them, were getting pummeled by four of the chunky dudes in tights. Scarlett held a couple of them off with her heat rays, but she couldn't take on the whole group by herself. Even from far away, you could hear her mouthing off.

One of the kids asked a nurse what Scarlett was saying, and I saw the nurse blush.

Ruth, strangely, was pointing her finger at the oldest, fattest Wrecking Ball. It looked like the two of them were engaged in a heated debate. She poked her finger into the two mounds of his chest, and they screamed in each other's faces.

I looked down at my boots and studied my shoelaces. Man, I'd really screwed up this time. The damage alone was going to cost more money than I could imagine, and here we were getting our asses kicked by a bunch of middle-aged guys in body Lycra. I wanted the soft, red carpet of the playroom to swallow me alive so I wouldn't have to look anyone in the eye ever again.

Two of the Wrecking Balls hoisted a crane into the air and aimed for Golden Boy and Larry. From the hospital we all watched helplessly at what was coming. Neither of the heroes would be able to dodge it even if they saw it. I wanted to yell out a warning, but I couldn't breathe.

One of the nurses screamed as the Wrecking Balls let the crane fly.

In a flash of fire and brimstone, Miss Scarlett yanked Golden Boy and Larry away in the nick of time. The last-minute save threw her off balance, and she tumbled with them into the river. The water instantly extinguished her flame.

Now the immediate threat was the two-ton crane hurtling through the air directly at the hospital. The floor shook, and we heard a great *kaboom* outside as the crane crushed the emergency room entrance, leaving nothing but a crater in the parking lot.

It was a miracle that no one had been standing there. The fear in the rehab room was palpable. The people by the window began to cry, some frozen, some screaming.

The Wrecking Balls saw that their opportunity to create mayhem had worked, and they weren't about to let up. The oldest Ball pushed Ruth to the ground and motioned for his cronies to leap over the fence and join him at the adjoining construction site. They followed him, and each one picked up a piece of heavy machinery: a forklift here, a bulldozer there. They aimed in our direction, straight at the hospital, ready to launch. Emergency sirens shrieked from all directions. Ambulances and police cars approached in the distance, but we all knew they'd be too late.

A skinny nurse with a terrified face tapped me on the shoulder.

"Excuse me," she pleaded. "Can't you help us?"

In theory I was supposed to help my team. But I was much safer in there with all the burned children and soft toys. Then I felt something softer than any of the stuffed animals touch my hand. I looked down and saw the little girl with half a good face. Her big brown eyes were filled with hope. My hands began to grow warm, and I could feel heat from the entire room swirling around my body. She smiled.

"Your hand feels good," she said.

Then a little boy limped over and grabbed her hand, and I felt a charge of fire course through my body. He reached over and held out his hand for another little girl in a wheelchair. Her bright green eyes peered through the thick bandages wrapped around her head, and she found his hand with the withered remains of her own. And one by one, the children in the unit linked up, drawn to each other's hands. Children calmly emerged from their rooms and wandered over in our direction, like they'd heard there was cake in the playroom, irresistibly drawn to the heat pumping in and out of my own hands.

I wanted to scream in agony each time another kid joined hands. The charge it sent through me was incredible, and I wanted to flail wildly on the ground. All I could feel were thousands of scorching flames licking at every inch of my body, my skin melting away cell by cell. My big left toe began to twitch. I knew in a second either the heat would overwhelm me, or a seizure would.

Both my legs were trembling now, and the nurses had noticed the unbreakable chain of melting kids attached to me. They ran in all directions for security guards, a doctor, or anyone to pull us apart. My vision grew dim, the edges of my sight cloudy and dark. I could just make out the line of scarred children joined hand to hand as it extended down the hall.

And then my body went numb. I crossed a threshold, and the pain suddenly didn't bother me anymore. I only wanted one thing. I looked at the Wrecking Balls across the way, and I prayed they wouldn't throw the machinery at us. I prayed they'd just leave us alone and go away. I prayed that any great power, anywhere in the universe, would come down and stop them in any way possible.

My eyes fluttered up into my head so far I thought I'd be able to see my brain, and then all of a sudden I felt an explosion somewhere deep inside me, like all my organs had burst with joy and anguish and happiness and pain, like I'd ripped all the ligaments in my body in half and the pain was amplified to infinity.

And that's all I remembered.

"Well, it could have been worse." Larry said, and dabbed his leaky nose with a frayed tissue.

Each of us fired looks at each other. Kevin at Scarlett, Ruth at Kevin, Scarlett at me, me at Ruth, then all of us at Larry with one question on our lips.

"How?"

Apparently I knocked out the power a whole half mile in diameter. Of course the cameras and news crews carried their own power and recorded everything, and I do mean *everything*. From The Wrecking Ball's escape to Miss Scarlett's infamous slap—the one she gave local award-winning news reporter Bruce Barry from *Channel Four's Eyewitness News*.

"Look, my jacket was unbuttoned and God knows what they could see, and there I was passed out on the ground with a camera up in my face. Sorry, but he deserved it." Miss Scarlett fastened the top button of her delivery jacket. "Is it cold in here?"

"You left a second-degree burn on his cheek," Golden Boy said.

"So, he can grow a beard," Scarlett said. "He should have thought about that before he started poking around my privates." She pulled out a thin bottle of nail polish remover from her utility belt and dabbed a cotton ball with the liquid. The acrid smell filled the room, and she rubbed the chipped paint off her nails. "I don't know why you're on my case anyway. Thom's the one who screwed up."

All eyes turned to me.

No one understood how I was able to absorb all that hurt at once and incapacitate everyone around me with it. If I could have controlled the outburst and confined it to only the Wrecking Balls, it would have been a clean capture. Instead I'd knocked everyone out and given some people seizures. Thank God I'd been in the hospital, because if the reporters had got my face on camera, Dad would have found out about my new extracurricular activities in an instant. I'd have to be more careful in the future. Maybe I needed a mask.

"If you can't stand the heat," Scarlett said to me, "stay out of the steam room." She tossed a dirty, red cotton ball over her shoulder and smeared her nails with a clean one.

"Let's try to keep this constructive," Golden Boy said. "We all could have done better. Larry, what did you give them, anyway?"

"Diverticulitis." Larry bit the inside of his cheek. "It can be very painful once it sets in." Scarlett rolled her eyes.

"*Once it sets in* isn't really good enough in a fight scenario," Golden Boy said. "They gave us a good thrashing."

"Hey, if Thom had been where he was supposed to be—" Larry held his hands up, innocent, and he was right. For all the minor contingencies that occur in a fight, after months of training I knew better than to let my guard down and abandon my post, no matter what the circumstance. I should have been there to help them.

Everyone looked at me again, and I didn't know what to say. I couldn't lie. Everyone had seen I wasn't where I was supposed to be.

"Well, Thom, we're now a full two hundred points behind all the other tryout groups." Golden Boy read from the incident form. "All our faces, except yours since you were conveniently out of the battle by that point, have been plastered all over the local news as the losers who bungled the capture. Have anything to say for yourself?"

I'd been throwing up at regular intervals since the incident. I'd never used my powers that way, and I had what could only be described as the world's most wicked hangover from doing so. I really didn't want to have this conversation now, while I was still recovering from the rebound effect of my powers. I belched and held my lips together and fought off the urge to barf. To add insult to injury, we were the laughingstock of the League and it was all my fault. What do you say?

Out of the blue, Ruth blew her rape whistle. Loud. I could hear Silver Fox and the Sonic Ear howl in pain three whole floors above us.

"Maybe you all didn't notice, but when that hospital was about to crumble with all those innocent people inside, Thom was the only one who stopped the Wrecking Balls. The only finger I feel like pointing right now is my middle one, at all of you, bunch of ungrateful wretches, if you ask me." Ruth struck a match off the bottom of her heel and lit a cigarette.

"Now, maybe he doesn't fully know how to use his powers yet, sure. Maybe he should have found a way to stop them without blacking out half the city, without sending everyone into convulsions. But the point is, all those people lived because he stopped the Wrecking Balls. So let's suck it up and give a little credit where credit's due. I mean, diverticulitis? Seriously, Larry, what were you thinking? Why not just give them a real bad case of dandruff? Scarlett, you dropped the kid three stories into a crowded hospital. You're lucky no one was killed. And Golden Boy, if you weren't so busy trying to be a one-man rescue machine . . . Well, there may be no 'I' in team, but apparently there's a real big one in 'Kevin.' If you're so goddamned worried about our PR then go get a job on *Entertainment Tonight*, because last I checked this gig was about helping people, not helping our image. By the way, all those kids in the burn ward have been making remarkable recoveries, up to seventy-five percent in some cases, nothing short of a miracle in my humble opinion. If you ask me, you're all just pissed off 'cause you had to change into a new pair of pants when you woke up after the seizures. Welcome to my world. I have to do that every time I laugh real hard at a good episode of *Jake and the Fatman*."

Wow.

That actually shut the rest of the group up, and I wanted to kiss Ruth right then and there.

"I didn't see *you* do anything, either," Scarlett said under her breath.

Ruth whipped around.

"What did you say to me?"

"I said I didn't see you do much of anything, either."

Ruth exhaled cigarette smoke and a sly grin crept over her face.

"That's because I knew we'd win."

After the meeting wrapped, Golden Boy offered Scarlett a fast ride to work. He said if he really turned it on, she'd make her shift on time. She thanked him without any hint of real gratitude, and when he scooped her up for the ride, she checked to make sure the buttons of her jacket were fastened tightly and warned him that if he copped any sort of cheap feel, she'd roast his ass. And then they were gone.

I waited for Ruth by her car in the parking lot and looked at my watch. It was late, and Dad was going to ask about basketball. Summer League was almost over, so I was going to have to come with a new excuse soon anyway. Ruth limped with a sore hip over to the door of her car and fumbled for the keys with crooked, arthritic fingers.

We got in and drove without a word for a long time.

"Hey, Ruth," I said finally, "why were you arguing with that one guy, the old Wrecking Ball?"

Ruth didn't take her eyes off the road.

"I used to work with him."

I thought about it for a second and it didn't make a lot of sense to me.

"He used to be one of the good guys?"

Ruth took a long drag on her cigarette.

"No." She exhaled smoke through her nose. "He didn't used to be one of the good guys."

Oh. If he hadn't been one of the good guys, then she must have been—

"It was a long time ago, and I don't want to talk about it."

So we didn't. We didn't say another word the whole way home.

CHAPTER THIRTEEN

"DO YOU EVER HAVE that one asshole on your team that just hates you for no other reason than you're you?"

God, did I ever. I wanted to tell him all about Scarlett.

"Remember that short kid?" Goran dribbled the ball in perfect figure eights between his legs. I thought he was trying to distract me by talking. "The one who called you a homo?"

Yeah, I think I could dig that one up from somewhere in the deep recesses of my memory.

"Little guy? Looks like Gary Coleman?"

"Yeah, that's him. I think he hates me because I'm white." Goran chuckled and shot the ball. "Which is a real laugh, because where I'm from no one thinks we're white."

The way Goran sneered gave off the impression that he didn't have a whole lot of respect for most of his teammates.

"You Americans," he said, "think you have some sort of patent on poverty if you're not an NBA pro or some rap star by age twenty."

Goran shot a three-pointer. "If he thinks it's so tough, he should try growing up in a country where genocide is still in full swing." The ball swished.

Goran and I had been meeting every morning at the rec center ever since I joined the League tryouts. We'd push each other through drills, wind sprints, and lots of punching-bag work. He was even teaching me how to spar with boxing gloves. You'd think with my secret League hand-to-hand combat training that I'd have been able to take him pretty easy, but he always knocked me on my tail by the end of every session. It was like he wasn't even trying that hard to win; he was mostly amused by my efforts to go after him. Then when it was getting time for me to leave for work, he'd read my balance during a lunge and somehow kick my feet out from under me. And the next thing I'd know I'd be flat on my back looking up at his nostrils, which weren't even flaring because he wasn't breathing that hard. Me, on the other hand, I was always drenched with sweat by that point. And no matter what kind of workout we did, we always ended with a little one-on-one.

"Sometimes you have to be your own best friend," he said as he sank another three-pointer.

"Some team player you are," I said, and dribbled between his legs and drove for the basket.

"Better to work alone," he said, and blocked my shot with his fingertips. "You're the only one who has absolute control over your own actions."

I snatched the rebound and dribbled it back up to the top

of the key. I bounced the ball and tried to figure out how I'd pass him on my next run to the basket.

"You sound like my dad." I faked a hard drive to the left, spun right, then pulled up short at the foul line to sink an easy two. "I guess that's what happens when you become a dad. You get all bitter, have to be the family martyr at all times. Can't ask for anyone's help."

Goran took the ball and stopped. He didn't turn around, but looked far off down the hallway for something I couldn't see.

"Yeah," he said. "Dads are weird."

Goran's brother suddenly bounded onto the court in his karate uniform and stole the ball. Goran broke into a broad smile and chased the kid around the court. The little guy squealed the whole time, until Goran caught up with him. Then Goran picked him up and held him above his head and threatened to dunk him with a maniacal grin. The kid howled and laughed, and Goran swung him around like a sack of potatoes and pretended he was going to toss him into the basket until the kid just couldn't laugh anymore. When Goran put him back on the ground, his brother was so dizzy that he had to drop to one knee to keep from falling over.

"Go get your lunch box and I'll walk you to camp," Goran told him. "I'm still down two points."

His little brother scampered off in a zigzag, still dizzy, and Goran took the ball at the top of the key.

"So you really think that guy hates you because you're white?" I asked him as he dribbled.

"That's part of it." Goran faked and spun right, but I was

there. He dribbled another few steps, faked and spun left, but I was there, too.

"That's what he says, at least. The real reason he hates me"—Goran bounced the ball through the space between my legs, picked it up behind me, and sprinted to the basket—"is because he thinks I stole his girlfriend."

He dunked the ball and smacked the ground when he landed. Like he'd been waiting to do that all game.

He looked up and saw my back as I headed for the door.

"Hey!"

I called out "I gotta go," gave him a half-assed wave over my shoulder, and left him there alone in the gym with the basketball still bouncing.

I ran down the hall, past the Student Life Center where I tutored, out into the parking lot. I couldn't turn around, I couldn't do anything but run. I sprinted the entire way home, but this time I wasn't soaring.

I hadn't realized it would bother me that much to hear him say the word *girlfriend*.

"You don't belong here," Warrior Woman said to me, her fists propped on her golden girdle.

"I was just studying," I said. "I thought it would be okay."

"Do that on your own time. Headquarters is off limits after hours. Your presence here is a privilege, not a right."

Thank you, Ilsa the Super Nazi.

I filed the archives back on the shelf. I'd been going through old articles and pictures since I got there.

I'd come home from the rec center to a dark house, because Dad was working late again. I'd run a glass of water under the faucet and noticed the kitchen sink was grainy and dry. Neither of us had been home long enough to use it for days. I felt the weight of silence bearing down on me, and I kept hearing Goran repeat the word "girlfriend" in my head. I had to get out of there, and I went to the one place where I felt at least a little bit at home—the League library.

Each member of every tryout squad was required to take a test on League history. If you could read, you could pass it. But I'd taken a real interest in the League's history and pored over the archives every chance I got. A sea of glorious victories from World War II. Parades. Trickster villains defeated either by wits or through their own folly. Throngs of adoring fans. Newspaper photos of the team in poses that promised better lives ahead for all of us. I would spend hours alone with the books, my only company the hum of the air conditioner. I hadn't seen much about my mother yet. Saw plenty of my father. Very little about the tragedy, no mention of his disgrace. His status was merely listed as inactive, which I guess was a step up from revoked.

Warrior Woman apparently didn't trust me to leave on my own. She waited by the door with her trigger finger on the light switch.

She smiled as I walked out the door, and I thought she was going to say something kind.

"Maybe you should spend more time learning how to use your powers instead."

Everyone's a critic.

I walked down the corridor to the locker room to get my dirty clothes. Even Typhoid Larry said they smelled bad, so I knew it was time for a wash, probably time to keep more than one change of clothes in the locker, too. I held the old clothes to my nose. They smelled sour and stale.

The laundry room and janitor's closet were on the top floor, near the exit to the observation deck. I thought I'd just drop the stuff in the wash before I left, and I could put it in the dryer when I came back the next morning. The hall was slick and clean, and I could hear my boots squeak. When I turned the corner, I saw a light coming from a crack in the door to the observation deck.

I poked my head inside, and the hinges squeaked as the door crept open.

"Come in," Justice said without turning around.

He stood with his back to me, his hands clasped and resting on the small of his back. I could tell his chin was lifted, his face raised to the heavens. A giant plate glass window stretched out in front of him. I hadn't realized the headquarters was this vast. He stared out into space. A giant telescope, something you'd see in a planetarium, stood on the other side of the room, pristine and ready for someone to look through it. I wondered how far away he could see with X-ray vision and a telescope.

"Go ahead and take a look if you want." His body didn't move when he spoke.

I walked over to the telescope, my boots still squishing, and brushed a tiny cobweb away from the lens and looked through it. I probably let out a gasp. I'd never seen space like this before, not on any field trip, not in any sci-fi movie. I stood there for I don't know how long, but it must have been a while because the moon had moved across the sky when I finally took a step back.

Justice remained perfectly still the entire time. Suddenly I felt like a big stone that had plopped down into a placid, calm lake, wrecking the smooth surface with a cannonball splash. I took a deep breath and almost gagged. I was still holding my dirty clothes.

"Sorry about the clothes," I said. "They really stink."

"You all smell to me."

I blinked a few times, repeated his line in my head. Did he just say we all smelled to him? He could see what I was thinking.

"I'm not from this universe. The whole planet smells different to me."

Oh. Okay. It's true that he was from another planet.

"You've been doing a good job, Thom, even at the hospital. You're doing a lot better than you think." He turned to look at me and gave me a gentle smile.

"Your mother would be very proud of you."

Holy shit. I'd almost forgotten.

"You knew my mother."

"A very special woman," he continued, his eyes glued back on the stars. "She served on our stealth squad longer than any other member."

That didn't make sense to me. At least the timing of it didn't. When did she serve? Was she still doing it after she got married? When I was born? Could she have hidden something like that from us? Did Dad know? And what about Dad, why didn't Justice talk about him?

"Do you know—" I had to take a breath to get the whole question out. I wasn't used to asking questions about my mother. "Do you know where she is?"

Justice sighed and rubbed his eyes. Maybe superbeings from other planets got eyestrain just like the rest of us.

"I wish I knew, Thom." His eyes drifted back toward the universe, and I knew there was something he wasn't telling me. "Do you want a drink?"

"Warrior Woman told me I had to leave."

Justice chuckled. "Warrior Woman's a bitch."

I laughed.

"Well, sometimes. I mean it in a good-hearted way; don't tell her I said that. Our secret." He winked at me, and I nodded.

We sat on the ledge of the terrace, and he handed me a ginger ale.

"Aren't you going to have anything?" I asked. I took a sip and felt the fizzy air tingle in my nostrils.

"I don't need sustenance the same way you do, but if it makes you feel more comfortable . . ." He suddenly had a drink in his hand. I hadn't even seen him get it. Superspeed takes a long time to get used to. I didn't know he had that power. I guess there was a lot I still didn't know about him.

"You can go ahead and ask," he said, and looked at my probationary ring. "I can see the question in your mind." Justice took a sip of his drink and pretended to taste it.

"Why don't you and my dad talk anymore?"

Justice stared down into the bubbles of his drink as they rose to the surface and popped.

"That's something you should ask him. I don't want to get

between father and son. Family's the most important thing, you have to respect that."

I nodded and tried to hide my disappointment. Doing the right thing was always a lot easier when you weren't dying to know what really happened.

"I'd give anything to have my family back," Justice said, a sudden confession. He looked up at the sky, and I saw a great sadness tugging at his eyelids. "My whole planet, everything I ever knew, everyone I ever loved, gone, just like that."

We all knew the legend. How his parents had sent him out in a rocket ship the very last minute before the planet exploded, how he'd been found in a crater and taken in by a kind, elderly couple.

"I can't look at the stars without thinking about my home planet." He drifted for a moment in an ocean of memory. "I couldn't get back to that part of the universe even if I wanted to. It would take a force so great . . ." He lost himself in the thought, then cut a glance over to me.

"Something else is bothering you." His focus came back to me, and then to my ring. "Want to talk about it?"

I did. I wanted to talk about everything, to tell him all about growing up with this crazy crush on Uberman, about how much I wanted to count in the world, about how bad I wanted to make the League because it was the only thing that really meant anything to me, and about this tall, lean foreign guy I played basketball with every day and how it really bothered me to hear him say the word *girlfriend*, and I wanted to tell him that my dad really sucked because he was all closed up and walled off, and I could never have a conversation like this with him.

I looked into his face and saw honesty. Justice really wanted to know, and believe it or not, that was good enough for me because it was the first time in a long time I felt like anyone genuinely cared about me.

We sat and sipped our drinks and stared out at the stars and let the silence speak for us.

The moon was even lower in the sky, and I felt much better now, maybe a little high from all the sugar in the ginger ale.

"I guess I should get going," I said, and hopped off the ledge onto the terrace.

Justice nodded and took my glass. I picked up my clothes, and he said, "Your father doesn't know about any of this, does he?"

I stared down at the bundle of dirty clothes in my arms.

"Don't worry." Justice patted me on the shoulder. "I won't tell him, that's up to you."

Our secret.

Dad was setting his alarm to go to sleep when I tiptoed upstairs. I could hear the ancient bleeps of his old digital clock radio, his ten-year anniversary gift from the factory.

"That you, Thom?" he called from the other side of his door.

"G'night, Dad." I kept on going to my room. I closed the door and stretched out on my bed and thought about Justice and our talk. I reached under the mattress and took out the old pictures of Mom.

She smiled back at me in her slick, trim costume, a teen fashion model caught in a coy pose. You'd never know what was really lurking in her mind, behind the magazine smile held up to keep you out. Had she been a part of the League's secret espionage squad even then? Who would ever have suspected that a sweet girl fresh out of teachers college was sneaking around behind your back? I guess it was a good cover.

Then it hit me that there was only one way Mom could have made her cover better: have a kid. Who would suspect a mom? In between running carpools, cutting cookies, scheduling appointments, and returning library books, who'd find the time to be a world-class spy? Was I part of the perfect cover? And why would she leave the note and the pictures for me? Maybe she didn't disappear of her own free will. Maybe she wasn't even alive.

I held the picture to my heart and let the air out of my chest. I couldn't think straight I was so tired, and my eyelids felt heavy. I lifted my head up and looked at the door. Ever so slightly, I heard the soft scraping of Dad's callused feet on the carpet outside in the hallway. He was good, but I was his son. I knew he was on the other side of the door, his hand raised in a fist, deciding whether to knock. I suddenly wondered if he knew I was listening, if he was waiting to see if I wanted to talk, too. I wondered if he knew how much I wanted to grab his melted hand and test my strength and show him what I'd learned to do, and pour all of my power out until his hand healed completely. But we remained on separate sides of the door in silence.

This is how we played the game, neither of us saying a word. A few moments passed and I heard Dad scuffle back to his room and crawl into bed.

* * *

I kicked ass the next day at tryouts.

Justice called all of the groups together and announced a competition, an old-fashioned field day with long jumps and egg tosses and hot dog eating contests. They cranked up the S.T.A., and suddenly we were in the middle of a perfectly manicured field of spring greens and golds.

No one was allowed to use powers, that was the only rule. The object of the game was to have fun, blow off a little steam, foster a little camaraderie.

"Hope you don't screw this up too," Galaxy Girl said to me when we lined up for the fifty-yard dash. Trash talk from a girl with a ring orbiting around her face. Spectrum fired the start gun, and Galaxy Guy stuck out his foot and tried to trip me as I took off. No way was I going to lose to those twin assholes. I leaped over his foot and sprinted like I'd been doing every morning at the rec center with Goran, and when I crossed the finish line, I turned around and saw I was a full two lengths ahead of my nearest opponent, Mr. Mist.

Ruth awarded Galaxy Guy and Girl their ribbons.

"Hey, fourth and fifth place is better than no place at all." She draped the ribbons over their heads, careful to avoid the moons. Galaxy Girl's got hung up on the ring around her head. She yanked it off and tossed it on the ground.

"We're still two hundred points ahead of you, you old bag."

Ruth suddenly doubled over and dropped to the ground.

"Ruth, what is it? Are you okay?!" I ran over to help her up.

"I see . . . I see . . ." Ruth grabbed her temples in pain. "I see the future, and it's a League with no twins."

"Very funny." The Galaxy Twins backed off and headed over to the refreshment table.

Ruth called after them, "If you're really good, I'll let you know which soap star is going to host your *Where Are They Now?* special!" She scanned the grass around her feet. "Where's my flask?"

Miss Scarlett and Golden Boy showed up for the wheelbarrow races.

"Where have you two been?" Larry asked.

Scarlett smeared cherry lip gloss on her lower lips with a hot-pink applicator. "I had to work late." She smacked her lips.

I called a last-minute substitution during King of the Mountain and had Larry stand in for me. Powers or no powers, we won because nobody wanted to get near him. He sat on top of the hill and looked out at all of the heroes and rested his chin in his hand with an Is-that-all-there-is? look on his face.

By the end of the afternoon we were neck and neck with the Galaxy Twins' team. The day's winner would get a bonus two hundred points, which would put us back squarely in the running with the other teams in the overall tryouts. All we had to do was win the last event.

Warrior Woman marched onto the field with two large banners and announced that the final, deciding event would be Capture the Flag, another game I hadn't played since I was a kid. The Galaxy Twins walked by our team with their flag. Galaxy Girl accidentally-on-purpose hit Scarlett with the end of her flag as she passed. It caught Scarlett right below the ribs.

"Oh, I'm sorry."

Scarlett's eyes went white hot with anger.

Galaxy Girl adjusted the buttons on her custom-designed Gucci costume, taking extra care to show off her trim, bare midriff. Scarlett eyed Galaxy Girl's tight, exposed stomach and wrapped her arms around her own waist. The twins reeked of privilege, expendable incomes, and inheritance—bags under their eyes from too much champagne too late at the clubs, never from a late shift or an early shift. They had a different high-end designer do a new costume for every new moon cycle. Word was they had their own reality series in the works.

"Nice jacket. Do they make you wear it all the time, even when you're not delivering pizzas?"

Scarlett tugged at the dirty, long sleeves of her jacket. It made me uncomfortable to watch Galaxy Girl strike a nerve, even in someone I didn't like very much. Scarlett's jacket was always wrapped around her like she had nothing else to wear, and it had the stains to prove it.

Scarlett lunged at Galaxy Girl, but Golden Boy intercepted her at full speed before her nails could gouge the color contacts out of Galaxy Girl's eyes. Golden Boy yanked Scarlett by the waist over to our side for a huddle. The twins moved on.

"Hey, Star Girl, I'm gonna take our flag when we win and shove it so far up your—!"

"C'mon, people," Golden Boy cut her off. "All we need to do is find their flag, bring it to our base, and we're back in this thing. Let's do it!"

We put our hands in the huddle with a go-team gesture. I looked down at Ruth's old withered fingers, Scarlett's bloodred nails, Golden Boy's tightly gloved fists, and Larry's hand, held safely away from the rest of ours. Go team.

Scarlett was seething, and the words sprung out her mouth like flames shooting off her tongue. "Let's crucify them."

We were down to the last five minutes of the game, and only four of us remained: me, Scarlett, and the Galaxy Twins. Ruth had been the second to go, but she didn't seem to mind much, because she sat on the sidelines and introduced Larry to her favorite cold remedy, a mixture of lemonade, a cough drop, and whatever was in her flask. Golden Boy had been a surprise victim of the Twins' subterfuge. He'd been sneaking around their territory, no superspeed at all, when Galaxy Girl accidentally-on-purpose created a miniconstellation to draw him out of the shadows, where her brother easily tagged him out. We tried to call a foul since she'd used her powers, but she lied and said it was just the reflection from the sun off her Fendi bag. Warrior Woman judged it fair play and had us continue.

But then Scarlett just got plain reckless. She ventured into their territory without any sort of plan whatsoever, calling out, "All right, who wants some?" Then she sent out an energy blast from her hands and burned Galaxy Girl's Fendi bag to a crisp. In the process she left a red, stinging mark on Galaxy Girl's naked belly. Scarlett was tagged out in a second, but didn't seem to care.

Meanwhile, I'd been busy sneaking around their turf, and I finally located their flag. Galaxy Guy was guarding it in a thicket by the river. He bent over the stream and hummed a tune and studied his reflection. He flashed a series of smiles and poses for himself. I tried to creep forward silently to grab the flag while he was preoccupied, but I stepped over a log and broke a twig in two with a loud snap.

"Hey, sis, I was thinking about getting my teeth bleached again. Think I need it?" Galaxy Guy studied his smile in the reflection. "Sis?"

He turned around, but I was already taking off with the flag. I ran as fast as I could. This was just another sprint, and even though I'd been giving it my best all day, I could still put on some extra pepper when we needed it most.

Galaxy Guy was catching up to me, and I knew I had to kick into high gear. I dodged a few of his teammates effortlessly, my basketball moves coming in handy. The crowd was cheering my name, and I saw all the League lined up out of the corners of my eyes as I raced toward our side. Galaxy Guy used just enough of his stellar overdrive to make up for lost time without tipping off that he was using his powers. In a few seconds he'd tag me out if I didn't do something.

Then I looked forward and saw Uberman by the finish line, waiting with a dazzling smile on his face. I couldn't imagine anything better than winning the game in front of him and putting our team back in good standing. The cheers echoed in my ears, and it wasn't like the goofy cheerleader squeals of a basketball game. This was different, these were the heroes I'd grown up admiring my whole life, and they were cheering my name.

But Galaxy Guy was right behind me, and I could feel him reaching over to my shoulder, inches away from snatching back his flag. The cheers grew louder, and I focused hard on Uberman's crystal blue eyes and his radiant smile, and made my legs kick me ahead faster and faster. And then I saw Galaxy Girl fly into space in front of me. It was a clear violation of the no-powers rule, but I knew that if I didn't get the flag over to my side, she'd find some reason to talk her way into victory, and I couldn't let that happen. I couldn't let my team down. She swooped down, low enough to dive-tackle me. I mustered every last iota of energy in my thighs and jumped above her as high as I could, like I was in my third and final try at the long jump at the Olympics and this one was for the gold.

I heard the crowd gasp and collectively hold their breath as my trajectory sent me high up in the air. I barely cleared Galaxy Girl, and I landed on the other side in a tumble and rolled over to the flagpole holder without spearing myself. Galaxy Girl ended up connecting headlong with her brother, who chipped his front tooth on her satellite when they collided. My forehead smacked the leather shin of Uberman's boot, and I looked up.

"Hi, there." Uberman looked down at me and grinned. "Looks like you're the winner."

I popped up on my feet and lifted the flag into the air. The crowd went wild, and it felt great. Even Scarlett and Golden Boy were whooping and hollering. Everyone in the world should have at least one moment in their lifetime when an entire crowd of people cheers them on for something, one moment to feel exceptional, one moment that lets you know you really do mean something in the universe.

"Uh, you still have to put the flag in the holder, you know," Uberman reminded me, never breaking his smile. Of course I did. I played it up for the audience. I gripped the flagpole with both my hands, held it high above my head, and swung it around. The cheers grew louder. I went to plunge the pole into the holder, Beowulf delivering the final blow to Grendel, and swung down with all my might.

The flag never reached the holder.

A lone, impossibly strong hand grabbed my wrist in a vise grip and stopped the flag in midair. I looked up, startled.

It was my father.

CHAPTER FOURTEEN

DAD'S EYES GLARED, and his voice shook with anger.

"Get home. Now."

I swallowed and my heart caught in my throat.

I stared into his eyes; they were bloodshot and wild.

"I know *everything*." His hand trembled with fury around the flagpole. The crowd of heroes around me stood in stunned silence. I'm not sure they recognized him yet.

"I found the pictures."

Out of all the times I'd seen him fly into a rage, I'd never seen him this angry. It scared me more than when I was a kid and he'd grabbed the thick leather belt, snapped it loud to instill fear.

My mouth was open, but no words came out. I didn't know what to say to make this better. I looked around and saw my team gathered nearby. Uberman looked on with curiosity and then stepped in.

"Excuse me, sir, why don't we escort you both to our reception area, where we can talk this out." He put a calming hand on Dad's shoulder.

Dad's head whipped around and he pushed Uberman away, the way a drunk in a bar would start a fight with someone who didn't see it coming. I heard a few gasps in the crowd. Warrior Woman was on us in a flash, Silver Bullet and the Spectrum close behind.

"I don't know how you got in here, but this is a private function. You are not welcome!" Warrior Woman turned my father around by the shoulder, ready to kick him out.

I saw the three heroes' faces drop and their eyes widen as they recognized my father, years older and still wearing the factory uniform from his shift. A tiny word of recognition escaped Silver Bullet's lips.

"Hal?"

Dad spoke to Warrior Woman through clenched teeth.

"Get your hands off me, and give me back *my son*."

He swung her arm off his shoulder by her golden bracelet. If she hadn't been a demi-immortal, he would have dislocated her shoulder. His stare was still fixed squarely on me.

"We'll talk about this at home."

I looked around, mortified. A wave of whispers spread through the crowd, and I saw Golden Boy explaining to Miss Scarlett exactly who this middle-aged man in front of them was. I saw Scarlett mouth, "No shit!" Ruth stood back from the crowd, her face lowered, and I wondered if she'd seen this coming. And if she had, why hadn't she warned me? I stared at her for a few moments, hoping to make eye contact, but she never looked up.

"Dad, hold on, let me explain!" I didn't know what I was going to say, but I had to try something. I'd worked too hard to lose everything now. Uberman was piecing together who Dad was. I suddenly understood the lure of my mother's power. All I wanted to do was disappear.

Dad grabbed me roughly by the bicep and started to drag me toward the door. I knew my arm would be badly bruised tomorrow, but I was numb to the pain. All eyes were on me, and I wanted time to stop so I could run away. I was humiliated, disciplined like a little boy in front of the entire League and all its tryout squads. He yanked at me so hard that I stumbled over my feet and fell toward the ground, but he kept his grip on my arm so I didn't hit the floor. I skidded along the ground as Dad pulled me toward the exit. I wanted to yell for him to stop, that he was hurting me.

"Hal."

Everyone looked up to see Justice lower himself from the sky and hover over the ground in between us and the exit.

"Let's go someplace where we can talk about this privately." Justice glanced at me with a look of sympathy. "Please."

My father's jaw clenched with rage, he shook ever so slightly, and I thought he might explode.

"How dare you tell me what to do with my son." Tiny lines of spit flew from Dad's mouth at Justice. "You."

"Dad, please . . ." I begged him to stop.

"Thom, you shouldn't have lied to your father, but that was your choice." Justice remained calm. He held his hand up like a teacher cautioning a hyper child to take a time-out. "Hal, think about what you're doing. Think about your son for a minute." Justice actually landed his two feet on the ground in front of my father. He placed his hands on his shoulders. I couldn't tell what he was doing, if he was maybe using his powers to quell Dad's rage.

"Listen to me, Hal. He's good. He's got a lot of potential." I watched my Dad listen with his best poker face. Totally still. Maybe Justice was getting through. "He could really *be* something, Hal."

I watched Dad and tried to figure out what he was thinking. If he could be turning a corner in his brain. Maybe he was beginning to believe there was a place for his son on the very team he so hated.

And then the unthinkable happened.

Dad slugged Justice. Square in the jaw, an old-fashioned right hook, something straight out of the boxing ring. The force of the blow knocked Justice over, and he stumbled backward. The entire crowd gasped. I didn't turn around, but I heard the commotion of murmurs behind me.

Justice looked up at Dad from the ground and rubbed his chin. All of us knew a mere punch couldn't harm him physically, but still, no one had ever seen him take a sucker punch straight to the face like that. It was a shock to everyone, and silence filled the room as people waited to see what he would do next.

Dad stood over him, fury in his eyes, his feet poised to move, his arms held up like vipers ready to strike. Justice slowly moved to get up.

And then I grabbed Dad's arm.

"Stop it, Dad!"

I knew better than to touch Dad when he was in one of his combat rages. The minute I grabbed his arm, I triggered his natural defense, a reaction as instinctive as his desire to protect me. He whipped around and grabbed me by the collar and pinned me against the wall with his fist raised. I saw his nostrils flare, and a network of blood vessels bulged out from his forehead, seething red.

I closed my eyes and held up my arms in defense—not that they would have done much good against a crushing blow from him. I waited for the impact, but it didn't come. When I finally gathered the courage to open my eyes, I looked through my fingers and saw my dad.

His paternal instinct had won out, just barely. His chest heaved with effort as he tried to breathe himself into submission. I looked in his eyes and instead of rage I saw fear.

Then I scanned each and every face in the crowd, from Golden Boy to the Galaxy Twins to Warrior Woman to Uberman to Justice to Ruth—a guilty and pained expression on her face—to every last person who thought they could one day live up to the title of hero. I felt their collective look bear down upon my father. That look reminded me of the way he'd stared at me after that basketball game where we all pretended not to hear the kid who called me the gay guy. Although their reactions varied slightly according to personality, there was one common denominator.

They all looked at my father with contempt.

He relaxed his fighting pose and tried to hold his head high. He looked at me and slowly reached out his hand.

"Let's go, Thom," he said softly.

I ran out of the room and didn't look back.

It had started to rain, so I hitchhiked home. It was the first and only time I'd ever done anything that stupid. The old guy in the car seemed nice enough and tried to strike up a conversation, but I just watched the windshield wipers go back and forth as they squeaked against the glass. If I opened my mouth to say anything, I was afraid I would cry or scream out in frustration.

He let me out by the highway exit near our neighborhood. I walked the rest of the way in the rain, and I couldn't tell if it was warm or cold outside. I pushed open the front door and ran upstairs, two at a time, and stopped in the hallway. I looked at the trail of pictures that led from my room to his.

I reached down and carefully picked up each picture, tears streaming from my eyes. He'd ripped a few, crumpled some others, but I vowed to straighten them out and tape them up and fix them later. They were scattered all over his bedroom; he must have thrown them at the wall in his rage. I reached under his bed and found some more. One had even made it all the way under the closet door.

I opened the closet to get the photo and picked it up. It was the shot of my mother at her graduation from teachers college. Although Dad had torn it in two, you could still see Mom. She looked up at me with a sly grin on her face like we now both knew what she was smiling about. I looked up and saw Dad's old costume hanging up in front of me in its fresh dry-cleaning bag.

Seconds later I darted downstairs to the refrigerator and

grabbed a pan of leftover lasagna and two jars of tomato sauce. I took the stairs four at a time as I raced back up to his bedroom. I ripped the flimsy plastic off his old costume and yanked it out by the hanger and threw it on the floor.

I opened a jar of tomato sauce and slung it at the jacket. Red sauce sprayed across the lapels as if a sword had sliced through the front, and blood and gook had gushed out of the wound. I threw the other jar on the costume lengthways, all the way down one of the pant legs. Then I dumped the old lasagna on the outfit and jumped on top of it to mash it in. When I felt like I'd ground in as much as I could, I hawked all the phlegm I could gather in my throat and spit on it.

I stepped off the old costume, pulled back, and felt my heart pounding in my chest. My mind flashed to the image of my father standing over me, his fist raised to strike, his breast heaving as he struggled to control his anger. I didn't want to be like him that way. I looked at the mess, took a few deep breaths, and carefully put the ruined suit back inside the cheap plastic wrapper and hung it in the closet.

CHAPTER FIFTEEN

I SHOULD HAVE CARRIED an umbrella with me. It was still spitting rain outside, but I'd left in a hurry because I didn't want to be there when Dad got home. The patter of the rain was growing into louder thumps against the rusting green enamel of the generator. I watched a few cars come and go, then finally worked up the courage to hop off the generator and go inside the Purple Cactus.

I probably looked like death, and I really could have used a breath mint, but I hadn't thought about any of that when I left the house. I tried to block the whole day out of my mind; if I didn't go in now while I had the courage to do it, then I never would. I put one foot in front of the other, and before I knew it I was walking toward the entrance.

The direction of my feet articulated my thoughts. This was not my crowd. I did not belong here.

Maybe I should just consider lifelong celibacy, join a monastery, and I'd be much happier, all my problems solved. The rain began to come down in sheets. I started to run, but I was soaked before I even got past the first row of cars. I shoved my hands in my pockets and slowed down to a bitter, soaked trot.

I rounded the corner and almost smacked into a car as it pulled out from its space. It screeched to a halt, and the passenger-side window rolled down.

"You okay?" the driver said from inside.

"I'm fine." Jerk. He should pay better attention when he drives.

I turned to walk away, but I was surprised by what he said next.

"Need a lift?"

I looked down at the driver. He was cute. Broad shoulders. About ten years older than I was. Maybe a little stocky. Maybe a little short; I couldn't really tell since he was sitting in the car. The car looked warm and dry inside, and I was soaking wet and shivering, and it was a long way home. It seemed stupid to get into a car with a stranger, but I could handle myself.

I bit my lower lip and thought about it for a second. He reached over and pushed the door open.

"What's your name?"

Since I'd never done this before, I didn't know if it was bad protocol to lie.

"John," I said. I counted the streetlights and tried to relax.

"I'm Simon," he said. He unwrapped a peppermint and

popped it in his mouth as he drove. I think he noticed me looking at the candy longingly. "You want one?"

I nodded, and he handed me a mint.

"That place is kinda cheesy, huh?"

"Yeah, I guess." Like I'd ever been inside.

I looked over at Simon and noticed how pale his skin was. I bet he wouldn't get tan if he spent a whole summer on the beach. The streetlights made his skin glow even whiter, and the reflection of the raindrops trickling down the windshield gave the impression that his skin was weeping. His face looked kind but maybe a little tired, like he worked nights or something. He put his hand on my knee and gave it a light pat.

"Relax," he said. "I don't bite." He crunched on his peppermint. "So where do you live?"

In an instant I knew I had a choice to make about what I wanted to say. Now or never.

"Let's go somewhere else," I suggested.

He raised an eyebrow and grinned. "How old are you?"

"I just turned twenty-one last week." I was getting good at lying.

"Happy birthday," Simon said. "You look familiar. Have I seen you in there befo—"

"No." I was too brusque, and he could tell. An awkward silence followed.

"You sure you don't want me to drive you home?"

I stared straight ahead.

"We can just talk if you want," he offered, and I could tell he really meant it. That was a nice thing for him to say.

"Let's go somewhere else," I suggested again.

God, why'd it have to be a church. Simon explained that he'd recently kicked his two roommates out after a big fight, and they were still packing, so we couldn't go there. I couldn't tell if they were linked romantically or by business, but it was clear he didn't want to dwell on it, so I didn't. He suggested we find a quiet place to park, and I looked at his chest and muscular thighs and thought that was a great idea, but c'mon, a church?

"No one'll bug us here," he said, and pulled into the parking lot. Then a thought entered my mind: maybe he came to this church for a reason, maybe he was the preacher, or maybe he taught Sunday school or something and got off on coming here to—

He caressed my cheek. His hand felt warm and good. "You all right?"

I looked up into his eyes and nodded. My mouth suddenly went bone dry, and I really wanted another peppermint.

He leaned in and tilted his head slightly, and I closed my eyes and thought that I should really take note of what happened next, because this was my first kiss. Well, my first kiss with someone I really wanted to kiss. There'd been a lot of girls and make-out sessions once I'd hit puberty, but nothing I'd really wanted to do. Mostly it was just at the end of some stupid party and we would have paired off arbitrarily, and I'd just end up kissing them because I didn't want to be responsible in any way for their low self-esteem or future eating disorders or whatever.

I ran my hand through his hair and imagined Uberman. Simon's hair wasn't as thick or as long, but it was blond, so that gave me something to go on. That was probably a shitty thing to do. Not that I was an expert on kissing, but to think about someone else while you're kissing didn't seem right. I let the moisture of his lips soak my own. He was gentle. I was used to adolescent girls who wanted to get in as much action as they could before curfew, but he took his time. He had his thumb and forefinger under my chin and gently smoothed his lips over mine. His saliva tasted slightly metallic.

His other hand crept around my waist, and he pulled me in close. My back arched slightly at his touch. I'd never felt a sensation like that, someone else in the driver's seat, but I liked it. His hand untucked my shirttail and he began to run his fingers across the small of my back, and I could feel tiny hairs stand on their ends as he touched me. Not wanting to be one-upped, I reached my hand under the back of his sweater and ran my hand up the smooth curve of his back. I stopped short at the back of his neck and opened my eyes when I felt a strange, coarse patch on his skin so dry it was almost scaly.

He could feel me stop for a second.

"Sorry," he said, embarrassed. "Just a little eczema."

I pulled my hand out of his sweater, and he started kissing my upper lip, tiny wet nibbles, then deeper lunges with his tongue. The force of his tongue kept my own firmly in my mouth. My eyes were slightly open, enough so I could see through my eyelashes. That way, I could take everything in, and if he opened his eyes to look, he wouldn't catch me staring at him.

He opened his eyes to see if I was getting back into it, if I hadn't been too grossed out by his back. I saw the insecurity in his eyes, and suddenly I wanted him to feel good. He'd been kind, and he was cute, and I liked the warm feeling I felt rising up in me while I was kissing him. I'd always felt like I didn't measure up, like I wasn't good enough or that I'd never be loved the way I wanted to, and the last thing I wanted to do was make someone else feel self-conscious or bad. So I leaned into him and pushed my tongue down his throat, swirled it around, deep and vigorous, so that he'd think he was the be-all and end-all of kissers, when really he was up to this point the only one I'd ever experienced. I think I must have really caught him off guard, because while my tongue wandered around the inside of his mouth I felt the edge of a sharp tooth and he recoiled, and I fell back in my seat.

"What was that for?" I landed on the seat belt, which was poking me in the back.

He wiped the spit off his lower lip like a kid would wipe away chocolate icing when he was caught sneaking a lick from the cake. He shrugged.

"It's nothing."

We sat perfectly still for what seemed like a really long time. When he finally started talking again, he pretended that he wasn't weirded out and we were just getting to know each other and maybe we should just talk. He asked me again how old I was, and I think he was embarrassed when I told him the truth. I can't even remember what we talked about, maybe he asked me about what music I liked. I didn't really notice. I did notice that his mouth had gone really dry, and when it did he had the ever-so-slight hint of a lisp.

He eventually popped another peppermint in his mouth

and worked up enough saliva while he fiddled with the wrapper so that he spoke more easily. In that time, I also began to notice that he looked familiar. Maybe it was the way he nervously fiddled with the wrapper. It was on the tip of my brain. He looked a little bit like that substitute teacher from my U.S. history class. Maybe he'd pushed me away because he recognized me too. But I didn't bother asking him about it, because by that time he'd already asked me where I wanted to be dropped off and had the car in drive.

We drove in silence. I didn't like the empty space. I wanted to tell him that I'd like to take him to dinner and get to know him, and that even though I didn't have a lot of money, I'd find a nice pizza joint and we'd both have fun. I wanted to tell him to drive us straight to the beach and we could check into a motel and talk all night and walk by the ocean until the sun came up.

But I guess if you don't really feel that for someone, then you shouldn't say it. I wasn't saying it to him, and he wasn't saying it to me, either.

I had those feelings for someone else.

I unbuckled my seat belt and opened the car door. Of course he knew that I didn't live at this 7-Eleven, but neither of us was going to say anything about it.

"See ya later," I said to the guy who gave me my first kiss.

"Yeah. See ya."

I went inside to buy a Slurpee but remembered I didn't have any money. The downpour had diminished to a fine, misty drizzle, and I felt like I was moving through a cloud as I walked out of the parking lot. The street ahead was long and lonely. The only thing I could hear was the splash of an occasional car driving past a few streets over. I looked ahead and saw a tree planted firmly in the middle of the road. I thought that was strange.

The closer I got to it, I realized it wasn't a tree at all but a mannequin. Why would someone put a mannequin in the middle of the street? Maybe it was some elaborate Saturday night high school prank, and it was about to explode with firecrackers, and somewhere there was a minivan full of teenagers screaming with laughter. And wasn't that where I should have been myself, out having a fun time with friends? Not worrying about saving the world or hooking up with some guy in a parking lot? I watched my feet hit the pavement as I walked and avoided the puddles. Eventually, I got tired of walking around them and just waded through the water. I looked up and saw that the mannequin was almost directly in front of me. The students had wrapped it with black cloth. I wasn't sure how that fit into their prank.

The mannequin suddenly raised its cowl and stared at me. The glow of the streetlights reflected off the wet streets and off those piercing eyes. I stopped in my tracks.

Dark Hero shook his head. Slowly and deliberately, back and forth. Measured. Burning. Like my father at his angriest. He didn't need to say anything.

How long had he been trailing me? What exactly had he seen? Did he watch my first kiss?

I'd had it with this guy. I shot my hand out and reached for his cowl to yank it off his face.

He batted my hand away so hard that it stung.

In the split second it took for me to recover from the shock of the blow, he'd disappeared into the night. I tried to follow him, but all I heard was a distant splash in a faraway alley.

Fuck him.

It started to rain harder, and I put my hands in my pockets and continued on through the puddles. It was a long walk home.

CHAPTER SIXTEEN

I WOKE UP IN the backseat of Dad's Camaro with a mean crick in my neck. Apparently it was not possible for someone over six feet tall to find a comfortable sleeping position in a Camaro—a piece of information that might come in handy now that I was sure to be homeless.

My mouth was coated with morning scum and I really wanted to go inside and get my toothbrush, but if the car was in the driveway, that meant Dad was home, and I wasn't ready to see him just yet. Maybe he knew I'd spent the night in the car, and he wasn't ready to see me just yet, either. I slipped out of the car quietly, careful to close the door firmly without making a noise, and I cut through the neighbor's backyard and headed to the nearest pay phone in front of the rug store at the strip mall.

I reached in my pocket and was once again reminded that you can't do much of anything in this country without money.

I was the only kid in my class without a cell phone, so I had gotten pretty good at finding pay phones. I knew how to use one, too. I bet all the cell phone users in my class couldn't have made a collect call with a gun to their heads.

"Hi, yes, I'd like to a make a collect call, please, to a Ms. Ruth Whitliff," I requested.

The operator asked me to hold as she connected the call. I heard the phone ring and ring, and I prayed for her to pick up. I don't know why, but I just felt like she was the only person I could call, the only one I could talk to. She was the only one whose reaction had been slightly different when Dad showed up at the League, and that had to be a sign. I needed to find her. Pick up, pick up.

"Sorry, no one's answering," the operator said.

I asked for her to let it ring a little longer, told her that sometimes it took Ruth a while to make it to the phone.

"Sir, there's still no answer. Would you like me to try another number?"

"No thanks." I slammed the receiver down hard and kicked the concrete trash can and almost broke my toe. Damn. I sat on the curb to untie my shoelace and look at my bashed toe.

That's when I saw Ruth's old, army green Gremlin parked diagonally in the handicapped space. She leaned out the window, grinning with a Pall Mall stuck to her bottom lip. I was shocked for a second. Then she waved me over and I got in the car.

"How'd you know I was here?"

She took a drag of her smoke and tapped her temple with her forefinger.

"I see things, remember?"

* * *

The woman drove like a maniac, nearly running down two dogs and knocking over a group of power cyclers as we careened into Riverside Park. She pulled out a bucket of fried chicken, led me over to a picnic table, and handed me a drumstick.

"You want your corn cobbette?"

I shook my head no, and Ruth leaned over and snatched it.

We ate and watched the candy-colored paddleboats glide across the river. I was famished. I hadn't eaten since lunch yesterday, so I wolfed down the drumstick and devoured two thighs and a breast. I looked up at the sun bearing down on us and took a deep breath. It felt good to breathe easy for a change.

"Quite a show you and your dad put on yesterday," Ruth said. I didn't say anything.

"You have some choices to make," she said.

I looked down at my greasy fingers and really wanted to wash them.

"You know what I'm talking about, don't pretend like you don't. That whole evasive, wounded, sensitive-guy thing you go into. I know everything, remember?"

I looked up, startled.

She saw the panic in my eyes.

"I'm not talking about that. That's not a choice. Don't listen to the bigots or the zealots; you like what you like. Don't let that distract you." Ruth handed me a moist towelette for my fingers.

I couldn't believe someone was actually talking about this with me. I'd never told anyone about my feelings before, and apparently she didn't need me to tell her now. I always thought somehow it would be more cataclysmic when someone finally called me out for liking guys, where I'd have to make some kind of epic confession. She glossed right on past it, grabbed another drumstick, and took a bite.

"For someone who's supposed to be a healer, you're really clueless sometimes."

Now I was totally confused. What was she talking about?

"It's like this: everyone's got a tremendous amount of pain; that's how life works." She waved the drumstick, punctuated her sentences with it. "Take me, for instance. And I'm not talking about what happens to my stomach when I eat a green pepper and drink a Pepsi at the same time. I'm talking about *pain*. The real stuff."

"Are you gonna tell me about that guy in the Wrecking Balls?" I asked.

"Christ, kid, hold your horses, I'm having a moment here. Now, where was I? Oh yeah, so when I was young—and yes, it was obviously a long time ago, so don't give me that look. Anyway, when I was just a little older than you, I fell in love, ran away, and eloped."

She stopped and polished off the little bit of meat that remained near the knuckle of the drumstick. Then she stared out at the river and watched the boats.

"Is that it?"

"No, smart-ass, that's not it. That's where you, the sensitive healer, are supposed to step in and figure out that I'm hurting deep down inside and pinpoint what it is. Jeez, kid, do I have to do everything?"

I hadn't thought about that part of my powers before, but I guess she was right. I did it with the coach that time I saw his heart condition. I wondered if he'd ever gone to get help. It was pretty shitty of me not to follow up on that, especially knowing how bad off he was.

I stared at Ruth hard for a minute. I tried to see past the nylon, flower-patterned pantsuit that reminded me of the couch my parents had in all my baby pictures. I studied her face and tried to look deep into her eyes, back into the past, and I found something floating around inside her body. It wasn't like with Coach; it wasn't attached to any one organ or anything specific like that. It was a peculiar haze, and it permeated her entire body and coated her with a grayish hue.

"Got it yet?"

"It's a deep pain in your stomach, in your head, and in your heart . . . like you've been holding something inside so long that it just ruptured. Seeped out into your body."

Ruth tossed the drumstick into a trash can with a resounding clunk.

"That's what happens when you let something fester inside you your entire life."

She fired up a cigarette. "I want you to tell me if you can see what happened."

I looked deeper and I started to feel a little faint—I'd never used my powers like this before—but suddenly I began to see Ruth without wrinkles, with big, bright eyes and full cheeks and soft skin. I dug deeper inside her, and sobs began to echo in my ears, and all of a sudden I latched on to a feeling.

"What was his name?" I asked softly.

"Jerome. Jerome Freeman." Ruth looked out at the paddle-boats and sighed. "He was the one. The only one. We met right after he got back from the war. We kept it from our parents for as long as we could, and then we eloped."

"Why'd you keep it from your parents?"

Ruth ran her finger across the graffiti on the picnic table, carved deep into the wood like wounds.

"He was black." She took a drag from her cigarette. "And I wasn't." She took another drag from her cigarette, like she couldn't get enough air. "Back then, that was enough." She looked at the river passing by and lost herself in thought.

I didn't want to intrude on her memories, so I waited for a while and watched her stare at the water currents as they drifted by us.

"What happened to him?"

She turned ever so slightly on the picnic table, just enough so I couldn't see her face.

"My father was a prominent man in our town. He was the president of the bank, and it wouldn't do for the president of the bank to have a daughter who ran off with a colored man. That's what they called them back then, colored, I mean. So my father hired a party of concerned citizens to track us down and bring us home."

I thought about how she'd felt the need to explain to me what *colored* meant because people didn't use the term anymore. I wondered if the same thing would happen one day to *faggot*.

"I kicked and screamed, but they pulled me out of the motel and put me in a car and took me home and locked me in the attic for weeks. And the whole time I kept seeing Jerome as he called out for me over and over again, while those men pummeled that perfect, smooth face."

I was afraid to ask the next question.

"Go ahead," she said. "I know you're going to ask anyway."

"Why didn't you go back?"

"They let me out of the attic after they were sufficiently convinced I wouldn't go after him. They told me it was no use to go looking, I'd never find him. Sometimes I'd get spitting mad and break things and threaten to leave and find him, but my father would just chuckle and go back to reading his paper or ignoring my mother. I never liked the way he did that, like he knew something I didn't."

"But you could have looked, couldn't you? I mean, didn't you even try to—"

"I was afraid."

And there it was. Her confession.

"Did you ever see him again?"

"A few years later I took a trip to Natural Bridge. My girlfriend and I spent the day hiking up the mountain. After we crossed the bridge, we went to the gift store at the foot of the hill, and I found a cute little glass dome with a picture of Grandfather Mountain that filled up with snow when you shook it. I went to the cashier to pay for it, and the guy behind the counter told me five dollars or some such outrageous amount for the time, especially considering we weren't even at Grandfather Mountain, we were at Natural Bridge. But the guy was a real prick and said he was charging double, specially for me. I didn't like that at all so I pretended to reach for my bag, and I knocked the bauble off the counter.

"It shattered into a million tiny pieces, indiscernible shards of glass across the wood floor, past the point of any fixing. I put on my best face and apologized like a sweet girl my age could always get away with. The guy behind the counter was so mad he shook.

"He shouted out toward the back room at the top of his lungs, 'Boy, get out here!' and a door opened in the back and his janitor hobbled out, limping on one leg, a knobby walking stick in his left hand as a cane.

"'Yes, sir,' he said as he came over and started to sweep up the mess with his bare hands. The cashier yelled at him to use his pea brain, and threw a dustpan at him so he wouldn't shred his hands to pieces. The janitor was slow to react, and the pan knocked the stick out from under him. I didn't like to see people treated like that, not one bit, especially to clean up my mess. I grabbed the dustpan and began to clean it up myself. I picked up his walking stick off the floor, and when I handed it to him I got a clear look at his face."

Ruth took a deep breath and didn't say anything for a minute. I let her take her time. And just when it looked like she might find tears that had dried up years ago, she continued with her story.

"He looked about twenty years older than I was. He'd put on at least fifty pounds, and his bottom lip hung low in a way it never had before, like an unseen force pulled it toward the ground. I reached out to touch his face, that face I'd remembered so differently, and he pulled away like he didn't recognize me. That was when I noticed the scars. All over his face. A number of crude zipper scars, the kind of thing you'd see on a horse when a country vet stitched it up. I tried to speak but the air was trapped inside me and I couldn't make a sound. He looked at me for such a long time, and then, slowly with that long lower lip, he spoke.

"'Ruth,'" he said.

"I wrapped my arms around him as tight as I could and prayed for the kind of power you hold in your hands today, that I could go back and make everything okay again.

"I didn't want him to see me cry, I didn't want to upset him, so I told him I was going to go outside around to the ladies' room to powder my nose. I'll never forget what he said to me next."

Ruth stopped and looked up to the sky.

"What did he say?" I asked. It was a while before she answered.

"He said, '*I'll wait for you*.'"

Ruth scratched the corner of her eye. I wanted to ask her what she did next. She turned and answered as if I'd asked it out loud.

"I ran outside and stole a car from the parking lot and drove away and never looked back."

We didn't talk for a while after that. We just watched the wispy clouds float by overhead. We watched kids playing with their parents on the paddleboats. Young couples splashing in the water. Whenever I got a chance, when I thought she wasn't looking, I tried to steal a good look at Ruth.

"I had started to get pretty good at seeing things by then, and I decided to get back at the world by robbing banks." She said it casually, like it was the obvious next step. "I started with my father's."

Good. I hope she bankrupted him and ruined his life.

"I hooked up with Joey my second year as a two-bit hood. He actually came and found me when he heard that I could sometimes see codes in my head when I looked at the lock on a safe. He was all muscle, and he needed some brains."

I remembered Ruth arguing with that big old Wrecking Ball in front of the hospital that day I screwed up.

"Had a real violent streak, that one." She shook her head. "That's why we split."

Her tone was matter-of-fact, a simple retelling of events, but when I looked at her I saw pain, that same grayish hue, flow in and out of her body. She was very good at not letting anything show on her face, but I could see through it now.

I reached out and gently placed my hand on hers. I thought I saw a faint smile begin to appear on her lips, I hoped it was one of comfort. I concentrated on the grayish hue and thought about making it burn away, and then I felt my palm start to sizzle where it met the sunspots on the back of her hand.

And suddenly she yanked her hand away.

"A while back I decided to start using my powers for something good for a change. I'd been using them to get back at this shitty world ever since the day I stole that car, when the only person I had to blame was myself. I'm old, I'm alone, and I have no one but me to thank for it. That's what I'm trying to tell you, Thom. You've got to make choices in life. And then guess what happens after that. You have to make more choices, and more after that. Sometimes you'll make good choices. . . ." She ripped open a moist towelette and dabbed the spaces in between her fingers. "And some will be bad. It's up to you."

I nodded. I understood as much as I could without having lived a minute of her life.

"You can't go on like you're going to start really living one day, like all this is some preamble to some great life that's magically going to appear. I'm a firm believer that you have to create your own miracles, don't hold out that there's something better waiting on the other side. It doesn't work that way. When you're gone, you're gone. There's no pearly white gates with an open bar and all the Midori you can drink. You only get one go-round and you gotta make it count. I know that sounds harsh, but it's true. *Don't wait.*"

"Ruth."

"Yep."

"Why are you telling me all this? What did you see in my future?"

She leaned back on the picnic table and lit another cigarette. I could tell she was proud that I was asking the right questions now; I was learning.

"You have your path, Thom. It's full of twists and turns and choices, but ultimately it's all up to you."

Apparently that was all I was going to get out of her right now.

"What about you?" I asked.

"You have your path," she repeated and looked up at a flock of birds flying high above in a perfect V-formation. "I have mine."

Then she hopped up from the picnic table, ready to go.

"Those damn birds start dropping on us, I'm gonna have to get my .22 out of the trunk."

She nearly wiped out a stop sign when she turned in to my neighborhood.

"One more thing," she said. "If you really want to be a good healer, you gotta know who needs healing."

"Okay, sure." Easy enough.

She tapped the steering wheel with her fingernail.

"Which means you can't be so obsessed with your own little problems and your own little world all the time, or you'll never be as good as you want to be. If you opened your eyes, you might see some hurt you could actually fix."

Ouch.

"Like what?"

She breezed past another stop sign. An oncoming car slammed on the brakes. She kept going.

"You're not very nice to Scarlett."

I'm not very nice to Scarlett!

"Ruth, you've got to be kidding me." I looked at her to see if she was joking.

She pulled into my driveway and stopped the car.

"Are you serious?" I asked. *"Scarlett?"*

"You're the healer. You figure it out."

I got out of the car and walked up to the porch.

She started to back down the driveway, rolled down the window, and shouted, "Even at my age, some things still manage to surprise you."

She backed over our mailbox on her way out of the drive-way and sped off.

CHAPTER SEVENTEEN

I HAD MY FIRST out-of-body experience when I walked in the door. I'd wiped my feet on the doormat and taken a second to muster up the courage to face my father. I took a deep breath, pushed the door open, and found Golden Boy sitting on our living room couch next to Dad. They had a bunch of old pictures spread out on the coffee table in front of them. I blinked a few times to make sure it was really Golden Boy sipping a cup of coffee with my father.

No one ever sat in the living room. Every once in a while my dad would meet with his insurance agent or financial planner, but it was rare. We barely even vacuumed the rug because no one ever walked on it.

And they were *laughing*, of all things. Together. Or at least trailing off. From the look of it, Dad had said something that had Golden Boy in stitches. I don't think I'd ever seen the guy laugh. In fact, if there had been a contest for most humorless League member, he certainly would have received my vote, and mine wouldn't have been the only one. Golden Boy stood up when he saw me.

"Hello, Thom," he said. He shook my hand, formally, like he was being interviewed and wanted to make a good impression.

"Have a seat," Dad said.

I wanted to ask Golden Boy what the hell he was doing here, but I was speechless. I sat in the armchair that matched the couch.

"I was just showing your father my scrapbook from when I was a kid."

Golden Boy held up an old photo album with a collage on the cover of Major Might in various poses, cut from cereal boxes and magazine articles.

"It's been a real honor to show them to your dad. Man, the stories he has, I mean, I used to dream about this when I was a kid."

Dad chuckled, slightly embarrassed. "Yeah, after girls and baseball games, I bet," he said. "I know where I fell on the totem pole." He grinned. "Who wants more coffee?"

I hopped up and offered to help Dad brew a fresh pot in the kitchen. It was comforting to know they had common things like coffee here in the Twilight Zone.

"Dad?" I said, once we were alone in the kitchen. "You aren't mad at me?"

Dad went about preparing a nice tray of snacks for his guest.

"Why didn't you just tell me about the team, Thom?

I thought you were answering to that Froot Loop Uberman. Your team leader's great. Not at all what I would have expected."

Did this mean he was okay with what I was doing?

"So you're not mad?"

He pulled some dirty mugs from yesterday's breakfast out of the dishwasher and rinsed them off in the sink.

"No, I'm extremely mad that you lied to me. I'm extremely mad that you put me in a position where I looked foolish for trying to do what's best for my son."

"You and Mom never told me the whole truth, either."

Dad turned off the faucet and leaned against the sink with his back to me. I had a very good point, but it probably wasn't the best time to bring it up. A few moments passed, and he dried off the mugs, put the tray together, and began to walk back to the living room. His jaw was clenched, and I think he counted to ten in his head.

"I've been a little tired from working late every night. I'm sorry I overreacted. Let's try to stick to the truth with each other from now on. Deal?"

"Deal," I said. But I would never be able to tell him everything.

At Golden Boy's request, my father told us a few stories from his halcyon days as America's premier crime buster. I'd never heard any of them. I sat captivated at every detail—the way he'd frozen Sig-Sig-Sputnik's jet pack with his own dry ice so he couldn't escape with the loot he'd stolen from Fort Knox. The way he'd found those creeps the Brothers Grimm who kept kidnapping children from the tristate area with various fairy-tale ruses. He said he'd come this close to strangling one of the Brothers with their own bean stalk when he saw what they'd been doing to those kids.

I scanned all the old photos on the coffee table and thought how handsome dad looked in his old costume. Mom must have fallen for him hard.

"Sorry to crash your house like this," Golden Boy said to him.

"Don't be silly, Kevin," my dad said. "You're welcome here any time."

Kevin? They're on a first-name basis now? *I* didn't even call him Kevin.

"No, I should get going. But I will take you up on that offer for a return visit." Golden Boy stood up, fluffed our pillows, and stacked the coffee mugs neatly on the tray.

"You sure you have to go?" Dad asked. I'd never seen him so eager to tell his stories. Maybe he'd been afraid that no one cared, that no one wanted to listen. "You're sure there's nothing else you want to know?"

"Well, there is this one thing," Golden Boy said. "If it's not too much trouble, sir."

Sir? Oh, brother.

"Sure—what is it, Kevin?"

Golden Boy smiled. "I feel stupid asking, but I always wanted to see your costume."

Uh-oh.

I looked to Dad, unsure how he would respond.

"No problem, let me go get it."

My heart dropped and my toenails went white. I remembered what I'd done to his costume.

"Wait!" I yelled.

Dad turned around on the stairs, shocked at my outburst. I had to think up something quick to keep Dad from going upstairs.

"It's just, it's just that . . ." God, I really was the world's worst liar.

"I think I know what Thom's trying to say," Golden Boy interjected.

Really?

"It's something I want to talk to you about, too, sir."

Dad raised an eyebrow.

"Hal," Golden Boy continued, "I don't want you to think that I didn't have another motive in coming over here today. One thing I learned from looking up to you all those years is honesty." Golden Boy gave me a sideways glance, and I thought it was really weird to hear him call my dad by his first name.

"We want you to let Thom come back to the team. With your approval, everything out in the open. We had no idea you weren't in the loop on all this. Sir, if you would please just think about it."

Dad looked over at me and studied my face. He could always see right through me, and I knew he could tell that I didn't have anything to do with this request. It was as much as a surprise to me as it was to him. Dad gave Golden Boy a firm look.

"Let me get the suit," he said. Then he disappeared upstairs.

I collapsed into the armchair and waited for the explosion when Dad saw what I'd done to his costume.

Golden Boy's pleasant demeanor dropped the minute my father left the room. He leveled a stare at me. "Don't you think you could at least pretend to be a little bit grateful here? I'm saving your ass."

I wanted to cover my ears. Waiting for Dad to find the suit was like watching one of those bad slasher movies when the killer has zeroed in on a victim, and you just know he's gonna get it, but you don't know exactly where it's going to come from. A machete to the neck from behind, a hatchet to the head from above, an ice pick to the ear from the side.

"You shouldn't have come here," I said to Golden Boy. I wondered how long it took him to cook up that fake scrapbook with all the old clippings. "You shouldn't have stirred him up."

He looked at me like I was insane.

"What are you talking about? He's going to let you come back."

I shook my head and buried my face in my hands and waited for the bomb to drop. The sound of Dad's footsteps creaked in the ceiling above our heads, then I heard him come to a stop. I knew at that very moment he'd opened the closet door and pulled out his costume. He'd probably think the dry cleaners started using a new red logo on their plastic covers at first, and then he'd get a good look at it in the light and think someone must have snuck into the house and defaced it. Then the reality of what really happened would sink in and he'd picture me sitting down in the living room. Guilty.

I heard the floorboards move above us, then the muffled sound of the closet door as he shut it. His footsteps grew louder as he descended the staircase. He appeared in the doorway and stood there.

I had expected to see him shaking with anger. We'd basically spent the last few hours dredging up his past, all about who he was and what made him great, only for me to remind him that he was now nothing, a single parent who could barely afford the payments on his shitty house by working his shitty factory job, with a shitty son who took a giant block of salt and ground it in the gaping wound that had become his life. Way to go, Thom.

Dad hadn't spanked me since I was a kid, but I wished he'd hauled off and hit me right then and there. It would have felt better than watching him hold all that hurt inside. Betrayed and reviled by the public, sure, that was the pain of his life. He'd learned to endure it, and the power of family had helped. When Mom left, I didn't think he'd recover, but he did. He got better because he still had someone left, a son to live for. And that son had just dropped his pants and taken a big shit on the last, treasured remnant of his father's greatness.

I looked up at him, trying to explain with my eyes how sorry I was and how inadequate any sort of apology would be. If I'd been a telekinetic I would have raised his hand with my mind and made him give me a hard whack to the face.

Dad stepped into the room, stood behind the chair, and placed his hand on my shoulder.

"My son can go back to your team if that's what he wants." He looked down at me, and our eyes connected. "I trust him."

Then Dad put on his long peacoat to go to work, and he reminded me on his way out the door that tomorrow was trash day. I sat perfectly still, afraid if I moved or spoke Dad would burst back in and kill me. Golden Boy thought it was a strange reaction to good news.

"Well," he said, "what are you going to do?"

I listened to Dad's car back out of the driveway. He needed a new muffler but got me a laptop instead. I stood up.

"I'm going to take out the trash."

Golden Boy flew up and down the driveway at superspeed, and one by one, overstuffed bags of cut grass and leaves appeared curbside.

"Kevin."

More bags stacked up on the curb.

"Kevin." I called out louder.

The stack of bags grew taller.

"Kevin!" I stuck my foot out, and a blur of golden costume tripped over me, and the recycling bin exploded open, which sent coffee cans and empty soda bottles and newspapers all across the yard.

"What?" Golden Boy was already picking up the mess.

I scanned the yard. "I don't think I can go back to the team."

Golden Boy looked at me for a minute and wondered if I was pulling his leg.

"You're not serious."

I was serious, and he saw it.

"Why not?"

I bent down and gathered six crushed cans of Milwaukee's Best Light.

"Who rigged up that ridiculous scrapbook?" I asked with

a little more edge than I'd intended, because I was really mad at myself for doing such a stupid, childish thing to Dad's costume. "Tell me who did it. Miss Mural? The Color Chameleon? SculpTOR?"

I chucked a mayonnaise jar in the bin.

Golden Boy looked up at me with a peculiar expression.

"It's mine," he said. He stepped toward me and clenched his fist. "Are you making fun of me?"

"It's really yours?" Honestly, I thought he'd made the whole thing up.

Golden Boy didn't answer. He took the question as an insult. He crouched down and gathered pages of newspaper that were flying around the yard. He didn't use superspeed.

"You kept a scrapbook?"

He continued to clean up in silence.

"About my dad?"

He winged some bottles into the recycling bin. The glass shattered.

"You may find this hard to believe," he said, "but not everyone in the world gets to grow up with all this." He waved his hands around and motioned to our modest house, the paint peeling on the shutters.

"I used to dream about growing up in a place like this, having a parent who looked after me. Hell, you even have your own yard."

I didn't know much about Golden Boy, other than what most people knew. He'd suddenly appeared as Silver Bullet's ward a few years ago. Like most sidekicks, he'd just popped up on a caper and now he was there for the duration, until he was killed or moved on to some new identity of his own, or until some younger, usually brattier, upstart took his place. I had no idea where he actually came from.

"Your dad was the only hero who knew what it was like to grow up in an orphanage. He knew what it felt like, not being wanted."

I tossed an empty pickle jar into the bin. "I hadn't realized . . ."

Golden Boy listened to the clank of the jar as it landed and knocked around glass bottles and metal cans. "They could never figure out what race I was. The black people didn't want me because they thought I might be Puerto Rican or something. The Latinos didn't want me because they thought I might be Middle Eastern. And the whites didn't want a question mark." His eyes avoided mine. "My nickname was *Mutt*."

I didn't know what to say to that.

"Your dad made it out, and he didn't even have a superpower." Golden Boy started gathering the bottles that had rolled down the driveway to the curb.

"So yeah," he said as he threw the cans in the bin, "the scrapbook's mine."

I felt lousy for jumping to conclusions. I felt lousy for taking so much for granted.

"What about everything that happened to my dad later?"

"I don't know what really happened that day. I wasn't there, were you?"

And that was the end of the conversation. We sealed the cover on the recycling bin tightly and wheeled it over to the curb by the trash bags. I guess he had a good point. I'd never considered the possibility that there were people who took my father's side.

"I don't care what anyone says." Golden Boy wiped his hands on the side of his pants. "He's still a hero to me."

Then he sat down on the curb. I joined him.

We watched the ants run around rivulets of dirt in the gutter.

"You know, the reason I'm your team leader is because you got me demoted."

I looked up at him, surprised.

"When we rescued that bus full of people, I should have been more focused on helping the injured. I didn't even notice that woman had been hit at first. When you have superspeed and superreaction-time, you have to look for these things. You're held to a different standard." He paused. "You wouldn't know anything about that kind of responsibility yet."

When he spoke, the muscles in his jaw moved in straight, sturdy lines. Out of all the tryout candidates, Golden Boy worked the hardest to maintain perfect physical condition. He took all parts of the job seriously. Monitor duty. Post-training cleanups. Even the public service announcements about preventing forest fires and obeying the speed limit. Conventionally handsome like a soap star, nothing objectionable, an even smile, narrow eyes, a strong shock of curly black hair on his head, and that beautiful olive, golden skin.

"We have to do better than everyone else, you know. It's not enough to be good. We can't afford to make any mistakes in this business. Ever."

That was true. Dad was living proof.

"I'll be back at tryouts tomorrow," I said. "Thanks for getting my dad to let me do it." It was really nice of him. I thought about asking him if he wanted some pizza or a beer or something.

"If it had been up to me alone," Golden Boy said, "I would have kicked your ass off the team myself. But the rest of them wanted you back, and a good leader keeps his team happy." He looked at his watch, pulled his golden mask up, and stood to leave. "I need to go, you've already kept me too long. Can I offer you a friendly piece of advice?"

I had the feeling he was going to give me the advice whether I wanted it or not. I wasn't sure it was going to be friendly, either.

"All I know is," he said, "if I had a father, I'd show him a little respect."

Ouch.

CHAPTER EIGHTEEN

I SHOWED UP AT the rec center early in the morning, like I'd been doing every day, to train in the boxing/martial arts room, lift some weights, and run the one-on-one game with Goran. He didn't show up in the martial arts room, so I trained with the punching bag alone for about half an hour. Then I moved on to the weight room, and there were a few meatheads with tiger-striped pants on, but no Goran. Finally, I headed to the basketball court thinking I'd do some wind sprints to make up for the basketball I'd missed. Maybe he was sick. I wondered who took care of him when he was under the weather.

I heard the ball bouncing against the wooden floor of the gymnasium, and what I saw inside stopped me in my tracks. Goran was there, dribbling the ball at the top of the key, making a circular path with the ball inside and around his legs while he decided what to do. I'd seen him do this a thousand times and I still couldn't read whether he was going to drive straight to the basket, right or left, or pull back for a jumper. Usually, I was up in his face, trying to make him think I could read him, and that I knew exactly where he was going and exactly how I was going to stop him.

But instead of my hand in his face, it was that little shithead's, the Gary Coleman look-alike.

Goran dribbled the ball, but his posture stiffened, like he was suddenly aware I was standing in the doorway, like he could hear me breathing. The Gary Coleman look-alike didn't notice me at first. He was too busy trying to read Goran's moves. His face was scrunched up in frustration, the bratty kind of look a kid gets when his mom won't buy him the candy bar in the checkout line and he's about to throw a tantrum. My guess was Goran must have been beating him badly, not holding back, and this guy didn't know what had hit him.

The ball bounced in a perfectly even cadence. It's rhythm lulled me, hypnotized me, made it hard to complete a thought. It made it hard for me to think of any reasonable explanation why he'd betray me like this, play with this idiot instead of me. And then it dawned on me.

He'd been waiting for me to see this.

He'd done it on purpose. To hurt me.

The Gary Coleman look-alike noticed me, out of the side of his eye at first. Then he did a double take, and a spark of recognition lit up his face.

Just then, Goran turned around, slowly, deliberately, and leveled his stare at me. Without taking his eyes off me, he jumped into the air, smooth and strong, and shot the ball from three-point range. As the ball soared, the Gary Coleman look-alike opened his mouth and began to say, pointing at me, "Hey, there's the gay g——"

The ball sailed perfectly through the center of the basket, and the sound of the swish drowned him out.

I slammed the door shut as hard as I could. Goran watched me through the small square window in the middle of the door, his stare perfectly fixed, unmoving. His face reminded me of the first time I met him, when I thought he was going to hit me. I tore myself away and pushed off from the rusty metal bars of the door. I felt the concrete walls of the hallway close in on me, the fluorescent lights beat down hard, like I was a specimen under a magnifying glass. I ran out of that place and never looked back.

Later that day I called in to the Student Life Center to tell them I wouldn't be coming back to tutor because my family was moving to another town.

CHAPTER NINETEEN

DAD DIDN'T COME HOME that night, so I was alone when I got the call. I had slipped into his bedroom and crept over to the closet to take his ruined costume out. I'd planned on bringing it to the cleaners. I'd made a few phone calls and found a place that specialized in fabric repair for old military outfits, but they were very expensive. After paying to get the computer out of the shop, this would drain my savings, and I knew I would have to find a way to fit in another part-time job on the weekends. But it was worth it. You can't put a price on your father's dignity.

I'd just grabbed his costume and looked out the window to make sure he wasn't driving up the street when the phone rang. I jumped.

"Hello?"

"Thom, it's me," Golden Boy said. "Hold on for second."

I could hear the urgency in his voice, and it rattled me.

"Why, what is it?"

Suddenly I felt a hand on my shoulder, and someone said, out of breath, "Thom—"

"Holy—!" I wheeled around and saw Kevin standing there. I was so scared I dropped Dad's costume on the floor. I almost dropped a load in my pants, too.

"Don't do that! You scared the shit out of me."

"Sorry," Kevin said.

I reached down and picked up Dad's costume and tried to hide it behind my back.

"What's that?" Kevin pointed at the dry cleaning bag.

"Nothing." I stuffed it back in the closet before he had a chance to say anything more about it.

"Justice called an emergency meeting, all members, reserve and probationary, too."

"Why?"

"There's been a murder."

They'd found King of the Sea floating lifeless, decaying, his scales sloughing off one by one in the harbor, next to the planetarium. Two girls had been working on a high school science project on the deleterious effects of the nearby power plant on the life in the water. They'd hoped for a major exposé, maybe even an award at the state science fair or a spot on the local news, something to make them a shoo-in on all their college applications. They found a lot more than they'd bargained for.

His gills had been sliced, and the coroner said that he'd been cognizant, immobile, and in immeasurable pain. What was more disturbing was that his ganglia had been severed in just the right place to paralyze him.

This was troubling because his murderer had placed his school of sea nymphs and his mate, a mermaid, on the side of the shore; King of the Sea had been forced to witness as they helplessly flipped and flailed just a few feet away from the precious water that would have allowed them to live. His only son, a sea horse, had been turned inside out by the pouch. They were cruel deaths, even by supervillain standards.

Ruth stirred some nondairy creamer into her Styrofoam cup and said hello to me without looking up. I sat between her and Scarlett, who was her typical warm, loving self. She sneered the second Golden Boy and I appeared, rolled her eyes, and looked the other way. I thought about what Ruth had said to me about how I treated her, and I still couldn't make sense of it.

I said hi back to Ruth, and then Kevin nudged me to lean in so he could whisper something to me; but Scarlett shushed us before he could say anything.

"Shut up, they're about to begin," she said. "Show some fucking respect."

I'm pretty certain I wasn't showing any disrespect, and I wanted to tell her so; but I saw Ruth shoot me a look, and I just swallowed my comment and tried to pretend I wasn't stewing. Justice descended from the air and hovered behind the podium. I looked around the room; I'd never seen such an assembly of heroes in my life. There had to be every living superhero, every champion who'd ever had any sort of association with the League. I recognized a few old faces from Mom's secret pictures. Mostly it was the costumes I recognized, not the faces. The faces and bodies looked like someone had left them in the microwave too long so that they'd melted at the jowls, waistline, and ass.

Justice held up his hands and the crowd grew silent. He looked weary, his tone was solemn.

"As I'm sure you all know by now, a hero has fallen." He took a second to let the gravity of his statement sink in. "He was one of our greatest champions." He pinched the narrow bridge of his nose between his eyes. "And he was our friend." The Aqua-teens and the Nereids wept openly in the front row.

"We will of course host the appropriate memorial services; everyone will have time to pay due respect." His solemn eyes narrowed.

"But there's another reason you're here tonight." He took a long breath. "We have reason to believe this may not remain an isolated incident."

Ruth looked over at me like she knew what Justice was going to say next and was sorry for it. Golden Boy leaned forward in his chair. Even Scarlett was engaged, fixed on his next words. Justice picked a spot in the crowd, probably the leg of a chair or the sparkle off someone's cape, and stared at it to avoid looking anyone in the eye.

"Unless we act now, find who did this, there will be more." He hovered slightly above the floor.

"Friends and colleagues, someone may be killing the heroes."

Our patrol began shortly after midnight. Justice's plan involved the entire League and its affiliates. We were to apprehend each and every supervillain in existence and bring them in for interrogation. Justice suspected that one of them had snapped—a death as cruel as King of the Sea's could only be the result of a supervillain with a major grudge to settle. Some suggested maybe it was the work of a group of supervillains who had banded together. I heard a few of the old-timers complain that in their day there would have been no meeting, no assignments, no teams or plans. Very simply, the supervillains would have started disappearing, maybe in concrete blocks at the bottom of the ocean, maybe in a black hole, and no one would be the wiser. Vengeance wasn't the kind of thing you announced.

I thought these were awfully aggressive tactics, atypical for the League. When I said something about it later in our team meeting, Golden Boy cut me off and told me it wasn't my position to question the League's authority. But if I wanted to be the sole person to go tell them their plan was bad, he had said, "Be my guest. Maybe they'll tell you to go find your own team, and you can come up with your own plan."

So assignments had been handed out to all groups, and our little team of neophyte heroes had been given the task of staking out a ramshackle building on the other side of the river, where three villains were purported to reside: Transvision Vamp, Snaggletooth, and Ssnake. Golden Boy explained that we'd been assigned these three because, as a result of my previous run-in with them on the bus, I'd be able to identify them quickly, even in their civilian identities.

"I bet they gave us loser-patrol because 'Mr. Sensitive' over there can't handle the big guys." Miss Scarlett crossed her legs and sat sidesaddle atop a streetlight across from the building. She clipped her fingernails.

"Ow." A pinky nail caught Typhoid Larry in the eye.

Scarlett had been calling me "Mr. Sensitive" ever since I got stuck in the burn unit at the hospital while she and the rest of the gang were fighting the Wrecking Balls. It would have been fine as a nickname from a teammate on your basketball team, typical ribbing from someone who counted on you for at least twenty points a game. But out of Scarlett's mouth, the name dripped like venom, with a slow, deliberate, effeminate drag on the S's.

"Keep your eyes open, people," Kevin said from behind his binoculars.

This was our third night keeping watch over the apartment, and no sign of anyone looking like the villains yet. We were the only tryout group who hadn't apprehended our targets.

"Maybe they slipped in and we just didn't know it was them," Larry said.

Golden Boy asked, "Is that possible?"

Everyone turned to look at me. I was, after all, the only one who'd been engaged directly in combat with them. But it had all happened so quickly on the bus that night, and God only knew what they looked like out of costume. I didn't want to let the League down now, in its time of greatest need, but how was I supposed to recognize them if they weren't in costume? I peered through my binoculars as someone with a banged-up metal trash can in his hand opened the front door. As far as I could tell, it wasn't Snaggletooth, Transvision Vamp, or Ssnake. The guy dropped the lid of the trash can, and it sounded like a cymbal when it crashed on the cracked pavement.

I shook my head and let the others know I didn't think it was one of them.

"I'm going home." Ruth flicked her cigarette in the gutter.

"We have another three hours until our shift is over," Golden Boy said.

"*You* have another three hours until our shift is over," Ruth said, and zipped up her pocketbook. "Tomorrow, that's when everything will go down."

Our group exchanged looks. We'd been up all night for three nights in a row and really needed a break.

"Now she tells us." Larry rolled his eyes.

"Well"—Golden Boy eyed Ruth suspiciously—"if you say so."

"I say so." Ruth slung her arm around his neck. "What say you give a tired old woman a lift home. My car's in the shop."

Golden Boy nodded, picked Ruth up, and in a blur they were gone. I didn't like seeing him go, because he was my ride home, too.

"See you tomorrow," Larry said as he peeled off in his Trans Am. He coughed at the exhaust the car spewed out. I shouted for him to wait, but over the revving of the engine he couldn't hear me. There went my other ride.

That left me and Scarlett.

I didn't even want to acknowledge her presence. But I needed a ride home.

"Hey, Scarlett?"

Scarlett's car was a lot like she was. Pretty on the outside, a mess on the inside. It was a gold SUV, one of those cars you'd see on the highway and wonder why anyone needed one that big. She said she kept the outside waxed and clean because it was leased. She did not apply the same logic to the inside of the car, which was covered in a blanket of fast-food detritus and half-empty makeup containers. She pulled over at a gas station and asked me to pump while she cleaned the windshield.

I milked the nozzle for every last drop of gas before returning it to the pump. I found a cluster of dirty cotton balls from inside the car stuck to my shoe, so I pulled them off and noticed that Scarlett was inside paying at the counter. I saw her lean forward by the cigarette lighter display, in her usual flirting mode with the cashier. I carefully screwed the cap back on the gas tank, and suddenly Scarlett burst out of the door, shouting back at the cashier two steps behind her.

"Your machine is broken!" she screamed. "My cards are good!"

The cashier, a dark-skinned, middle-aged man with a full beard but no hair on his head chased her. Scarlett kept shouting as if she could drown out his presence with the sound of her own voice, and hopped in the driver's seat of the car.

"Get in!" she shouted at me.

The cashier pounded on her window as I climbed in. His eyes looked less angry than desperate. The money would have to come out of his pocket, and judging from his job—the graveyard shift at the Pump'n'Fill—and from the size of Scarlett's gas tank, it would probably mean he'd have worked this whole night for nothing. Scarlett screeched out of the gas station onto the road.

"Jesus," I said, more out of shock than out of judgment.

"I didn't see you offering to pay, either!"

I didn't really have a chance to, but I didn't think it was worth mentioning right then. The car started stalling, and Scarlett popped the gearshift into neutral, revved the engine, and popped it back into first, which sent us lurching forward.

"Don't mouth off to me in my own car, got it?"

I stared at my hands folded in my lap and thought about not asking what I really wanted to know. I finally decided I didn't have anything to lose.

"Can I ask you a question?" I said.

"It's your mouth."

"Why do you hate me?"

Scarlett gripped the steering wheel with white knuckles and ground her teeth.

"Why the fuck does everything have to be about you all the time? God!"

The engine began to sputter. Frustrated, she slammed her foot on the gas pedal, but I knew that was a mistake.

"You're going to flood it," I told her.

"Will you shut the fuck up! I'm trying to drive!"

The car conked out completely, and we coasted over broken glass from a streetlight onto the shoulder and came to a stop by the guardrail.

"Fuck!" She smacked the steering wheel as hard as she could, and then buried her face in her hands and began to sob. I studied the sleeve of the pizza delivery jacket that she never took off, how it was frayed at the edges, how the ends of the sleeve were stained with sweat and dirt and sauce. I looked closely at her hands and saw for the first time her fingers up close, chewed down at the cuticles, bright red spots of raw flesh exposed. She always exuded so much confidence, I couldn't imagine her in a private moment gnawing on her hand, much less crying like this.

I tried to put my arm around her, a natural instinct when someone's sobbing, but she winced and jerked away.

I didn't know what else to do. This was someone I didn't really like much, someone who went out of her way to make me feel awful most of the time. And still I couldn't stand to see her cry like that.

So I reached out and held her hand.

And that's when I noticed it.

There was a color, a swirling of substance all around her body. It was different from the sickness I saw in Ruth. In Scarlett's case it was a mixture of colors, some of them bright. I couldn't tell what it was at first. Her stomach seemed troubled, like she'd been throwing up recently. Her bladder seemed swollen. Her head ached, and hormones raged up and down her tiny frame. Still I couldn't pinpoint the source. I squinted and looked deeper.

There was a darkness, too, a thick blackness. But it didn't go with the color, like they were two separate forces working against each other. I couldn't make sense of it, but I concentrated and pushed my powers as hard as I could without passing out.

A mild electrical shock jolted me. I gasped and pulled my hand away from hers. Scarlett looked at me, and I looked back into her eyes, fierce and wet, and finally understood what it was.

There was something cruel and defiant growing strong inside her.

CHAPTER TWENTY

SCARLETT SAW RIGHT through me. "If you tell any-
one, I'll kill you, I swear it." Then she added in a tiny voice,
"Promise me."

"I promise."

What else was I going to say? I'd never had a friend sick
like that before. In fact, I wasn't sure I would call Scarlett a
friend, regardless of her health. Still, I didn't have any plans to
mention it.

"How long—?"

"I don't know." She reached into the backseat and pushed
away a few empty Diet Pepsi bottles and came back with a cigarette. She pressed it hard against the back of her hand and lit
it. "Doctors don't know shit." She inhaled deeply, and the ember
glowed against the smooth white skin of her hand.

I wanted to tell her that I didn't think she was supposed to be smoking, but so far this was the most we'd ever talked without any outright hatred, and I didn't want to ruin the moment.

She saw me staring at the cigarette.

"Don't judge me," she said, and took a long drag. "There's some things you don't know." She unbuttoned the top button of her jacket. "You ever wonder why you never see me without this jacket?"

"Once or twice, maybe." Of course I wondered, everyone did. Especially considering the grungy sleeves. I never understood why someone who cared so much about her appearance would wear a pizza delivery jacket with sleeves full of muck.

"You think I'm too poor to buy a new one, I can tell." That thought had crossed my mind, I have to admit, but I didn't say it.

"When I was a little girl," Scarlett said, "I woke up one morning and discovered I had breasts. I was in the sixth grade, and my dad had already left, and my mom resented me because I started to get attention from her boyfriends." She scraped around the floorboards searching for something as she spoke.

"About a year later, I started getting really high fevers, the kind they take you to the hospital for. One night at the emergency room they got worried that my temperature was so high I would die, so they put me in a tub full of ice." Scarlett found what she was looking for, a small plastic disk of blue and pink eye shadow. She adjusted the rearview mirror so she could see her eyes.

"It only took me a few seconds to melt the whole thing. I burned the nurses' hands when they tried to take me out of the water." She dug into the disk of eye shadow with the applicator.

"My mother was horrified; the hospital told her they couldn't do anything else for me, so she took me home." Scarlett carefully applied the makeup to her eyelids. "They wouldn't let me back in school because they thought I'd burn it down. I'd already tried to once, and that was before I even had powers, so I guess I can't really blame them. I spent a lot of time at home." She flung the case of eye shadow somewhere in the backseat and reached down for a bottle of makeup remover.

"Finally I got this scholarship to a special school for people like us, where they train you to control your powers. It was a bunch of spoiled rich kids, but it was okay, I didn't need to stay too long to get the hang of my powers." She reached over down by my feet and felt around. I scooped up a handful of cotton balls and handed one to her.

"I came home during the first Christmas break and found out that my mom was real sick, and she wasn't getting any better. The doctors said that it had been exposure to my high levels of radiation, before I'd learned to keep it under control.

"And then I started throwing up every day." Scarlett doused the cotton ball with makeup remover and began to wipe away the trails of mascara left on her face by her tears.

She tossed the used cotton ball in the back and I handed her another one. "You know how expensive it is to get chemo? Even with government aid, it still costs a shitload. And Mom's too tired to work most of the time because of it. I picked up four extra shifts last week just so they wouldn't repossess her wig."

Scarlett pulled a mascara wand out of a pocket inside her jacket and began to apply it to her lashes.

"What about you?" I asked.

Scarlett stopped with the mascara and turned to look at me. She shook her head. "You still haven't figured it out, have you?"

I scratched my eyebrows. I thought I knew everything, thought I was a smart kid, but there was still more to her story, another surprise. She unbuttoned her jacket all the way and opened it up. I looked at her belly in shock. The bag spread over her stomach like a pouch of colorless Jell-O and rested in her lap.

"It's a colostomy bag," she said.

"What does that mean?" I asked.

"It means I won't be winning Miss America this year." She dipped her mascara wand into the tube. I'd heard the term before, but I didn't know what it really was. She could see the confusion on my face and sighed.

"It means I shit through a tube in my stomach, okay?"

Oh. I stared straight ahead.

Scarlett turned her attention back to her eyelashes in the mirror and began reapplying the mascara. She applied countless layers of black on her lashes, trying to make them longer and longer.

She saw my eyes grow wide as I stared at the bag, and I knew I should have hidden my reaction. I thought she'd kick me out of the car right then and there, but she didn't.

"He took me to dinner a few times, made out through a couple of movies, and we talked about our first time being special. But that night we both got out of work early and I started kissing him, working on his neck—he can't resist that, it drives him absolutely crazy—and we couldn't help ourselves. So we went at it right there in the parking lot." She blinked her eyelashes and began to wipe away the excess.

She said that last part wistfully, and it surprised me—that she'd waited a long time for anything she really wanted. It was the first time I really identified with her. I knew what it was like to wait for what you really want.

"The parking lot's full of gravel, you know, so he didn't really say anything when I told him I wanted to keep my jacket on; who wants a bunch of gravel digging into your skin? I told him to take it slow, because he's usually so fast about everything else. I really wanted to enjoy it." She rested her head against the windshield and sighed. "I'd been waiting such a long time. I was so into the moment, I didn't care that he was getting close to my bare stomach. Maybe I even wanted him to find out." She stared at her eyes in the rearview mirror. "I thought about how the scene would play out when he reached down and felt the bag. I could picture the look on his face, the shock of discovering it." She suddenly pushed the rearview mirror away so she wouldn't have to look at herself. "Then I thought, well, if that's the worst thing that could happen, what the fuck. Better to know now than later. But the more I thought about it, I realized there was something even worse he could show."

"What?" I asked.

"Pity," she said. She turned and stared directly into my eyes. "And I will not be pitied. Ever." She took a deep breath, which made her chest look even bigger.

"So I told him to get his fucking hands off me, got in my car, and went home." She stared out the window.

"I don't even know why the fuck I'm telling you this."

It made me mad for her to clam up suddenly like that, but I thought about what Ruth had told me and decided what I'd do next. I reached out my hand and, without using my powers, squeezed Scarlett's hand, and this time she let me.

"Why would you ever let someone fall in love with you if you aren't going to be around to enjoy it with them? I know you think I'm pretty cruel sometimes. It's true. I can be. But I'm not that cruel. I wouldn't wish this on anyone."

We breathed the same air for a minute, and I watched Scarlett stare out the window.

"Maybe you should talk to him," I said. I hadn't read the handbook for these situations. "Maybe if you saw him and told him what was going on, I don't know, maybe he's just waiting to see you again to talk about it."

Scarlett took her delivery cap off. Underneath she was patchy and bald from chemo. Her blond ponytail was a hair extension woven, rather sloppily, underneath the cap. She reached under her seat and pulled out a new cap with a blond ponytail.

"What are you talking about? I see him every night," she said, and adjusted the cap so the ponytail looked even in the back. "So do you."

I didn't want to hear what came next, but she said it anyway.

"It's Golden Boy."

CHAPTER TWENTY-ONE

I MET SCARLETT at her house, the prettiest trailer in the park, at exactly 7:30 a.m. the next morning. Scarlett said if we went early, maybe she'd get out in time to take a nap so that no one at tryouts would notice how exhausted she really was. "They're always 'running behind' at the doctor's office," she said. "Not exactly what you want to hear when every day could be your last."

On the way she stopped at a 7-Eleven for some biscuits and a Diet Dr Pepper. She spooned some extra-spicy salsa out of the nacho fixin's container onto the biscuits.

"What do you care?" she said, when she saw me make a face at her breakfast. "I'm just going to throw it all up anyway."

We parked the car across the street, and she asked me to find her appointment card in the backseat while she wolfed down the last half of a biscuit. I found the small card underneath a repossession notice for the car. I decided not to bring that up. One crisis at a time. I read the card, which said we were about half an hour late.

"Oh, I almost forgot to ask," she said. "I need to borrow two hundred and fifty dollars."

I thought she had to be kidding. She waited until now to ask me to pay for it?

"Hey," she said, and shrugged, "good chemo ain't cheap."

I calculated how much I had in my savings and told her I'd write her a check. Thank God for those extra shifts I'd picked up to pay for Dad's dry cleaning. She said she'd pay me back as soon as she could, but I knew better.

"This wasn't part of the deal," I said while scribbling out the check. "I said I'd drive you because you were too tired after the treatments to pull it together for practice."

"Yeah, okay, whatever." She snatched the check. She wasn't even looking at me.

"You got a girlfriend yet?" she asked me as she yanked open the door to the concrete building. My heart dropped a little, my usual reaction to this question.

"Uh, no," I said.

"Well, when you do," Scarlett said as she tossed the remains of her ham biscuit in the waste bin, "try to pick one whose insides aren't rotting."

In the waiting room, I flipped through a *Reader's Digest* and found myself lingering on a page called "The Lighter Side of Life." Scarlett had been uncharacteristically restrained with the woman at the front desk, who castigated her for being late. She said it meant she'd have to wait a while longer because they were "running a little behind." Scarlett turned to me and grinned when the receptionist said that last part.

Scarlett went behind the closed doors, where husbands, partners, friends, and I were not allowed to enter. The excessive number of young people in the waiting room made me wonder what the hell we'd done to the world that this many kids were getting chemo. You could tell by the varying degrees of hair loss approximately how long each one had been in treatment. I scanned the room, and each one was too embarrassed to make eye contact with me. One of the teenage girls sat rocking back and forth like she had a bad cramp in her stomach and was waiting for it to pass.

I didn't realize how rude it was to be the one healthy kid staring at all the patients until I got to the last guy in the room. Apparently, he'd decided to make a joke out of the whole process—he'd painted arched eyebrows where his real ones had been, and he wore a towering bouffant wig on his head. He was grinning at me, waiting for my eyes to come to a rest on his. His middle finger was raised in my direction.

I laughed out loud—I couldn't help it—and saw that the entire waiting room was staring at me like I was crazy. This wasn't the kind of place where you laughed. I didn't have time to apologize. The emergency alarm on my ring went off.

The doors busted open, and Scarlett came running out, clenching her ring finger.

"We gotta go!"

She almost knocked over the crabby receptionist, who fell back in her seat. Scarlett grabbed my arm, yanked me out of my seat, and the next thing I knew, we were sprinting down the hallway.

The window at the end of the hallway was open. Good thing, because Scarlett heated up, lifted me off the ground, and seconds later we were flying through the air.

CHAPTER TWENTY-TWO

"LOOK WHO DECIDED to show up," Golden Boy said. He eyed me and Scarlett suspiciously. She set me down, and I saw Golden Boy's eyes on our clasped hands. Scarlett knew he was looking, and gave my hand an extra squeeze for emphasis. She barged past Golden Boy.

"Where's the fire?" she said.

Golden Boy pointed toward the parking lot of the ramshackle apartments we'd been staking out. Scarlett turned on the heat, yanked me up into the air with her, and we were suddenly off again.

I tried to focus on the emergency, but I couldn't help but think about Scarlett. Was it safe for her to be back in action this soon after the procedure? I was about to ask her if she was okay, when she did something that threw me for a loop.

She dropped me. I whizzed through the air and thought for

sure I'd splatter on the pavement, so I closed my eyes. Instead, I landed on top of someone and thought I heard a bone crack. It knocked the wind out of me, and when I finally caught my breath, I saw that I'd landed on Snaggletooth. And the cracking sound I heard wasn't his bone, it was his tooth. I'd landed right on the back of his neck and driven his tooth straight into the concrete sidewalk.

A pair of quick hands lifted me off the ground.

"Get up," Golden Boy shouted at me as he whipped around Snaggletooth at superspeed and tied him up. "We're supposed to apprehend them, not kill them." It was the first time I'd seen him since Scarlett had told me her news. He eyed Scarlett again as he wound up Snaggletooth.

Typhoid Larry was leading Transvision Vamp to Ruth's car. Her hands were tied behind her back, and Larry told us he'd first given her a wicked case of glaucoma so she couldn't resort to her usual eye tricks, and then he'd given her a debilitating case of tendonitis so she couldn't run. Larry was getting smarter with his powers. He'd also tied a bandana around her head to cover her eyes. She stumbled and hit her head on the roof of the car as she climbed in the backseat.

"Right on time," Ruth said. "I was waiting for you two to show up."

Golden Boy didn't offer me a hand to get up. I got the message loud and clear and got up just fine on my own.

"Where the hell were you two, anyway?" he said.

It wasn't my place to tell him.

"Shouldn't we get these guys to headquarters?" I wasn't very smooth at dodging questions, and he could tell.

His demeanor changed immediately. His molecules slowed down and he actually came to a full stop. He looked at me. I could tell he was wondering exactly how much I knew about him and Scarlett.

"Hey! Wake up!" Ruth shouted from her car. "We got trouble!"

She pointed down the street, where Scarlett had pinned Ssnake in an alley. She was pummeling him with her fists. Her arms flung wildly, weaving trails of flame in figure eights, and from the force of her blows, she didn't seem to care if she broke her hands or his ribs. She tore into his stomach like it was a punching bag.

"Stop her!" Ruth shouted.

Golden Boy got to Scarlett, who was still ripping into Ssnake with no intention of stopping. She was lost in rage, and it was our job to get her back before she killed this poor loser. Golden Boy grabbed her by the shoulders and pulled her back. She whipped around, her eyes lit up with flames.

She looked around frantically for something to hit, her chest heaving, and she tried to get her bearings. Ssnake crumpled against the wall and slid down to the ground in a motionless heap, like a giant spitball thrown against a blackboard. Scarlett pushed Golden Boy to the ground, and I saw the shock on his face. Flames escaped from Scarlett's mouth as she seethed. I ran over to her and grabbed her, like my dad had grabbed me the first time I'd ever had a seizure.

"Scarlett, listen to me," I whispered into her ear. "Everything's going to be okay." My hands were burning, and I couldn't tell if it was my powers or hers, but it hurt like hell.

More than anything in the world, though, she needed to know that she wasn't alone, so I took a deep breath, braced myself for the pain, and hugged her tightly.

My skin sizzled as she sobbed into my chest. The burning was almost more than I could take—the worst pain I'd ever been through up until this point—but I held on tight. She was trying to spit some words out, but she couldn't manage to catch her breath from all the crying. "Shhh, you don't have to say anything." I stroked her hair and tried to ignore the fires burning my skin.

"But—" Scarlett gagged and sobbed. "I—" She choked back more tears. Then she got fed up with herself, shut her mouth, looked up at the sky, and counted to ten to catch her breath. She put her mouth next to my ear, and before the sobbing took her over again, she managed to get out one sentence.

"I left my purse at the clinic," she whispered. I saw Golden Boy, still on the ground, his eyes burning with envy that she was confiding in me and not him.

I held on to her as she began crying again, and told her not to worry about it, I'd take care of it. She cried and cried.

By now, Ruth and Larry had caught up with us. They'd hoisted Ssnake to his feet, lifted his arms over each of their shoulders, and helped him to the car. Larry tried to latch the Power Inhibitor around Ssnake's neck, but Ruth motioned for him to stop. It was an unnecessary precaution. He wasn't going anywhere.

I made eye contact with Ssnake; I was glad he'd regained consciousness. Underneath his mask he had cloudy, listless eyes, and the minute he saw me staring at him, he turned his swollen head away in shame. I guess supervillains could get embarrassed, too.

After Ruth and Larry escorted Ssnake away, Scarlett looked up from my shoulder and her face grew still.

"The fuck are you looking at?" she asked Golden Boy.

He stood there, silent. For a long while they stared at each other. I didn't know who was going to move first, and I wanted to be anywhere but in between them. I made my best effort to back away without drawing any attention to myself. I looked at Golden Boy's face, strong and earnest, but rattled. Then I saw Scarlett's face soften for just a second, and it made me think about how long she must have waited for the right moment to let him know how she felt about him, how long she must have waited for their first kiss. Kevin took a step forward and opened his arms up to hold her.

Scarlett pushed him away as hard as she could. He crashed into some empty metal trash cans and fell on his ass. Then Scarlett burst into flames and disappeared into the sky without looking back.

As I stumbled toward the clinic, I realized I hadn't been this sick since I was a kid, since before my powers had developed. My head was pounding, and I felt feverish and weak. I'd woken up in the parking lot on the hood of Scarlett's car just a few minutes earlier. Maybe the day's events had taken more out of me than I thought; it was a vicious rebound effect. Or maybe I was recovering from Scarlett's burns, healing myself. Either way, I wasn't sure how long I'd been out, and I'd never been knocked out like this before.

Inside the clinic I waited for the elevator and felt like I was being watched. The light had burned out in the hall, so it was difficult to see. I looked down the corridor and was convinced I heard something around the corner. Footsteps. I peered down the hallway but didn't see anything except the door to the stairwell.

I looked up the shaft of empty space made by the staircase as it spiraled up. I swore I saw something move. I lifted my foot up to the first step as quietly as I could and slowly began to ascend the stairs. About halfway up, I was certain there was someone else in there with me, but I couldn't tell if they were ahead of me or behind me. I stopped for a minute to listen, but I think they stopped each time I did. All I could hear was faint breathing, and I was sure it wasn't my own. Stairwells are dark, creepy, and claustrophobic, especially when you could have someone a flight above you or a flight below. Panic seized me, and I held my breath so long that I thought my lungs were going to burst, and all I could think about was getting out of there.

I raced up, three, four stairs at a time, and threw myself against the exit door on the sixth floor.

I tumbled forward and knocked over a coffee table, which sent plants and magazines spilling out onto the floor. I looked up and saw the entire waiting room staring at me. The receptionist stared at me, horrified, her ear to the phone.

"Uh," I said. "My friend left her purse."

It wasn't much hassle to get the purse back. The receptionist handed it to me without asking a single question. The guy with the bouffant wig was still there. He didn't bother to look up. To leave, I took the elevator. I kept an eye on the stairwell as I exited the building.

The street was empty, and the parking lot across the street was full of cars, but no people. I crossed the street and crouched down to look under the cars.

The coast was clear. I didn't see any feet, so I got up and headed toward Scarlett's car. I didn't like walking around in public with her purse. I tried to hide it under my arm, but there was just no way to look manly with it. I hurried to her SUV.

I stuck the key in the lock and whipped my head around. I was sure I heard footsteps this time. I thought about jumping into the car and fumbling with the keys in the ignition, like a stupid victim from a bad slasher movie. Then I stopped. I got out of the car and shouted into the parking lot.

"What is your problem?"

I heard the flutter of a cape, and turned around. Maybe I saw a corner of fabric flow and disappear around a Subaru. For the first time I wasn't scared. I didn't care who was following me. I felt tired and empty, and sort of hungry. I wish I'd kept a biscuit for me.

Things had to change. Time for me to start taking control of my own life. I got in the car and drove.

CHAPTER TWENTY-THREE

"WHERE HAVE YOU BEEN?" Ruth pulled me aside. "There's been another murder."

The press was waiting inside the League headquarters press room. The meeting hall was packed with reporters and news cameras.

"Who are all these people?" I asked.

"Justice called a press conference. We've been trying to get hold of you since you left."

"Is Scarlett back?"

"No," Ruth said. "But listen to me. There's something you should know—"

Larry interrupted her. "Did Ruth tell you yet? Isn't it exciting?"

Isn't what exciting? I looked at Ruth. She hadn't told me anything.

"We caught the murderer!" Larry wheezed with overexcitement and asthma. "Can you believe it—us?"

The Galaxy Twins strutted past, and Galaxy Girl threw us a distinct "Hmph" over her shoulder.

"Those jerks always laughed at me." Larry ratcheted his voice up a few decibels so they could hear. "Didn't think we could do anything. Yeah, well, who's laughing now?"

I was confused.

"Who was murdered?"

Ruth pulled me aside again. "The Spectrum," she said. "Justice said the Spectrum had found something last night during the autopsy on King of the Sea, but he wasn't exactly sure what it meant. They found his body this morning in the color lab. Listen, that's not the important part—"

"Thom, can I talk to you?" I looked up at Golden Boy, who was stone-faced, utterly serious. He pulled me aside by the shoulder with more force than necessary. I looked down at his hand on my shoulder.

"Where's Scarlett?" he said. His thumb pressed into my bicep. "Where is she?"

I looked over at Ruth and hoped she would rescue me.

"This is serious, Thom." I turned to leave, but he grabbed me by the shoulders.

"Get your hands off me." I was fed up with being pushed around.

"Where were you two today?" He was losing it. I'd never seen him unravel like this. "Where were you two yesterday?"

He was interrogating me. I knew where he was going with this.

"You have to tell me, because I know she won't." His eyes grew red. "Tell me!"

I squinted and looked at him to make sure I had this right. He thought that Scarlett and I—me, the guy with a thing for cowboys and Uberman—were doing something we shouldn't have been doing behind his back. Then his rigid posture melted and his shoulders slumped. "If you two have something going on, just say it."

He had no idea. He didn't know a thing about what was really going on.

Then he grabbed me by the collar and stared at me with fierce eyes. "Okay, that's total bullshit," he said. "You tell her I won't give her up, certainly not to you. I'll fight for her. You hear me?"

Then a strong, tanned hand thrust a powder puff between us.

"Justice wants you on camera with the whole team," Uberman said, and nodded at the puff. "Here, you don't want to look too shiny."

Golden Boy and I looked up at him, and Uberman saw the red in Golden Boy's eyes. He disappeared for an instant, and then he was back with a tiny bottle of Visine.

"Allergies," Uberman said, loud enough for the reporters to hear. Then he leaned in and whispered, "We're all sad about it. It's okay to cry." He put his arm around both of us. "Thanks to you, there won't be any more tears." I held the powder puff in my hand, not really sure what to do with it.

"I'll help him with that." Ruth barged in and yanked me aside.

"Listen, just shut up for a minute and hear me out." She dabbed my face with the puff. "I've been trying to tell you since you got here, I saw something, just a quick glimpse forward, but it was clear. I think you know something. You're about to discover it, and it's something only you will know." She glanced down at her watch. "In a few minutes, it's about to happen." She smacked her watch a few times and shook it. "Or maybe it already did, damn this old thing."

"What's about to happen?" I asked.

"Christ, kid, I don't know. What am I, psychic? Just keep your eyes peeled."

Uberman escorted us to the podium, and I walked in a daze. Under normal circumstances, my entire body would have lit up the minute Uberman's perfectly toned arm met my perfectly willing shoulder, but this whole scenario was too strange. The world had suddenly flipped upside down and all around, and I couldn't think straight. I wondered about Ruth's warning, and if I'd already seen whatever it was and just didn't know it yet. I kept my eyes peeled, trying to get a clear shot of every face in the crowd as Uberman parted the sea of reporters and mourning teammates.

Justice descended from the sky. The cameras rolled and flashed and snapped. A hushed silence overcame the audience. Justice raised his head and addressed the room.

"I'm sorry to see everyone on such a tragic occasion." As Justice spoke, I huddled in line next to the rest of my squad. We stood behind Justice, so the lights from the cameras cast a harsh glare on us. The lights blinded me and the glare shot a sharp pain through my temples. No matter how hard I squinted, I couldn't see out into the crowd. I leaned a little to the left to hide my eyes behind Justice's shadow. "I think it's important to let everyone know that the Spectrum died a hero, and his death will not be in vain." He moved slightly to the right, and the light hit my eyes again. "Behind me you will see our newest group of recruits. These are the brave souls who apprehended the vicious criminal responsible for these heinous acts of vengeance on our greatest heroes."

As Justice droned on, I gave up trying to scan the crowd for something that I didn't even know I was looking for, and my mind drifted. Standing up onstage with those spotlights on us made me feel exposed. I tried to think of dark, soothing things to shield me from the lights, and my brain filled with images of black capes making shadows in the night. The images felt peaceful and cool.

I was sweating from the lights, so I bent my knees slightly to keep the circulation going in my legs. I didn't want to pass out in front of everybody.

My mind leaped forward in a stream of thoughts, and soon the capes swept away the darkness, and there stood Goran, basketball at his hip. Suddenly I knew for certain why it bothered me so much when he'd said he had a girlfriend, and it wasn't a thought I wanted to hold on to right then, with everything else going on. I tried to think of something else.

I had to clear my head, keep focused. So I thought about Scarlett.

I pictured her jacket. How she must have struggled those first few days with the colostomy bag, staring down at the hole in her belly, connected to a pouch of sterile plastic. How she'd probably stayed up all night trying to think of an outfit that would hide it properly. Looking at herself in the mirror, crying. Forgetting about it momentarily, only to look down at her belly and to be reminded that a synthetic leech had attached itself to her and wouldn't let go.

"Allow me to introduce you to the killer," Justice continued.

I snapped out of my daydream when I saw Justice gesture toward a curtain off to the side, which lifted to reveal Ssnake, via satellite, in the League's containment facility. He sat in a chair, his head hung low, a curly mop of messy blond hair. He reminded me more of one of those hostages you see in the Middle East than a supercriminal. I couldn't even tell if his eyes were open underneath his mask.

The cameras went wild, hundreds of hands shot in the air, and the reporters buzzed with questions. I took a step back and ducked behind Justice's shadow again.

"I won't be taking any questions today, but I will indulge you with one answer." Justice levitated a few more inches above ground. I couldn't tell if it was deliberate or if he was just getting worked up. "We will reveal the identity of the killer. There will be no more hiding today. Silver Bullet, if you would, please." He nodded to Silver Bullet, who disappeared in a shiny blur and reappeared next to Ssnake on the monitor.

Silver Bullet tore off Ssnake's mask, and ice shot through my body.

"Ladies and Gentlemen of the world, allow me to introduce you to the killer—Ssnake—Simon Hess." Silver Bullet lifted the man's face to camera level by tugging back on his pale blond hair.

I recognized him immediately, even with all the bruises.

How could I forget the face of the man who gave me my first kiss?

CHAPTER TWENTY-FOUR

THE FIRST THOUGHT that runs through your head at these critical junctures in life is usually neither logical nor wise. In this case, all I could think about was that he'd actually told me his real name. I had lied and told him my name was John that rainy, wet night in the church parking lot.

After that shame passed, a new one overwhelmed me. I felt worse than I'd ever felt in my life. On the one hand, I was scared to death that Ssnake would recognize me and talk. Guilt rolled through me and gained the momentum of an avalanche. He'd go down swinging, I'd be outed, and they'd kick me out of the League faster than I could say *homo*.

Belonging to this group was the only good thing in my life, and I was about to lose it all. My father would disown me, I'd be reviled by everyone I ever knew—forever linked to the notorious hero killer. The muscles in my legs shook, and I prayed I wouldn't pass out. The camera lights were cooking me up on that stage, and I desperately wanted to run off somewhere cool to get a glass of water.

Then again, maybe he wouldn't say anything. Maybe if I just avoided him. After all, it was *my* first kiss, not his. It couldn't have meant as much to him, and therefore there was a good chance he'd never connect my face to the goofy, nervous kid with the dry mouth in the church parking lot. Maybe all I had to do was wait this out. Keep quiet and it would all go away. Heck, he was an accused killer. Maybe he really did it. And if he didn't actually do this crime, surely there were other reprehensible acts in his past.

I was starting to breathe easy again.

The crowd went nuts with questions. Justice raised his hands to silence them. "Because of the nature of his alleged crimes and his threat to public safety, Ssnake will await trial in our containment facility, where we can safely keep him."

Ruth slipped beside me and gave me a nudge.

"You're white as a ghost. See anything yet?"

I couldn't breathe again. An idea was forming in my head, a seed sprouting tendrils that bored into my whole body, and suddenly I was terrified to move or do or say anything.

"Well, what is it?" Ruth whispered in my ear.

I couldn't think straight. Was this the big surprise, or was there something more?

Finally I blocked all my problems out of my head and thought about it clinically, logically, without emotion. I focused on Ssnake. Something wasn't right. Okay, so the guy I happened to have my first kiss with turned out to be the worst villain in the universe. Big deal. There was more at work here, and I needed to pull my head out of my ass if I was going to see it.

"That will be all for today." Justice wrapped things up at the podium. "I can assure you of this: these murders will not go unavenged."

I didn't like the way that last word sounded. *Unavenged.* A promise. I saw Warrior Woman grip her sword handle at her side and slide her hand down its sheath.

That couldn't mean anything good for Ssnake. What about, I don't know, a fair trial? Maybe it wouldn't be one of the heroes in this room to exact revenge, but someone would. Maybe it would be a convenient accident when he was transferred from the containment facility to the prison facility. Maybe they'd blame it on a disgruntled former colleague, frame Snaggletooth for it. Who would doubt it? I couldn't see the future, that was Ruth's department, but in my heart I knew that someone somewhere would make this man pay for assassinating two of our world's finest heroes, whether he'd actually done it or not.

Ruth's watch had stopped again, and I saw her smacking it as she tried to get it going. I stared at the watch, and that's when I realized what it was that didn't add up. The timing.

He couldn't have done it. I was *with* him the night King of the Sea was murdered. But then the horror sank in. What was I going to do with this information?

Telling the truth, the whole truth . . . could I do that? What if I pulled Justice aside? I'd be risking everything I ever worked for. They'd kick me off the team for sure. Jeez, what the hell would Uberman think of me? My team? Golden Boy already hated me, but did I need the rest of the League to hate me too? This would change my whole life forever. There would be no turning back.

And then the horror turned to something worse. Pure panic.

What would my father think?

I looked over at Ruth, hoping she'd seen the future and could tell me what to do next. I held up my hands to shield the light, and closed me eyes. I wasn't going to turn to anyone else. This was all up to me.

Once in a while, life gives you a chance to measure your worth. Sometimes you're called upon to make a split-second decision to do the right thing, defining which way your life will go. These are the decisions that make you who you are.

I felt a surge of energy well up from my feet, through my heart, to my head. I willed myself to take one step forward. That first step was the hardest. I felt like my feet were glued to the floor. But after that first step, I walked with a little more assurance, and the next thing I knew I was at the podium next to Justice.

I grabbed the microphone.

"I'm sorry," I said into the microphone. "But you have the wrong man."

Stunned silence as I looked out into the audience, the heat of the lights bearing down on me.

"It couldn't have been Mr. Hess, at least not for the King of the Sea murder. I know it for a fact—" I paused and felt the heat of the lights bearing down on me. I knew this was the moment my life would take a turn forever. I pushed thoughts of everyone else out of my head—the League, my teammates, Goran, my mother . . . Dad—and I took the plunge. "Because I was with him that night."

A tidal wave of response from the press hit me. If they'd been wild with activity before, this was a full-on feeding frenzy.

Silver Bullet whisked me away into the pantry before I could open my mouth to respond. He looked at me like I'd been possessed by Dr. Psycho. He scooted a metal chair underneath me; the chair knocked the back of my knees and I collapsed in the seat.

Warrior Woman appeared moments later.

"That little stunt is going to cost you," she said, and reached for the golden scepter fastened to her belt.

Silver Bullet stopped her from raising the scepter.

"What the hell was that?" he said.

I knew they didn't want to hear it, but I was just telling the truth. They did have the wrong guy, and I couldn't let him suffer for something he didn't do. Besides, it meant the real culprit was still out there. Didn't they care about that?

By now, the rest of the League was crowding into the pantry. Arms folded, they stared at me from below the shelves of cereals and canned goods. Warrior Woman scowled at me beside a can of chunky soup.

"What I'm asking is what did you mean by that? What do you mean *You were with him that night?*" Silver Bullet demanded. But these were rhetorical questions. They all knew exactly what I'd meant. In fact, their minds had already taken it much further than the botched kiss it actually was. But to protest their assumptions would only make it look like I'd done more than I really had, so I decided to keep my mouth shut about the details.

Next came a battery of questions, rapid-fire. Where was I that night when it happened? Why was I with him? How was I so sure of the time? Could someone else vouch for my whereabouts? That last one threw me a little. As if my word alone weren't good enough. Simon would be able to confirm it, and I told them so. Dark Hero would probably be able to confirm it, too, but I thought it wasn't such a hot idea to bring him up right then.

Uberman stepped forward from a wall of Jell-O cartons.

"Is it true, Thom?"

He spread out his arms as if he were ready to embrace a new explanation, anything but this truth right in front of them. He wore disappointment like he did every other emotion, handsome and strong. I wanted to revoke what I'd said somehow, say anything else to please him.

But I was done with lying. I was scared about the future, but it felt nice to breathe. I nodded and folded my hands in my lap and stared down at the floor.

I waited in the pantry for nearly four hours while the League questioned the rest of my squad. I was looking around at the bright-colored packages of processed foods when it finally struck me that I'd been imprisoned. I didn't like that thought at all. This wasn't the high-tech containment chamber on the third level designed by Brainzoid and the Machine-Meister, I had to remind myself. These were just cans of SpaghettiOs, not walls of deadly laser beams. My legs were crossed because I'd had to take a leak for the last half hour and I didn't want to get up. I think I was afraid that I'd find out some hero had been posted outside the door to keep watch over me, to make sure I didn't run. I didn't want to be reminded that they'd lost that much faith in me, so I rocked back and forth and tried as hard as I could not to think of waterfalls.

What I did think about was that my confession was probably all over the news by now, already whittled down to a perfect ten-second sound bite. I wondered if the news had reached Dad at the factory. They had a TV in the cafeteria, something his union had fought for that summer they were on strike. I wasn't naive enough to believe he had any friends at work, but I wondered if maybe one guy respected him enough to pull him aside to explain that his son was all over the news.

It was more likely, however, that he'd notice the entire floor whispering and looking at him. At first he'd check to make sure his fly wasn't open. Then he'd take his meal break alone, as always, and eat the turkey sandwich he'd made for himself in our kitchen that morning, and he'd glance up at the news while chewing, because damned if that face on CNN didn't look exactly like his son's. A few jerks at a nearby table would snicker at him as he stood up and watched the news, open-jawed.

The door to the pantry opened, and the first-string Leaguers streamed back in. I'd never seen Uberman look tired, but now there were bags under his eyes.

"The press is finally gone." He leaned against the doorway. "I did the best I could with them," he said, and then looked at me. "Given the circumstances."

Warrior Woman gave me the eye. "Your teammates could neither confirm nor deny," she said. "And what about your missing teammate? Miss Scarlett—where did you take her this morning, and where is she now?"

God, not this again. That was Scarlett's business, and I wasn't about to get into it. Warrior Woman saw me roll my eyes.

"You'll have to ask her," I said.

Warrior Woman turned red. "You will not make a mockery of this. I asked you a question!" She started for me, and I was sure she was going to pick me up by the neck and shake the answer out of me.

Suddenly, a pair of feet poked through the ceiling above us. Justice phased through the floor and floated down between us, calmly, quietly.

"That will do," he said.

Warrior Woman backed off. Justice studied me for a while, deciding what to say. He circled the room again and again, and I thought about how much he reminded me of Dad. Any second now he could explode.

But then he helped me to my feet and walked me out of the room.

"How long have we kept you waiting in here?"

Justice floated beside me as I walked down the hall. He asked that I accept his apology on behalf of the team for keeping me holed up in the pantry like a criminal. He explained that even though they'd been defenders of the galaxy for more than twenty-five years now, they still encountered a few situations that weren't in the manual. I told him I understood.

I kept waiting for his disapproval, but it never materialized.

"I'm sorry if you feel judged, Thom. I wouldn't do that to you."

He surprised me. I'd been sure he'd kick me out, right then and there. I'd figured he'd put the right spin on it, but I'd know it was because the League didn't know what to do with me anymore. I'd made them . . . uncomfortable.

His feet touched the ground and he walked alongside me. "I know what it's like for people to distrust you because of your differences, Thom. That happens when you're from outer space, too."

I thought about us sipping ginger ale that night we stared out into the stars as he longed for his home world.

"Of course, your revelation today does raise an interesting question. If Ssnake didn't do it," Justice said, "then who did?"

In those hours I'd sat in that pantry and worried about my future, the thought hadn't even crossed my mind.

"Where has your father been lately?" he asked.

What did he mean by that? Was he worried about my father's reaction? Or was there something more he was searching for?

"I'm sorry to raise the question about your father's whereabouts. I know you two will have enough to talk about after today." He placed his hand on my shoulder.

"I understand what it's like to be different." He stared out the window at the stars in the sky.

Maybe his time on our planet had opened his mind. Maybe I'd been the one who misjudged him.

I knew I couldn't stay inside the League headquarters forever. I'd made a decision up at the podium today that would affect the rest of my life, and there was no point in hiding from it any longer.

"Can I go home?" I asked.

I found Ruth and Larry smoking cigarettes in the parking lot beside her car. Larry coughed on his.

"Where's Golden Boy?" I asked.

Ruth shrugged. "I think he went looking for Scarlett. "

An awkward moment ensued as we stood in a huddle.

"You just had to say something, didn't you?" Larry finally said. Then he sighed. "I'm sorry. You did the right thing, I know. It's just that—" He kicked Ruth's tire. "We were so close this time, I could taste it!" Ruth and I stayed quiet. We let him have his outburst, recognized the need to vent. "We were so close, you know?"

I knew.

Larry said to call if I needed anything. He didn't seem to care about which team I was batting for. It made me feel that much worse that I'd robbed the guy who'd always been the poor sickly kid his first chance of being a real hero.

"Here, this'll help you sleep." He slipped a Xanax in my palm when he shook my hand good-bye.

Ruth offered me a ride home, but I told her I was going to take the bus. I needed to be alone for a while. I needed to think about what was coming next.

CHAPTER TWENTY-FIVE

IF DAD HADN'T FOUND out while he was at work, he'd certainly figured it out when he got home. With our ratty old scrub brush and a dented metal pail, he was trying to wash the spray paint off the garage door. So far he'd only managed to blur the letter F in FAGGOT. Smudged, it looked more like an "E." A minivan drove by our house and I pictured the kid in the backseat: "Mommy, what's an 'Eaggot'?"

Dad stopped scrubbing as soon as I walked up the driveway, but he didn't turn around. I stood behind him for a long while. What was I supposed to say?

A lump caught in my throat every time I tried to say even a word. I knew this wouldn't be easy, but I wasn't prepared for what he did next.

He stood up with the bucket, swung it above his head, and

slammed it into the driveway with such force that the metal pail shattered into bits.

He walked inside, both his good and bad hands shaking. I noticed a deep cut on his good hand. I couldn't tell if it was from the pail shattering, or maybe he'd cut it at work, fixing a faulty gear or crank, or maybe I didn't want to know where the gash came from.

He couldn't even look at me.

My chest felt hollow. I didn't think I could ever feel worse.

I looked down at my shirt, stained with the sudsy paint lather sprayed from the bucket. I gave Dad a few minutes and then I crept inside, careful not to make a noise.

All I could think about in that moment was to get clean. I took my stained shirt off in the laundry room and dropped it in the washing machine with Dad's foreman uniform. He hadn't run it yet, so I filled a cup with dry detergent. I looked in the washing machine and was puzzled by what I saw.

I pulled out his uniform and took a closer look. It was perfectly clean.

I stared at the tiny pebbles of detergent caught in the crisp folds of the uniform and wondered why he was going to such great lengths to make me think he'd been wearing it. And the cut on his hand—it would have been a common enough injury when he was working the lines, but not now that he was a foreman. He was lying to me about something.

I remembered what Justice had asked me, and I stared at the uniform for an answer.

Where has your father been lately?

* * *

Ruth called and offered me the couch at her place, and I would have been happy to accept the invitation. Dad hadn't exactly left suitcases in my room as a hint, but obviously he would be happier not to see me for a while. Still, I turned down her offer. I told Ruth I wasn't going to run. I was done with hiding who I was—that was the old me.

I lay on my bed and fought off the urge to cry. I watched the moon move above the horizon and thought long and hard about what my life would be like from now on. Anyone I'd meet would know me from the news—would know my biggest secret. It would taint everything, from going to school, to picking up food at the grocery store, to getting a job. I'd experienced a taste of the public's disdain from watching Dad over the years, but I had a feeling that wouldn't hold a candle to being the target of contempt myself.

Finally I willed myself to head for the attic to get my suitcase. Maybe I wasn't as brave as I thought. Maybe Mom had the right idea about running away, after all. I walked down the hall, and I was certain Dad would be able to hear me move across the floorboards. His door was closed, his light off. I stopped in front of the door and raised my hand to knock.

I wanted to talk to him so bad, to hear him tell me it was all going to be okay, that he knew what it was like to have everyone think so poorly of you, but that life goes on, and there are good things ahead. I wanted him to split a beer with me and talk about it. It was probably way too soon, but he had to know his son was suffering, that I needed him more than anything else.

Against my better judgment, I knocked. I waited a beat

and held my ear to the space at the bottom of the door. With one ear on the fuzzy carpet, I listened. I felt cool air from the fan against my ear as it poured out from the other side. A couple of seconds went by, and I told myself he was probably just thinking about the right thing to say. Then a minute went by, and still no response. I thought maybe I'd knocked too lightly, maybe he hadn't heard it, so I knocked again. Nothing.

Still no response. Hell, maybe he wasn't even in there. I could have checked the driveway for his car, but I didn't. Instead I reached up and yanked the cord dangling from the ceiling and pulled down the stairs to the attic. I climbed up the rickety wooden steps, the springs groaning under my weight. I grabbed a dusty suitcase.

Back in my room I unzipped the suitcase on my bed and started to pack. I stuffed my socks in the corners of the case, a space-saving technique Dad had taught me. Suddenly I felt cold and dug around for a sweatshirt to put on. Then I realized that the window was wide open. This struck me as strange because I was almost positive that I hadn't opened it.

The air from outside was chilly and fresh. I took a deep breath and it smelled good, like the garden my mom used to keep. It reminded me of helping her pick weeds in the summers.

The gardenia bush was Mom's favorite, and she taught me to take special care of it. On warm summer days, I still had vivid memories of lying on the carpet in the family room, the fresh-cut gardenias floating in tiny glass bowls of water, their scent wafting into my nostrils. The smell always made me sleepy, at peace, and some days Dad would come home from work and stop short of tripping over me in a deep sleep on the floor.

The first time I'd been old enough to save enough money from doing chores around the house and yard, I bought my mother a special birthday gift, a vial of drugstore perfume, gardenia scented. Mom unwrapped the lumpy paper, delighted at what she saw. (I think Dad had given her a waffle iron that year.) She hugged me and wrapped her pinky around mine, our secret shake. She sprayed a thin mist into the air and stepped through it. She'd worn only that brand ever since.

"Thom?"

I turned around and thought I was imagining things. Maybe I'd finally lost it. I'd been through so much that day, it wouldn't have been such a stretch to start hallucinating. I couldn't remember when I'd last had something to eat or drink.

I turned back to the suitcase and began laying my underwear in neatly stacked piles.

"Thom?" the voice called again.

This time I knew I wasn't hallucinating. I felt her hand on my cheek. I knew that voice. And I knew the smell of that perfume.

"Mom?"

CHAPTER TWENTY-SIX

WHAT A BABY, I kept thinking to myself, but I didn't really care. I couldn't stop crying. Mom held on to me tight, and I kept my eyes closed, my head resting on her shoulder as I sobbed quietly. She stroked my hair and kept telling me in soothing tones that everything would be okay.

If I'd been thinking straight, I would have launched into the hundreds of questions I had always planned to ask in the event I ever saw her again. The questions suddenly seemed silly and stupid, and the only thing that mattered was that I felt her right there in front of me.

Even if I couldn't see her.

"Mom." I caught my breath. "Can't you, you know, turn it off for a minute?"

I felt Mom pull away, and I heard the floorboards creak

over by the window. I saw a spark by the floorboards, and then I watched a match light itself in the air. The tiny flame met with a cigarette floating beside it. I saw a stream of smoke coming out of where her mouth would be, but I still couldn't see her.

"I missed you," she said.

There was something sad about the way she said it.

"I found the pictures," I said, proud of my discovery. I wondered if it was possible to hear someone smile.

"I know," she said, and another stream of smoke shot down, this time I figured through her nostrils. "I've been watching you."

Of course she knew. Mothers know everything. But it did make me wonder exactly how she knew. I remembered the night Justice had told me he'd known Mom, that she'd been a crucial member of the League's espionage squad. She probably knew lots of things. She'd probably seen me on the news.

"How long have you been watching me?"

"Don't worry about that right now, it's not important." She said it quickly, like she'd been ready for the question and had no intention of giving me the real answer.

"Mom?" There were so many things to ask, but I started with one question. "Where have you been?"

I heard the distinct sound of ice cubes clank and tinkle against a glass. Then I turned and saw a glass filled with brown liquid floating in the air. I sniffed and noticed the faint aroma of Scotch and soda on top of the gardenias and cigarette smoke.

I think Mom saw me sniff at the air. An old electric fan floated out of the closet, perched itself on the window ledge, plugged itself into the socket, and clicked on to blow the smoke out the window.

"Promise me one thing, Thom," she said. Then I felt her heavy breath on my neck as she whispered the one thing. "Promise you won't judge me."

I thought about that for a while and decided she was right. She had her reasons for leaving, and even if they didn't sound great to me, I shouldn't judge her. Hard as it was to put into practice, that much I'd learned.

"Dad's asleep," I said. "You want me to wake him up?" I walked over to the door to go get him.

"No, no, no," she said. "Don't do that."

I stopped with my fingers on the doorknob. I turned around and faced the open window, the fan whirring on its ledge.

"Why did you leave?"

Okay, maybe I wasn't done with the questions yet.

Mom didn't say anything right away. This was a question I was sure she had expected, so I knew she must have had some sort of answer rehearsed. Why the hesitation? Was she cooking up something else? Was she considering telling me from her heart, not from a scripted explanation?

"Meet me tomorrow," she said, "at the Wilson Memorial."

A glass of water floated into my hand, and I saw the pill Larry had given me resting on the windowsill. How long, exactly, had she been following me?

Then I felt a kiss on my cheek, and just like that, the fan clicked off and I knew the time to ask questions was over. She was gone.

CHAPTER TWENTY-SEVEN

THE NEXT MORNING I put on a baseball cap and pulled it down to eye level before I got on the bus. The last place on earth I wanted to be recognized was at the Wilson Memorial.

Especially after what I'd found when I stepped out of the front door. Our yard had been rolled. Long streamers of toilet paper dipped and swayed in the breeze, which made our tree look like a synthetic weeping willow. I was in such a hurry that I stepped on the morning paper, which turned out to have a big ol' picture of me on the front page making my confession. In a small corner was an old, extremely unattractive picture of my father. It was shot lit from below, giving him the sinister look of a kid shining a flashlight under his chin while telling a ghost story.

What bothered me the most, though, was the certified overnight delivery envelope that I found wedged in the screen door. The return address said it was from the League's human resources department. My heart sank. I tucked it under my arm, unopened, and ran to the bus.

I arrived shortly before the 10:15 tour, and the girl in the ticket booth sneezed on my tickets as she handed them to me. I wasn't thinking when I bought two tickets. Invisible people usually get in for free.

I sat on a bench and looked for a sign of Mom, but I didn't notice anything. Two teenage girls sat down beside me and spilled a bag of M&M's out into their laps and began separating them by color while they gossiped.

I looked at the envelope in my hands, rubbed my fingers around the sharp corners, and wished it would just disappear. But I'd decided I was tired of running away from things, so I bit down and tore open the pouch with my teeth.

One of the girls did a double take when she noticed me.

"Hey," she said. "Aren't you—"

Then she stopped like she'd lost her train of thought, and popped a green M&M in her mouth as if it would help jog her memory.

God, this is exactly what I wanted to avoid. I tried to pull my cap even lower, but it couldn't swallow my face. Where was Mom?

Inside the pouch was a notarized letter from the League's human resources director, with their legal counsel copied at the bottom of the page. The letter was short but not sweet. It was notice of my termination from the League's probationary team. I folded it carefully, slipped it into my back pocket, and tried not to think about it.

"Aren't you in my English class?" the girl said through a mouthful of M&M's, chocolate and colorful candy bits stuck between her teeth.

"No," I said.

I got up and asked the girl at the ticket counter when the tour was supposed to begin. She pointed to a group that had already started toward the entrance of the site and told me I'd been waiting with the wrong group. I rushed over and positioned myself on the outskirts of the group.

"Excuse me? You, in the back, do you have a ticket?" the tour guide asked.

I pulled both tickets out of my pocket and held them in the air for her to see.

"Marvelous," she said. "Now, if you'll follow me. Please remember, there's no smoking, chewing gum, or food or beverages of any kind allowed. You'll notice a number of people here paying respects, so please keep your voices down and your cell phones off, thank you."

She smiled tightly through bleached teeth. "This is, after all, a shrine to the dead."

We passed by three students who were meditating by the entrance. They'd pasted together a banner that read NEVER FORGET out of death certificates and held it spread out between them. I was the last to go inside, and I was careful not to let my foot catch on one of their candles as I stepped past them.

"Built in the early seventies," the tour guide began, "the Wilson Tower became the tallest building in the world, and stood as a monument to technological advancement and economic prosperity."

I was bored already. I'd come here on a field trip once when I was in the fourth grade. After the rambunctious hour-long bus ride into the city, our class quickly discovered this tour was anything but fun. I remember it even made Angel Stanton, the toughest girl in our class, cry because she'd lost her aunt in the tragedy. Before the trip, I'd been afraid to show my dad the permission slip because of where we were going, so I forged it myself. I wished I'd stayed home from school.

We entered the Corridor of Names, a well-intentioned but tacky holographic memorial that listed the names of all the innocent people who'd perished that day. I stood there and felt conspicuously lit up, the glow of the names reflected off my face.

"We lost approximately nineteen thousand citizens that day, perhaps more." The tour guide gestured to the lists upon lists with a flick of her wrist. "It was impossible to tell, given the degree of devastation."

"What'd I miss?" my mother whispered in my ear.

"Where have you been?"

A family of tourists with matching oversize T-shirts and fanny packs that read THE EVIL SHALL BE PUNISHED turned around and glared at me. The mother of the group held her finger to her lips and hissed, "SHHHH!"

The tour guide continued walking, and I hung a few lengths back with Mom so we could talk.

"Look at this place," Mom said. "They keep it like a tomb. No air."

Well, I thought, a whole load of people tragically died

here. At least it wasn't a McDonald's or a Wal-Mart. Yet. I heard the tour guide's voice echo down the tunnel, and both Mom and I stopped on her words: "Major Might."

"Sounds like the tour is just about to get interesting," Mom said. I saw the strike of a match and then I smelled cigarette smoke.

"You're not supposed to smoke in here," I reminded her.

"Who's going to see?"

"They'll smell it and think it's me."

I saw her take a sip of something out of a flask. What was she drinking? Suddenly it really annoyed me that she wasn't visible.

"Mom, why won't you let me see you?"

I heard her take another swallow. "It's not that simple."

"Sure it is, just make yourself visible."

I heard another gulp. That flask must have been endless. Maybe there were two.

"I can't," she snapped at me. Then she changed her tone back to the one I remembered. "Let's catch up with the tour, I want to show you something."

She took hold of my hand and led me forward. "Besides, we don't want to miss the part where they start trashing your father."

We caught up with the tour a couple of flights up in the memorial tower, built after the tragedy in a space directly across from the site, so you could still see the crack in the earth where the top half of the Wilson Tower had landed.

"As a result of Major Might's failure," the tour guide said, "the government drafted the ban on non-superpowered champions, which outlawed so-called 'heroic' acts by people like Major Might, who lacked the necessary powers. If it hadn't been for the major's hubris that day, some argue we could have averted all casualties entirely. Can anyone tell me in which branch of the U.S. military Major Might earned the rank of major?"

Silence from the audience.

I wanted to raise my hand. Dad was in the army, and he won a Bronze Star for Valor the night his camp in Vietnam was overrun, and he was only my age at the time.

Some goober with a trucker's hat affixed just so over his two hundred dollar haircut raised his hand and took a stab. "Coast Guard?"

What an idiot.

"No," the tour guide responded slowly. She relished the chance to play teacher.

The youngest kid from the fanny-pack family stuck her plump ham hock high into the air.

"The Boy Scouts!"

Her family snickered at such a cute response. I didn't think she meant it to be cute. I think she was just plain dumb.

I felt Mom let go of my hand, and someone smacked the top of the chubby little girl's head.

"Ow!" She turned around and scowled at her brother. "Mom, he hit me!"

"No, I didn't," her brother squealed.

Their mother admonished the brother despite his declarations of innocence. When he wouldn't shut up about it, she finally had to slip him a Twinkie while the tour guide wasn't looking.

"No, not the Boy Scouts, silly," the tour guide said. "You may find it interesting to know that his wasn't a military rank at all; his rank was *self-appointed*." She raised her eyebrows and dragged out those last two words, as if to say, Yep, you heard it here first.

"That's not true," I said. What about the war? What about the Bronze Star? "He was in Vietnam."

Mom squeezed my hand. The crowd whipped around and stared at me like I was a lunatic.

The tour guide sneered; she wasn't used to being challenged. "Actually, although he did serve a tour of duty in the army," she continued, "he was only a sergeant. *Major* Might was a moniker he gave himself before he'd ever joined the armed forces." She gave me a look of false sympathy, like it was a nice but pathetic attempt to correct her.

Well, no shit, he made it up—it was just a name. That's what people did when they became superheroes. They gave themselves catchy names bigger than life, to intimidate criminals into thinking twice before they robbed that liquor store or snatched a purse. What about Captain Victory? He'd been in the navy in World War II, but he was never a captain. Was this woman also going to attack Captain Kangaroo? What about Cap'n Crunch?

"Some people find it a little offensive," she said in a loud whisper in my direction to rub salt in the wound. "It's not exactly the best way to honor those in the military who put their lives on the line every day so that we may enjoy freedom."

Who actually talks like that? Yet most people in the crowd nodded along with her and agreed. The fanny-pack father looked at me and shook his head, his disapproval of Dad aimed clearly at me. I wonder what they would have done if they'd recognized me from the news, if they'd known I was his son. Burned me at the stake and sung the National Anthem?

Mom pulled me back as they started up the next flight of stairs.

"Let it go," she said in a reassuring tone. "We have bigger fish to fry."

I had to listen to that tour guide drone on for another two hours as we wound our way up the tower, before my mother finally pulled me aside and told me to crouch down and pretend like I was tying my shoe.

"Why should I do that?" I whispered.

"So the guide won't see you, and if anyone turns around, they won't get suspicious."

"Suspicious of what?"

She knocked me over and rolled me through a door into the emergency stairwell, which ran hidden, parallel to the main staircase.

"Let's go," she said, and I felt her grab my hand.

We climbed down what must have been at least twenty flights, then down again, into the catacombs below the memorial. I couldn't see anything, but Mom seemed to know the way. For a time, Mom's hand separated from mine, so I followed the sound of her voice in the darkness.

"It wasn't his fault, you know," she said. "The way he chose to handle it, that was his fault. But the event itself, he did the

{ 295 }

best he could with an awful situation. History forgets that part. Watch your step."

We stepped up and into a new corridor.

"You can't believe everything everyone tells you. Sometimes you just have to trust your gut. Do you honestly think your father would have needlessly risked all those lives just because he thought he was powerful enough to defeat that creature on his own?"

Of course I didn't think that. I always believed the best of Dad. It was the rest of the world who couldn't see him the way I did.

"You want a bottled water? You look thirsty." Mom handed me a plastic bottle of water. I felt for the cap, twisted it off, and took a gulp; the cool liquid felt good as it sloshed down my throat.

"The two things I've learned to hate most after all the years on this job are magic and outer space. Never did understand a damn thing about either of them. That goes triple for time travel."

We continued on through the corridor. Maybe my eyes were playing tricks on me, but it was getting lighter.

"Your father, though, nothing ever intimidated him. He was on the scene before anyone else in the League had a chance to respond. Even before Justice."

"Where were you?" I asked.

Mom stumbled slightly over a step, and I saw her catch her flask.

"Justice had me on assignment." Then she added softly, "Justice had me on a lot of assignments."

"Meaning what?" I wanted to know.

"That," she said in between drags, "is a story for another time."

I tripped over the same step that made her stumble and stubbed my toe. I gritted my teeth and tried not to care.

"This is it," Mom said, and flung open a door. "Cover your eyes."

My eyes immediately hurt. I squinted, but still it was impossibly bright. Shafts of light shot up through the cracks between the floorboards and pierced the darkness all around us.

"What is it?"

A crowbar floated over to the corner, and I saw that we were in what looked like the biggest basement I'd ever seen. It went on so far in one direction that I couldn't even see where it ended.

"This was the concourse level of the tower," Mom sighed. The crowbar dug into one of the floorboards and pried it up. Brilliant light burst forth into the room, and I shielded my eyes. "This is what's left of that creature after it tried to go super-nova. Crystal."

It was beautiful. I couldn't understand why anyone would cover it up, keep it hidden underground.

"Here, give me a hand while I tell you a story." The crowbar presented itself to me, and I grabbed it. I looked down at the floor for a good spot to pry open.

"Go ahead. Don't be gentle." I felt Mom's hands grasp mine, and she plunged the crowbar into the floor and showed me how to give it a good yank. The boards were surprisingly ramshackle and brittle, not as strong as they looked, like someone had been more concerned with getting it covered up fast than covered up well.

Another crowbar appeared, and Mom began working beside me.

"The first time I met your father I was in complete awe. I didn't even think I could bring myself to say hello. All I could think of was that he was so much more handsome in person than he was in the newspapers.

"After a few months on the probationary squad, one day I gathered up the nerve to ask him to help me with my hand-to-hand combat training. No, actually, I just worked up the nerve to say yes when he offered to teach me. I'd had my ass handed to me when I'd tried to stop an attempted break-in at Fort Knox by some two-bit hood that wore a glorified doggie costume and went by the name Anubis the Jackal. Unfortunately for me, his bark wasn't worse than his bite. Your father showed up with the rest of the League before the guy could do any permanent damage to me, but I was pretty beat up. I'll never forget the drubbing your father gave that man. Captain Victory had to pull him off the mongrel.

"I spent a week in the hospital, and your father came to visit me every day and read me the minutes from the League meetings I'd missed. He offered to teach me to defend myself better, and I knew I needed the help if I wanted to make the big time. He'd been generous the same way with Right Wing when Right Wing was his sidekick, always showing him ways to make himself better, not to rely solely on his powers. Honestly, I don't know where your father found the time, but he always made a point to be there for anyone who needed him.

"So he made time for me, a second-stringer. We began a daily routine, staying late after League meetings every night when he'd teach me how to work the punching bag."

I thought about Goran. I'd never had much of a right hook until he showed me how to push off with my back foot.

"I started to get pretty good. In a few weeks, I could beat the stuffing out of that bag. It did not go unnoticed that I was better in my fights with supervillains, too. I moved up the ranks, and your father kept practicing with me after the rest of the Leaguers had gone home. One night, later than usual, he told me it was time to learn to kickbox. He said I had great power in my legs and could do more damage with a kick than with a punch, and he didn't want to see me ending up on the wrong side of a fight with someone like Anubis ever again. At first I thought this was criticism of my punching skills from the master, but it was really something else. I figured out later that your father lived in mortal fear that something bad would happen to me. So kickboxing was the next answer to the question of my safety in the field.

"I didn't take to it at first. In fact, the first few times I tried to kick the bag, I was so shy that I stayed invisible. I didn't want to look stupid in front of him, especially with my legs splayed out in different directions. You have to understand, Thom, I'd had a deep crush on this man for a very long time."

I understood what it was like to have those feelings for someone. If she'd stuck around the past few years, maybe she would have known just how much I understood.

"Your father asked me, very politely, to make myself visible so he could see me to make sure I was doing it right. I became so self-conscious with him watching me that when I tried the kick, visible, I completely missed the bag. I lost my balance, and instead of connecting with the bag, I kicked him in the gut, knocked him to the ground, and fell over on top of him.

"I was so embarrassed I thought I'd die. But he didn't laugh at me. He was careful with my feelings back then, really kind. I was so mortified that instead of getting up off of him, I just lay there frozen. My hands were still resting on his chest, and I must have had this look on my face like a little girl who'd been caught with a broken cookie jar she'd knocked off the counter. He gently placed his hands around my wrists—your father had such strong, smooth hands—and asked me if I needed help getting up. I couldn't move, I was utterly enthralled. When it became clear that I didn't have the where-withal to pull away from him, he leaned up, his face inches away from mine. And then he kissed me."

I found myself wishing that I'd asked Goran to show me how to kickbox back when we still worked out together. I wondered if I'd ever have the chance to see him again.

"Are you listening, Thom?"

"Yes." I stopped thinking about Goran and pulled up another board.

"So our late-night workouts turned into dates. We'd work out, clean up, then go out to a midnight movie or dinner at some quiet café, where no one would see us. We kept our relationship a secret from the rest of the team for as long as we could. This was my request, not his. No one would take me seriously as a hero, I thought, if they knew what was really going on. Plus, I didn't want people to think I was trying to sleep my way to a top spot on the League. Do you remember Velvet Vixen? No, of course you don't, you're too young. Well, she was a real slut, and I didn't want anyone thinking I was easy like her.

"And we were still taking the training very seriously. The more your father grew to care for me, the more he cranked up our workout sessions. We did a pretty good job keeping our relationship under wraps, but it became a problem sometimes during fights. He literally wouldn't let me out of his sight, he was so protective of me. God knows how he could see me, but somehow he always knew where I was. Some of the Leaguers began to notice that he was often out of position during combat. Right Wing especially: he even brought it up in a meeting.

"We couldn't keep it a secret forever, now could we? One night, Justice—sorry, Right Wing—walked into the gym. I'll never forget the look on his face. Your father and I were kissing—your father's back to the door, and mine against the punching bag. I was the first to see him. Then he started at your father.

"'I was wondering why you weren't training with me anymore,' he said. Our eyes locked—mine and Right Wing's—and I saw something in his eyes. Betrayal. Your father turned around and hurried over to explain. More for me than for him. I don't think he thought it was any of his sidekick's business who he decided to fall in love with. And I was right: Right Wing did feel betrayed. But not by your father. Neither of us found out about that part until later.

"Before long your father convinced me that we should come clean with the League. He made a smiling announcement in front of the members that after years of my refusing his advances, he'd finally worn me down. Your father could still charm the socks off of any group back then, and nearly everyone in the League was nothing but happy for us. But there was strain. Between your father and his sidekick. They no longer trained together, no longer sat together at League functions; they didn't even go out on patrol at night anymore. Right Wing made up excuses at first, but then he just stopped showing up entirely.

"Captain Victory assured us that this was all natural. He pointed out that your father had done the very same thing—pulled away from him—when he was ready to move on from sidekick to a full-fledged hero in his own right. So your dad let Wing have his space. Which gave him more time for me. This is all going somewhere, don't worry."

"I'm not." I wanted to know where I came from.

"I wanted your father to ask me to marry him so bad. We'd been together for over a year, and we'd started to talk about marriage, what it would mean for us to build a life together. He resisted the idea at first. Not because he didn't love me. I thought he wanted the tension with Right Wing to die down first, but then I realized there was more to it than that."

Mom stopped talking. I looked up from the boards, in the direction where her voice had been. I knew that pause of hers. It meant she was looking at me.

"Children," she said. "He was thinking about our children, and what it would mean for two heroes to raise a family. You don't have to be Einstein to do the math from there. We weren't your average couple. One of us would have to retire. You can guess who was the logical choice."

Yeah, I could guess. Dad was old-fashioned in so many ways. Mom knew what I was thinking.

"Your father was never sexist, mind you. Quite the opposite, in fact. He'd been the first to throw his support behind the idea of letting women enter the League. That was a big deal back in his era. And he wasn't just thinking of the ones who wore fishnet tights as part of their costumes, either.

"Our discussion about the future was more about what our commitment to a family would mean. And there wasn't much question about which one of us would step down. Your father was the world's biggest hero. I was still second rate at best.

"Second rate?" I asked, somewhat defensive. She didn't sound second rate to me.

"Oh, I found out I'm good at *lots* of things the League isn't capable of, don't you worry."

Was she grinning? It's hard to tell when your mother is invisible.

"But don't get me wrong, I was thrilled to step down. I had gotten what I wanted: your father.

"Once we talked the family part through, we started talking nuts and bolts. When and where to get married, where to live. But there was one thing your father wanted to save as a surprise for me.

"Lift with your knees, Thom, not your back."

I bent my knees and not my back and yanked up another floorboard, letting more light into the room. "What didn't he want you to know?"

"The proposal. He wanted to keep that part a surprise. He was a hopeless romantic, your father. You'd never know it now."

But I did know it. She left—I stayed, and I knew. He kept all of her clothes in the closet, just as she had them. He even dry-cleaned them once a year so they'd be fresh, in case she ever came back. He didn't know that I knew this, but I'd learned from him to see what people didn't want you to see. I saw him at night sometimes, looking out into the backyard through the window over the kitchen sink, watching tree branches blow in the breeze, the wind rustle the sheets on the hanging line, hoping it was Mom slipping back to the house, finally returning home.

"How'd Dad do it?" I waited for an answer. "Mom?"

"Sorry, honey, I was just thinking. I've been wondering the best way to tell you this part. Bear with me, okay?" I heard her take a long drag of her cigarette. "When you can turn invisible, you learn that nothing is as it appears.

"Right Wing had the bright idea of holding a celebration for his promotion at his adoptive parents' farm in Kansas, so that people could see that even heroes from another quadrant of the universe have parents just like everyone else. He could always come up with a masterstroke of public relations in a pinch, and he was still a little uncomfortable that some viewed him as an alien."

Mom ripped up two floorboards in one swift yank and continued. "We followed the balloons on the signposts and turned down dirt road after dirt road until we finally came to the farm. We drove under a welcome banner to park in the field. Your father grabbed my hand and we began the long walk down the path to the farm where Right Wing's parents had adopted and raised him, ever since he'd crash-landed on our planet so many years ago.

"Your father picked a handful of wildflowers for me along the way—he loved to do goofy stuff like that—and he opened the gate to the front yard for me. I had no idea what was waiting for us inside.

"After we'd devoured a pig on a spit and mounds of potato salad, we settled down for cake, and washed it down with that God-awful punch made out of ginger ale and sherbet. Captain Victory got up on a platform and thanked Ma and Pa Wing for welcoming us to their modest dwelling for such a momentous occasion. That little town had never seen so much press, but there they were, right on the farm, ready for the big announcement.

"So Captain Victory introduced your father, who gave a very moving speech about his sidekick, the plucky young Right Wing, who'd been training hard and developing a whole new host of superpowers that had manifested themselves once the kid had reached adulthood. 'At his age,' Hal said, 'most of us are just starting to shave. But this kid has to orbit the planet at least once a day for the sun to recharge his battery.' The crowd laughed. Corny jokes were the hallmark of most League events. At this point, I was almost asleep in my chair. 'Ladies and gentlemen, we proudly introduce to you our newest full-fledged member, *Justice*.'

"And Right Wing flew onto the stage as Justice, and I woke up. He nearly took my breath away. I couldn't believe what I saw. The boy who'd been bugging your father for so long, interrupting our time together, well, he'd grown up. And out.

His muscles bulged out of his new uniform, a more modern look than the rest of the League. And he was the only one who didn't wear a mask, so you could see just how handsome a face he'd grown into. He wasn't a boy anymore; he was a man.

"The press went wild, snapping picture after picture. Justice looked truly spectacular. I remember your father and Captain Victory standing on the side of the platform with beaming smiles on their faces. They were proud of their new hero, a product of three generations of training, and here the press was eating it up.

"'Before I give you a demonstration of my full, new array of powers,' Justice announced. 'I'd like to bring someone back to the front. Hal?'

"He drew your father next to him and put his arm around his mentor's shoulders. 'This, my friends, is the greatest hero on the planet. All my life I've dreamed of being half the hero he is. I just wanted to say thank you, Hal, from the bottom of my heart. I owe it all to you.'

"The crowd applauded. I, of course, stood up from my seat and whistled. I thought it was a sweet gesture from Justice, especially considering how strained things had been between him and your dad since I'd entered the picture.

"Justice glanced out at me and looked quickly away. 'I'd like to give my mentor back the floor.' Then he ducked offstage.

"Your father stepped up to the microphone and said, 'Thank you, Justice, I know you'll make us all proud. To shift gears a minute, I'd like to point out a very special woman in the audience tonight. Lila?' Your father craned his neck. 'Has anyone seen Lila?'

"That got a laugh from the audience. Even Warrior Woman chuckled.

"Well, yes, I'd turned invisible. I still used to do that whenever I felt the least bit embarrassed, and suddenly all eyes were on me, so what'd you expect me to do?

"When I returned to view, my cheeks were beet-red.

"'Lila, would you please join me onstage?'

"And that's when the pictures started snapping. Your father reached for my hand, but the paparazzi were focused on their newest hero, Justice. Whispers spread throughout the audience like wildfire. I didn't need superhearing to know what they were saying. They thought I'd been brought up onstage because I was the faithful girlfriend."

"So what's wrong with that?" I asked.

"Because they thought I was the faithful girlfriend"—she took a full swig of her drink—"of Justice.

"Before I knew it, the press had descended on us; they were up out of their chairs, and we were mobbed. Let's get one of you with your arm around her! How about a kiss, you two! I held my hand up, I said no, but nothing seemed to work. Justice pulled me over and whispered in my ear. 'Don't worry, Lila. Just go with it. Give 'em what they want, and they'll be gone in an instant.'

"I stood there, dumbstruck at the attention. I searched for your father through the glare of the lights. I thought I saw him disappear behind the refreshments table, and that's when the money shot happened."

"The money shot?" I'm not sure I wanted to know the rest of this story.

"He kissed me. Justice planted a big one on my lips. It took me by total surprise—I wouldn't lie about that—and I just closed my eyes and went with it. The crowd went nuts. Cameras flashed like crazy. I knew immediately I'd made a terrible mistake.

"And when it was all over, and the crowd had cleared out, I finally saw your father by the punch bowl. I ran over to him as fast as I could; he was uncharacteristically silent. Although he was never prone to outbursts—as you know, *in*bursts are more his speed."

She sure got that part right.

"He said he needed some air. I told him I'd come with him, but he said he wanted to walk alone."

"And you let him go?" I asked.

"Of course not." Mom yanked up another board and winged it aside for emphasis. "I said lift with your legs, sweetheart, not your back.

"You'll discover one day, Thom, if you haven't discovered it already, there's one thing we do when people tell us no. It's in our blood."

"What's that?"

A bottle of water appeared in the air in front of me. I downed all of it in one full gulp.

"We do it anyway." Then a hand towel floated toward me and wiped the sweat off my forehead.

"They didn't call me Invisible Lass for nothing. I followed your father for the rest of the day, and he had no idea.

"He walked around back, where Captain Victory tried to calm him down. I listened to the Captain defend me. That I couldn't possibly have known that Justice was going to plant one on me. But he knew as well as your father there was one thing I hadn't done."

"What was that?" I wanted to know.

"Turn invisible," she replied.

"He left Captain Victory and walked down to the river. I'd been following about thirty feet behind, but when he stopped to watch the current, I gathered my courage and decided to reveal myself to him. I moved toward him, confidently, and then I saw him reach into his pocket. What he did next made me stop dead in my tracks.

"He pulled out a modest but elegant diamond engagement ring. He held it to his heart, then balled it up in his fist and launched it into the river. He watched as the current carried off the small ripple of water.

"He turned around to leave, but by that time I'd disappeared again. Your father spent the rest of the day alone, wandering around the fields and woods. Finally, hours later, as evening was about to fall, he came across an enormous crater. It was probably the one left after Justice's escape pod crash-landed into earth all those years ago. He stood on the lip of the crater and looked down as far as he could, and then he began the long climb down to see how far it would go.

"He said it took at least two hours before he could finally make it to the bottom. At the very bottom, he spotted something."

I looked up from the floorboards, interested in what came next. We'd pulled up enough boards now that the room was glowing bright.

"It was a spark of purple, a beam of color shining through the darkness. He reached down and tried to grab the light, and when he stood back up he found the most peculiar rock in his hand. He said he could barely exhale because he was so taken with the rock's beauty.

"He sat it in the gravel and watched its purple glow for a long time, long enough for the sun to drop in the sky, and he thought about what to do with his life. He made a lot of decisions that day, some I didn't find out about until much later."

I didn't want to leave a mess, so I began stacking the discarded floorboards.

"Don't worry about those," Mom said, and ripped up another one.

"He didn't tell me about what he'd found that day. After we got home he took the precious stone to every geologist he could find, but none of them could identify it.

"It was about that time that your father stopped talking. Eventually he took an official leave of absence from the League, which wasn't all that uncommon for our rotating roster. He said he needed space, and I respected that. But what bothered me the most was that he didn't take calls and he wouldn't answer his door. He wouldn't even talk to me."

"How'd you get him to come out?" I asked. We'd kept yanking up the floorboards, and we had a quite a collection of them. I felt like I was a little boy again, and Mom had laid out the Concentration cards on the floor and I was trying to remember where all the pairs were. We plucked the boards up, pair by pair, until eventually there were only a few left.

"He showed up at school one morning. There was a knock on the door while I was teaching fractions, and when I opened it, there was your father, kneeling on one knee, dressed in a clean, pressed suit, a bouquet of daisies he'd picked in one hand, and a small jewel box in the other.

"I opened the box. In it was a beautifully carved ring with the most curious glowing purple gem mounted on top. A perfect circle of violet radiation. The kids in the class oohed and aahed. Your father explained he'd found a stone that no expert had been able to identify. He said that it was the only thing worthy of giving me, that I was as unique as the stone itself, perfect and beautiful and bright and special, and he wanted to spend the rest of his life with me."

I laid the crowbar on the crystal floor and couldn't help but smile. This was what every child wanted to hear. That they were born of a perfect love, a perfect union.

We were coming to the end of the floorboards.

"Your father had spent that month holed up in his apartment carving two matching wedding rings out of that strange, beautiful stone. He was so damn proud of those things that he could barely wait for us to put them on. We got married at city hall the next afternoon."

"I didn't know Dad could do something like that."

Mom chuckled.

"Your father can do just about anything when he puts his mind to it, powers or no powers."

Her comment should have sounded like a compliment, but somehow it didn't.

"When he explored the crater and discovered that rock,

that sparkle of indigo, he said it gave him the one thing he needed most of all: hope. Hope that we could make a new life together. Hope that our love for each other would be enough.

"Later, when I looked down at the ring on my finger, the stone sometimes felt so heavy that I could barely lift my hand. It can be an awful responsibility when you're someone's only hope. But that part didn't come until later, when your father came to this very site." She attacked the last floorboard with extra vigor and pitched it across the floor. "Here we are."

The light was blinding, and I had to cover my eyes until they adjusted. We stood on a bright, smooth crystal floor, and as I stared beneath me, the crystal seemed to continue down for miles.

"They'll tell you the monster flew back to whatever crab nebula it crawled out of, but don't believe a word of it. That's what they want you to think. Because if people knew that that thing was still here, no matter what state it's in, if people knew the danger . . .

"Here's what really happened, Thom. When there was no other option left, with the entire world at stake, your father plunged his hand into the creature's heart. They called those things Planet Eaters for a reason, you know—he really didn't have a choice. There wasn't time to wait for the rest of the League to show up. Your father had been first to respond to the crisis. Despite his lack of superspeed, he was always vigilant that way. It was a last-ditch effort at saving the world. Blowing up a few buildings is a lot better than an exploding planet, but people aren't very interested in simple arithmetic when there's blame to assign. Sometimes what you choose to do in a crisis can change your whole life in a single instant." I now knew a little bit about what that meant. I missed my dad right then.

"When your father's fist struck the Planet Eater's heart, something happened. Maybe it was your dad's hand, maybe it was the ring on his finger, nobody knows. But we all know the result. Somehow your father's fist fused with the creature's core seconds before it was about to achieve meltdown and consume our planet, and this was the result. Instead of incinerating the planet, the creature instantly crystallized into a dazzling rock that extends to, well, you know what? No one's ever been able to figure out just how far down it goes. Or, fortunately, how to reactivate it. This crystal is that creature, frozen in time. It was about to destroy our planet, and your father stopped it."

She narrowed her eyes and peered deep into the crystal.

"There was a high price, though. The shock of that creature turning into crystal emitted such force, almost everything in the immediate vicinity was obliterated. The Wilson Tower vaporized. So many died."

I tried to look deeper, but the crystal got brighter the farther down it went. I held up my hand to shield my eyes, but Mom tugged my hand away, and I felt her breath in my ear.

"Look closer," she said. "What do you see?"

I strained my eyes and looked as far as I could stand to, and suddenly I noticed something that was out of place. Something that twinkled a different color light.

Something purple.

"The ring." I said, excited by what I saw.

"Must be right where that thing's heart was, where your

father lost his hand. When the force of the explosion demolished the Wilson Tower, the only person Justice had time to rescue from the nova blast was your father. If he'd been a split-second later, your father would have lost more than his hand. You know the rest, about all the casualties, more than we'd lost in several wars. I tried to protect you from that when you were a little boy, but how do you keep world events on that scale from your child?"

She wasn't really asking me. She was trying to apologize for being a shitty mother. Or justify her actions. I didn't care that she couldn't keep it from me when I was little. I cared that she left.

"Mom, why are we here?"

A flamethrower floated in front of me. I saw the shoulder strap reach around the space where Mom's neck would have been.

I stared down at the endless chasms of jagged crystal edges, impossibly sharp, that lay beneath the smooth surface.

"You're the only one who can get it back." She lit the tip of the flamethrower.

Me? I managed to form a few sentences of protest.

The last question I asked—"But *why* do you want it back?"—received a response that ended the discussion.

"No judgments," my mother reminded me. "Remember?"

I peered into the crevices below the polished surface; their sharp edges glittered back up at me like razor blades. No human could make his way down there. Fractured corners threatened to slice through my flesh like a ripe tomato every millimeter of the way.

"I'll slice my arm off. If I hit a major vein, I'll die within minutes."

"Oh, don't be so dramatic," Mom said. "I know you get that from me, but it's not one of my finer points. Haven't you ever thought about using your powers on yourself?"

Actually, up until that point, I hadn't. It made me wonder how long she'd been watching before she revealed herself to me. How much did she know about what I could and couldn't do?

FWOOSH! The flamethrower shot a jet stream of fire and melted a broad opening through the smooth surface, exposing the deadly crevices below.

"Here, this should help," Mom said as she sprayed fire liberally and melted a few of the sharp edges near the top. "If you get cut, it'll be sterile, minimize the risk of infection."

I couldn't believe I was really going to do this. "What if someone comes?" I asked.

A welder's mask descended on top of Mom's invisible head, and she cranked up the juice on the flamethrower.

"Don't dillydally."

As I crawled down into the cavern of jagged edges, sharper than a giant cheese grater, a skin-shredding coral reef, I tried to review how I got here. A searing pain shot up through my leg. I pushed back on my heel for better leverage, and I was pretty sure I severed my Achilles tendon. There's no limit in life to the things you'll do for your mother.

I zigzagged slowly through the crystal crevice, but not carefully enough to avoid the slices. I practiced biofeedback breathing and felt my skin get fire-hot as my power began to heal my shredded flesh. I ignored the blood, which gave the path a rosy glow as it dripped down toward my purple destination.

I imagined what my father must have felt as the flesh melted away on his hand when that creature exploded. Did his life pass before his eyes? Did he think about me, the son he'd never get a chance to have? When did he first look down to see that his hand had melted away to a clump of scarred flesh? And when did the thought finally strike him that his wedding ring was gone forever? I stretched and strained and ripped my skin as I pressed on. Mom was right. I could heal myself. I didn't want to get too cocky about it, though. No reason to test my abilities on a severed carotid artery.

Sweat beaded up on my forehead, and I reached to wipe it off before it dripped into my eyes. I looked at my fingers, crimson-stained and wet with blood. I told myself over and over the story of my father proposing to my mother as I crept lower. I thought about the depth of Mom's love for Dad, and how it was beautiful and sweet, if a little unhinged, that she still wanted the ring, the perfect symbol of their perfect love.

I stretched my hands as far as they could go, my fingers shaking; and ignoring the slices to my knuckles, I hooked my middle finger around the ring and pulled it back. I heard Mom shout praise and encouragement down the crystal chasm.

Mom was waiting at the mouth of the crevice with enough gauze to mummify me. But I was getting good with my powers. I barely bled at all.

Exhausted from burning up so much power, I handed her the ring and fell on the floor to rest. I felt almost as drained as I had when I'd gone back to the oncology ward to get Scarlett's purse. I thought I saw Mom's hand tremble as she held the ring, but in a moment she'd disappeared. I sat up on the floor and held my head between my knees to catch my breath and get my bearings.

Mom tried to wipe a cut on my forehead with the bandage, but I jerked away. I wasn't sure why I didn't want her to touch me. She took the hint and backed off.

"Your father was a good person; he didn't deserve all the shit that happened to him." The ring slid down a long string of leather and the two ends lifted into the air.

I didn't like to hear my mother use crude language. She'd never been this coarse when I was young, at least not around me. I didn't care what she'd been through since she'd left; she was still my mom, and my mom didn't talk like a truck driver.

"He shouldn't have taken it out on me, though," she said.

I didn't want to ask, but I had to know. "Did he hurt you?"

"Of course he hurt me." She was quick to say it. "But not the way you're thinking. He never laid a finger on me. You can't let your problems eat you up from the inside like that without it affecting other people in your life. He couldn't take all his anger and frustration out on the world around him, so he took it out on me. You, too."

I was so mad I thought I was going to explode. I wanted to hurt her.

"So you left me with him. Alone."

I shook my head, disgusted by her selfishness.

"You can't run away from your problems, either," I said. I spit some blood on the crystal.

It was a long while before we said anything else.

"Why'd you leave?" I asked again.

Mom sighed a deep breath. "Because I loved him."

That didn't make any sense. "You left because you loved Dad?"

"No." What she said next echoed in the crystal abyss. "I left because I loved Justice."

I felt just a sliver of the dread my father must have felt when he found out.

"I couldn't have picked someone who would have hurt your father more if I tried." She paused. "But sometimes you don't pick these things, sometimes they pick you."

What a crock of shit.

I grabbed her hands and pretended to hold them to comfort her, and I rubbed her fingers. I felt kinda shitty for doing it, but I had to know. I felt around her knuckles for it, but it wasn't there.

"What happened to your ring?" I asked.

"It disappeared," Mom said, and pulled her hands away. "That happens when you're invisible all the time; you lose things."

I didn't buy that. At least not all of it, and I told her so.

"I took it off the first night I moved in with Justice," she said. "And then I couldn't find it by the sink the next morning. I never saw it again." I could tell by the echo of her voice that Mom had turned to the wall when she told me that, ashamed to look me in the eye.

"Are you and Justice still, you know—?"

"God, no." She laughed the kind of laugh you give when you encounter someone who doesn't know anything about life.

She took a swig from her flask. "We had one Christmas

together before it ended." She got lost in her own memory for a few moments, and then started to tie the loose ends of the leather string together. "Some things you lose are gone forever."

She pulled the knot tight. The necklace hovered above my head for a moment.

"You'll do better than I did. You won't end up like this."

I thought I heard her sniffle back a tear. She knew I heard her, and she coughed and tried to cover it up.

"Damn it," she said. "I think I'm finally getting some of that crud that's been going around lately."

Then I felt her hands on my shoulders as the leather necklace settled around my neck. The ring rested perfectly in the middle of my chest.

I heard Mom wipe away something on her face, and I felt the warm, tiny remnants of a tear land on my cheek.

"You have to promise me one thing, Thom. No matter what."

"Sure," I said. It hurt me deeply to see her in pain.

"You can't tell anyone about this."

I looked up and tried to make sense out of what she was saying. "Not about me, not about the ring, not about anything. You can't tell your friends, you can't tell your teammates, and you can't tell your father." She cleared her throat and added, "Especially not your father. Promise me."

"Okay," I said.

"You can't even *think* about it. Understand?"

"I promise," I said.

"I mean it," she said louder. "You'll know what to do when the time is right." I felt her fingers stroke my cheek. "That's my boy, my dear, sweet boy. Now, promise me."

That I'll know what to do? About what?

"Okay," I said. "I promise." I held out my pinky for her. "I pinky-swear it."

I waited for a beat, but I never felt her pinky grab mine like we did so much when I was a boy.

I reached out to grab her hand, but in my heart I knew she was already gone.

I clutched the ring and slipped it in under my shirt. I'd keep her secret for her, but I decided it was time to make some changes. I stood up and felt for the piece of paper—the official termination notice from the League—in my back pocket. I took it out and folded it into a paper airplane and sailed it down the crevice into the abyss.

Time to take control.

CHAPTER TWENTY-EIGHT

I STOLE THE BALL from the half-court line and drove it all the way to hoop. I was on fire.

Goran had been in the middle of a scrimmage with his team, the Gary Coleman look-alike included. I guess Goran had figured this was a safe place for his team to play now that I was gone. I snatched the ball during a fast break and challenged Goran to a one-on-one. The Gary Coleman guy snickered. The rest of the team looked on with delight when I pulled two twenties out of my pocket and held them in my hand.

"Don't worry," I told his teammates. "This won't take long."

I played better than I'd ever played in my life. I got to twenty before he even made it to double digits.

"Why are you doing this?" Goran whispered when we scrambled for a rebound. He was imploring, not asking. I didn't even give him the courtesy of looking him in the eye.

On my last two points I threw him an elbow to his gut before sinking a jump shot from the top of the foul line.

I walked out of the gym with the rest of Goran's team laughing. The jeers and the names were obvious. They were laughing at Goran's expense. It was worse than losing to a girl.

He'd been beaten by the town faggot.

I left the rec center—this time I promised myself it would be the last time ever—and I passed Goran's little brother in his karate uniform at the drink machine. He was fighting to get his quarters back.

He gave the machine a good thwack and then he saw me. "Hey, you're—"

Yeah, yeah, yeah, even the little kids had seen me on the news. I'd reached a new high: taunted by a second grader. My adrenaline was still pumping from the game, and I found myself restraining an urge to tell the kid off.

Then he finished his sentence.

"You're my brother's friend."

I turned around and looked at him.

"What did you say?"

"You're Thom," he said, delighted to be talking to one of the big kids. "He talks about you all the time." He punched the ancient drink machine, then swung around and gave it a good kick. "I'm gonna be a hero one day, like my brother."

Not a very good one, I thought. He'd dented the side of the machine, but his drink was still lodged inside. I rubbed my hands together and placed them on each side of the machine.

"My mom and dad were soldiers," he said.

Okay. Not really sure what to do with that information, but thanks.

"They're dead." He smacked the machine hard.

I shook the machine as hard as I could, heard some clunking around inside, and an orange drink dropped into the receptacle. I handed it to the boy.

"Cool!" he said. "Thanks."

And then with a high kick into the air, he scampered off to the basketball court to find his big brother.

Sometime soon I'd have to think through what Goran's brother said, but I didn't have time right then. It would have been particularly bad form to be late to a meeting I had called myself. Especially when I wasn't even officially a member anymore.

I began a swift jog out of the parking lot and glanced down at my watch. If I picked up the pace and skipped the shampoo in the shower, I could arrive at least fifteen minutes before my teammates.

Two high-top sneakers dropped from the sky and landed on the pavement in front of me. I looked up and saw that the shoes were attached to Goran. He'd leaped out from behind a row of cars.

He stood very straight, his chin held high, and stared into my eyes. I tried to move past him, but he jumped in front of me and blocked my way. I felt his shoulder crash into my collarbone. I ducked to move past him on the other side, but he pushed me back. My body trembled with fury, ready to fight, but all I could do for the moment was stare back at him.

Then he touched me again, but not to fight.

He reached out, grabbed my hands, and lifted them up to his face. He took my left hand and placed it palm down over his mouth, he took my right hand and placed it palm down over his forehead. He pressed my hands tightly against his face. I felt the warmth of his palms on the back of my hands, and the feeling shot a fiery sensation throughout my entire body.

He leaned forward, his eyes straining as if they were asking me to see something. I stared for a long time at those dark, deep-set eyes peering out at me from the tiny window made between my hands. I couldn't take my eyes off his. I didn't know what he wanted me to see, but I was transfixed. I gazed deeper and deeper into his eyes.

A car door slammed on the far side of the parking lot, and I suddenly pulled myself away from him. He continued to stare at me, and I didn't take my eyes off him, either. I kept looking back at him as I slowly made my way out of the lot. He was still staring at me when I turned the corner.

I sprinted the rest of the way home.

"But we've been disbanded," Larry said through a hacking cough. "Technically, this group doesn't even exist anymore." He spit a phlegm globber into the face of a cartoon mouse printed on a thin paper napkin.

"I have to say I don't understand why we're here, either," Golden Boy said. "Especially after the stunt you pulled."

It was hard to hear over the din of video games, but the backroom of the Chuck E. Cheeze was the only place I could think of to meet where no one would expect to see us.

Ruth offered Golden Boy a slice of pizza. Her way of shutting him up.

"We're here because there's a killer on the loose," I said with as much authority I could muster. "It's up to us to stop him."

"But we're going to be reassigned to other tryout groups," Larry said. "Well, most of us, at least, and I don't want to risk another shot to make the team."

"The League says we already have him." Golden Boy folded his arms.

"I've been through this before," I explained for the umpteenth time. "I was with him at the time."

"How can you be so sure about the time?" Golden Boy challenged me.

"It's on the autopsy report," Ruth said in between drags on her cigarette and crunching on the fried zucchini.

"But how can you be sure, Thom?" Larry continued.

"Just ask Ssnake," I said.

"You ask Ssnake," Golden Boy said. *He's your boyfriend*, I could hear him saying to himself.

"Dark Hero was there too," I said. "He could vouch for the time." Golden Boy rolled his eyes.

"Dark Hero? That's your alibi?" Golden Boy pushed his chair away from the table in disgust and stood to leave.

"With all due respect, Thom," Larry said, "how do we know the League isn't right on this one?"

"We just have to trust him."

We all turned around, and Ruth nearly fell out of her metal folding chair. It was the first time we'd seen Scarlett since she'd left.

No pizza jacket, either.

She made no effort to hide her colostomy bag.

"I don't know about the rest of you suckers," she said to Golden Boy's stunned face, "but I'm with Thom."

It was my idea to start off by talking to the victims' families. I suggested we track down a relative of Captain Victory first.

"But he wasn't murdered," Golden Boy said.

"Maybe," I said. "Maybe not."

The old captain didn't have any immediate family. He had outlived his two children: one had died of meningitis at a young age and the other died a middle-aged spinster. His wife had died of breast cancer before she was fifty. But we did manage to track down his great-grandniece, a dietician in a hospital cafeteria in Poughkeepsie.

We invited her to lunch so we could ask her a few questions about her illustrious relative. During the meal, she kept probing us for information about his will and how much money he had left. Apparently she'd only seen him a handful of times in the past thirty years, but she knew she was his closest blood relative. She accidentally spit a small glob of sloppy joe on Scarlett's hand when we told her we didn't know anything about Captain Victory's estate.

"Sorry," she said, and offered Scarlett a napkin.

Larry offered her an antacid, but she refused. Ruth returned from the lunch line with a warm plate of chocolate-chip cookies.

"Oh no, I couldn't possibly—well, maybe just one."

I deliberately reached for a cookie at the same time so our

hands would touch. Once I had contact, I sensed a deep anxiety within her; her heartbeat quickened, and I wondered if she was hiding something or if the palpitations were just a result of a bad diet.

"Are you sure there's not anything else you could tell us?" I asked. "Any detail would help, no matter how small you think it is."

The great-grandniece chewed on her cookie and thought long and hard. Then she leaned forward in her seat.

"Fine, you got me." The rest of us perked up. "The last time I went to visit him," she said, "he told me I wasn't in the will at all."

King of the Sea had a brother who ran a successful pet shop in the city by the seaport. As soon as we walked into the shop, the customers whipped around to check out our costumes. Ruth found the brother working behind the counter, and we took our places at the end of the line.

When we finally made it to the front, King of the Sea's brother didn't look up from the puppy chow.

"So what'll it be?"

I introduced myself and our group and asked him if we could borrow a second of his time. He looked at the long line of customers behind us. Then he took a beat to recognize my face from the news.

"Get out of my store."

That was it for the day. We piled into Ruth's car, and on the way back I told the gang we'd meet up first thing in the morning and continue down the list. I told them not to be discouraged, this was part of the process. We might have to get through a lot of people who didn't have information before we got to the people who did.

Larry sighed loudly as we pulled into the parking lot. Golden Boy hopped out and raced over to open the door for Scarlett before the car had even come to a full stop.

"I can let myself out, thank you," Scarlett said, and then she blew right past him and went to her own car. It was almost hard not to feel a little sorry for Golden Boy.

Almost.

The house was dark when I got home. Dad was out again. It smelled like the neighbors had been burning leaves, which I thought was strange because it was the wrong time of year for that. I walked up the driveway, and inside, I turned on the front porch light for when Dad got home. I noticed something out of the corner of my eye.

The front yard, illuminated by the porch light, had been torched. Deliberately. The burned pattern left a message.

YOU'RE NEXT, FAGGOT.

I dragged the thatch through the yard in the middle of the night. My hands ended up blistered and bleeding, but that would be small potatoes for my healing powers. I wanted to finish the job before Dad got home.

The wind rustled in the trees, and I looked up and saw shadows moving. Could have been a cape, could have been a tree branch, could have been nothing.

"Bring it on," I said out loud to the wind, out loud to who-ever left the message.

Bring it on.

I got up the next morning before dawn to get an early start with the rest of the group. Dad still wasn't home yet from his shift. I caught the bus to Ruth's place and rang the doorbell at the front door of her townhouse. I heard a dog bark next door. She didn't answer. I knocked hard on the door, but she still didn't answer. Suddenly I got nervous and raised my foot to kick the door in; then I noticed her car across the parking lot.

The old engine was thrumming, so she couldn't hear any-thing. I walked over and tapped on the windshield and flashed her my best early morning smile.

"Who wants to capture a villain today?" I said, and held up two fresh cups of take-out coffee I'd picked up on the way.

Ruth jerked her head around; she hadn't seen me until now. Her mascara ran tiny black rivulets through the deep crevices in her face. She'd been crying.

I rushed over to the passenger side and hopped in.

She sniffled and wiped her nose on her elegant sleeve. It was then I noticed she was dressed to the nines.

"Wow," I said, referring to her dress. "What's that?"

"Vintage Chanel," Ruth said, and smiled weakly. The red of her dress matched her lipstick. "A girl doesn't need a specific reason to look her best, does she?"

I shook my head no. I guess not. Still, I wondered when the last time had been that she had worn that dress, and what had been the occasion? When had been the last time she had danced? And when she danced, did she think of her poor, lost fiancé?

"Give me the coffee," she said, and grabbed it from me, cupped it in her hands, and took a long sip. "Here, hold this." She tossed her makeup bag into my lap and adjusted the mirror to see herself. "I've got to put my face back on before we see the others."

She reached over and pulled out a cleansing pad and wiped the dark smudges off her face. She swabbed at her cheeks with so much force that I thought she was trying to smooth out her wrinkles. I wanted to say something to comfort her, but I'd learned that sometimes it's just as good to sit by someone's side, just to let them know you're there.

"Hand me my base."

She looked into the mirror at her face. The makeup brush shook in her fingers. She didn't know where to begin.

"Ruth," I finally said, "what's going on?"

"I'm a little tired, that's all. I've been up all night. Writing."

"I didn't know you were a writer."

"I'm not." She snuffled and lit a cigarette off the car lighter. "Now, be a lamb and put those in the mailbox for me." She pointed her thumb hitchhiker-like toward the backseat.

I turned around and saw neat piles of carefully sealed letters in the backseat of her sedan.

As I walked to the mailbox at the end of her sidewalk, I wondered what had made her break down like this. Had she seen something in the future? Did she know about the message I'd found waiting for me in the yard? Whatever it was, I wasn't going to get it out of her. She clung to this one herself. Whatever it was, it was hers and hers alone to carry.

After I'd filled the mailbox with all the letters, I hopped back into the car.

"Thanks," she said, and revved up the engine.

I strapped on the seat belt and noticed Ruth wasn't wearing hers. "Ruth," I said, "seat belt."

"Don't worry about it." She put the car in drive and sped off in her vintage red Chanel.

We met up with the rest of the team and spent the entire day talking to near relatives and close friends of the deceased heroes. Unfortunately, we hit five more dead ends in a row. One of the relatives, a groundskeeper for a state-run golf course, actually sprayed his water hose at us.

Still wet, we piled into Ruth's car.

"I'm gonna say one thing and one thing only," Golden Boy announced. "This is all a big waste of time."

Nobody said anything, and the silence stretched out for a long time. My plan wasn't yielding results, and the troops were getting restless. Scarlett looked exhausted. She glanced at her watch.

"I've got chemo at five, and a mani-pedi after that, so let's make this the last one for today." She rested her head against the window and closed her eyes to catch a nap on the way.

We'd learned that our next target, the Spectrum's daughter, was working at an elementary school fair sponsored by the PTA, so we crashed it. Ruth asked a PTA member if she knew the person we were looking for, and we were directed to the bake sale. A concerned group of parents looked at our costumes curiously, and a few minutes later I saw them sidle up and whisper to a security guard. We found the bake sale. To break the ice, I thought it was a good idea to buy a whole tray of Rice Krispies Treats. I offered them to my teammates, who took one apiece, somewhat halfheartedly.

Golden Boy hesitated before he took a bite of his square. He looked off to the trees on the outskirts of the school.

"What's up?" I asked.

He looked around the fair, past the student raffle, past the moonwalk, craning his neck in all directions.

"Nothing," he said, although he sounded like he was trying to convince himself.

The woman behind the bake-sale counter was busy counting money. She thanked me for our generous contribution and asked if we wouldn't like to try the lemon bars.

"Actually," I said, "we wanted to talk to you for a minute."

She put down her wad of dollar bills.

"You want to talk to me?"

"Yes," I said. "It's about your father."

She went back to counting her bills.

"I've talked to enough of you people already. Please, if you'll excuse me."

Larry suddenly coughed up his Rice Krispies square into the trash can. "Jeez, how much butter did you put in these things?"

Scarlett elbowed him in the gut. I noticed Golden Boy was looking off in the distance again.

Ruth stepped in. "You know, I think I will try those lemon bars. How many can I get for a twenty?" She handed the Spectrum's daughter a crisp twenty-dollar bill.

"I already told you, I have nothing to say. I'd appreciate it if you left me alone now."

She turned to go, but I put my hand gently on her shoulder.

"We're very sorry about your father. He was a great man, and we want to honor his memory by stopping whoever did this from doing it again."

Her eyes darted around the fair, like she didn't want anyone to see her talking to us.

"My father's identity was secret; you have no right to be here." She leaned forward and whispered, "I don't want my children to find out."

"That your dad was one of the world's greatest heroes?" Ruth asked. "Funny, I'd be proud of it."

The woman's face dropped and she stared at the lemon bars, lost in her thoughts. "I am very proud of my father," she corrected Ruth. "It's not that at all—"

"Guys, something's not right," Golden Boy said. "I'm gonna do a quick loop around the school."

Scarlett smacked Golden Boy hard on the shoulder.

"What the fuck is your problem? This dumb woman was finally about to talk and now you fucked it up!" She swatted him again.

"Cut it out," Golden Boy said under his breath, and backed away.

"Easy," Ruth said. "We got an audience."

The Spectrum's daughter was understandably offended. She yanked the tray of lemon bars away from Ruth, tossed her cash back at her, and started to move away.

"You can keep your money."

"Wait!" I stopped her. She wheeled around and dropped the tray of lemon bars, the metal tray making a tremendous clatter as it hit the ground. The crowd looked over, and I saw the security guard making his way toward us.

"Please." Tears pooled in her eyes. "I don't want my kids to see me like this."

"I don't want to upset you," I said. "We're on your side."

I put my hands gently on her arms and felt the pain of a little girl who'd lost her father. As she looked back at me I think she knew that I recognized what she had lost. Maybe it was the power in my hands, maybe it was the feeling in my heart; but she opened her mouth to talk. I had the feeling she was about to tell me everything.

She didn't get a chance to say a word.

"Go away!"

Scarlett was screaming at Golden Boy. Our probationary team already stood out in the crowd. The shouting wasn't helping us blend any better.

"Talk to me," Golden Boy said to Scarlett. "That's all I want. Just talk to me about it."

"GO AWAY!" Scarlett pushed him away and tried to blow past him, but he moved at superspeed to block her path. We were gaining a real audience at the fair.

"Talk to me," he said again, and she pushed him away again, and he appeared in front of her again.

"Talk to me."

"I can't." Scarlett finally gave in and stopped pushing him. She sounded so tired.

"Why can't you?" Golden Boy said, trying to make eye contact with her. He reached out and held her hand.

"Don't you get it?" Scarlett said. She wouldn't look at him.

"Tell me," Golden Boy said.

Scarlett eyed Golden Boy's hand on hers, then she looked at her stomach.

"It hurts to be around you." Scarlett pushed his hand away.

They stared at each other for a while. None of us knew what to do; this was between them. I glanced at Ruth, hoping she'd have a bright idea, but she was massaging her temples like she had a major migraine. At first I thought she was faking it: some kind of distraction to get us out of there. But she didn't wink or anything. Something was wrong with her.

Larry and I both noticed the security guards calling us in on their walkie-talkies. He whispered to me, "This is not good. What do we do?"

Then Golden Boy took an awfully big chance.

He stepped forward, put his hands around Scarlett, and kissed her gently on the lips. She closed her eyes and melted into the kiss.

She opened her eyes and blinked after Golden Boy was finished with the kiss. He smiled at her, his arms around her shoulders.

"LEAVE ME ALONE!" Scarlett heated up her arm for extra strength and pushed him away. The force of the blow knocked him into the crowd; he could have been seriously hurt if the Spectrum's daughter hadn't been there to cushion his fall.

He landed on her head.

Larry and I helped the Spectrum's daughter to her feet. She'd been knocked to the ground like a bowling pin when Golden Boy landed on her. Her upper right cheek was cut and bleeding.

She touched her fingers to her cheek and saw the blood. "Oh my God!"

"Kevin!" I was desperate for help. I saw the cops getting out of their car in the parking lot.

I hate to admit it, but there were times that Golden Boy was an invaluable asset to our team. He had the most experience of all of us, and that counted for a lot under this kind of pressure. Before the police car doors had even slammed shut, he'd scooped each of us up and had us waiting on the far side of the school, where no one could see us by the edge of the woods.

Ruth was getting her bearings and starting to stand up, so Larry came over to see about the Spectrum's daughter. Scarlett was crying softly into her hands, and Golden Boy stood behind her, patiently waiting for a chance to comfort her. I was trying to figure out who to tend to first.

"Can you help me? God, look what you've done! Can you fix this?" The Spectrum's daughter held her hand up and looked at Larry.

"Actually, I make people sick," Larry said.

I pulled her aside, took her by the hands, and went to work on calming her. Her posture relaxed, and the panic evaporated. The wound began to heal, and she could feel the smooth skin seal over her cheek.

"Believe me, I've seen much worse," I said. "There, good as new."

Her eyes were now grateful and calm. She cleared her throat and rubbed the smooth skin of her cheek.

"He called me that night from his lab and said he couldn't tell me too much. He said if anything happened to me, he wouldn't be able to bear it," she said. "I asked him what he was talking about, and he told me he couldn't tell me who did it, warned me that the person he thought had been killing the heroes could read minds. He said we were all in danger, and he told me to take the kids to the mountains until things settled down." She took a deep breath. "He said I couldn't even *think* about what he told me."

That last sentence echoed in my mind. *You can't even think about it*, my mother had made me promise.

I went to Ruth's side. She grimaced like her head hurt—or like she was seeing something else. Then she looked at me like she wasn't sure who I was. I thought maybe she was having a senior moment.

"Thom!" Ruth called out. "I can almost see it!" She furrowed her brow and squinted. "I think I know who it is."

"Guys," Larry said, "something isn't right. Look at the sky."

"C'mon, Ruth, you can do it," I said. "You're almost there."

We could hear the loud rustle of the wind as it whipped through the trees.

Golden Boy raised his head from Scarlett and looked to the clouds that had suddenly begun to cover the sky. Even Scarlett took her face out of her hands and looked up. Now the trees were bending in the force of the wind.

"Oh!" Ruth cried out and dropped to one knee. I rushed to hold on to her. Her red dress flew behind her in the wind like a cape.

"Guys, something is really wrong!" Larry shouted over the wind.

A panic seized Ruth; I could feel her whole body go rigid. She grabbed my collar and looked at me.

"It's coming."

Larry pointed at the sky, the dark clouds parting. We stared up, Scarlett lit up with flames in a defensive pose, and Golden Boy clenched his fists and readied for the strike. I squinted and stared into the clouds to see what was coming.

"Something's wrong with my head," Golden Boy shouted.

Scarlett raised her hands to her temples in pain. Larry and the Spectrum's daughter quickly followed.

All of a sudden, thoughts were screaming through my mind: *You're going to die. All of you are going to die. And it's all your fault.*

I raised my hands to cover my ears. Agony seized my brain, but my powers quickly took over and my hands began to sizzle on my head. Then my stomach dropped at a sudden realization.

Those weren't my thoughts. Someone was putting them in my head.

The heavy clouds finally cleared in a burst, and then I could only see a dark blur. A blur that whizzed past Larry and a forearm that sliced toward him. Larry flew back, his hands around his neck as he choked and gasped for air, his windpipe suddenly broken.

In the second it took for me to turn to grab the Spectrum's daughter, I saw Golden Boy pick her up and speed her away to safety. This time he'd remembered the innocent bystander first.

Scarlett's body lit up in flames, a natural defense mechanism. The dark blur circled her but was careful to avoid the fire. Instead I saw it cover and wrap her in a giant, clear plastic tarp, like she was being spooled into a huge roll of Saran wrap at ultrafast speed. I'd barely even taken a step toward her when the dark blur snatched her up and hung her high in a tree, impossible for me to reach. Her flames were quickly being extinguished by the lack of oxygen. She gasped for air and began to suffocate as she desperately tried to rip open the plastic.

I didn't even have time to panic. I started for Scarlett, and I spotted Ruth making a break to help Larry.

The dark blur disappeared, and Ruth and I made sudden eye contact before we could make it to our friends. One of us would be next. Then Ruth's fear melted away, her face muscles relaxed, and I saw a peace overcome her. She looked at me and smiled. It was the most serene expression I'd ever seen on her face, and it made me realize how beautiful she must have been when she was young, why that man had risked his life to be with her.

In a flash she was gone. Just like that. One minute she was standing there, and the next she was hurtling through space directly toward a giant oak tree, carried by a dark, inexorable force. I saw her brittle body smack against the wide trunk of the tree at full force and then collapse, utterly limp, onto her face in a mat of pine needles. Chills shot their way through my body. My teammates were getting picked off one by one, and I couldn't act fast enough to save them.

Then I felt the searing pain of two hands beginning to crush my head. They lifted me from the ground by my face, and I wondered if my head was going to pop off my neck. Suddenly I was airborne, being propelled through the air at an impossible speed. I managed a glance behind me and saw another massive oak fast approaching. In a moment my body would be crushed against it like Ruth's. In front of me was nothing but a dark blur.

I struggled as much as I could, kicked my legs. In a few seconds I would be pulp. It couldn't end like this. My teeth managed to grab hold of a finger, and the hand pulled away from my head. Then I felt a different pain. The hands gripped my neck and squeezed. The pressure of those hands was incredible; they pushed so hard that I could feel them drive the ring on my necklace clear into the skin, right into my throat.

And suddenly, just short of impact with the tree, the hands pulled away, the dark blur whizzed back up into the sky, and the clouds disappeared. The ring fell back down and hung on my chest.

I tumbled to the ground, somersault over somersault. I finally stopped rolling and looked up, dizzy, and saw the sky spinning bright blue. The dark blur was no where in sight.

I tried to see straight. I saw a shining golden arc shoot toward the tree where Scarlett hung. Golden Boy tore open her tarp and sped her safely to the ground, where she gasped for breath.

I heard the chokes and wheezes of a dying man and saw that I'd landed close to Larry, who was straining for every last breath he could manage through his windpipe. I was on top of him in a second, my hands gently around his neck, and I felt his trachea spring back to its proper shape in the heat of my grip. He began to breath evenly again, though clearly it was still painful to take in air.

We saw Ruth crumpled by the oak tree she'd been smashed against. She lay in a limp, fetal position.

I raced over to her. Larry tried to keep up. Golden Boy scooped up Scarlett, and we were all beside Ruth within seconds.

We stood around her, sure of the worst. Her frail body didn't move.

Scarlett buried her head in Golden Boy's chest. He wrapped his arms around her, and she let him. Larry choked back a tear. I crouched down and put my ear over Ruth's mouth and prayed that I'd hear some breathing.

She suddenly sat up like she'd found a good yard sale.

"What's everybody looking at? I ain't dead yet!" She struggled to catch her breath and wiped a clump of oak leaves off the side of her face. "Knocked the wind out of me, that's all."

Scarlett laughed through her tears. Larry and Golden Boy and I all shared smiles of joy and relief. Ruth began to push herself off the ground to get to her feet.

"Help a tired old lady get up, will you, kid?" She reached out a hand in my direction.

Our expressions suddenly changed. Scarlett's jaw dropped, Golden Boy turned white, and Larry actually gasped out loud. I grabbed Ruth's hand, but I didn't help her up. She looked at me curiously as I began to lay her carefully on her back on the soft mat of pine needles.

"What?" She didn't like what she saw in our expressions. "What is it, what's wrong?"

Then she saw that my hand was covered with blood. Her blood. Her eyes moved in a trail as she followed the blood from my hand to hers, from her hand up her arm, and from her arm to her chest.

We hadn't seen the blood at first because it matched the red of her dress.

There was a hole in her chest the size of my fist, and just inside it we could see the broken-off end of a sturdy oak branch. It had impaled her and broken off when she slammed into the tree. Scarlett covered her mouth, trying her best not to let the horror show on her face.

I reached into the wound and yanked the chunk of wood out of Ruth. I covered her chest cavity with blazing hands. Golden Boy disappeared in a flash to get an ambulance, and Scarlett cradled Ruth's head. Ruth gripped my wrists with vise-like desperation.

"Don't let me die," she whispered. "I thought I was ready for this"—she gulped in as much air as she could hold in her leaking lungs—"but frankly I'm a little scared." Then she began to choke on her own blood as the life ebbed out of her.

I focused all my energy into the healing power of my hands. I tried to deny the thought going through my head, that this had been what Ruth had seen this morning when I found her crying. That there was no use in trying to save her, that she'd seen this clearly, the moment of her death.

Through bubbles of blood, she spoke. "Don't worry, I'm a tough old broad."

But her eyes betrayed her fear, and she began to whimper in pain. The more blood she lost, the more her grip relaxed on my wrist.

Her breathing soon went from shallow to nothing.

"She's not breathing!" Scarlett screamed.

I strained with all my might to make my hands as hot as a white star. The damage was so massive inside; I'd never been able to heal anything that bad. I couldn't even keep up with all the bleeding, much less try to heal the severed organs.

Larry rose to his knees and began administering CPR on her rib cage above my hands. Scarlett laid Ruth's head back, pinched her nose, and put her mouth over Ruth's crimson lips to give her mouth-to-mouth.

"C'mon!" My voice broke like a little boy's. "We're losing her!"

Larry's CPR compressions shook her body. I thought I heard a rib crack. I could feel Scarlett's breath blow out of the hole in Ruth's chest.

"WHERE'S THE FUCKING AMBULANCE!" Scarlett screamed.

Then Ruth coughed and suddenly came to, and opened her eyes for just a moment. She began to say something through her bloodstained lips, and Scarlett leaned in close to listen. I kept my hands welded to Ruth's chest, covering the wound, and then I experienced a new sensation I'd never felt when using my powers before.

My hands went cold.

Ruth struggled to whisper a few words to Scarlett. I leaned over and looked right into her eyes.

"You've got to help me, Ruth! Fight it!"

I didn't want her to see me cry. Scarlett was bawling, and Larry put his arm around her.

The corners of Ruth's mouth raised ever so slightly, and she looked at me with heavy, sleepy eyes.

"I was wrong," she said, her voice weak, barely audible. "About what happens after . . ."

"Don't go, Ruth! PLEASE!"

Her eyes suddenly lit up as if she saw something else. Her face looked joyful, and tears of happiness, relief, and joy rolled down her cheeks. She whispered her final words to me.

"He's there, Thom," she said. "He waited for me."

Ruth's eyes rolled back in her head. I gently closed her eyelids.

CHAPTER TWENTY-NINE

RUTH'S FUNERAL WAS a simple, unadorned affair, much like her life. Even though it was summer, the day was gray and a chilly mist drizzled in the air. The funeral home attendant asked if I'd like to say a few words, but I declined. Ruth had always been the one with something to say.

Scarlett wore a black dress that was far too short for a funeral, and bawled throughout the ceremony. She wouldn't let Golden Boy stand near her. Each time he approached to lend her some comfort, she'd slip through the scant crowd to another pew. Larry sneezed uncontrollably throughout the whole service.

Ruth deserved a better memorial than this; Ruth deserved a better life. She was my friend, and she never gave a shit that I was gay. She actually believed in me, and now I didn't see how I was going to go on without her. There was a tremendous bouquet of expensive flowers on the altar from the League. How generous. It was so big that it dwarfed the casket. In fact, it took me a few minutes to realize there even was a casket. A reporter or two lingered by the door. No one from the League bothered to attend.

I turned around and scanned the crowd. Maybe I hoped to catch someone from her life lurking in the background. A relative, her old partner from the Wrecking Balls, anyone I could share a memory with. Anything to keep her memory alive just a little bit longer.

I thought I saw someone dressed in black hiding in the foyer. I excused myself and stole out of the pew to see who it was. My shiny black Sunday school shoes looked brand new, and they were smooth on the bottom because I rarely wore them. As a result I slipped on the carpet in the middle of the aisle, and everyone saw me drop. Shit! The last thing I wanted to do was make a mockery of Ruth's service. As I started to get up from the floor, I made eye contact with Scarlett, who grinned and stifled a laugh.

I thought for a second and realized that no one would have enjoyed me sprawled out on the floor of her funeral more than Ruth. She would have been cackling louder than anyone. I chuckled and began to push myself off the floor.

And suddenly I was standing face-to-face with a new guest.

"Hello, Thom," my father said.

Dad always looked good in his black suit. His broad shoulders filled out the jacket, and he looked more comfortable and relaxed than he ever did in his starched factory uniform.

"Sorry I'm late," he whispered. "How's it going?"

A real barrel of laughs, Dad, it's a funeral.

"Where have you been?" I asked, loud enough for the people in the back of the chapel to turn around and look at us.

Dad tilted his head and stared at me. It sounded like an accusation from his own son, and I didn't mean it to come out that way, but I'd been thinking about it since Justice asked me the same question. I thought about the clean uniform in the washing machine and how I'd seen so little of him lately.

I rubbed the back of my neck, felt the leather string of the necklace Mom had given me. I went to reach for the ring, to feel the perfect circle between my fingers, but I stopped short. I couldn't tell him about seeing Mom. I kept myself from even thinking about it.

We hadn't really talked about anything since I'd decided to step forward at the news conference. I bit down on my lip to stop it from quivering.

I looked up to him with sad eyes. Neither of us said a word for the longest time. Neither of us moved.

I couldn't read his expression. It was solemn, his eyes deep with pain. But there was something more in his face, and I couldn't tell if it was disappointment, fear, or something worse, maybe anger. His chest heaved as he drew in a long breath. I thought he wanted to speak to me, but maybe he didn't know what to say.

I didn't know what to say either, but I knew one thing with all my heart: I needed him to hold me. Like all those times when I was sick and he came upstairs to my room and held me through the night and told me everything was going to be okay. I was racked with pain and guilt and grief, and I missed Ruth so much. If he just held me I could cling to the idea that my father could somehow fix everything.

As he looked at me, suddenly I caught a glimpse that he was fighting just as hard as I was to hold back tears. But he didn't move forward. His arms remained at his sides. He couldn't bring himself to touch me.

I reached out to hug him, and the minute I stepped toward him I knew it had been a grave mistake.

He winced and pushed my hands away.

Without meeting my eyes, he turned his back on me and walked out of the memorial chapel with strong, even strides.

I stood alone in the aisle, stunned. I knew everyone in the chapel had seen it, but it didn't matter what they thought. *I* had seen it.

The service ended, and Larry called me over to a side exit with Scarlett and Golden Boy. We snuck into the back room, where Ruth's casket had been taken. Larry looked to Golden Boy, who did a quick loop of the place.

"We good?" Larry asked.

Golden Boy nodded.

"We only have a minute before they take her away," Larry said, and opened the lid of her casket.

Ruth was perfectly white, her skin alabaster, her face at peace, her cheekbones smooth and lifted, her lips so full and red that you couldn't even tell where they'd been sewn shut by the embalmer. Unfortunately, they'd smeared a shade of tacky green eye shadow on her eyelids that she'd never have worn herself. Sure, she was a ballbuster, but she had terrific taste. She always knew how to work with what she had, and she was a great lady.

Scarlett leaned over the casket and placed her hand gently

on Ruth's. She ran her young, slender fingers over Ruth's spindly digits, and then held up Ruth's limp hand and stroked it like she was caressing a baby. She stopped at Ruth's ring finger.

The only piece of jewelry Ruth wore was her League probationary ring. We looked at each other, and then at Ruth's four bare fingers. None of us said another word. We didn't need to.

Scarlett slid the League probationary ring off her own finger and held it up with a sad but determined look on her face. Larry, Golden Boy, and I slid our rings off our fingers, too, and held them up.

Scarlett whispered something into Ruth's rosy, powdered ear and slid her ring onto Ruth's pinky finger, then stood up to make room for Larry. Larry leaned over the casket, gave Ruth a sweet kiss on her forehead, and slipped his ring onto Ruth's middle finger. He smiled a little that he'd got the one finger she'd used the most in life. Golden Boy moved up, careful to step around Scarlett, and gently held Ruth's hand and slipped his ring on her index finger. He laid her hands back on her chest in a crossed position and closed his eyes, his lips moving in a silent prayer.

Then it was my turn. I reached in the casket and grabbed hold of Ruth and hugged her as tightly as I possibly could without snapping any of her brittle bones, and I slid my League ring onto her thumb and carefully laid her back on the worm-proof satin cushion, and closed the lid.

We stood there for a long time over our fallen teammate. We didn't need to speak. We all knew it was over. Then slowly, one by one, we each went our separate ways without saying so much as good-bye.

I couldn't bring myself to leave the funeral home. As soon as I saw the last car leave, I doubled back round to the delivery docks by the garage. Ruth's casket was sitting alone on the loading dock, waiting to be taken to the cemetery. Ruth didn't have any sort of life insurance; the League had paid the amount necessary to meet the minimum of the state health board's burial requirements.

Maybe the funeral home had forgotten about her and left the casket, and it would remain on the loading dock until someone bothered to ask what the hell it was doing there. Maybe there'd been a shift change, and the guys who left her there had already gone home.

Fire welled up in my belly as I watched Ruth's casket sit there for what seemed like hours. I told myself if someone didn't come soon I was going to drag it to the road, hail a cab, and bury it myself in my own damn backyard.

But two guys in drab uniforms finally pulled up in a paneled truck. One of them wasn't much older than I was. They lifted Ruth's casket and loaded it into the back of the truck, which had no sign painted on its side. It could have just as easily been delivering newspapers or cupcakes.

I'd picked up a few things about sneaking around from my father that came in handy from time to time. The workmen had no idea I'd slipped into the back of the truck when they closed the door and drove off.

* * *

We came to a bumpy stop at the burial site, and I quietly slipped out the back before they came to get the casket. I stole behind a large headstone and watched them carry Ruth's casket to the spot they'd dug.

What a shitty job, hauling caskets that nobody cared about. The older workman huffed and grunted as they lifted Ruth's coffin. His mottled forehead was wet, and I couldn't tell if it was sweat or drizzle. The radio blared from the front seat of the truck.

A few feet away from the hole, the old-timer tripped over a clump of dirt and stumbled to the ground. The young guy tried to keep his end of the casket up, but the sudden shift in weight was too much for him. Ruth's coffin went tumbling out of their hands, and the lid flew open when it hit the ground.

It took every ounce of self-control I could summon to remain still for the following seconds. They looked at the casket on its side. I could see Ruth's pale, limp arm stretched out on the ground, her forearm covered with grit that slowly melted into a muddy trickle in the drizzle.

They stood and stared at the mess they'd made, and the young guy got this look on his face, his eyes squinting in a fond memory.

"Looks kinda like my grandmother," he said.

They stood for a moment and watched. Then the old-timer patted his partner on the back. "C'mon, let's do this."

He knelt down in the dirt and carefully lifted Ruth's arm. Holding her hand up, he saw the five rings. He licked his thumb and began wiping the mud off them. Then he motioned to his partner.

"Get my bag."

The young guy disappeared in the back of the truck and came back with a huge toolbox. He reached in the toolbox and pulled out what I thought was the biggest pair of hedge clippers I'd ever seen. The handles were long, but the blades were short nubs, a tool perfectly designed to cut something thick and tough.

The old-timer slid our four rings off Ruth's hand, but he couldn't manage to pry my ring off her thumb. The woman was tenacious, even in death. The young worker pulled open the long handles of the clippers, and the old-timer steadied Ruth's hand so that the blades zeroed in on Ruth's thumb.

I yanked the clippers out of the young guy's hands by the sharp end and whacked him across the face with the heavy wooden handles as hard as I could. I heard something crack as I hit him.

I wheeled around and swung at the old man. His mouth was open in astonishment, and I swatted him down like a fly. He hit the ground and I kicked him into the open grave. He landed on his back with a dull thud.

Blood dripped down from my hands, still gripping the sharp open blades of the clippers, but I couldn't feel anything. I grabbed the clippers by the handles and raised them high in the air with the full intention of driving the blades down and spearing the old man through the heart like the vampire he was.

The old man looked up from the grave, his eyes pleading for mercy, and then he passed out.

I stood there, my hands raised, ready to plunge down—but I couldn't.

Something grabbed my shoulder and whipped me around, and I stumbled in the mud and dropped the giant clippers. I stood and found myself face-to-face with Dark Hero.

I reached for the clippers with my slashed hands, ready to fight. He'd been begging for a dose of his own medicine for a long time now. Who the fuck did he think he was, following me around everywhere, dishing out his own brutality whenever he saw fit? I wasn't going to kill either of these two bozos, and I certainly didn't rough them up any more than he would have. In fact, I was a kitten with them compared to what Dark Hero would have done if he'd stumbled across the same scene.

I knew he was the faster one, the better fighter, and he'd get in the first shot. But I was possessed, ready to inflict some serious damage. I could probably manage one good slash with the cutters before he put me down. He'd never forget messing with me.

I raised the clippers in front of me, and he batted them out of my hands. It only took him a millisecond to grab me.

And he brought me in to his massive, dark body and hugged me as tightly as I'd ever been held by anyone in my whole life.

I was so shocked by this move that my body fired off like I'd been plugged into an electrical socket. My toes began to twitch. For Dark Hero, holding me must have been like trying to contain an earthquake.

But he held tight. The twitch moved up my legs; my fingers began to jerk and shudder. I knew this feeling from before, and I desperately wanted it to go away, but he grasped me tighter and clung to me.

And finally I let go. I forgot about my body entirely—the convulsions, the rage, the despair over Ruth's death, all of it—and I let myself disappear and melt into him. His embrace was vast and inviting.

I gave myself over to him and absorbed all the warmth of that massive dark body as it poured heat into mine. It felt warmer and better than the morphine drip when I'd had surgery, better than the feeling of utter peace I'd had when I fell asleep in the backseat of the car as my parents drove me home from my sixth birthday party at the miniature golf course.

The next thing I knew, tears streamed down my face like I was a giant leaking bag of saline. Dark Hero held me as long as it took to empty every last bit of pain inside. He clutched the back of my head and I sobbed into the refuge of his broad, safe shoulder.

When I grew calm, we collected Ruth with great care, fastened the lid of her coffin to last forever, and lowered her into the grave. Dark Hero had removed the unconscious old man from the hole and put him in the back of the truck alongside his partner. I heard the clang of the young man's head smack against the side of the truck's door as Dark Hero tossed him inside. Whenever those two finally woke up, they'd think twice about robbing anyone again, dead or alive.

The mist lifted, and the sun eventually came out from behind the clouds, although it hung low in the sky. Sweat dripped from the ends of my hair, and I felt grime on my neck where my necklace was fastened. I'd been shoveling for two hours and I was finally done. I knelt down to Ruth's grave, kissed the dirt, felt the granules of earth stick to my lips, and said good-bye to my friend.

I stood up to leave and observed a perfect stillness throughout the cemetery, row upon row of uniform headstones. I looked for him, but Dark Hero was gone.

A note lay on top of Ruth's headstone. I opened the slip of paper, and the words leaped out at me.

Follow your father.

CHAPTER THIRTY

FROM STUDYING MY father's old case files in the League archives, I learned that the secret to following someone is simple. Never get too close. It sounds easy, but it requires a surprising amount of patience, and it's why most people can't do it. Your instinct is to watch them so closely that the only person who's really on display ends up being you. Sometimes you have to fight the urge to do something, fight the urge to go when your body says go. More often than not, you have to fight the ever-present need for instant gratification.

I sat at a bus stop and waited for hours until I was certain Dad's shift at the factory had begun. People came and went from the seat next to me on the bench. The last woman, an elderly lady with a three-pronged cane, offered me her elbow and asked me if I needed some help when the bus pulled up and I didn't move. I looked at my watch and told her no thank you. Even though I knew Dad's shift had already begun, I decided to wait for the next bus, just to be sure.

I arrived outside the factory and spotted the light on inside the security guard shack. It was laughable how easy it was to pass by security. The chain-link fence had a thin layer of barbed wire strung across the top like one long pathetic strand of Christmas tree tinsel. There was a black-and-white-striped rail that blocked incoming cars from entering. I waited and listened to the two security guards shouting at their portable TV in the guard shack—a basketball game not going their way. Since I wasn't in a car, I just walked inside around the rail. The security guards never even looked up.

Security wasn't much of an issue inside, either. The real problem was figuring out where to go. The first time I passed a factory worker in uniform, I breathed deep and easy and walked by as if nothing were out of the ordinary. No one said anything to me. They weren't paid enough to care if something seemed out of place.

I passed by an austere cafeteria, which looked like something from two or three decades ago. It boasted modern technology in the form of a giant microwave, surely one of the first models ever made, because it was as big as our laundry machine. In the corner a TV was broadcasting mostly static, and a guy fiddled with its antenna. Maybe we weren't the only people in the world without cable.

I passed down a narrow corridor, turned the corner, and found myself at the door to the factory floor. The hum of machinery became a roar whenever someone opened it, and I had to restrain myself from covering my ears—a sure tip-off that I didn't belong there. I peered through the window in the door and saw hundreds of workers spread out among stations across a vast floor. It reminded me of the ant farm I'd had when I was a little boy, the sand and dirty caverns replaced with chrome and concrete. This was the world in which my father struggled to make sure I would have a better life.

My eyes tracked up high above the workers and found a windowed box hanging in the air. I decided this was the owner's office, because a grim man in an ill-fitting pin-striped suit stood on a platform adjacent to the box and watched over the work below.

The factory owner stood up straight, his legs stiff, his hands clasped behind the small of his back. He had two deputies that leaned against the rail in front of him. I wasn't sure what they were looking at, or why they needed to maintain a vigilant watch. Was it really necessary? I looked for my dad on the floor, but there were too many people, and from that far away it was next to impossible to see faces, especially those covered with hard hats and goggles.

I turned to leave and smacked into a worker. Major points for stealth.

"What's your problem?" the guy said.

"Sorry, I'm new."

The guy raised the brim of his hat to check me out. His cheeks were covered with acne—he was barely a year or two older than I was.

"Oh." He eyed me up and down. "Where's your uniform?"

I hadn't thought of a good excuse, because I hadn't really counted on stopping to talk to anyone. He sensed my hesitation. I looked at the door and figured I could make a break for it.

"The hell are you waiting for?" he said. "Let's get you suited up."

Brad Stemple took me back to the locker room and let me borrow his spare uniform. We stepped out onto the factory floor, ready for the shift, and I was careful not to look up at the factory owner and his deputies. I didn't want to look like one of those tourists wandering around the city who's never seen a skyscraper. I kept my eyes peeled for my father as we lumbered on toward our station.

It was difficult to take in the sight of all the workers at once. I tried to observe them individually, see if I could pick out familiar traits that would give away my dad, but it was hard to see them as a whole. It also made me very uncomfortable to pose as one of them when I hadn't worked as hard as any of them.

Suddenly we were in a sea of workers, which made it next to impossible for me to make sure I didn't bump into Dad. I strapped on a pair of goggles.

"You don't need those," Brad said.

"Oh," I said, but kept them on.

We stood in line to grab crates. I have no idea what was in them. It was our job to hoist the heavy boxes off the conveyor belt and carry them to another conveyor belt on the other side of the room. Why they didn't have a conveyor belt to connect the two, I don't know.

By around my third or fourth box, I thought I was going to die. All my intense physical training with the League, and here I was teetering on the edge of exhaustion because I faced a shift of heavy lifting. Thoughts of permanent damage to my back consumed me for the first hour. How did these guys manage? I remembered my mom telling me to lift with my knees not my back.

I have no idea at what point during the shift I noticed a big, powerful man a couple of stations over who worked twice as fast as everyone else in his group. He carried two boxes at a time.

I pushed the construction cap down over my eyes as far as I could go without totally blocking my vision. Brad was midsentence when I interrupted him.

"Who's that guy?" I motioned toward the powerful man.

Brad took his eyes off his crate and looked over at me. "Him? He's a real hoss, isn't he? A brick shithouse. Far as I can tell, everyone here thinks he's the best employee in the plant. Never misses a day of work. Always gets the twenty-dollar bill at the end of the year for perfect attendance. You like beer?"

I kept working as Brad rattled on about his prodigious capacity for malt liquor. And I kept watching the powerful man's massive frame move gracefully across the floor as he deposited two crates at a time on the conveyor belt, smooth as a card dealer. Once I thought I saw him glimpse up at the factory owner on his stage up in the sky.

I followed his line of sight and saw the factory owner unclasp his hands from behind his back, step forward, and whisper to one of his deputies. The man disappeared down a winding metal path of stairs and catwalks. As I picked up another crate and hauled it across the room, I spotted the deputy crossing the floor toward the powerful man.

A siren wailed, and everyone in our part of the plant

seemed to know to stop working, so I stood there with my box pulling my arms to the floor until Brad told me it was okay to set it down. The deputy called for everyone's attention. Even the whir and grind of the machines ceased to echo.

He raised his hands, apologized for the interruption, and announced that unfortunately one of the toilets in the men's room had exploded and he needed a volunteer to clean it up. I thought that was a really strange reason to stop work on the floor, but I kept my mouth shut.

No one stepped forward, no one said a word, and all eyes zeroed in on the powerful man. The duty was meant for him alone. I didn't want him to have to clean up a room full of shit, and I stepped forward to volunteer, but Brad yanked me back.

"What are you, crazy?" he whispered.

The deputy foreman handed the big man a mop. He took it and, keeping his head high, walked out of the room to clean up the mess. The factory owner, high above on his platform, looked pleased.

The machines buzzed back to life, and everyone went back to work, business as usual.

I leaned over to Brad. I felt like I was one of the last remaining humans in *Invasion of the Body Snatchers*, and someone was going to point the finger at me and scream any second now.

"What was that all about? What's he doing on bathroom patrol—shouldn't he be running this place?"

Brad lifted my crate off the floor and handed it back to me. "He just worked his way up to foreman after years on the floor." Brad dropped a crate on the conveyor belt, and it landed with a heavy thud. "But he lost it."

"Why?"

Brad looked over to make sure the foreman wasn't watching. He took a breather and rubbed his back before picking up another crate. "His kid likes dick."

"Oh." I nodded.

Shit.

My heart sank and I wanted to ask what the hell that had to do with anything, but I knew better. It had everything to do with everything. We picked up our crates and began to carry them across the room.

"His kid likes dick, said it on national TV or something," Brad continued. "The owner's a big Christian, has a lot of power in that world, his pop was a famous televangelist, you know."

My heart sank further into the crate as I laid it on the conveyor belt and watched it make the slow journey toward the door, where my father had disappeared.

"They demoted him for that?"

"No." Brad's eyes lit up, delighted to tell the rest of the story. "That's the punch line. After twenty years on the job, he'd just been promoted to foreman. Everyone was sure he'd lose his job, all things considered. But rumor has it the factory owner pulled him aside when the news broke about his son and said he understood, because he has a daughter who's been a heroin addict for years, stealing shit from him and his wife for years, in and out of jail. After that thing on TV, he called the guy into his office, lit up two cigars, handed him one. Said he knew what he was going through, these kids choosing to go to hell after all the sacrifices they'd made for them. The owner gave him the break of a lifetime and offered him an even bigger promotion—asked him to run the *whole goddamn plant* for him. Said it was the right thing to do for someone going through the same thing as him."

"So what happened? What did he say to the owner?" I asked.

"Nothing, the way I heard it," Brad said. "He punched the shit out of the conveyor belt. Then he went in the locker room and put on his old workman's uniform. Picked up crates and started working."

I looked up at the factory owner watching over his domain. My father returned to the floor, his head held high, to grab a bucket. I knelt down to tie my shoe so he wouldn't see me when he passed by us. I noticed Brad shut up and start carrying his crate at an extrafast pace as my dad moved by. Brad was suddenly a soldier on his best behavior.

The factory owner stared down at Dad, and Dad refused to look back up, refused to make eye contact with the man as he left the room. Stone-faced, the owner turned and disappeared into his window-box office.

After my father had left the floor, Brad revved up the engine on his mouth again.

"Phew," he said. "Close one."

I looked at Brad's face and recognized what he'd felt as my father passed. Fear.

"What was that about?" I asked. "So what if he heard you talking?"

Brad swallowed and set his box down carefully, motioned for me to lean in closer.

"Don't you know who that is?" he whispered at me, his eyes wide. "It's *Hal Creed*, man. Major-fucking-Might!"

* * *

I changed back into my clothes during our fifteen-minute break, and I remained in a stall in the men's locker room when the whistle blew to signal the break had ended. I could see Brad's shoes scamper up and down the floor as he looked for me, and I lifted my feet up out of sight. He was the kind of guy who'd check the stalls, no matter what he heard coming from them. I heard him walk out and the door shut behind him. Then I waited. Better safe than sorry.

I quietly opened the stall door and froze when I heard the locker room door slam open. I stepped back in the stall, leaving the door slightly cracked. I pressed my back against the wall and saw my father through the slit in the door. He sat on the bench and rested his head in his hands.

I listened to the sound of my own breath, the sound of my own heart beating, and I prayed he wouldn't hear me. I tried to absorb the weight of my father's sacrifices for me, the idea that I'd misjudged him.

Dad changed out of his shit-stained uniform into a new one. I saw him pull a crisp foreman's uniform out of his locker, and he adjusted it on its hanger to make sure the pleats hung evenly. This would be the uniform he'd bring home, the one that he'd toss in the laundry to make me think it was business as usual, another day as shift manager down at the plant.

I waited for him to leave before I slipped out. That's the key. It had always worked for Dad, and now it worked for me.

Never get too close.

CHAPTER THIRTY-ONE

I ARRIVED HOME to no graffiti, no car in the driveway, no lights on inside. But I didn't feel I was alone. I was sure I saw movement near the bushes around the side of the house. I doubled back through the neighbor's backyard, picked up a baseball bat lying in the grass, and crept into my own backyard. If those graffiti artists and hatemongers were back, I was going to give them a surprise they would never forget.

I moved quietly, but I didn't see anyone. As I crossed the perimeter of the yard, I remembered the last message etched on the lawn. *You're next.* Maybe it wasn't hateful little bigots after all. Maybe I should have been more worried.

I turned when I saw the weeping willow swaying in the breeze. I squinted to see if someone was hiding behind it. I could have sworn I saw someone move the branches. I snuck up to the trunk of the tree, the baseball bat held high in my hand.

In the back of my mind I prepared myself for the possibility that this might be a fight to the end. I clutched the necklace my mother gave me, put my hand on the bark, and took a deep breath, ready to strike. Then I jumped around the trunk and swung the bat with all my might.

The swing didn't connect. In fact, I looked down at my hands to find the bat was missing. I turned around and saw it floating behind me.

"Hi, Mom."

"Thom, listen to me, there isn't much time."

"I did everything you said." I felt the ring on the necklace resting on my chest. "I haven't even thought about it."

"That's my boy."

I heard a gulp, but I couldn't see her flask.

"There's something you should know, Thom. You're the product of both me and your father. Now, I know you'll be doing the right thing, heroics and all that. You get that from him. But you are also the child of invisibility. It's very important you never forget that. The powers, Thom, they're a gift."

Yes, I knew that. "I'm learning more about how to use them every day. You'd be surprised by what I can do."

"No. I wouldn't. In fact, I'm counting on it. But powers are also a tremendous responsibility. There's a price to pay for using them. It's not good to hide behind them all the time, Thom. If you hide too much"—I saw the spark of a match light her cigarette—"you can lose yourself entirely. Remember how you never thought I could see you when you wrapped yourself up in your blanket as a little boy?"

"I'm not hiding anymore." I said it firmly and I meant

it. I was through with hiding. That was her department now.

"These powers, they're just a part of you, Thom, but they're not all of you. Do you understand what I'm getting at?"

Not really. Was she drunk?

She patted my head.

"Don't worry," she said. "You will. You still have so much to learn about who you really are."

She flicked the cigarette in our neighbor's yard, and I reached out and gripped her forearm. I didn't let go.

"Mom, what's going to happen? Why did you say there isn't much time?"

I felt her jolt when I grabbed her. She was surprised I'd been able to measure where she was by her cigarette. In a second, she yanked away.

I turned around in the yard, looking for a sign of her. "Mom!"

A weeping willow branch whipped up into the air, and I took off after it. I was running blind, following an instinct, but I was determined to catch her.

When I neared the deck, I knew I was right behind her. I heard her footsteps race along the deck. I leaped over the rail and ran toward the door. The door swung open before I could get there. She was in the house, but which way had she turned? She was better at this than I was, but I was fed up, angry that she kept leaving, and that anger kept me going.

I thought about what my dad would do and inhaled deeply, smelling gardenia and liquor. I jumped over the couch in our modest living room to follow the scent. I knocked over our family pictures and heard the glass frames shatter on the floor. I swung to catch her, but she was one step ahead of me, and I stumbled.

I looked up and smelled the trail of the scent leading to the front door. No way. Not this time. I took off like an Olympic sprinter. I was going to stop her before she got to that door, before she disappeared into the night, before she could leave me again. I was going to find out what the hell she was talking about once and for all.

The front door tore open in front of me. I dove forward, my hands outstretched to stop her. I flew through the air.

And I landed on Goran.

I helped Goran up to his feet and apologized for knocking him over. I explained we'd been having a little trouble with vandals lately, the whole while straining my eyes to look for a sign of my mother. I sighed deeply, troubled that she was gone.

Goran had a sheepish look on his face. He picked up a mashed flower arrangement and held it against his hip, the same way he held a basketball. He cleared his throat. "I heard you lost your friend."

He looked down at the bouquet of flowers, not the cheap kind from the deli or drugstore, either; these were from a real florist. They must have set him back a lot, on his budget. I felt bad for landing on them.

"I just wanted to say I'm sorry," he said. "About everything."

My feelings for Goran were complicated. Tied up in a tangled network of impossibilities. I had never let myself fantasize about being with someone my own age, because it stopped being a fantasy at that point. It entered the realm of possibility, and that's where you can really get hurt.

I hadn't seen him since I'd closed the door on my emotions. I hadn't seen him since I'd wanted to hit him in the parking lot. Since he'd put my hands on his face.

"What do you want from me?" I asked.

He looked off to the side, into the darkness. "Can I come in?"

"Can you make this quick? I've got some other things going on right now." I looked up and down the empty street one last time before letting him in and closing the door.

He looked around the living room and asked if he could sit down. I swept the broken family pictures under the couch with my foot and stood. He laid the flowers on the coffee table and looked at them instead of me.

"I promised my mother and father that I would take care of my brother, and I'm afraid I haven't been doing a very good job."

What the hell was he talking about? He was the best big brother I'd ever met. It was one of the things I loved about him the most. I'd always dreamed of having a big brother like him, someone to look up to, someone tough and cool, not afraid to tell it like it is, and with the strength to back it up. My mind flashed to a picture of his little brother doing a high kick to the drink machine.

"You're crazy. That kid's great."

I pulled the curtain open to check the front yard. As far as

I could tell, there was no one out there, but I didn't want to take my eyes off the darkness.

"What kind of a role model am I," Goran said, "if I'm a liar?"

"What are you talking about?"

He leaned forward on the sofa, rested his elbows on his knees, and interlocked his fingers. "When I was my brother's age, my parents decided that it was better to join the war as soldiers than to wait in our basement for someone to kill us. They made me promise to take care of my little brother if anything should happen to them, to do whatever I had to do to take him as far away from there as possible."

He pretended to study his hands, but his mind was somewhere else. "They would leave for days at a time, but they'd always come home. Then they were gone for three whole weeks, and I didn't know if they were going to come back. I was afraid to light candles at night—no one had electricity anymore, because someone would know where we were. I played games with my little brother, sang songs quietly to him until he fell asleep. Sang songs to keep my mind off the decision that faced me. Do I wait for them to return? Or do I honor their request to take my brother as far away as possible? We had almost run out of food, and I decided to let that make the decision for me. We would wait as long as we could make it through the last three cans of beets.

"We were down to the last quarter of the last can when my mother returned in the middle of the night."

I sank down into a chair and listened to him continue.

"She had fashioned together a crutch from two fence slats

and a silk pillow and some cord. Her left leg was covered with bloody bandages. She wasn't alone. A group of soldiers was with her, some dressed in civilian clothes, but all with guns. My father was not there.

"My brother was crying, and I was trying to be brave. She said we must hurry. She handed me over to one of the men, and then she handed over my brother, and they loaded us into the back of a dented van, the sides fortified with metal sheeting.

"The van began to pull away, and my mother was not inside. My brother and I howled. What a cruel trick for her to come back, only for us to be separated again. I scrambled to the back of the van, put my hands up against the cold glass of the window, and saw my mother getting smaller and smaller in the distance. She climbed painfully into a small car with a sunroof.

"I heard the whistle of the mortar as it shrieked through the air. It hit our block and exploded. I held up my hands to shield myself from the blast, which blew out the back window of the van. I managed to grab hold of my brother as the van flipped over and over. When we came to a stop, I pulled him out of the car, and we saw our driver's mangled body crushed into the steering wheel. I turned to look back at our house, at the tiny car my mother had gotten into.

"There was nothing left."

He stopped speaking, and silence filled the air between us. I wanted to tell him that I knew a little about what it felt like to have your mother vanish, disappear without a trace. I thought maybe I could find a way to explain that to him later, but right then I wanted to let him know I was listening. "What did you do?"

Goran made eye contact with me without moving his head. He spoke slowly and surely, miles of subtext under his words.

"I did what I had to do to get us out of there."

That was it. I wasn't going to find out what it was he'd had to do. Those were his own ghosts, his own personal haunting, and he wasn't going to share that with me.

I walked over to the couch and did the only thing I knew to do at that moment. I sat down next him and didn't say a word.

"It is very difficult for me to continue," Goran said. "I do not have the same words as you to express how I feel."

I didn't question him. I just wanted to sit there beside him.

He leaned back into the safety of a shadow cast by the unlit lamp on the table beside him. He looked down at his feet.

"There's so much I want to tell you," he said in barely a whisper.

I turned on the lamp and looked into his eyes. There was something so intense boiling up inside him, and the more I stared into those eyes, the more I saw something familiar, something I understood.

"I can't lie to my brother anymore," he said. His jaw was clenched and the muscles in his neck rippled as he spoke.

"About what?"

I suddenly had to know. I would leave him some of his own personal ghosts, but not this one. He was silent.

"About what?" I said again. I wouldn't let him take his eyes off me.

I was fed up with waiting for people to tell me things, fed

up with being scared of what might come next. That was no way to live.

"About what?!"

I got up in his face and challenged him. He turned to look away, and I grabbed his chin and turned it back toward me so he had to face me. I felt the warmth of his jaw on my thumb and forefinger. He didn't pull away.

I wasn't going to let him off the hook. I felt he could read my thoughts.

He opened his mouth to speak.

And then the earth shook.

We ran outside and shielded our eyes from the skies. A sharp, bright light exploded from the city, and the ground reverberated beneath us. You could feel it all the way up through your feet to your stomach.

"Was it a nuclear bomb?" I asked.

Goran studied the sky. He was serious, detached again, the walls back up as strong as before.

"There's no cloud," he said.

Car and house alarms went off throughout the neighborhood, and the neighbors poured out into the street to see what the commotion was. Instinct took over, and both Goran and I broke into a sprint in the direction of the light. We had made it a couple of blocks when it became clear to both of us that the disaster was somewhere far off in the city, somewhere we couldn't get to on foot. We were embarrassed to look at each other. I couldn't tell if it was because we'd broken into a pointless sprint, or because we'd been so close to saying something that scared us.

We stopped by a pickup truck that had pulled over on the side of the road. The driver had opened the windows and turned the radio volume up, and a small crowd of motorists had gathered around to listen, people seeking safety in numbers.

A helicopter news report informed us that there had been a blast downtown. The reporter had no idea about the damage or the casualties, but the area under attack surprised us all.

The Wilson Memorial.

A woman clasped her hand over her mouth when they announced that a twelve-story building near the memorial had just crumbled to the ground. A grocery deliveryman had dropped his bags, and milk pooled around his shoes. A scared child clung to his mother's leg, and I saw the fear in his eyes. The mother looked at Goran, then at me.

Another whistle pierced the air; then what sounded like a thousand missiles screamed over the sky above us.

"It's the end of the world," the mother said, dry-lipped, and pulled her child into her closer.

We all stared up to see the missiles of mass destruction fly overhead. But what appeared over the tree line wasn't missiles at all.

It was the League.

I could tell, even from this far away, that Uberman led the charge. They flew in a perfect pattern, hundreds of heroes, all the League's allies over the years, and its many probationaries. Whatever it was in the city, the crisis had to be big. I'd never seen this many heroes in one place in my life; I didn't know that many even existed. I touched the skin on my finger, the empty space where the League probationary ring used to be.

It was a dazzling sight. Legions of colorful costumes skimmed across the horizon, flying like fighter jets in tight formation.

I looked around me, and all of a sudden I knew what I needed to do, where I should be. I turned to Goran.

"I have to go," I said to him.

But he was already gone.

I raced into the house without closing the door behind me and bounded to the top of the stairs before the screen door had even slammed.

I burst into my father's room, threw open the closet door, and reached inside, grabbing a handful of plastic dry-cleaner bags. I found what I needed and threw it on the bed, then rifled through my father's change dish on his dresser for his car keys.

Shoving the keys in my pocket, I ripped open the plastic and stared down at my father's uniform.

I stomped on the gas pedal of Dad's Camaro to make it go as fast as it could. Dad was always careful to observe the speed limit. You should have seen the papers the time he got a traffic ticket for rolling through a right-hand turn on a red light.

There was a line of traffic stopped ahead, a row of police cars blocking the road in front of them. I pulled over onto the shoulder and sped forward to the front of the line. A cop rushed over and waved his hands for me to stop.

"You can't go into the city," he said as he walked over to my window. "The governor has declared a state of emergency. We can't let anyone in or—"

He stopped short when he saw what I was wearing.

Although it was a little broad in the shoulders, my father's old costume fit nearly perfectly.

"Where are *you* going?" A stupefied grin appeared on the officer's face.

I put the car in first.

"I'm going to save the world."

Then I floored it.

It took me forever to get to the center of the city. Although incoming vehicles were blocked, there was a steady line of traffic to get off the island. I rarely encountered another inbound car, but I did have to be careful to stay out of the way of ambulances and fire trucks, and there was the occasional impatient departing motorist who decided to use the lane of the oncoming traffic. I saw this maneuver result in three accidents; one took out a police car. It was an appropriate amount of chaos for the end of the world.

I circled around the outer loop of the downtown area; every road into the center was blocked off by police. I decided to go the rest of the way on foot, but by the time I was halfway to the Wilson Memorial, I couldn't remember how many turns I'd made. A nagging doubt entered in my head—that I wouldn't be able to find my way back to Dad's car.

I encountered masses of oncoming foot traffic as panicked people fled the scene. Other people seemed glued to the spectacle, and I pushed into the crowd as close as I could get to the Wilson Memorial building. People stared up at the building, sirens blared, and policemen and firemen rushed inside.

Emergency service workers tried to tend to the wounded and get them into ambulances.

"It's going to fall! Just like last time!" a man in a pinstriped suit shouted, sheltering himself under his briefcase as he fled from the scene.

I heard other fragments from the crowd, and I couldn't tell which were silly and which were true. A bearded man with a homemade poster that read JOHN 3:16 in Magic Marker shouted at our section of the crowd.

"Repent! Repent!"

A stray chunk of debris came tumbling down from the sky directly toward the crowd. I shouted for everyone to move and did my best to shove as many people as I could off to the side. The chunk of debris landed and exploded into dust, and tiny sharp bits sprayed the crowd. People screamed as they were showered with shards.

I tried to decide which person was the bloodiest, who needed my hands the most.

"It's the remains of that Planet Eater. It's an alien reactor, and it's been activated," a fireman covered in a chalky layer of dust told me. "Someone stirred it up again." I saw a trickle of blood drip down his forehead from under his hat. Hands burning, I reached up to shift the hat and help him. The bleeding stopped.

"Who stirred it up?" I asked.

The fireman charged back up into the building before I could get an answer out of him. I looked around and saw too many victims for me to help. Maybe instead I should try to get everyone out of here as fast as possible before another explosion.

But if what the fireman said was true, nowhere on the planet would be safe from the next explosion.

I looked up at the Wilson Memorial, looming high above. It blocked the morning sun, and its shadow felt cool on my face. I could hear the cops shouting over the din of the sirens and engines. They did their best to control the crowd, to move people out, keep them away from the building. Round after round of firefighters charged inside. You could tell that most of them were remembering the event of the first disaster on this site, because they wore doom on their faces.

At the very top of the Memorial building, towering high above us, Justice stepped out. More accurately, he hovered out onto the ledge. Instantly the crowd recognized him by the unmistakable color and pattern of his cape, and cheers erupted.

Thank God, I thought to myself. Justice made it here first; of course the entire League was inside under his command, repairing the damage in superhuman time.

Justice surveyed the crowds beneath him, then looked up into the sky. I couldn't pinpoint where he was looking. It was difficult to see his expression from so far away, but I could read something in his posture, something resigned, almost sad. It reminded me of the night I'd interrupted him while he stared out into space.

And suddenly the Wilson Memorial was a beehive, and we the people on the streets were the foolish, curious children who'd knocked on it to see if there really were bees inside. Hundreds of heroes came flying out of the building and flew overhead.

The crowd looked up in awe, and the applause diminished.

Fantastic colors and capes swarmed high above us and gathered in a single, unified swirl of heroes. Uberman was in front, his proud chest puffed and leading the way. There was something different about the way that he flew, though. He had the same righteously powerful posture, not too graceful, not too rough, but there was something missing in his face. Then it dawned on me: what was missing was his kindness.

The swirl of heroes changed direction and swooped down on the crowd. The people froze, caught in a single, spectacular, breathtaking moment, the moment their heroes became kamikazes and their city became Pearl Harbor. There wasn't even time to scream.

Gamma rays, supercold charges, and bio-blasts rained down from the sky and blew holes in the ground around us. I saw a NO PARKING MON/WED/FRI sign vaporized. A goateed man on his Vespa was instantly frozen in a block of ice. A group of tourists dropped to their knees and grabbed their bleeding ears at the howl of a sonic scream.

"Move!" I yelled at the top of my lungs. "Move!"

People scattered and ran helter-skelter, and I saw a few trampled in the stampede to escape. Another wave of heroes was swooping in for the next round of attacks. Victims littered the streets everywhere. I needed to get the crowds to safety.

Warrior Woman pulverized the entire top floor of an office building and toppled over a giant underwear billboard. The billboard caught on the side of the building, but threatened to fall and flatten a circle of ambulances and emergency medical technicians. I raced to the group and yanked an EMT's hand away from a resuscitator.

"Tell everyone to hold hands now!"

She looked at my hand, then at me like I was a nut job.

"NOW!" I yelled, and looked up at the billboard. She saw the threat and screamed for everyone to take cover by her ambulance. We grabbed each other's hands and joined in a chain right as the billboard dislodged and careened down toward us. I shouted for everyone to hold on tight, and I heated up and sent my power through the chain just as it crashed onto us. Under normal circumstances we would have been crushed to death, but it took only a split second for me to concentrate and make us whole. Still holding hands, we stood up and shot clear through the remains of the billboard. I'd never pulled off anything like that kind of healing before, and I was a little surprised at how simple it had been. I even felt energized by the action. All I had to do was keep my cool and focus. Maybe it really was as simple as my dad said it was. Maybe all you really need to do is believe in yourself.

I didn't stick around for congratulations, and the EMTs went right back to work on their patients. I had to be extra fast because people were understandably dumbfounded, which made their reaction time slower. They couldn't imagine why their greatest heroes had turned on them. It didn't make any sense to me either, but I had to focus on the task at hand. Rescue. I could think about the rest later.

Across the street the Galaxy Twins, blank-faced, had cornered an entire waitstaff in the vestibule of their restaurant. The Twins hovered in front of the potential victims and reached out to join hands and ignite.

God, how I missed my team. If Golden Boy had been there,

he would have been on top of the Twins in a second flat, Scarlett would have flown the group to safety, and Larry would have given the Twins a mean case of shingles. Actually, no one would have been in any serious danger in the first place, because Ruth would have spotted the whole thing minutes before it happened.

But I was alone, and it was up to me to stop the carnage. I tried to break through the chaos to get to the Twins, but there was no way I could make it there before they blasted the restaurant workers to smithereens. The Twins rose up into the air to improve the trajectory of their blasts.

Suddenly a dark cape materialized out of the shadows of the building behind them. I was just halfway across the street when I saw Dark Hero palm each of their heads like they were two coconuts and smash them together. The Twins spiraled through the air like crumpled paper airplanes and careened down into a Dumpster.

Dark Hero disappeared into shadows, and I turned and saw Warrior Woman high in the air. She had drawn her sword and was diving down toward a tour guide and a group of school children huddled pitifully with their teacher under a thin, glass bus stop.

"You get the kids, I'll take that pushy broad."

Next to me a big, bald bruiser was rolling up his sleeves. It was Ruth's old partner, the Wrecking Ball. I guess there's not much thrill left in robbing banks if the world has been destroyed. We raced toward the bus stop at full speed as Warrior Woman neared her target. Her aegis, full-body armor, and battle helmet reflected the glare of the sun, and she looked more missile than woman. I yelled at the school group to move, to get away from the glass. The Wrecking Ball grabbed a stop sign and yanked it out of the pavement like he was pulling a dandelion out of his garden.

I pulled the children away from the bus stop at the same moment the Wrecking Ball leaped up onto it. He turned his shoulders, wound up, swung with all his might, and hit Warrior Woman with the stop sign like she was a softball, knocking her out of the park. The sound of the sign connecting with Warrior Woman's armor produced an eerie metallic clang that traveled up my spine.

The Wrecking Ball hopped down off the bus stop.

"That'll teach her," he said, and wiped the rust off his hands. "Who's next?"

I looked around at the tour group. We were standing in the middle of the street. Devastation all around us. A tremor in the ground knocked a few kids off their feet. We were exposed, and I had to get them to safety.

I wasn't sure where to take them. Hundreds of heroes were attacking in the streets. Hiding them in a building might be our best bet, but I couldn't tell which ones were safe. Blue Lightning blew up a bagel shop. Ethereal Empress evaporated a shoe store. There was so much more, it was difficult to take in all the destruction at once.

I shielded my eyes to block the sun and looked up once more at the top of the Wilson Memorial building. Justice still hovered in front of the building. Why hadn't he put a stop to the threat inside yet? What could be so insurmountable that even he couldn't stop it? I thought about charging in as soon as

I'd helped these kids to safe ground, but what chance did I have of stopping those alien remains from blowing if Justice himself couldn't do anything?

The tour guide was in a panic. She grabbed the epaulets of my father's costume and tugged at the medals.

"You have to help us, you have to help us!" I saw the panic in her eyes and recognized her as the same haughty tour guide who'd led me and my mother through the Wilson Memorial days ago.

My mind turned to thoughts of my mother. What had she done? What was happening in that crystallized alien core? Was this all part of her doing? I hoped she wasn't responsible. I couldn't imagine her falling this far. Instinctively, my hands went to my chest, and I fingered the ring on the necklace she'd given me.

Justice turned and looked down. He raised his arm and pointed his finger at me. The boom of his voice echoed in my ears as he looked right at me and shouted "Boy!" with anger and disgust on his face. The sound of that accusation chilled me. Every hero stopped when they heard it, and the swarm turned their attention to me. They swooped in our direction from all sides. The kids screamed.

I saw a shadow appear at our feet, and it was growing in diameter fast. I didn't stop to look up; I dove to the right.

The Wrecking Ball was caught underneath the thirteenth floor of the Bascom Accounting Firm building, which Warrior Woman had launched from the next building over.

I peeled myself up off the ground and saw the kids, their faces drained of all color as they looked at the pile of rubble. All that could be seen of the Wrecking Ball was a hand, its palm still smudged with rust.

I grabbed as many of the children as I could and started running. I couldn't see a building that wasn't under siege; hell, I couldn't even see a free door. I was about to fumble the small child in my arms when a cowl suddenly whooshed in front of me. Dark Hero lifted the child over his shoulder before I dropped her, and motioned for us to follow him.

The heroes gathered in a swirling vortex and began to form an attack aimed in our direction. I shouted for the teacher and the tour guide to hurry. The tour guide kicked off her heels so she could run. We sprinted down an alley along the side of a factory building. Dark Hero yanked open a fire exit and directed us to hurry up the stairs. We grabbed the kids and raced up three flights as fast as we could. We burst out onto the fourth floor, and Dark Hero gathered us in the middle of the room and shoved heavy metal file cabinets around us to provide some shielding. The teacher hurried the children into the makeshift bunker and told them all to sit quietly. The tour guide cried hysterically.

I thought I heard a scraping noise above us, but I assumed it was the building settling under all the duress of the battle outside.

Dark Hero put his hand over the tour guide's mouth to shut her up. He needed to listen. We all looked up at the ceiling, at the sound of something moving above us, something like claws scraping across a metal floor. Dark Hero rose and walked directly beneath the sound.

A carved circle of concrete dropped out of the ceiling, and the Badger and the Weasel dropped through the hole and pounced on top of Dark Hero, taking swipes at him with their claws. The kids squealed and clattered to the other side of the room. Dark Hero drew the rodents away from the children and engaged them in hand-to-claw.

A sudden blast rattled the building. The children screamed, and the floor began to crumble and disappear beneath us. I yelled for everyone to roll with me to the side of the floor that still remained intact. I grabbed a little girl by her tiny arm to stop her from slipping into the abyss. The other children reacted quickly, and no one fell. Another sonic boom rattled the building, and the floor across the room collapsed. Suddenly we were struggling to stay on a tilting plane that sloped directly toward a yawning chasm, a certain plunge to death. The children didn't scream; all of their energy had been spent climbing up to safety.

There was a little boy who looked like he hadn't changed clothes in a few weeks trying to scramble up the sloping floor, but he was dangerously close to the edge. The tour guide was close enough to help him, but she was frozen with fear. I scooted down closer to him, only a few feet away, and stretched out my leg so he was almost able to reach it. I called out for him to hold on, that I was coming. The building shook again, this time with a heat blast. I felt my eyelashes singe in the heat, but I kept crawling closer and closer to the boy. Dark Hero had his hands full trying to dodge the Weasel and the Badger, all the while keeping them away from the kids, but he managed to throw me the end of his cape, so I could hold on and dangle near the boy. Just a few more feet—I was going to reach him and save him.

"Thank you!" The teacher cried big grateful tears as the boy reached to grab my foot. "Thank you!"

Then the center of the floor gave way completely.

Everyone screamed, and we saw the boy, his eyes big as saucers, disappear in the darkness.

But something stopped him in midair.

A massive, sinewy hand grabbed the edge of the floor and pulled a husky frame onto the remaining ledge. Under the rescuer's other arm—which ended in a lump of flesh that could have been a hand—was the little boy, frightened but unharmed.

Dad.

"Are you an angel?" the filthy little boy asked my father. He must have thought he was already dead.

Dad wiped a smudge of dirt off the side of the kid's face and mussed his hair. He lifted the boy up, sat him down safely next to me, and in the next second my father was upon the Badger and the Weasel.

The Weasel gnashed his razor-sharp teeth at him. Dad picked up the Badger and threw him at the Weasel, knocking them both to the floor. They never had a chance to get up. Dad grabbed each by the foot and tossed them into the hole. I counted to five before we heard their bodies smack the bottom.

Dark Hero motioned for us to follow him. Dad picked up the tour guide, helped the teacher to her feet, and we led all the kids toward Dark Hero, who had found an emergency fire door leading to a metal walkway that connected with the building next door.

I wanted to stop and catch my breath, but Dark Hero kept urging us forward. Dad and I each had three kids in our arms, and we herded the rest along quickly. Dark Hero led us up a dozen flights of stairs to the roof and began to lower the children over the side, onto the roof of the next building.

Dad told us to hurry, we had to get the kids across into the next building and out the first-floor exit before the heroes found them. The building was severely damaged, more a husk than a building, really. I hoped it would hold long enough for us to escape. The tour guide didn't want to drop over the wall to the next building, so after all the children were safely on the other side, Dad picked her up, still squealing, and tossed her over into Dark Hero's arms.

Just then we heard the roar as the building we'd just left collapsed. We turned around to watch the floors crushing down on each other like a petrified stack of pancakes. We didn't wait to see the top floor hit bottom; we disappeared below.

The power was off, so we hurried in and out of shadows as we poured down the stairwell. It's a good thing missing chunks of walls allowed some light to stream in, because we'd never have been able to see otherwise.

Dark Hero led us out onto the tenth floor and motioned for us to be quiet. He and Dad listened. Nothing. The silence made my hair stand on end.

"What the hell is happening?" I asked in a sharp whisper. "Who's doing this?" But I already knew the answer, and so did Dad.

He looked out of a missing chunk in the wall, and I followed his gaze up to the alien who hovered over the Wilson Memorial.

Justice.

Dad rubbed the corners of his eyes like he always did after a bad day at the factory.

"He always was a real bad penny."

"I don't get it," I said. "How's he doing this?"

Dad stared off into the sky, crowded with hundreds of heroes, destroying the city.

"Mind control." Dad sighed and shook his head. "I *hate* mind control."

"How do we fight it?" I laid my hand on a little girl's forehead, and a cut stopped bleeding and sealed.

"We're fine for now. He's working in large numbers."

"What if he tries to get in our heads?"

"Simple," Dad told me. "Don't think like everyone else." He grabbed my wrist. "Let me see your hand."

"Why?"

"Where's your ring?"

I didn't want to tell Dad that it was buried with Ruth. That was none of his business.

"I don't have it anymore."

"That's how he does it, I bet. How he controls the League. The rings," Dad said. He was looking up at the sky, watching the "heroes" of the world weave in and out of air currents as they wreaked mass destruction. "It's how he always knows where you are. That's just his style, too. He made a big production out of giving it to you, didn't he?" Dad couldn't hide the disgust on his face. "Like it was some special treasure."

"Why's he doing this?" I asked.

"He's going to blow up the world," Dad said, as if it were a simple, obvious truth. "So he can go home."

I thought about the night I'd caught Justice staring off into space.

You all smell the same to me.

"He can't get there on his own—even he doesn't have that kind of power. He needs something big to propel him."

Dad looked me up and down.

"Nice outfit."

Up to that point I'd forgotten that I was wearing his costume. I would have felt less embarrassed if I'd been standing in front of him naked. He stared at the faint outline of the marinara stain around the abdomen. The dry cleaners had done a good job, but they weren't miracle workers.

Dark Hero was crouched near the missing chunk in the wall. He never took his eyes off Justice or the Wilson Memorial. So far we were lucky, no one knew where we were. Yet. I wrapped my hands around two sprained ankles and then cupped my hand around the teacher's shoulder blade. She said she thought she'd broken a rib in the scramble when the floor fell. I did what I could for the pain.

"Who's your friend?" Dad motioned to Dark Hero.

"Oh, that's Dark Hero," I said, like I was introducing a new friend I'd brought home from school.

"Nice to meet you," Dad said, and extended his hand. "I'm a fan of your work." Dark Hero stood up and shook my father's hand. "Very result oriented."

"So," Dad asked himself, his eyes narrowing, "what are we gonna do here?"

We were a motley group of leftovers, saddled by potential victims—kids, no less. Simple, I thought, we'll get the kids to safety, take out the hundreds of heroes on our own—surely three of us should be enough—then we can stop Justice from destroying the planet. If we mind the time, we may even be able to make it home in time for dinner.

In response to Dad's question, Dark Hero made a wringing motion with his hands like he was snapping a neck in two. I assumed he was referring to Justice.

Dad motioned for us to crouch down on the floor with him. He took a stapler off the ground and used it as a pointer.

"If Justice is here"—he stood a hole puncher on its side to represent the Wilson Memorial building—"and we're here"—he grabbed a dented pencil sharpener to stand for our building. Then he stopped and rubbed his chin and thought about it for a second. Dark Hero silently pointed out some possible maneuvers.

"Too many of them," Dad said. "We'd never make it inside in time to stop Justice."

The building lurched and tossed us to the side.

"We don't have much time," I said. The children clung to the teacher and the tour guide.

I stood up with Dad and Dark Hero, and we stared at the impossible number of superpowered beings who swarmed the sky, sowing destruction.

"So *many* heroes." I looked up with wonder. I didn't need to look over to Dad or Dark Hero to know that we were going to try anyway. This was crazy. This was suicide. But we didn't have a choice. How the hell were we supposed to get past them?

I heard the distinct shuffle of footsteps coming from the stairwell.

"Get ready," I said. "They're coming."

Dad turned, ready to strike. Dark Hero had already disappeared into the shadows.

The door to the room burst open.

"Fuckin-A, I'd give my left tit for a working elevator!" Miss Scarlett rubbed her sore feet, heels in hand. Typhoid Larry filed in close behind her and propped himself up against the doorway to catch his breath.

"I said I'd carry you up," Golden Boy said as he zipped into the room from behind them.

"And *I said* I got it!" Scarlett threw a shoe at him. The shoe missed and stuck by its stiletto heel into a pushpin board next to the tour guide's face.

Golden Boy saw me in Dad's costume.

"Thom, that's your father's—" He stopped short when he saw my dad.

He stood up straight and saluted.

"Sir," Golden Boy greeted my father.

"Kevin," my father greeted him back.

Scarlett yanked Kevin's hand away from his forehead. "At ease, soldier."

"So," Larry said. "How can we help?"

CHAPTER THIRTY-TWO

DAD WAS THE TACTICAL genius, so we all looked to him for a plan. He surprised me by what he did next—he asked for suggestions and looked directly at me. I told him the situation reminded me of a simulated training exercise during League try-outs, on a much larger scale, of course. He nodded for me to go on.

"Well." I cleared my throat. "Our goal is to stop the maniac commanding all this. So we shouldn't try to defeat all the heroes together; all we really need is a distraction so some of us can get inside the Wilson Memorial. We have to stop that alien reactor before it blows."

The group nodded. Dad listened as I continued.

"We have this one maneuver we do—our team—we call it the Shake 'n' Bake."

"Oooh, that's a goodie." Scarlett rubbed her hands together and Kevin nodded. Larry tugged at his collar like it was too tight around his neck.

"I think we could adapt it for this situation. Scarlett, you and Kevin take on the first wave, pay close attention to the A-level superpowers. Larry, you know your part. That'll give Dark Hero and Dad time to get inside and take care of what needs doing." I knew they would have no qualms about killing a renegade hero to save the world; they should be the ones to go inside.

"You're the healer. You have to come with us," Dad said to me. "In case one of us falls."

I took a deep breath and nodded, not sure if I had what it took to do this.

"Great," Scarlett said. "We're the world's last hope: Disease-boy." She nodded at Larry. "A homo." That would be me. "History's biggest failure." That would be Dad. "A big fat asshole." She shot a mean look at Kevin like we wouldn't have figured out who she meant.

"And wait, I'm sorry, who the hell *are* you, anyway?" Scarlett asked Dark Hero. He kept his mouth covered with his black cowl.

"But," Larry began to protest, "there's no way, I mean, there are so many, I don't know if I have that kind of power. They'll *kill* us." He gulped and then said out loud what we were all thinking. "We're going to die trying, aren't we?"

Our silence gave him his answer.

Scarlett and Kevin stole a glance, and just as quickly, she turned to look away.

The building shook again. This time it was a direct hit. The children screamed. The heroes had found us.

* * *

We stood at the bottom doorway, ready to go. The sunlight poured inside and lit up our faces. We looked up at the swarm of heroes gathering in the air above us.

"Let's do this," I whispered to everyone.

The teacher was already scurrying out the back exit with the children and the tour guide.

Larry stepped forward. "I just want to say if we're gonna go out of this world swinging, there's no group I'd rather go out of this world swinging with."

Larry put his hand in the middle of the group, and the rest of us followed and clasped his fist in a huddle. Even my dad put in his good hand. I grabbed each hand and let the warmth of my power flow through them. I was protecting them from what was to come, passing along the extra immunities they'd need if our scheme was going to work. I looked into each of the faces around me, grateful for the people in my life. Here at the end of the world, during these final moments of our time on this planet, they were all I had, and it wasn't a disappointment. It was family. Scarlett's eyes brimmed with tears. She clasped Golden Boy's hand tightly, with affection. He looked into her eyes to see if she meant it, and she did.

"Let's do this for Ruth," I said. "On my count."

"One—"

We stood at the door, our muscles tensed, ready to break forward, the heroes fast approaching.

"Two—"

BAM! Scarlett ignited and flew into the air in the middle of a throng of heroes and met them head-on with the biggest blast of fire I'd ever seen.

Golden Boy sprinted into the crowd and clocked each hero

on the ground. Then he zoomed up the side of the building and jumped onto Uberman's back. He whipped up Uberman's cape, covering his head with the fabric, and tried to steer him like he was riding a bull at the rodeo.

Larry turned and ran back up into the building. I heard his footsteps echo up the stairs.

On the way to the Memorial Tower, Dad and Dark Hero had taken down six heroes, three apiece, before I even had a chance to engage my first one, a reserve member known as the American Agent. He had bored me even during his prime—all he had was some superstrength serum and an inordinate sense of pride, that was about it. I kicked him in the groin and went on to the next challenge. I had some catching up to do.

In fact, there were even more renegade heroes than we'd thought, and we still had to clear most of them to get to the Wilson Memorial. I saw about fifty of them descend on Dark Hero. It was straight out of a zombie movie as he disappeared under a sea of heroes, who tore at his flesh. I couldn't imagine how he was going to survive.

The fight in the air wasn't much better. You could see more costumes than blue sky. Golden Boy propelled the blinded Uberman through the masses of floating heroes and gave Scarlett some breathing room. He zipped across the horizon and was gone.

Scarlett screamed like a battle-crazed soldier and blasted Warrior Woman clear across the harbor. But the odds were against her; tens of heroes became hundreds, and soon she had to shift into desperate defense mode.

Nothing seemed to stop Dad. He had an uncanny knack for

engaging the heroes one at a time. He'd dispatch them faster than they were able to realize he was standing in front of them. He'd be on to the next before the last one hit the pavement. Still the numbers were stacking up against him. He had hundreds more to take out if we were ever going to make it to the Memorial, and we simply didn't have that kind of time.

Where the hell was Larry, anyway?

I dodged a catarang and took a talon across the face from the Lynx. She moved impossibly fast, and my reaction time was nothing compared to hers. I looked up for help, but Scarlett had disappeared in a swirl of capes high above, Dad was busy dodging and striking at least a hundred high-powered heroes, Golden Boy was zipping across the horizon, still trying to subdue Uberman, and I hadn't seen Dark Hero since he'd been overwhelmed by the masses. We needed a miracle.

And then I saw Larry out of the corner of my eye. He stood on the edge of our teetering building, our crumbling refuge. He raised his chin and faced the sky. He surveyed the incredible destruction around him. Then with the grace of an Olympic diver, he jogged a few paces back and began his approach. He ran with a determined look on his face, planted his feet on the concrete ledge, and leaped off the building in a perfect swan dive.

He flew through the air at an impossible speed toward the ground, and I thought about Larry the night I owned up to who I was, when he slipped me a Xanax and sped off in his muscle car—the young man who so desperately wanted to be a hero. This was his chance, and he plummeted toward the ground like he had at last found his purpose. I closed my eyes and said good-bye to my friend.

Larry splattered on the pavement into a million globular particles of pink goo that bounced out in all directions and permeated the air everywhere. I covered my mouth with my mask, and I saw Dad take in a deep gulp of air so he could hold his breath while he fought.

Then I watched the domino effect as hero after hero doubled over in pain, some with the bubonic plague, some with dysentery, others with the bird flu. They dropped in droves, and soon the hundreds of heroes who had been blocking our way to the Wilson Memorial were merely objects to be stepped over on our way inside the building. On our way to stop Justice.

The plan worked. Larry had cleared the way for us on the ground, and I'd given us just the right amount of my power so that we were immune.

But the heroes in the sky were unaffected by Larry's sacrifice. Even though Golden Boy's hands were moving at superspeed to pull Uberman's cape over his eyes, Uberman was about to get the upper hand. Scarlett tried to keep a hundred flying capes at bay, but I could tell she was reaching the limit of her powers, because her flame was beginning to flicker. Uberman finally managed to pull free of his cape. He swatted Golden Boy off his back with a speed that would have made Kevin jealous— if he'd had time to see the punch that sent him flying.

Scarlett yelped when she saw Kevin belted into the sky. She knew in a few seconds he would begin a deadly descent, so she summoned all the fire she had left and raced through the air to catch him.

She caught him about ten feet from the pavement. Hundreds of heroes swirled after her. I watched her fly up into the air and then into a narrow space where two buildings almost touched. In mass formation, the heroes couldn't fit through the narrow crevice, and this bought her a little time.

But there weren't any more miracles left for Scarlett and Golden Boy. As they disappeared over the top of another building, I saw a flock of heroes overwhelm and crush them to the ground, like they were trapped in the bottom of an hourglass with sand pouring down on them relentlessly. The light from Scarlett's flame flickered one last time and then disappeared for good. I closed my eyes and prayed for their safety. I had to remain calm and focused on the task at hand.

I raced to catch up with my dad as he sprinted toward the building. Scarlett and Kevin and Larry had bought us the time we needed—they'd distracted the heroes, and it was up to us to do the rest. Dark Hero was nowhere to be seen.

In seconds, I found myself staring up at the Wilson Memorial. It glowed with radiation, and I felt the warm light on my face as I gazed up at my destiny.

"Ready?" Dad looked at me, eager to charge.

I nodded, and he ripped open the front door.

Warrior Woman appeared in the doorway, her shield and sword raised for battle. She lifted her helmet and proclaimed, "This domain is mine and mine alone to protect!"

Dad glanced over his shoulder at me with his best you-cannot-be-serious look. Then we leaped at Warrior Woman.

He punched high and I kicked low. My kick bent her bare knee backward, and Dad took advantage of the open helmet to knock her in the face and send her flying across the room. She didn't get up.

Dad and I raced up the stairs.

"This domain is mine and mine alone," Dad mumbled to himself as we took the stairs three and four at a time. "What a ridiculous thing to say."

I didn't think I could maintain this pace after the first fifty floors, but Dad showed no signs of slowing down. I struggled to keep up with him, and I thought I was going to barf. Suddenly I realized that Dark Hero had slipped in with us—when, I don't know. He stuck to the shadows even though there weren't many left, with all the radiation glow. The space around us became brighter the higher we climbed, and we charged up directly into the light.

When we yanked open the door to the floor below the observation deck, we had to cover our eyes. The crystallized formation had overtaken the building all the way up to the top. Gingerly, we stepped onto the smooth surface of the crystal.

"We don't have as much time as I thought," Dad said. "He's right above us."

We needed an inspired plan, one of those great, heroic last-minute Hail Mary passes that wins the Super Bowl. The kind of brilliant move that would give us the upper hand against impossible odds. The kind of idea that would make us icons for years to come and yield a succession of blockbusters and action figures. I wished I could think of one.

"Let's just take our chances," I said, ready to charge up to the last floor. I clutched the ring around my neck and thought maybe this was when I would need the ring. Mom said I'd know what to do with it when the time came, and since the world was about to end, this seemed as good a time as any.

"I have the ring," I told Dad. "Let's go."

"What ring?" He looked at me, puzzled.

"Mom told me not to think about it. But she said I'd know what to do with it when the time came, and this has got to be it."

"You've seen your mother?" Dad stepped toward me.

"She told me not to think about her." And here I was talking about her, thinking about her yet again.

Dad grabbed me by my shoulders. "You've seen her?" He began to shake me. "Tell me, where is she?"

"I don't know, she can't make herself visible anymore, she came back and had me get the ring." I could not have picked a worse time to spill all this, even if I thought it would help.

Dad turned white, the muscles in his face froze, and his whole body became rigid. He could barely breathe, barely allow himself to hope.

"But she was here," he said to himself, lost in thought, then faced me. "Where's the ring?"

I lifted it out of my shirt and showed it to him. He couldn't believe what he saw. He gently took the ring, the wedding gift he'd made for my mother, and cradled it in his palm. Suddenly, his fingers snapped shut around it, a Venus flytrap ensnaring its insect victim, and snatched it off my neck. The ends of the thin leather straps stung as they snapped against my skin.

Dark Hero suddenly appeared and pushed us apart, motioning for us to be quiet.

"What?" Dad said, perturbed at the interruption. He shoved the ring into his pocket. "What's he trying to tell us?"

I studied Dark Hero's face as he scanned the corners of the brightly glowing room. My eyes followed his.

"He thinks we're not alone."

I didn't say it out loud, but I wondered if it was Mom.

Smack!

Silver Bullet slammed me against the wall. The force knocked Dad to the floor, and I saw him struggle to catch the wind that had been knocked out of him. It was sloppy for Dad not to notice the impending attack, but he had been distracted. Silver Bullet had his hand halfway in my father's pocket before Dad could react.

Silver Bullet was fast, but Dark Hero had instincts so sharp they could slice a wall of steel. He kicked Silver Bullet clear to the other side of the room and reached into Dad's pocket and took out the ring.

Dark Hero stood in the middle of the room and held the ring up like bait, like a matador brandishing his red cape. He sprang up over a flash of silver and landed unharmed.

I saw him count three beats to himself, then he raised his arm and threw a right hook to the air.

Silver Bullet's face slowed down enough to become a recognizable metallic blur as it connected with Dark Hero's fist. He came tumbling to the ground, out cold.

Dad picked himself off the glowing floor, and I peeled myself off the wall.

"I know what to do." I looked at the ring in Dark Hero's hand.

Then I looked into Dark Hero's face. "Give me your clothes."

Dark Hero took a step back. I took a step forward.

"He won't know who we are if we change clothes. It'll give us the element of surprise."

Dark Hero shook his head, but I persisted. I didn't care if he thought I was a big old gaybag.

"C'mon, man, this is the end of the world. I don't care about your secret identity."

I faked right so that he'd move left, my old reliable basketball maneuver, and he fell for it. I grabbed the back of his cowl and pulled it off. In an instant, all the air flew out of my lungs. That face was unmistakable. I should have recognized his eyes all along. They bore a hole down to my heart.

"Hello, Thom."

Goran's face glistened in the bright glow of the alien crystal.

CHAPTER THIRTY-THREE

SUDDENLY SILVER BULLET came to and disappeared in a flash. That was bad; he was free to warn Justice.

"I'll stop him." Dad's voice echoed in the stairwell as he raced down the steps. His focus was back.

Meanwhile, I stood directly in front of the only person who'd been able to open my heart, the one person I could never get out of my head. I couldn't believe he was the one who'd been following me all this time. It suddenly made so much sense, and I felt like the biggest fool. This is what he'd been trying to tell me when he put my hands over his face and above his eyes.

We heard a steely clang echo from the stairwell, like sheet metal ringing a bell.

The space between us was filled with electricity and

anticipation and embarrassment. All my emotions were laid bare. I couldn't move.

I knew we didn't have any time, the world was depending on us, but I had to do what I did next. I could hear Ruth in my head. *Don't wait.* I reached out and put my hand on the side of his face. I had to touch him, to make sure he was real, to make sure he was there right in front of me.

"He won't be telling Justice anything." Dad entered the room.

I pulled my hand away, but it was too late. Dad had seen it. He cleared his throat. He knew he'd intruded on a moment of unguarded intimacy. It was impossible to mistake. He'd loved, too.

Dad struggled to hide his emotions. But I could tell that he was trying as hard as he could to understand. In an instant he was back to business.

"My suit, please."

I handed Dad his old costume, and he suited up in the uniform. He didn't bother to put his mask or gloves on; he shoved them in his belt.

I slowly pulled on Goran's cape and cowl.

Goran discreetly took Dad's work clothes and put them on. Then Dad snatched his wedding ring back from Goran with his good hand and pointed upstairs with the melted lump of flesh.

"If we're going to do this," he said without looking at me, "let's do it now."

The observation deck to the Wilson Memorial was alive with radioactive crystal that would soon detonate and take our planet with it. This was an unfortunate side effect of Justice's plan to create an explosion that would propel him into the stars and home. The human race, the one that smelled, was apparently an acceptable loss.

He stood, arms folded, waiting, and stared out into the sky. Dad and I crept onto the deck.

"Is this all I'm going to get from this planet?" Justice sighed. "An old has-been and his lackey. How's the wife, Hal?"

Dad didn't stop inching toward Justice.

I could now see that Justice was sitting on a strange apparatus. It looked like a miniature rocket, and he'd strapped himself into it. I'd always thought heroes on his level could do anything, and here he had to strap himself into a rocket and explode our planet to go to some remote sector of outer space? His planet wasn't even there anymore. Maybe he should have used his big mental powers to wrap his head around that one.

My dad carefully observed his every move as Justice punched a code into a keypad on the rocket and unbuckled the harness. I watched Dad turn the numbers over in his head. Justice hopped off the rocket.

Dad tensed, ready for the first move, and I tried to withdraw into a shadow in my best Dark Hero style. Unfortunately, there weren't any shadows on the deck, and as I stood in the light I thought Justice was right. We weren't much of a cavalry.

Dad struck first. A quick left jab, which Justice easily blocked by raising the palm of his hand. But the jab was just a distraction so Dad could deliver a swift kick to the groin. Normally the move worked like a charm, but it was little more than an annoyance to someone with indestructible testicles.

Still, it took Justice by surprise, which gave Dad enough time to spin and land a high kick to Justice's face. Justice stumbled back and rubbed his eyes, temporarily blinded by the blow of Dad's boot to his pupils.

I raced in to join the fight, but almost tripped over my long cape. Dark Hero knew how to use the costume to his advantage, but I had trouble with it. Before Dad could pummel Justice any further, I took a swing.

Justice didn't even look at me. He palmed my forehead and gave an effortless push that sent me flying across the room. I landed on the crystal floor with a thud. The cape floated down after me like a deflated parachute.

"Be patient," Justice said to me. "You're next."

Dad jumped on Justice and delivered two quick chops to his windpipe. The moves would have killed most people, but they didn't have much effect on someone who didn't breathe. Justice tossed Dad aside, but Dad hopped up, ready to strike again and again, as much as it took. Justice rubbed his Adam's apple and then licked at something on his lip. He looked down at his tongue and was surprised by what he saw—blood. He didn't know that he'd bleed red in this atmosphere, and the discovery incensed him. His alien eyes bulged from their sockets; he clenched his teeth and lunged for my father.

Then Dad received a drubbing like I'd never seen before. Blow after blow at superspeed. Dad bent his knees and lowered his center of gravity to meet the force of the blows, reduce their impact. I couldn't believe he was still standing, still conscious. That didn't last. Justice blew on him and pinned him to the floor with his superbreath.

I hopped to my feet to help, but I stumbled over the cape and fell to the floor. Justice saw me trip out of the corner of his eye and momentarily stopped mangling my father to scoff.

"This has got to be some kind of joke," he said. His eyes searched the corners of the deck for a hidden camera. Then he turned back to my dad.

"So, Hal, where is the little faggot, anyway?"

I lifted the cowl off my face and let the cape drop to the floor. The brightness of the room felt good in my eyes.

I ran as fast as I could and body tackled Justice.

But he just stood up and dusted himself off.

"Stupid disguises for stupid humans. You'll have to do better than that."

Goran dropped down on him from the roof of the observation deck. God only knows where he'd been hiding or how he'd gotten there without our seeing him, but there he was. If he'd had his cape, he would have engulfed Justice in the flowing, dark fabric.

But that wasn't his job. His job was to fell him, if only for a moment, in order for Dad to get close enough. Justice, caught by surprise, lurched forward to the hard crystal floor. If not for his invulnerable bones, his cranium would have cracked like a melon. He quickly got to his knees and bent his nose back in joint. Even an alien with impenetrable bones had cartilage.

"You've always been a loser. You just don't know when to quit." He moved in to my father for the kill.

Dad smirked, which I thought was strange. Then I watched him reach into his pocket and pull out his wedding ring. He held it up to Justice—a vampire hunter presenting his homemade crucifix to Dracula. And Justice recoiled from its powerful glow.

Of course. This unique gem was a remnant of his home world, the last tiny chunk of his dead planet. The one thing in this world that was poison to him was now an inert wedding ring from a marriage long since dissolved. A few major villains had once dared to gather some of the precious material years ago, but the League had confiscated it all, sent it into the sun. And come to think of it, all of those villains seemed to have disappeared mysteriously over the years, or died suddenly—foiled robberies, car collisions, premature cardiac arrest.

Justice shrieked at a pitch that shook the city. We covered our ears, but still my left eardrum popped. Justice was in agony. He clawed large chunks of flesh off his neck and chest and arms, like he'd been poisoned with a topical agent and all that mattered was freeing himself from the prison of his own body.

He screamed at the devastating purple glow of the ring, and for a moment I actually felt sorry for him—despite his plans for mass destruction. He wanted to go home to a place that was no longer there, to re-create in a hopeless void some sense of belonging, because he didn't feel like he belonged anywhere here. I knew exactly how that felt. I watched the purple glow of the ring illuminate his face, his wrinkles and his fear. Dad walked steadily toward him, holding out the ring as Justice scraped and ripped at his skin; I thought it was an especially cruel way to go.

Apparently so did Justice. He mustered whatever strength he had left and stared at my father. His pupils were now gone, his eyes entirely milky white. Then he squinted and launched two lasers from those cloudy eyes. The beams shot across the room and severed my father's good hand from his arm at the wrist.

Dad's good hand flew to the far corner of the deck, on the brink of a large fissure that had opened up in the crystal floor. The fingers still clasped the ring tightly.

Dad muffled a scream and clutched his forearm above the cauterized stump. He dropped to his knees in pain, and Justice was behind him in a flash. Justice took Dad's arms, yanked them out of the sockets, and tied them behind his back as if they were rope. Then Justice did the same with Dad's legs, folded them like a pretzel. He dropped Dad face-first to the ground and made his way toward the severed hand.

Dad turned to me with anguished eyes and screamed. "The ring!"

Instead of going for the ring, I ran to my father. I put my hands on his face and let them burn; all I could think about was soothing the immense pain that racked his body.

"Thom!" Dad shouted. "The ring!"

Had I made the wrong choice? Was this the choice Ruth said I would face, and had I already failed it? I couldn't let my father die. I felt the heat of my power flow from my hands into his body, which drank it up like years of thirst in the desert. He was broken inside, dying, a lump of bleeding organs. I poured on as much heat as I could. I had to save him.

Justice moved cautiously toward the severed hand, toward the little piece of anathema it held, to remove it from the building. He approached it purposefully, but with extreme caution. He examined the ring, tried to figure out the best way to pick it up, as if he were a chef who had to determine the least painful way to take a steak off a fire-hot grill without any utensils. He reached down once or twice, tentatively, then withdrew his hand quickly. Touching it would most likely kill him. Instead of reaching again, he put his fingers to his temples and thought.

In the split second it took Justice to transmit a thought, Goran snatched the hand and made a run for it.

"Get it back," Dad murmured to me.

I wanted to help, but I couldn't let go of Dad.

"Thom, don't be foolish." Dad licked back a trail of blood that had spilled out of the corner of his mouth. "You have to stop him; it's more important."

I let myself go, poured on so much heat from my hands that I couldn't tell where I began and the heat ended. I struggled to stay conscious. I'd never used this much power before. I felt my toes begin to twitch, then my calf muscles tremored. Not now, I thought, not now, hold it together.

Goran had sprung out of Justice's reach, not an easy feat considering he was evading an alpha superhero with superflight, speed, and reflexes. As Goran zigzagged around the deck, Justice managed to gain on him. He was right behind him, and then Goran faked to the left and ducked right. My signature move. Justice shot past him and plummeted into the open fissure. Goran made a break for the exit to the stairwell.

He ripped open the door, and there in front of him stood Uberman. Goran, who never took shit from anyone ever, took a step back. This was not good.

Uberman swiped at him with superstrength and agility. Goran barely ducked in time. The blow would have knocked his head clear off his shoulders. Goran leaped up, and with one hand pushed off Uberman's shoulders into the air like he was springing from a pommel horse. With his other hand, he clasped the severed hand with the ring tightly to his chest.

"Go," Dad whispered to me. "Help him."

I felt Dad's insides coagulate, enough for me to remove my hands. I sprang to my heels. The sounds of crystal shattering emanated from the fissure, and I knew Justice was making his way back to the surface.

Dad's eyes went wide. He held up the nub of his forearm where his hand used to be. I think he actually thought he was pointing, that he still had his index finger.

"I see him, Dad, don't worry."

"No," he said weakly. "Behind you."

I whipped around and saw Warrior Woman, her sword raised high above my head, ready to bring it down executioner style, a one-woman guillotine. I sidestepped her as she swung, and elbowed her in the kidney. The crystal surface crackled with sparks as her sword plunged into it. She tugged on her sword, but it was stuck. She abandoned it and wheeled around to swing her scepter directly into my face.

Instinctively, I raised my palm to absorb the blow and caught the scepter like a catcher would take a fastball in the strike zone. It didn't hurt. Instead I felt immense and strong. I tossed the weapon aside and decided to return the favor with a right to Warrior Woman's jaw.

I was shocked to see how effective I was. Somehow my body coursed with strength I'd never felt before. My powers had developed. I'd learned to transmute the energy I'd absorbed from healing, and the results were incredible. Warrior Woman flew across the room upon impact. I'd never seen her felled by pure strength before; she was nearly indestructible. She coughed and pushed herself up and reached for her magic lariat. I wasn't sure what I was going to do if she lassoed me. I wasn't sure how to use my newfound strength to avoid it.

She swung the lariat high above her head, and then all of a sudden it escaped her fingers as if pulled by an unseen force. In an instant, the lasso wound itself around its owner. It wrapped Warrior Woman like a child would thread a spinning top, cocooned her in her own weapon. With her feet tied so close together, Warrior Woman teetered and tried to maintain her balance.

Then an invisible blow knocked her to the edge of the observation deck. Her eyes filled with panic as she tipped over and began her fast plunge to the ground below.

Where the hell did all that come from?

I looked around in time to see Uberman pin Goran to the floor. Goran, quick as ever, threw the severed hand as far away as he could. Uberman took his boot off Goran's sternum and started for the hand.

Goran shot up. He sprinted and snatched the hand away from Uberman as he reached for it. Goran sped toward the ledge, grabbing his cape on the way. He held the severed hand, fingers still twitching, high above his head, taunting Uberman with it. He kicked something with his foot, but I couldn't see what. My eyes were focused on the hand. And so were Uberman's.

Justice pulled himself out of the crystal hole the instant Uberman flew after Goran. Goran fastened the ends of his cape to his belt and bounded from the building as if he were hang gliding. Uberman followed him down into the sky, and they both dropped into a billowing smoke cloud.

As Goran and Uberman disappeared into the smoke, Justice emerged from the crystal hole. Justice hadn't been as foolish as Uberman. He knew better than to fall for such a simple deceit. I looked over to my father, still recovering on the floor, trying to breathe. The ring lay a few yards away, where Goran had kicked it. It glowed and tempted me. He'd drawn Uberman out of the fight, and now it was up to me to get the ring and stop Justice.

I scrambled across the jagged floor for the ring, but Justice intercepted and kicked me across the face. The skin on my forehead ripped open, and I felt my skull crack. I reached up with burning hands and patched my forehead.

Then I caught a purple glow out of the corner of my eye. The ring was levitating into the air. Purple reflected off the crystal floor and cast us all in an eerie grape hue.

Suddenly the invisible force that had tied up Warrior Woman and pushed her over the ledge revealed itself. My mother willed herself to become visible. Her jaw was clenched with determination, her body shaking. Clearly the act of making herself visible brought her great pain.

Dad's lips parted, but his dry throat couldn't find a way to produce any words. Mom looked over in his direction, but she wouldn't make eye contact with him. Her head hung low.

"I'm sorry."

That was all she said. She held up the ring in Justice's direction. I lashed out at Justice with a kick, but without even looking at me, he stepped over my leg and made his way to my mother.

"Welcome back," Justice said, expressionless. "And goodbye."

He fired two death blasts from his eyes, and they found their way directly to my mother's rib cage. In the millisecond it took for the blasts to obliterate my mother, she raised her head and met my father's gaze.

"Hal—!" She threw the ring toward him before she disappeared.

The resulting explosion wiped her off the face of this earth.

Dad screamed out Mom's name as she vanished into the air—no bits, no pieces, no smell of gardenia—as if she'd never been there in the first place. My stomach dropped to my feet, and I went numb all over. I couldn't find the breath to scream. Mom was gone. The detonation blew a chunk of wall out of the monument steeple, which towered five stories above the observation deck. Debris showered us, and I could barely see my dad through the falling rubble.

The ring skidded across the crystal floor, slipped past my father, and landed on the ledge of the observation deck, eighty stories aboveground. It was now impossible for my father to reach it, even with his teeth, which was about all he had left to use.

I ran to help my father, still broken, and took the mangled ends of his arms in my hands.

"Dad!"

"Never mind, Thom. Get the ring. You've got to bring me the ring!"

I grabbed the two nubs where his hands used to be and squeezed and prayed with all my might that I had enough strength in me to do what had to be done. I ignored the pain for as long as I could—my hands almost caught fire with more energy than I'd ever emitted—and just before I passed out, I heeded my dad's advice and raced for the ledge to get the ring.

I nearly made it to the ring, but Justice fired an eye-blast that shot straight through my left arm at the bicep as I reached for it. I didn't wince at the pain; I kept moving. He clasped both hands together and brought them down on the back of my neck like a sledgehammer. I felt my neck snap and my legs go numb; then I crumpled to the floor.

He stood above me, his eyes lit with fury and rage.

"You."

He kicked me in the stomach, and I felt my organs burst and rupture. I opened my mouth to scream, but shut it because it was spurting out blood.

"What the hell do you care for the people of this planet?" He kicked me in the face as he ranted. "They hate you, they call you names and are ashamed of you. You know I'm telling the truth. You're all so stupid, you're killing this world anyway. I'm just giving you a little nudge, a gentle push."

He lifted me off the ground, pulled me up by my collar with one hand. I dangled like a noodle, my insides were lique-fying. I glanced at the hole in my bicep. It sealed, and I felt a strange crackle of energy work itself up from the base of my spine. I could wriggle my toes.

I spit a bloody tooth at him. I wasn't about to agree with him on anything, and I needed some time for my body to recover.

He then took two fingers and pushed them toward my eyes. I shut my eyelids as he thrust his fingers forward. I clenched my teeth and strained, and sent all the energy and heat and power I could muster to my face to defend myself. The pressure was shocking, unbearable. I struggled desperately in his grasp, but he clutched me tight and kept pressing, pressing. . . . I could heal fast, but not fast enough to survive this. I gritted my teeth but couldn't help crying out in agony.

This was the moment of my death. Ruth had foreseen it, and I had failed to prevent it. Get the ring or help my dad. I had chosen to help my father, and the choice had sealed my fate.

But suddenly the pain stopped. I opened my eyes and I could see again. Justice's fingers were gone. He dropped me and whirled around to face a new threat.

Dad stood behind him, two perfect new hands raised in fists.

"*Get—*"

He smashed Justice's jaw with his right fist.

"*Your—*"

He slammed him across the head with his left hook.

"*Hands—*"

A deep punch to the gut.

"*Off—*"

He brought Justice's face down to his knee and jammed it into his nose.

"*My—*"

He head butted him.

"*SON!*"

With that, Dad pulled the purple ring from his pocket and

plunged it into Justice's chest, where his heart should have been.

The death of Justice was anything but peaceful. His body convulsed and broke apart, and bright violet lasers shot out of him in all directions as the life poured out of his body. I saw a dazzling purple ray blow a hole wide open through the crystal floor in front of me. Beams of light tore out of him and ripped into the surrounding buildings. He gurgled and shook and wailed as his thunderous life surged into the world and dissipated.

I dropped to the floor to dodge the destructive force of the beams. Dad ignored them and held on to Justice tightly with one hand, while still pressing the ring into his chest with the other. The world depended on it.

With an ear-piercing shriek and a final giant blast of his life's essence shooting up into the Memorial steeple, Justice collapsed into a lifeless heap on the shiny crystal floor, his body a husk held together by powerless atoms. Dad finally let go of Justice and slumped to the deck. He grabbed his abdomen and struggled to catch his breath.

The steeple had suffered a crushing blow from Justice's final blasts of life, and it rocked and moaned and began to fall. I watched its shadow creep over my father. I felt the crackle of energy in my spine ignite every molecule in my body as my powers grew within me, and I leaped up and flew to the base of the steeple and propped the towering structure up with my back, like Atlas with the weight of the universe on his shoulders.

Not only did I have enough strength to keep the building up, but I could hear things, see things, like I'd never been able to before. Down below, I could actually see hordes of people staring up and pointing. I could see the details of their faces, their fingers. Photographers and cameramen documented every action. I wanted to tell them to move, to get out of the way. If the steeple came down, thousands would die. My thigh muscles shook, and suddenly I wished I wasn't alone, that there was another hulking hero standing beside me, someone else to shoulder the burden. I looked at my bad knee and prayed the joint would hold together. My legs bounced up and down with tremors. I couldn't let go, not now.

Dad pushed himself off the ground with his hand, one arm still wrapped around his stomach. He stumbled a little, held himself up on the ledge, and then stood up straight.

"Well, I'll be," Dad muttered when he saw me. His eyes moved from me up to the top of the steeple. It was so high that his pupils almost disappeared up into his head. "Nice catch."

"Dad, I—I don't think I can hold it."

"Of course you can," he said. "You're my son."

It was a matter of fact. Dad believed in me. And if he believed in me, I believed, too. He looked at me in that moment the way he had when I'd won each basketball game, when I was named citywide volunteer of the year, when I got second place in the forensics tournament, when I made him my first Father's Day card with construction paper, safety scissors, and glue.

My legs stopped shaking.

In front of Dad's feet lay Justice's body. Justice's index finger shook with a tiny twitch, a tremor. Dad and I stared and waited a tense beat to see if this was significant. Then Justice's entire hand twitched with spasms of life. Its fingers scraped at the crystal, looking for traction, a way to push the body up.

He was reanimating himself.

Dad's demeanor darkened, and he staggered with weariness, but he held his head high, his jaw resolute and strong.

He walked over to a spot on the floor and picked up the old gloves and mask from his costume. He wedged the gloves back into his belt. He used both hands to put the old mask back on his face, which had grown slightly too large for it over the years. When he raised his hands to put on the mask, I saw what he'd been clutching.

A crimson hole gaped wide open in his abdomen. He hadn't been able to avoid the blasts that shot out of Justice, at least not all of them.

"Dad?"

The pressure from the building on my back was enormous. It felt like it would snap me in two.

Dad walked over to Justice. Thick, dark blood leaked in waves from his stomach with each step, but he moved like it was nothing more than a hangnail.

"Dad!" I shouted, desperate. "Let me help you!"

He crouched down beside Justice and looked up at me. He knew as well as I did that I couldn't let go of the building.

He hoisted Justice by the back of his neck and dragged him over to the rocket. Then he turned to me with a sad smile.

"This is what we do, son—we save people."

He tossed Justice up onto the rocket, punched in the code with his fresh, new fingers.

"Dad." I began to cry.

He strapped on his old gloves, one at a time, and straddled

the rocket alongside Justice. He pulled the belt over his shoulder and fastened them both in.

"I will always be proud of you."

"Dad!"

"Promise me one thing, Thom."

"DAD!"

"Promise me"—he snapped Justice's neck out of joint. Then he took his wedding ring and thrust it down Justice's throat the way you force-feed a dog a pill—"that you will love as much as you can."

He looked up at me and waited for an answer. He wasn't going anywhere until he knew I wouldn't make the same mistakes he had. Justice's neck slumped over his collarbone.

My legs felt like they would buckle any minute. I struggled and strained, and tears trickled down my face. This was the real choice Ruth had warned me about. I wanted to save my father; I thought it was the only thing that mattered in the universe. But he and I both knew it wasn't.

I felt the air escape my lips. "I promise."

With that, Dad punched in the final numbers on the pad.

"Dad, please don't—" I begged and shifted my weight and tried to reach out to him with one hand. The building lurched, and I propped my back up against it. I couldn't move.

My whole life I had been convinced that my father didn't know me, didn't understand me. But the truth was that he knew me better than anybody, and he loved me more than anybody in the universe. He even knew what to say in his last moment.

"It will be all right, Thom." His eyes were fixed on me,

strong but gentle, and his voice was firm but assuring. I looked into his face and saw only truth.

I tried not to weep. I didn't want him to think I was a baby, that I wasn't strong enough to bear the hardest choices in life. But he could always see right through me, and this our last moment together was no exception. He said it one last time to make sure I knew it would be true. The first time he said it partly to convince himself. This time he said it to convince me.

"It will be all right."

The last thing I remember before the rocket fired was that he took off his mask, tossed it aside, and he smiled at me. The proudest look I've ever seen.

The rocket launched, and he graced across the heavens, and then he exploded like a million rounds of fireworks put on for everyone around the world to see. I watched the glorious display of light envelop the planet, and then waited breathlessly for them to fade. I stared into the nova where my father had been, and I quietly said good-bye.

CHAPTER THIRTY-FOUR

I KNEW IT MUST have been important when Uberman asked me to meet him on top of the observation deck of the Wilson Memorial. I hadn't been there since we'd saved the world.

"It's good to see you, Thom." Uberman flashed me a half-smile. I hadn't seen him smile since before the news coverage of the heroes' possession at the hands of one of their own, and the death and destruction they had unwittingly caused. Their names had been cleared ultimately, but their bravado had eroded along with the world's confidence in them. After she recovered from her injuries, Warrior Woman had returned to her island and vowed never to visit Man's world again.

I'd ridden a wind current down to the observation deck and spotted Uberman sitting on the ledge with his legs dangling off the side. He stared off in the distance, his mind somewhere else. It was strange to see him slouch.

"I have something to ask," he said. He kept his eyes on his hands, folded in his lap, and he picked at dead skin around the nails. "It hasn't been easy ever since, well, you know. I don't think people have much faith in us anymore."

His muscles had grown noticeably softer in the stomach and around his neck. He wiped a greasy streak of blond hair from his forehead.

"What I'm getting at is we really need you, Thom. People know what you did, what your father did, and well, you'd really help us out here if we could add you to our permanent roster. Now that you're A-level."

His nose started to drip. Jeez, what a mess. I pulled a tissue out of my pocket and handed it to him. He blew his nose, loud as a foghorn, and tossed the wadded tissue off the side of the building. A draft caught the tissue and carried it up. Uberman incinerated it with a weak blast of heat vision.

"Can't be seen littering," he said.

I thought about what he was asking, what it really meant. There was a time when all I'd dreamed of was an offer to join the League, when all I'd wanted was for the world to think I was special.

But everything had changed, and I was becoming more and more of who I really was, and less of this person I had thought I wanted to be.

"I can't join permanently." I tried to let him down easy. "I have plans, commitments."

He slumped even more and sighed.

"But I'd be honored to be included as a permanent reserve member."

He perked up, even smiled a little. They could use this with the public, with the media. And while I was in good standing I was happy to let them use me. But I didn't delude myself that it would last. Wheel of fortune, round and round and all that. The trick for me was to keep it in perspective, to know in my heart what was really important. I had my eyes fixed on new things. There was so much to do.

Then I raised my index finger and told him, "On one condition."

The doorbell rang as I carried the last box downstairs. I'd been packing all through the night, and I was glad that it was almost finished. I opened the door, and Scarlett handed me a cup of green tea and a bag of fast-food breakfast. She walked in, grabbed the bag back, and pulled out an Egg McMuffin.

"Look at you," I said, and pointed at her new costume.

"Hell," she said, chewing with her mouth open, "this is nothing; you oughta see the benefits."

New uniforms were part of the League's revamped image, and Scarlett looked great in clean threads that fit her. They'd even arranged for a celebrity hairstylist to come in and give freebies to the new members. Scarlett had been reluctant to let the stylist see under her wig, but to her pleasant surprise, her hair had started to grow back.

"I'm curly now, who knew?" She pulled a layered piece over her ear.

She wore an oversize League jacket over her costume, though. Some things never changed.

"Why don't you take your coat off," I said. "Stay awhile."

"Can't," she said. "I've got practice."

"So what'd I miss?" I asked.

I'd been out of commission for over a month while I was recovering in the hospital from having strained my powers so much. Patching up the tower, healing Scarlett, Golden Boy, and Dark Hero had taken a real toll on my system. The final straw that had broken my back, though, had been putting Larry back together after Golden Boy had raced around to find all his pieces.

One day when Golden Boy came by, I had gathered up my courage to ask him something that had been on my mind. "Did you find anything else when you were looking for Larry?"

"What do you mean?" Golden Boy asked. "Like what?"

"Like maybe . . . anyone?" I was reaching, and he knew it. "Like my mom," I finally admitted.

Golden Boy shook his head. "I'm sorry, Thom."

A body is very difficult to recover when it's invisible. Or atomized. I know my father would never have stopped looking for her, but she's been gone from my life for so long with so many unanswered questions, I've accepted that I simply may never know. She may be gone forever, or one day I'll smell a hint of gardenia and maybe it will be her.

"I don't know about what you missed," Scarlett said. "But I'll tell you what I missed." Scarlett reached into the bag and pulled out a hash brown and stuffed it in her mouth. "My period."

"You're kidding."

"The doctors said my remission is nothing short of a miracle. But this . . . if it's true, I can't wait to see the look on their faces."

I sipped on my tea and thought about how I had hugged Scarlett so tightly that day, the way she'd let my warmth envelop her.

"I never thought I'd have another chance at life." She reached for my hand and squeezed it tight. "Thank you," she said in a quiet voice.

"I've got to go." Scarlett glanced at her watch. "Golden Boy said if I'm late for practice I'll get demerits, no exceptions, especially for his girlfriend. Can you believe him? He's such a tight-ass." Scarlett threw her empty wrappers in the bag and balled it up. She stood to leave.

"By the way, if I really am late, you're the godfather."

I watched Scarlett heat up and lift off of the driveway. I called out to her in the sky.

"So what would you name my godchild?"

"Someone once told me I'd have a girl. I thought she was full of shit at the time."

She flashed me a proud grin over her shoulder and shouted back in midair.

"I'd name her Ruth."

"Do you think she could really be pregnant?" I asked Goran.

"I don't know," he said. "Anything's possible."

I'd learned that much was true.

Goran reached into the cooler and dug through the ice. He fished out a Pabst Blue Ribbon and tossed it to me. I felt the can and it wasn't very cold.

"How about a cold one?" I said. Without thinking, I shook the tepid can and tossed it back in the cooler. I wished Dad had been there to open it, to spray it everywhere.

Goran shoved a deviled egg in my mouth and shut me up. He made great deviled eggs. I watched him dig down deeper into the cooler. His jersey traveled up his back and revealed the very top of his butt, firmly muscled and peeking out from his jeans.

"Keep looking." I leaned back on top of the picnic table to bask in the warm sun and enjoy the view.

He reached behind the cooler into his backpack and tossed something at me. I put my hand in front of my face and grabbed it. Goran could really throw, and whatever it was had edges.

I looked in my hand and saw that I'd caught a carefully wrapped gift. It had been Goran's idea to stop for a picnic lunch on the way out to visit Dad's memorial site. He'd prepared all the food, and even bought flowers for the monument.

It had been my idea to have the picnic in the park by the railroad tracks where my dad used to take me to watch the trains when I was a boy. I wanted Goran to know everything about my dad.

"Go on," Goran said. "Open it."

I tore the paper open and found a simple box. I lifted the top and couldn't believe what I saw inside.

Goran smiled at me.

I pulled my father's mask out of the box and held it in my hands.

"You'll carry on his legacy," Goran said.

I carefully set the gift down, hopped off the picnic table, walked over to him, and placed my hands on his face. I had to make sure he was really there. With one palm over his forehead and the other palm over his nose and mouth, I looked into those deep, dark pupils and saw the way he used to look at me when he was Dark Hero, when I didn't know. Goran took my hand off his mouth and held it. He raised it to his mouth, placed his warm lips in the middle of my palm and kissed it. Everything I love about Goran was in that kiss. Equal parts soft and strong, tender and scary. Infinite.

I heard the whistle of a train as it approached the crossing. I reached my arms around Goran, pulled him in, and our lips met.

It felt like flying.